not good for maidens

not good for maidens

tori bovalino

PAGE STREET
PUBLISHING CO.

PAGE STREET
PUBLISHING CO.

Copyright © 2022 Tori Bovalino

First published in 2022 by
Page Street Publishing Co.
27 Congress Street, Suite 105
Salem, MA 01970
www.pagestreetpublishing.com

Distributed by Macmillan, sales in Canada by The Canadian Manda Group.

26   25   24   23   22   1   2   3   4   5

ISBN-13: 978-1-64567-466-5
ISBN-10: 1-64567-466-5

Library of Congress Control Number: 2021948387
Cover and book design by Julia Tyler for Page Street Publishing Co.
Cover illustration by © Peter Strain

Printed and bound in the United States

IN MEMORY OF JEAN, WHO SPUN
HER OWN KIND OF MAGIC,
AND FOR LEX AND DANA, WHO
WOULD ALWAYS COME BACK FOR ME

PART 1
Come buy, come buy

"O, WHERE ARE YOU GOING?" "TO SCARBOROUGH FAIR,"
PARSLEY, SAGE, ROSEMARY, AND THYME;
"REMEMBER ME TO A LASS WHO LIVES THERE,
FOR ONCE SHE WAS A TRUE LOVE OF MINE."

—"SCARBOROUGH FAIR," TRADITIONAL ENGLISH BALLAD

"LIE CLOSE," LAURA SAID,
PRICKING UP HER GOLDEN HEAD:
"WE MUST NOT LOOK AT GOBLIN MEN,
WE MUST NOT BUY THEIR FRUITS:
WHO KNOWS UPON WHAT SOIL THEY FED
THEIR HUNGRY THIRSTY ROOTS?"
"COME BUY," CALL THE GOBLINS
HOBBLING DOWN THE GLEN.
"OH," CRIED LIZZIE, "LAURA, LAURA,
YOU SHOULD NOT PEEP AT GOBLIN MEN."

—"GOBLIN MARKET," CHRISTINA ROSSETTI

May

Boston, Eighteen Years Earlier

MAY HAD WAYS OF COPING.

She ate. That was an improvement. She ate, and sipped the water that Laura kept pushing toward her. She looked out the window of the brownstone, watching the people down below. She kept looking for the city walls, but of course, they weren't there. The walls, the people, the market—they were all a world away.

May coped, and she slept, and she ate. She held her tongue until her voice was rusty in her mouth, until her vowels were unfamiliar and her accent heavy against Dad's. But silence was better than screaming, and if she opened her mouth, May was not sure what would come out.

She smiled when their father brought a new candy every day from the shop on the corner, presenting them with an endless rotation of American snacks that turned her stomach. She let Laura fret over her because it hinted at forgiveness awarded or forthcoming, even though it tugged at that deep guilt May couldn't shake.

When she was alone—which was rare, with Laura's fretting— she hummed to herself. She knew the songs, all of them, by heart.

Backwards and forwards and all the way around.

Are you going to Scarborough Fair?

No, May thought, staring down at the street as their father rounded the corner with a shopping bag hanging from one hand. *No, I've been to Scarborough Fair, and I'd not like to return.*

Sometimes, in the moments May forgot about it all, she woke up searching for something within herself she'd lost, only to realize all over again that it was gone.

Thirty-two days after they arrived, Laura knocked softly at May's door. "Are you in there?"

"Yes," May said. Where else would she be?

Laura came in. She was wearing a dress, green, that she didn't have in York. She must've bought it here, but May couldn't remember her leaving to get it. Perhaps she'd gone when May was sleeping. Laura looked better now. Less thin, less tired.

"I'm going out tonight," she said, nudging a fallen silk scarf on the floor with one foot. May had gotten it in Leeds four years before.

In their past life, in the times before, this would've been an enticing bit of information. May felt it tugging in her mind, that spark of something that would've interested her. It only lasted a moment in the current fog of her brain, the dimmest of embers in a pile of ashes.

But it was a fog she didn't like Laura to see. "Oh?" May said, remembering that she had to say something.

Laura nodded. "With a boy. He works at that bookshop on Newbury."

There was a pause, a pause May was probably supposed to fill. She stared at Laura blankly. Maybe she was meant to ask his name. May had never been to the bookstore on Newbury—

Laura had invited her, but May didn't like to leave. She felt the age of the city pressing against her skin. Not York old, not by a longshot, but the closest this country had.

All she could think was: *Don't stay too late, don't seek the market, you don't know if there's a market.*

Laura's smile faded. May had failed, she knew. She should've pretended, should've asked something. Anything.

"Are you okay with me going?" Laura asked. "I can stay."

Stay here, in her green dress, with Dad and his questions and haunted May? Stay here when she wanted to go, after she'd sacrificed everything for May? It would be a travesty, probably, to keep Laura inside. No matter how much she wanted to ask her to stay. No matter how much the idea of a house without Laura scared her.

She dreamt of her sometimes, in the haze of the market: Laura, brave and valiant. Standing tall, stained with the juice of cherries and shining with sweat, blood leaking out of a gash across one arm. Laura, always the stronger sister, always with the greater will; Laura, come to save her yet again.

Laura, who had given up the entire world for May.

"You go," May said. She tried on a smile, but her teeth felt dry and the corners of her mouth cracked and Laura looked even more wary. "Go and have fun." She turned back to the window so she didn't have to watch Laura leave.

Coping was an odd thing, May thought, as she watched Laura flit out onto the street in her green dress, into the arms of a kind-looking brown-haired boy with a mediocre silver car. Coping was pretending to listen to Dad as he chatted over dinner and nodding in the appropriate places, and returning to her room and the window seat as soon as she was able. Coping was watching the people on the street but not seeing them, not really processing, because she was trying too hard to see the horns and warts and pale green skin glamoured to look human; not thinking of the magic she'd lost or how Laura must resent her. It was not running through the spells that were once so familiar to her she practiced them in her sleep, not calling Mum every day to see what she was missing, what she'd given up, what she'd thrown away because of May's mistakes.

Coping was not thinking about the market, not thinking about the market, not thinking about anything other than the market.

When May slept, it felt less like she was slipping from consciousness and more like she was falling out of present time, back to somewhere else.

Well, not just anywhere else. Most times, her mind went back to the beginning. To York, her home, where the pavement smelled like rain and fog, where she knew the streets by heart. She closed her eyes and imagined standing in the shadow of the Minster with a girl by her side, unbloodied. In her imaginings, she and Eitra walked the velvet night, through misty rain and clear darkness, fingers entwined.

In her imaginings, Eitra did not die. May had that thrill of magic back, even if she could not use it. They were home, home, home, in the place where May could not return.

But in the end, May opened her eyes, like always. In the end, she was always banished, always alone, and Eitra was always dead.

An indeterminate amount of time later, long past dark, May watched the silver car pull back up to the curb. The boy got out, went around, and opened Laura's door. They kissed on the street outside.

May tasted a rush of goblin blood in her mouth.

She swallowed it down.

Minutes later, the door opened and shut, and Laura came in silently to sit on her bed. Her cheeks were flushed and her hair askew, and there was no point telling her that the buttons of her dress were not done correctly.

It was a detail she noticed, May realized, despite the fog.

"You look like you haven't moved," Laura said.

May shrugged.

Laura sighed, slipped off her shoes, and shimmied out of her dress. She pulled the pins from her hair and grabbed a spare shirt from May's drawer.

"Come to bed," Laura said.

May nodded. She slipped under the sheets, still in her jean shorts and tank top that Laura made her put on that morning. Laura smelled of cigarette smoke and lipstick, but it was okay. In a way, it was the first time she'd smelled normal since . . . since before.

Laura ran her fingers through May's hair, combing through the tangles. "You're here," she murmured. "You're safe. You'll never go again, May. Do you hear me? You'll never go to the market again."

May bit her lip. Because, though she was an ocean away from the market, though she may never see the walls again in her life, she knew the truth. She was a part of the market. Some part of her would always be there. Some part would never leave as her blood clung to Eitra's skin, as they decayed into flowers and moss together. Maybe, in her time away, some part of her had become the goblin's property, even if Laura had gotten her out.

When she closed her eyes every night, she fell into the same nightmare of the goblins grabbing Eitra's arms and legs and holding her down, pushing her into the grass of the park as she struggled against them. In her dream, May never closed her eyes fast enough, or perhaps she forced herself to watch.

Maybe she watched because she hadn't in real life, when it had really happened. She'd only heard the snick of the knife, had only imagined the hot splash of Eitra's blood, and heard her sharp scream cut off.

But in her nightmares, her eyes were open. In her nightmares, every night at the witching hour, May watched Eitra die all over again.

She'd never left the market. She'd never leave the market. And when it was time, when it came again, the market would take her back.

That was the truth of coping: it was just delaying the inevitable.

CHAPTER 1

Boston, Present Day

ON THE NIGHT THE MARKET CAME TO CLAIM WHAT IT WAS OWED, Louisa Wickett-Stevens was three thousand miles and five time zones away, trying to figure out how she had so many mothers who didn't understand her.

She stood at the Do Not Walk sign, dead phone clutched in her hand, and waited for the Walk sign to flash. It was one of those weeks in Boston when the city felt buried under a layer of heat, when she could almost smell the harbor all the way in the middle of town. Every few seconds, she pressed the home button and glanced down at her phone, only to be reminded all over again that there was no point. She'd forgotten to bring her charger to Dad's. Usually, she'd call Neela when she was walking home alone at night. Especially a night like this, when the city felt sleepy and silent, the weight of it pressing against her ears.

Lou shifted, wishing the light would just *change* already. Dad had offered to drive her home, but if she rode with him, there would be a guaranteed talk about how her stepmom Gen was just trying to do what was *best*, trying to be closer to Lou. As if closeness was what she needed.

The walk sign flipped on, and Lou jogged across. It wasn't a

TORI BOVALINO

far walk: a mile at best, from her dad's place in Beacon Hill to
the apartment in Back Bay where she lived with her mom and
aunt May, recently inherited from her grandfather. Sometimes,
Lou's feet still dragged her to the bus route that would take them
to their old place, and she had to consciously remind herself that
their cramped apartment wasn't home anymore. That they'd
relocated, shifted with all of their same problems and misshaped
dilemmas into the new, bigger place.

Lou took the longer route through the Gardens. Dark was
falling, and it probably wasn't the best idea, especially with her
phone dead. But she wasn't ready to go home yet.

It had started that afternoon, when Lou was at the hardware
store with her mom for more Command hooks and wallpaper
stripper to handle the upside-down bird wallpaper in May's
bathroom. She wished May was off work to go with them,
because it felt less like a chore when May was around and more
like an adventure. Lou went back for more painter's tape and
by the time she was done, Mom had found the paint section.
Before Lou could intervene, Mom was having a ghastly shade of
magenta mixed.

Lou raised her eyebrows, checking the paint chip in Mom's
hand. "Hot Lips. Sounds . . . inappropriate."

Mom only rolled her eyes. She finished up and paid, and she
and Lou set off for the car. "It'll look nice in the lounge," Mom
said in her broad Yorkshire accent. It was always softer when they
were out of the house, like she felt the need to hide some part of
herself, even if she was only talking to her daughter.

"It'll look terrible," Lou responded. She was tired and sweaty
and didn't want to spend any more time painting the house. May
couldn't do it, claiming the fumes were bad for her pregnancy, and

Mom was too busy with the unpacking and wallpaper stripping. So it had been up to Lou to paint the hall and the nursery in approved colors. If Neela had been there like she was every other summer, it would've been fun. But by herself, the whole thing was dull and annoying.

"If I spoke to my mum the way you speak to me, she would've left me for the fairies," Mom said airily.

Lou rolled her eyes. Sometimes, with the way Mom, May, and Nana Tee spoke, Lou wondered if they actually *did* believe in fairies.

She slid into the front seat, rolling down a window as soon as Mom turned the car on to get some of the hot air out. "About Nana Tee," Lou said, shooting a quick glance over at Mom. Though it wasn't a great opening, the threat of being taken away, it was better than nothing. "Neela had an idea."

Mom sighed, like she knew exactly where this was going. Neela, Mom and May's younger half sister, was just a year older than Lou. Usually, Neela came to stay with them in Boston for her six-week summer break, but not this year—she had a wedding to attend in India in August, and she was leaving for university at the end of break.

But Lou couldn't imagine a summer without Neela, her best friend.

"What if I go stay with them?" Lou asked, trying to keep her eyes on the road ahead. It was easier than looking at Mom, easier than seeing her quick refusal, or worse, her disappointment that Lou would even ask.

"When? Your dad has that Yosemite trip planned for August," Mom said. Lou couldn't miss the caution in her voice, like she was seeking an easy dismissal.

Lou picked at the frayed edge of her shorts. She'd rescued them from Neela two summers before, when Neela splattered paint on the front right side and was about to throw them away. Lou kept them; she thought the splattered paint and worn rips made the shorts look cool and edgy.

"Nee gets back August 10th. School doesn't start until the first week of September." Lou dug her nails into the meat of her palm. There were negotiations to be had, the same tired fight they'd struggled through Lou's entire life. "Why can't I go there?"

Mom's lips were thinned into a line, her knuckles white as she clenched the wheel. "You're with your dad then. The custody agreement includes—"

"I'm seventeen," Lou interrupted. "I get a say in where I go. And Dad won't care. Gen might, but Dad—"

"No, Louisa," Mom said. It was a sharp word, cutting through any and all arguments Lou and Neela had hashed over the night before. She felt that terrible knot in her stomach, the lump in her throat. Lou leaned her head against the window.

But she didn't want to give up, not this time. "I've never been to your hometown," Lou said, trying to keep her voice steady. "I don't know anything about where you and May are from. Don't you think that's a little weird?"

Mom didn't answer. Lou couldn't tell if she was ignoring her or not.

"Neela and Nana Tee come here every single year. That's not fair to them, and it's not fair to me. And it's not fair to Neela or me that we can't see each other because of your stupid rules."

"It's a lot of money to just go—"

"It can't be about money," Lou bit out. "Not this time." Not since Grandpa Jack had died and left his hefty bank account and swanky apartment to Mom and May. Yes, they'd struggled for Lou's entire life, living in the shitty one-bedroom apartment in Revere before Grandpa Jack passed away in the spring and left them the brownstone apartment that May and Mom had grown up in and everything else he owned. But money wasn't an issue anymore.

Mom turned onto their street. As soon as they were inside, this conversation would be over. Lou couldn't let this just slip under the rug, like every previous iteration of this conversation.

"Please," she said. She hated revealing any vulnerability, showing any loneliness to Mom and May, who got along just fine with themselves. But at least they had each other to lean on. Lou didn't even have Neela, not in real life. "I just want to visit for a few weeks."

She watched as Mom looked up toward their second-floor apartment. Lou could just see the outline of a hanging pentacle in one of the windows, meant for protection of the house.

"No," Mom said. "You're too young to go by yourself. Money or not."

"You were literally just a year older than me when you came here by yourself," Lou seethed. She couldn't stop the anger that flooded through her. "It's been enough time. Since whatever happened to you that you refuse to tell me about."

Let me in, she thought. *Let me see who you were, why you chose this, why you left.*

Mom's eyes cut over to her, hard and emotionless. "I wasn't alone. I came here with May to live with Dad. And look how that turned out."

The jab smarted, even though she knew her mother didn't mean it. When Mom and May moved to Boston as teenagers, the first thing Mom did was get pregnant.

Mom closed her eyes and pressed a hand to her forehead. The hairs along her neck had escaped from the bun on top of her head and stood out in frizzy curls. Sometimes, it felt like Mom's dark wavy hair was the only thing Lou had inherited from her. Like they were strangers, unrelated and unknowable, besides that dark hair.

"I'm sorry," she said. "I don't want you to go alone, not without May or me." Her accent was thicker, just like it always was when she spoke of home.

It was finished and done. Mom would not let her go to England to see Neela and there was no debate there.

Or so Lou thought as she angrily texted Neela from her room. But then Nee said, *Would your dad let you?*

So off Lou went to dinner at Dad's, where she was supposedly always welcome, even though she wasn't a permanent fixture there like her stepbrother, Peter. Except that plan wasn't great either, because Gen threw a whole fit about Lou even *considering* skipping the family vacation, and Dad had only shrugged and said, "Tough luck, Lulu. We can all go next year."

But next year didn't matter. It didn't even matter that Lou had dual citizenship if her parents didn't give her permission to go. And worst of all, Lou's phone died before she could even call Neela to come up with a new plan.

Now, alone in the dark, Lou let the full force of her misery settle into her bones. She'd never been good at friends. She didn't know what parts to show, what parts to keep. Maybe she'd gotten that from Mom, who held everything so close to her chest that Lou wasn't sure anyone knew her, other than May.

She pushed her hands into her pockets and left the Gardens, turning onto Comm Ave. This, at least, was well lit. There was nothing to worry about, not a soul to bother her. Sometimes, it felt like there wasn't another soul in the world.

The faster she got home, the faster she could call Neela. It was past midnight in York, but Neela was out with her friends. She'd be up.

Lou glanced up at the window as she approached their brownstone. Golden light filtered through the upstairs window. Mom was still up, or May had gotten home early. Lou chewed on her lip. She just had to get to her room, and she wouldn't have to talk to them.

She jogged up the stairs to the second floor and unlocked the door, excuses already prepared on her lips. But when she went in, the living room was empty.

Mom had pushed all the furniture to the center of the room and laid drop cloths. A ladder stood against one wall, and there was a pan with the offending magenta and an abandoned paint-brush left in it.

Lou paused, listening. The place was old. If Mom was here, she'd be able to hear the creaking. If May was back, then at least Lou could complain to her. Though May was like another mother to Lou, she also filled the role of fun aunt. She knew May would understand the injustice of it all.

Nothing.

The place smelled of burnt herbs. Mom must've cleansed the house while Lou was out. A few drips of paint marred the drop cloth. In the shadows of the ladder, they looked like spilled blood.

Lou tried her best to shrug off her sense of unease and shut herself in her room. It used to be May's, back when May was younger, and there was still plenty of her crap left here from nearly two decades ago for Lou to sort through and throw away before she finished unpacking.

First things first, she plugged in her phone. While she waited for it to come to life, Lou went to her windowsill and brushed away the salt—it was another of her mom's superstitions, meant to ward the house or something like that. Lou didn't keep track of all the weird stuff Mom and May believed it. Mom must've gone on a full spree earlier after cleansing. The salt looked new, and there was a new iron pentacle hanging over Lou's window.

She changed into soft shorts and a Boston University T-shirt before settling onto the windowsill. The air conditioning was flighty and old, so Lou preferred to sit here with her window open to cool down. She pulled her phone to her as it flashed, coming back to life.

It immediately started vibrating. Lou wasn't surprised to see the flurry of drunk messages coming in from Neela: three about someone spilling a beer on her shirt, one about a pretty girl in a bathroom. Nothing to say she'd made it home.

A few messages from Mom, too, and one from May. But Lou didn't bother to read them.

There were two voicemails, both from Neela. They talked every day on the phone or video chat, but it wasn't a big deal if one of them left a voicemail or WhatsApp voice memo. It was much easier than sending a million texts back and forth.

Lou pressed play on the first message.

"Oh my god—fuck. *Fuck.* Lou. Lou I need you to pick up, I need you to—" Neela's voice faded for a second and Lou heard something odd in the background, like screams mixed with muffled sobbing. Something scraped along a stone floor. Neela's voice came back, closer, like she was holding a hand over her mouth and the speaker.

"I need you. Help me. You have to get—" Neela cut off again. Something smashed, like breaking glass, and the line went dead.

Lou stared at the wall, uncomprehending. She listened to the message again, her fear deepening. What had Neela gotten herself into? And how was Lou supposed to help, all the way from *Boston?*

But there was another message. Her mouth tasted bitter, bile creeping up from her stomach. She didn't want to listen. She needed to call Mom or May or Nana Tee, someone who understood what was happening. Someone who could really help Neela with whatever had happened.

She pressed play on the second message.

Gaspy, breathless sobbing crackled through her speakers. "Please," Neela begged Lou or someone else, someone on the other side of the phone. "I didn't mean to. You have to get me *out.*"

Someone shouted in the background. There was a dull roar, and above it all, a cackling sound.

"I'm out of time," Neela said, her voice more forlorn than Lou had ever heard it. Lou's palms were slick with sweat. "I'm at the market, Lou. When they ask you where to find me, I'm—"

Something clattered. The phone, maybe? In the distance, Lou heard someone screaming. Her heart plummeted.

Neela.

The line was silent for a second, as if all the sound in the room had been sucked out. And then, just as Lou was about to start the message over again, a very different voice took over.

"Are you coming to Scarborough Fair?" the voice whisper-sung in a rusty alto. A chill ran down Lou's spine. Then, lower, almost inaudible, "We're waiting for you, Louisa Wickett."

The phone fell from Lou's hand. It had to be a prank, she thought, scrambling for her phone. She needed to know it was a prank.

Lou called Neela.

The phone rang and rang and rang and rang. No answer. Neela didn't pick up.

Don't panic, she thought. It had to be an ill-considered, drunk prank. It *had* to be.

But Neela sounded so awful. So scared. Lou dialed her number again, listening as it rang and rang and no one answered, no one came.

She sent a quick text before trying to call again: *What happened? Are you okay?*

Somewhere else in the apartment, the door opened. There was a clatter of keys hitting the table, the rushed babble of two nearly identical voices arguing.

"You literally *can't,*" one of them said.

"Ten years was up years ago. I'm not asking for your help . . ."

Once, Neela had complained that people calling the house could never tell her and her mother apart. Lou had never had that problem, and the mismatch of accents sometimes left an aching hole in her chest. Lou did not look like Mom and May, did not sound like them, did not have their easy relationship. How, then, could she belong to them?

If there was trouble, Mom or May would know. Lou launched off the windowsill, through her bedroom door and down the hall. Both fell silent when Lou slid into the room on her socks. May looked exhausted, as always, in her flower-patterned scrubs. She had one hand on her belly and the other pressed to her back. Mom, on the other hand, was tightly wound and closed off, with her arms crossed over her chest and a muscle in her jaw ticking.

"Have you spoken to Nana or Neela?" Lou said, the words coming out in a rush.

The silence stretched too long, long enough to realize that there were black streaks of mascara under May's eyes. She'd been crying.

Lou's heart thumped harder, a dark stone of fear rippling in her stomach.

"Is everything okay?" But even as she asked, she knew. It wasn't, it wasn't, it wasn't.

I'm at the market, Lou, Neela had said, her voice trembling with fear. But what did that even *mean?*

May's lip trembled. She pressed her hands to her face, a move both she and Mom did when they were stressed. "You decide," May said, probably to Mom, but Lou couldn't be sure. She wiped her nose on her arm.

"Of course I'll decide," Mom said quietly. "I'm her mother."

They shared another significant look, one that Lou couldn't even begin to interpret. Finally, Mom sighed. When she turned to face Lou, she looked infinitely more exhausted. "Something happened to Neela."

Lou felt like she'd been removed from her body, like she was watching the scene play out from above. She could hear her heartbeat. She could see the blank look on her own face. But none of it mattered, none of it was real.

I need you. Help me.

No. She couldn't get carried away. Everything was going to be fine. Of course Neela was okay. Of course she was fine. Lou could not exist in a reality where anything else was true.

Mom shook her head. "She's been . . . taken."

Something about the phrasing made Lou's stomach drop. She looked again between her mother and May, both grave and hopeless. "Taken? How? By . . . a gang? Sex trafficking? Like, that Liam Neeson movie?" Her mind spun in circles, grappling for purchase, for anything. Behind her mother, the magenta wall looked even more offensive after dark.

"Louisa—" May started, but Mom shot her a look that cut her off. May bit her lip, looking down at the floor. Her shoulders were full of tension. The way they stood reminded Lou of a picture of the two of them, right after they moved to Massachusetts to live with Grandpa Jack. In it, both sisters had looked drawn and pale, and May especially looked haunted. She'd had a hard time aligning her happy, joyful aunt to that image, but now—now, she saw it.

"Taken by what?" Lou asked, dreading the answer.

"Taken by—"

"May." Mom cut her off harshly, turning May's name into a ragged, wretched thing. Mom shifted her attention to Lou. "I'm going to handle it. You'll go stay with your father for a few weeks."

There was that spinning sensation again. "You're . . . Where are you going? To handle it?"

"York," Mom said, biting off the hard syllable.

Lou stared at her, waiting for an explanation, waiting for the words to make sense. Neela was gone—gone where, she did not know, but gone somewhere—and Mom was leaving. Mom was leaving her here, and she wasn't even leaving her with May.

"But Mom—"

It was too late. Mom was already gone into the kitchen where Lou could hear her talking to Dad on the phone. Lou stared at

May as if the answers would come from her, but May just shook her head.

"Neela called me," Lou said desperately to May. "She told me she needed my help."

May's face was carefully blank. "Laura will fix it," May said, darting a doubtful glance at Mom's back. "She'll fix it."

But that wasn't an answer; not even close. "What happened to Neela?" Lou pleaded.

May came closer, close enough that Lou could feel her breath on the top of her head. She leaned down to kiss Lou on the forehead. Her fingers squeezed Lou's hand once, briefly. They were ice cold.

"Be glad," May said, stepping away, towards her room, "that you never have to know."

CHAPTER 2

THE ROOTS OF LOU'S CHILDHOOD HAD BEEN TANGLED WITH secrets. She did not know why, when Mom was eighteen and May was seventeen, they moved from their mother's home in York to live with the father they barely knew. She did not know why they never went back. And most of all, she did not know why they could not explain any of these things to her.

But if Mom traded in secrecy, Lou reciprocated with a delicately crafted set of rules: She did not ask about York, not when she could fight the questions that bubbled up within her, because they would not be answered. If asked, they only put Mom in a bad mood and made May look weary and frustrated.

She did not ask Neela or Nana Tee, because they only responded with heavy silences. Lou wanted to believe that there was nothing Neela would hide from her, nothing that could come between them, but if it was not Neela's secret, she would not share it. So it was better to leave the questions unasked rather than feeling left out of her own family even further.

She did not question May's lines of salt and Mom's iron protection charms. She did not ask about the scars that covered their skin—Mom had made up an excuse once, but Lou couldn't be certain it was true. May had tried to cover them, tattooing both arms with wildflowers, but it hadn't hidden the worst of them.

She did not tell Dad that there was anything going on, that there was anything to be worried about, that she was so frustrated with her lack of knowledge she felt it itching under her skin. She laid awake at night puzzling through what could've happened. Did they break the law? Were they criminals? Had someone hurt them?

A final rule, but the most important of all: she did not let the secrets hurt her. If she let herself fall into the grief of unknowing, it would be worse than the pain of looking at her mother's face and barely understanding her at all.

In previous summers, Neela had haunted this room with her.

Lou's room at her father's house was small and painted dark green, and hung with framed embroidery that Gen gave her on every birthday. Lou sat on the bed, staring at the wall, listening to the voicemail on a loop.

She didn't know what she was searching for or what she expected to find. She only knew that there had to be *something* more, something she could do.

Lou had forced Mom to listen to the voicemails in the car over here, but Mom's face had been blank as May's when Lou tried to get an answer out of her. When they were done, Mom had only sighed. She didn't speak until they pulled up in front of Dad's house. Her suitcase was in the back seat. She was going straight to the airport after dropping off Lou.

"I can't expect you to understand," Mom said finally, and Lou felt that deep sinking within her, that realization that Mom had a whole other life back in York that Lou knew nothing about. She reached out, quick like a snake, and laced her fingers through Lou's. When she looked at Lou, her clear blue eyes were distant. "There are monsters out there. Is it so bad of me to protect you from them?"

Lou swallowed hard. "There are monsters *here,*" she said. "Criminals and gangs and rapists."

Mom leaned over and kissed Lou's forehead. Lou had the oddest feeling this wasn't a normal goodbye. There was something terribly mournful about the way Mom looked at her now. "It's not the same thing, duck," she said.

Now, Mom was long gone, already halfway across the Atlantic, and Lou was no closer to answers about what could've happened to Neela. May wasn't answering any of her calls. When Lou tried to call Nana Tee, it went straight to voicemail.

Something was terribly wrong, and there was nothing she could do about it.

And if Neela was—no. Lou couldn't even think of a world without her. She squeezed her eyes shut tight. Neela was the only person who really knew Lou, the only person who'd seen the hidden parts.

She remembered how Neela tumbled into Boston the summer before, in her cornflower blue sundress that looked impossibly perfect against her brown skin. They'd spent days lazing around the bookstores near Newbury Street and hunting bubble tea, laying in the sun in the Common and watching the swan boats from the bridge. Neela had been full of stories of her antics back home; she was brave enough to sneak into pubs, to flirt with older people, to go clubbing with her friends in London, and skinny dip in the River Ouse.

"Your life just sounds so fun," Lou sighed, shielding her face from the sun.

Neela lifted herself on one elbow. "It'll be different when you come," she promised. "We'll go to uni together."

"In Edinburgh," Lou said, vaguely proud that she knew how to pronounce the city like Mom did.

"Or Glasgow," Neela said, poking her ribs. "More potential for scandalous affairs in Glasgow."

Lou was quiet for a long moment—probably too long. But she told Neela everything. Over text or in their weekly phone or FaceTime calls, through any form of social media they could wrangle to get across the ocean between them. But this felt vulnerable in a secret, hidden way that Lou didn't know how to explain.

"I don't think I'm interested in, um, scandalous affairs," she said, trying to pick her words carefully.

Neela rolled over to look at her. Her hair was in a fishtail braid, artfully pulled apart, tendrils of it clinging to her neck. Lou scraped her own brown hair into a sloppy bun on top of her head, just to give her hands something to do.

"You alright, Lou? You look . . . sweaty."

Lou grimaced. She *felt* sweaty, which was utterly unfair with Neela looking wonderful, as usual. The effortlessly pretty genes had skipped Lou.

"I think I'm ace," Lou said in a rush. "Like, asexual."

"I know what ace is, darling," Neela said.

Of course she did. They went to many a Pride event with May and Mom and sometimes Nana Tee. May's bisexuality was no secret, and Neela frequently wore a pan flag bathing suit when they went to the beach. She was not an outlier and there was absolutely nothing wrong with her, so why was it so scary to tell Neela?

But Neela only sat up and turned Lou around, her hands digging the hairband out of Lou's hair. She was gentle as she redid Lou's bun. "I'm surprised you waited so long to tell me," she said.

Lou turned around to see her face, nearly ruining the efforts Neela was taking on her hair. "You *knew*?"

"Well, I wasn't going to assume. But I had an inkling." Because of course she had—even the things Lou couldn't bring herself to say, Neela had already known. And it was even *easier* after that, like Lou hadn't needed to hide a single thing about herself, like all of the pages in her book could be open to Neela.

That night, as they'd crammed themselves into Lou's bed back in Mom and May's old stuffy apartment in Revere, Neela had said, "It's so nice to sleep with the windows open. With the breeze."

Lou looked over at her. "Can't you open the windows in York?"

Something odd had flashed across Neela's face. "Old buildings, you know? We don't have screens. Bugs get in. But anyway, tell me more about your realization."

She thought that it was possible she could be romantically involved with someone, but she didn't need to be. Lou was happy on her own. The idea of sex wasn't repugnant to her or anything of the sort—God knew Neela talked about it with her enough—but Lou just didn't have interest in it.

It had taken her a while to figure it out, skirting around the Queer Club at school and going to virtual talks with Neela and in-person events with May, but once she tried the ace label on, she felt it fit her like a well-worn T-shirt. She didn't need a label to explain herself, but having "ace" felt like armor; it was easy to drop a word, to be somewhat understood.

And for Neela and Lou, that hadn't changed a thing. She hadn't yet told Mom or May, nor had she figured out all the nooks and crannies of her own identity. But Neela had known who Lou was, known before Lou even said it.

Neela always knew. Neela always understood. No matter how vulnerable Lou was, no matter how many fractions or scars she revealed, Neela did not change how she looked at or spoke to Lou. And Lou knew that if someone cut deep into her heart and searched for the pearl inside of it, the ounce of meaning, they would peel back the bloody muscle to find Neela.

And now, she was gone.

There was a feeling in Lou, a deep Unbelonging that she felt in school and at home and here, at her Dad's house, and when held up against May and Mom and their perfect, on-the-same-page sisterhood. But she'd never felt the Unbelonging when she was with Neela. She'd only felt like herself.

Again, she listened to the voicemail. *I'm at the market.* Neela said it so clearly, as if she expected Lou to know what that meant. As if it was easy.

But Lou didn't *know* York. She didn't know if there was any place called the market or if that was some kind of code. If Mom knew, she hadn't shared with Lou.

May might've known. After all, May and Mom shared everything. But May wasn't talking to Lou either.

It was all so *frustrating.* She had the key to where Neela was, the key to something, and she was stranded here at Dad's.

Lou called Neela's phone again, like picking a scab. It went straight to voicemail.

She couldn't just sit here and rot in Boston while Neela was in trouble, while Mom only chipped another inch in the distance between her and Lou. She'd have to break her own rules.

Lou slipped out of her bedroom, tiptoeing past the living room where Gen watched back episodes of *Say Yes to the Dress,* past Peter's room, to her father's office.

"What's up, buttercup?" Dad said, glancing up from his laptop. He was a hotshot corporate lawyer, but he always looked like a primary school teacher to Lou. Maybe it was because he was her father, and though he wasn't around as much as Mom, he was always warm and soft in the way she was sharp and resigned.

Lou wondered, when he looked at her, if he saw her as his daughter—or as her mother's daughter.

She sat on the edge of his desk. When she was little and she did this, back when he was finishing up law school and the bags under his eyes were dark as bruises, her legs swung over the edge, unable to touch the ground. Now, she could press them flat to the floor.

"I need to ask you something about Mom."

Lou's tongue was dry and heavy in her mouth. What if Dad didn't know either? She focused on a picture hanging over his head, from when they were on a road trip to Arizona and Neela tagged along. It was a little odd, having Neela and Peter in the same room together, two sides of her life merging, but it was . . . nice.

"Oh?" Dad said.

"Something happened to Neela," Lou said. She hadn't spoken the words out loud yet; they'd just rotated around and around in her head, one of those breaking news ribbons at the bottom of the evening news: *Something happened to Neela. Neela is gone. More at 7:00. Stay tuned for updates.*

Dad frowned, lines jumping into deep relief between his eyebrows. "I know. Laura said she was missing. Lou, if there's anything I can do, anything you want to talk about—"

Lou shook her head. "It's not like we can find her from here. But Mom . . . she acted weird about it." She chewed on her lip. In the past, it had seemed obvious: don't tell Dad about what Mom believes, what Mom doesn't say. Don't tell Dad, because what if he saw Lou differently? "Do you know why Mom and May moved here?"

The question was out. She'd never asked it before, not of her father. She'd never been brave enough.

Dad grimaced. "You know how your mother is. Everything is so close to her chest. You'd have better luck asking May."

Lou shook her head. "She's not answering my calls."

Dad's lips thinned into a line. If he had something to say about that, he kept it to himself.

"But I do have this," Lou said, opening her phone. "Neela left me messages last night, before whatever happened, happened. Have Mom or May ever mentioned some kind of market?"

Dad's eyes snapped to Lou's. "The market?"

Lou played the voicemails for Dad. He stared at the wall, chewing on his lower lip, tapping the highlighter to the page. When the second voice came on, the tapping stopped, and Dad took a sharp breath.

Are you coming to Scarborough Fair?

"I don't know the details, and what I do know was from the one time your mom was drunk with me—don't worry, it was before you." Dad cringed a little as he said it, as he always did when anything about him and Mom pre-Lou came up. "She told me that May had some sort of breakdown that caused them to leave York. And May—she wasn't in a good state before you were born. She was basically comatose. I didn't ask questions about it, not until that night. But your mom said . . ." He stared off into the distance.

Lou's fingers gripped the edge of the desk. May, like Mom, didn't talk about their childhood back in Yorkshire—but did that automatically mean something had happened to them? To her? "What did she say?"

Dad shook his head slowly, not to negate what Lou said, but like he was thinking something over. "She was afraid that something would come back for May. She was afraid the market would come back to take her."

The market. Something had happened to May nearly twenty years ago back in York, and now it was happening all over again to Neela. There was no other explanation.

"I'm not saying it's related," Dad said, as if reading her mind—or arguing a court case. "But for May to be . . . kidnapped, and then for the same thing to happen to Neela? It seems odd, doesn't it?"

Lou nodded, releasing a long breath. This was what had been irritating her: the idea that it was all connected, that everyone knew some lost secret that hadn't been shared with her.

She knew better than to ask, to prod, to seek, to find the buried truth underneath. But now, she felt the weight of the secrets buckling around her. Before, they were just stories. Now, Neela was gone. Something was wrong with her. And Lou needed to know what that was.

"Do you think it's connected?" Lou asked. "Not, like, a professional opinion. Just a personal one."

Dad tapped his pen on his knee. "It's too similar, Lulu. And even if they're not connected, there's something very weird happening there and you—" Dad frowned, his eyebrows pulling together. "You deserve to know who they are."

The oddness of the phrasing snagged on her thoughts. Did she deserve to know who her mother was? Or May or Neela or Nana Tee?

What if none of them were the people Lou had grown up knowing?

She nodded, trying to ignore the rolling of her stomach. She couldn't just get on a plane, not without further confirmation. And there was only one person who could tell her what may be going on with Neela, and why Mom reacted the way she had. One person who, for no apparent reason, wasn't speaking to her.

"I guess I have to talk to May."

CHAPTER 8

"YOU PROMISE YOU'LL CALL ME IF YOU RUN INTO TROUBLE?" DAD asked again. His face was tinted green from the dash, barely illuminated in the glow of the streetlight. They sat in the car outside the brownstone. The light was on upstairs, so May was home from her shift.

"It's *my* house," Lou said, unclipping her seatbelt. "I won't get into trouble."

Dad kept frowning anyway. "Are you sure you don't want me to wait? I don't like the idea of you being here alone."

"The light's on," Lou said. "May's there."

This didn't make Dad look any happier.

Lou offered a half-hearted smile. "I'll be fine, okay? But if you really want to stick around, at least go around the block. I don't want May thinking this is some sort of stakeout."

Dad sighed. Mom, May, Neela, Nana Tee—the true Wickett women, as Lou saw them—were all stubborn and independent. Lou didn't have that same bite, that sharpness, but she often *wished* she did. And yet, there was still time. Lou wondered if that scared him, if he expected her to grow up lonely and hardened. Not for the first time, she puzzled over how her parents had been as a couple. They'd split before Lou was born—barely even been together, really—and co-parented well, but they were always separate entities. Mom and May, then Dad and Gen. Never "parents." She'd spoken of it with Neela, of their separate parents and traditions, of not being a child of divorce or a former couple so much as they were a child of two totally independent people.

It was like that stirring of Unbelonging, of being placeless, of belonging to no one. If she didn't belong to her parents, then whose was she?

"Just call, okay?"

"Will do."

Lou slipped out of the car and into the humid darkness. She took the stairs to the door two at a time and got the correct key on the first try. Dad waited until she was through the double doors before he pulled out and turned the corner onto a side street. Their place was on the second floor, and Lou felt her heart pounding as she darted up the stairs to number 3.

She waited outside the door for a moment, listening. When May was home, it was usually possible to hear her straight away. When she was little, Lou thought it was comforting. In their old apartment, she'd fallen asleep to creaking floorboards as May moved around, or rushing water as she drew a late-night bath, or the hiss of the kettle as she boiled water for tea. Mom made fun of May, calling her *le chat,* as if she were a feral cat on a midnight run through the apartment. Really, May just liked dancing when she was cooking or drinking her tea or washing up after a long day at the hospital. Since they'd moved here, Lou had struggled with the extra space but hearing May moving around on the creaky floorboards late at night made it feel more like it was theirs, not like they were borrowing it from her grandfather.

Now, she didn't hear anyone shifting around inside. Perhaps

May had already gone to bed and forgotten to turn off the living room light.

She texted Dad *I'm in* and put her phone on silent. She started to turn the knob and hissed, drawing her hand back at a sharp, bright stab of pain. Something had cut the back of her fingers between her first and second knuckles. Lou knelt down and looked at the doorknob. There was something there: a sharpened bit of metal, positioned to catch the hand of anyone who opened the door. Lou realized there were nails too, hammered in a circle around the doorknob.

She was familiar enough with Wickett superstitions to recognize that the nails were iron. Lou sucked in a breath.

Her mother and aunt believed in the same things, but it had been May who'd taught her most of the superstitions. When she was younger, she and May used to sit in the corner with the radio between them and tie holly onto strings to hang over the doorways. She remembered, one time, looking up to see Mom watching the two of them from the doorway of the bedroom. Not angry, not concerned, but indecipherable. Eyebrows knitted together, mouth pressed in a line. When she was a teenager, Lou wanted to ask Mom why she lined the windows with salt and hung the doorways with holly and pentacles all by herself, why she never asked Lou for help, why she had to be solitary.

But maybe that was something May was more willing to reveal to her. Because, until now, Lou had always thought that May was the easiest to get information from. May was always the one with cracks, the one who revealed the truth when Mom only turned away, deeper into her secrets.

Careful not to cut herself again, she turned the doorknob with her fingertips and shut it as softly as she could behind her.

May was not asleep. She laid on the couch, not watching TV, not listening to music. She was just staring at the ceiling as if she'd been waiting for Lou for hours.

As if she'd been waiting for Lou to come, for her to seek the truth. Because perhaps that was what May wanted: to reveal it all, no matter how much Mom wanted to keep the past buried.

"May," Lou said. Words caught in her mouth. May looked like she hadn't slept since Mom left, dark bags marring the skin under her eyes. Thickly, she said, "You didn't answer my calls."

May shrugged. "I thought you'd come by," she said in an odd voice. She laughed, the sound sending a chill up Lou's spine. Wryly, she repeated, "Come by, come by. Come buy, come buy."

It was oddly, stirringly familiar, but Lou couldn't place the phrase. There was something terrible about May repeating it to her. Lou locked the door but stayed there in the entryway, halfway between the kitchen and the living room.

May was wrapped in her robe with a towel atop her head. The only jewelry she'd bothered with was a thin iron chain, dark against her pale collarbones. She must've just come in from her shift and showered before Lou walked in. A cup of tea sat on the floor next to her, milky brown, half-drunk.

"Well?" May asked expectantly.

Lou stared at her, wide-eyed. She wasn't sure what she'd expected, but it wasn't this. May looked . . . Lou didn't know. She didn't look like herself.

"I wanted to check on you," Lou lied, but right now, it felt like the thing to say. And she did want to check on May. "See how you were doing."

I need you to tell me what happened. I need it to make sense.

May looked at her, clearly not taking the bait. "That's why

you came at"—she glanced at the clock—"eleven-thirty on a weekday."

Lou gritted her teeth. She didn't like this, the way May spoke to her, the way May looked. Her aunt was never this . . . this . . . odd.

She perched on the arm of the couch. May went back to staring straight up at the ceiling.

"Has there been any news?" Lou asked. This was better. May knew why she was really here. She knew she was here for answers. Might as well get to it.

May glanced longingly at the kitchen, towards the Vice Cabinet. Lou knew that look—it was the first thing about this version of her that was familiar. The Vice Cabinet was where Mom and May kept the stronger stuff, like whiskey and cigarettes they claimed to have given up years ago. May sighed.

There was something May was hiding, that she'd been through, that shaped who she'd become. Lou chewed on her lip as she looked at May and then away, trying not to get caught studying her. But how could Lou be certain? May was acting strange, yes, but Neela was missing. If something had happened to May before Lou was born, she didn't know how to ask about it. There was that unapproachable bit of space, that unquestionable area of May and Mom's life that Lou didn't ask about.

She felt the need to move, to do something. Lou went into the kitchen, noting the dirty dishes in the sink. At least May was eating, but—no. Not all of it was food.

Lou poked at one of the plates, covered in ashes and half-burnt bundles of herbs. One of the bundles, perfect and whole, rested next to the sink. Lou picked it up for closer examination. They were dried, the ones May grew in the windowsill and hung upside down in one of the upper cabinets. For good luck, she always said.

A chill ran down Lou's spine. Parsley. Sage. Rosemary. Thyme. She brushed the cold ashes into the trash and, before May could see, tossed the unburned bundle in after them. She was no stranger to cleansing—Mom and May cleansed their house regularly—but she'd never seen this combination before. Never had Lou felt quite so haunted by a sprig of parsley.

The kettle was still hot, full of boiled water. Lou poured herself a mug of tea with extra milk and sugar. It was the same way May liked her tea. Her mother, who drank hers black, called this blasphemy.

When she went back to the living room, May sat up and tented her knees, leaving room for Lou. Lou sat next to her, each taking one arm while their legs alternated in the middle. They'd sat like this to watch TV as long as Lou could remember. Though May was not her mother, she'd raised Lou just as much as Mom did. Mom and May aligned their work schedules when Lou was younger so she spent days with May after school, going to the library and walking around parks, until Mom came home and May went in for her night shift.

Mom protected Lou from the truth when she thought it would hurt her, but May didn't. Not when Lou asked why she didn't live with both parents like the other kids, not when Lou wondered why she couldn't get new clothes for school every year, not when she asked how badly Grandpa Jack's illness was progressing. Not before, and hopefully not now.

But looking at May, Lou didn't know if she *wanted* the truth. Unfortunately, in equal measure, she knew she needed it.

Lou went to set down her mug on the coffee table, but it was too far away, pushed against the non-painted wall. The room was still arranged from the day before. She held onto the mug, even though the ceramic kind of burned against her fingers.

The unfinished magenta wall mocked them both, yet another reminder of Mom's sudden departure. Yet another reminder that Neela was gone. May examined it mournfully.

"Will you please tell me what's going on?" Lou asked.

"What does it matter? We can't help anyway."

Lou's heart sank. "Maybe. Maybe not."

But her aunt didn't answer. If anything, May's shoulders drooped even lower. Lou chewed on her lip. "Do you remember when you taught me to sew holly together and hang it from the doorways?"

May's eyes flicked to Lou's. She had the same eyes as Nana Tee, blue irises with dark, heavy lashes. "Of course. What about it?"

Lou traced a circle on her own knee. "Mom was mad about it. She . . . I remember you two argued that night. In the kitchen. And she said that she was doing what was best for both of us."

She wanted to look over at May, to see if this was getting through to her. But there was silence beside her. The room was filled with the incessant ticking of the clock and the clatter of traffic outside. Lou swallowed hard, searching for words.

"I never asked. I knew it was better not to, and it didn't hurt anyone. It didn't hurt you. Maybe when I was really little, Mom told me not to talk about York, and I just accepted that. But this isn't fair. This isn't protection. I need to know what's happened to Neela." Lou glanced over at May, noting the way her eyes darted over to the window, then to the door, then settled on Lou. Something about May was different and charged. "I need to know what happened to you."

May stared down at her mug. She seemed to make some decision and her shoulders sagged. "They come every summer."

They. Lou puzzled through who "they" could be. "What do you mean?"

"They come every summer and they sing at the windows; you can hear them on every street, if you're one of the girls they want, one of the girls they're looking for. They sing and they call and they cry and it gets to you. It worms its way inside of you and you *want*, and you hear them until you're so full of wanting that it's all you can think of. And you go, and they take you, and you never ever come back."

Lou stared at May, wide-eyed and unsettled. "Who are they, May? Who are you talking about?"

May looked straight at her, and Lou wished she wouldn't. She was the girl-in-the-picture May, the broken May, the May Lou had never seen before.

"The goblins," May said. "The goblin market."

Lou stared at her for a moment, uncomprehending. Goblins? Goblins weren't real, just like vampires and witches and demons weren't. They were relegated to nightmares and horror movies and dark novels. They didn't come in and snatch girls off the street; they couldn't have hurt Neela.

Except, she remembered the odd tone of that voice, singing to her over the line. Telling her to come visit. Lou's skin had prickled when she heard it; perhaps some part of her knew that it wasn't quite human.

"I don't know what you're talking about," Lou said. She ran her thumb over her scratched knuckles. There was iron nailed into the door, just as there were iron pentacles hanging over the windows. Wasn't that a faerie story?

May closed her eyes. Lou had never seen her look so miserable. "I promised Laura I wouldn't tell you," she said, voice cracking.

"I promised to *protect* you."

Protection. Iron nails in the door, herbs on the counter, salt lining all entrances to the home. Sometimes, when Lou went out in the morning after a particularly windy summer night, she'd find yeasty bread or a saucer of milk nestled next to the stoop. She could not visit her mother's hometown, she could not hear the truth of what her childhood was like or what happened to make them leave England in the first place.

None of this was protection. Lou felt quite tangled in a safety net that was meant to keep her away from the worst of the world. Instead, it felt like it was strangling her.

But . . . goblins? Maybe this was why she'd never broken the rules before, never asked. Some part of her knew she wouldn't believe whatever answer they gave her.

"Why should I believe you?" Lou asked. She clenched her hands into fists, nails biting into her palms. Something had sent Mom running back to York, even after years of staying away. But how could it be goblins?

"It's better if you don't believe me," May said bitterly.

Lou chewed on her lip. A plan was forming in the back of her mind. "So if Neela was taken by goblins, why did Mom go? What good could she do?"

"Laura's going to try to get Neela out of the market," May said. There was a hopelessness to her voice, utterly unfamiliar to Lou. An odd realization swept over Lou as she looked at May. In the same way that Lou revolved her world around Neela, counted on her and confided in her, Mom was the same for May. Without Mom, May was knocked off-kilter, unsteady.

Lou didn't have to believe in goblins or their market. Mom and May did, clearly, or else Mom wouldn't have gone. But if

Lou played along, if she kept herself open to the idea, she could get May to take her to Mom. She could figure out what was going on, firsthand, and . . . well, that was where the plan needed more work. Because if goblins were real, then Lou had to square with that. And if they weren't, she had to figure some other way to get Neela back.

"We have to go help her," Lou insisted. "You know we do."

May bit her lip. She was so small, shoulders tucked and knees up, hunched in on herself, made awkward by her baby bump. "I know," she said miserably.

A final thought crystallized above all others, nagging in Lou's brain. "How does Mom even know what she's doing?" she asked. Lou hadn't considered any kind of reality in which Mom was actively in danger, but if May was right . . . Lou chewed on the inside of her cheek. She couldn't think of a world in which something happened to Mom, just as she couldn't imagine a world without Neela. So she didn't. "How does she know how to get Neela back?"

May looked at Lou, haggard and miserable. "Who do you think came to save me?"

CHAPTER 4

May

York, Eighteen Years Earlier

THE FIRST BODY OF THE SEASON HAD BEEN FOUND ON THE BANKS of the river, in the shadows of the Ouse Bridge. At least, what was left of it had—and May wasn't sure just yet what parts those were. Judging by the rumors, it was a torso, neatly sliced from the head and lower extremities, with the organs removed and the chest left open like an armoire. In the back corner of the pub, the regulars nursed their ales and bickered over how many more would be found before the market packed up and left.

Even as they named their bets, they cast anxious glances at the front door because they knew, they knew, they knew.

May kept an ear on the conversation as she and Charlotte pulled pints and mixed drinks. She wanted all the details before she went to the Witchery that night, where the remains would probably still be laid out on a table in the back room, clean after Mum's inspection. She wanted to know now, so she wasn't confronted by the utter brutality of the killing when she faced it later.

Mom and Laura always told May that she didn't fear the market enough. That she spent too much time looking at the dark corners of the streets in the months of June and July, when monsters lurked in the shadows. That she didn't respect the sacrifice her ancestors had made.

Well, that was bollocks, May thought as she pulled a pint for Georgie, one of the regulars, who looked at her a moment too long.

She respected the sacrifice well enough. After all, magic came at a cost. For her ancestors to protect most of the city from becoming a hunting ground, the price was May's blood.

"Ye look like you're considering something you shouldn't," Georgie said as he set down coins for his drink.

May swept them up and deposited them in the cash drawer. Charlotte aimed a look at her. She was from out of town, only here for uni; she didn't understand the tone of Georgie's voice. Charlotte was just another outsider in this city, fearing a murderer.

The reality was much, much worse.

Or, at least, that's what everyone kept telling May.

"And what's that?" May asked, trying to keep her voice sickly sweet. There wasn't actually much wrong with Georgie. He was nice, and he'd stood up for May when a customer got too rowdy with her once earlier in the summer.

But Georgie only sighed. He sipped his ale. Some of the head stuck to his mustache, but he didn't seem to mind. "You mind your mother, love," he said wearily before returning to the table.

Charlotte waited until Georgie was well away before she came and nudged May's hip with her own. "What was that about?"

May shook her head. "He had a message for my mum," she said. For the thousandth time, she wiped the bar.

Charlotte leaned against the bar, not even pretending to work. "What do you suppose happened to that girl?" she asked, voice pitched low.

May shrugged. "Who knows if we'll ever find out." Of course, she knew what happened. The girl had gone to the market, by choice or seduction, and she'd overstayed her welcome. There would be nearly a dozen bodies like hers left within the walls before the summer's end.

The body was only public knowledge because it had been found by the wrong people. Between the solstice and Lammas, if a native of the city found one of the bodies within a faerie circle, they were more likely to go to the witches than the police. After all, during this time, the police were only going to take the body to the witches themselves.

But last night's body had been found by a tourist visiting the town. They'd screamed and drawn a crowd, and before Mum or Joss or any of the coven could intervene, the word had spread through the city, in fearful whispers, with darting glances by those who didn't understand, and with weary sighs and clenched fists full of iron from the locals.

It was foolish, May knew, to venture anywhere near the market. Anyone born here knew that.

Foolish, yes. But she wanted to all the same.

The little bell over the door rang. Charlotte glanced up, customer service smile in place, but it slipped when they saw who entered. It was only Laura, still wearing her apron from the corner shop where she worked selling cigarettes and newspapers. She nodded once to Charlotte and tossed a pack of rolling papers to May. May caught them easily and tucked them in her pocket, next to her tobacco and filters, and pulled Laura a pint.

She couldn't help feeling guilty. It was like every time May let the dark thought of the market cross her mind, Laura appeared. Like she knew.

A girl just died. You know what they'll do to you.

"Good day?" May asked as Laura leaned an elbow against the bar and surveyed the clientele.

Laura frowned. "Tense," she said. Georgie glanced over—don't speak of the market, not here on the streets, out of home, and not in front of Charlotte, an outsider.

"It's coming," Laura said, keeping her words vague enough that Georgie only sighed and went back to his drink.

"It's already here," May said.

Laura looked mournfully out at the street. Neither of them could strip goblin glamour away like Mum could—in this case, they were like every other vulnerable human on the street. A couple meandered down the street—odd, because there was nothing around here of any interest, not unless you had to be here—but not odd enough for May to worry. She was still watching them when the little bell rang again.

There was another girl now, a girl so beautiful that May felt something in her heart tug and pull in a way she wished it wouldn't; she didn't know what to do with it.

The girl was only just taller than May, by the looks of it, but had long and graceful limbs, tanned and toned. Her hair was purple and wavy, twisted through with the occasional tiny braid. She wore a tank top knotted at her waist, shorts, and ripped tights with sturdy boots.

May stared at her for two seconds before she knew she was panicking, and that she mustn't panic like this in front of Laura, who would see it on her face and know.

"Hiya, you alright?" she asked, forcing her best customer service voice, her truest smile. A few of the regulars looked over at her oddly and she knew she'd gotten it wrong. Too eager. Too loud. "Can I get you something?"

The girl smiled, one corner of her mouth dragging up, and May could only—maybe—no. But she swore, just for the fraction of a second, she could just see the tips of the girl's pointed teeth.

"Whatever's strongest," the girl said.

Neither of them pointed out that it was only passing three, that the sun was still bright in the sky. It was the time of year when girls like her disappeared in the dead of night, and May wasn't stopping this girl from drinking however much she liked to get through it.

"If ye insist," she said. She started fixing a drink the regulars called Goblin Blood for its ability to knock you on your back or get you in a fight.

As May poured the spirits in the glass, she felt the girl's eyes on her back. Had she seen the teeth? Possibly. And what was to say that they were really oddly pointed, that she didn't just have sharp canines? What if she was from the south and teeth sharpening was a new trend May had somehow missed?

And what if May was trying to make this girl some supernatural being in her mind because that would make it easier to explain the tingly feelings in May's chest when she looked at her?

Oh May, she thought, *you've really done it now.*

Because the truth of what May liked, what she wanted, was easier to swallow when it wasn't standing in front of her with rips in her tights and braids in her hair.

"Here you are," May said, turning and setting the drink down in front of the girl. "Four pounds even."

The girl nodded and took coins out of her pocket. May held out her hand, not focusing at all on how warm the coins were from the girl's thigh, not one bit.

"Thanks," she said. She went to the register where Charlotte lounged, eating a bowl of chips the kitchen had sent down.

May opened the drawer and started to pour the coins in, except—there were five here.

Four pounds, and one gold coin with a sword embossed on it. Goblin gold.

May looked at the girl. She smiled, all wickedly pointed teeth and devious green eyes. Holding May's gaze, she tipped the drink back and emptied it to the dregs. In her peripheral vision, May only just saw Laura's eyes fly open in surprise.

The goblin girl set her glass down on the bar and wiped her mouth with the back of her hand.

"Aye," she said, "thanks for the drink. I'll be seeing you."

May didn't have to look at Laura to feel her gaze piercing through her skin. She swallowed hard.

The girl sauntered out of the pub and into the sunshine. May watched until she turned the corner and disappeared.

There was a body in the Witchery, the body of a girl just like May, possibly the body of a girl May knew from school. There was a body of a girl who'd been tempted, maybe one who'd started just like this, with the promise of goblin gold. A body of a girl who'd played the games the market offered and lost.

A girl who'd made the decision May was wrestling with now.

"May," Laura said carefully, as if she could read her mind. "When are you done?"

"Oi, you go," Charlotte said. "It's getting on four anyway."

"Now," May rasped, throat dry. She closed her hand around the goblin gold, still burning with heat from the girl's body.

They'd be at her window tonight, singing and calling. May had no doubt of it.

Her only doubt now was what she'd do when they sang to her.

It was the market, the market, the market, and the night air swelled with possibilities, with things to come and mistakes to be made, hot with danger and clamorous with anticipation. The first victim had been slain, and many more would follow. If May wasn't smart, she would be among them.

It was the market, the market, the market, and the line between worlds was thin and hazy. When May swallowed, she tasted the metal of suppressed magic on her tongue and felt the singing of her blood. It was the market, and this was the year that everything would change.

CHAPTER 5

THERE WERE THINGS ABOUT MAY THAT LOU INHERENTLY KNEW. It was like every child with a beloved aunt, she supposed. She knew which of her mother's rules May would let her break, and how she took her tea, and the scent of her perfume. Lou knew all of May's favorite movies and had met every person she'd dated and let May keep her secrets when she wasn't willing to tell Mom.

But there were things about May that Lou struggled with, like how she and Mom had grown into one another over the years like roots of neighboring trees. Sometimes it was impossible to tell where Mom began and May ended, and who was smirking at what, and if they were ever really on Lou's side at all or just a united front to parent against her.

She puzzled over this as May stood in the kitchen, squinting at the laptop. "I think that's it. We're booked."

Lou looked up from the living room floor where she was folding clothes and shoving the piles into a suitcase. "Is there anything in particular we need to bring?"

"No." May sighed. She rolled her shoulders, cracking her joints. "Laura is going to *kill* me."

"Because you're bringing me?"

May looked at her, but Lou wasn't certain she was actually

seeing her. Perhaps she was looking through her. "I'm sure she's not keen on *me* going either," May said. She glanced away, face full of something like shame.

If Lou accepted the reality of the market and held it up against what she knew of May, she had to accept that it had changed her in some way. And yes, there were things they avoided discussing, talked around—but every family had that.

There were days when May couldn't get out of bed, mostly when Lou was younger, and when she'd go past, she could hear the sound of her sobbing. As she grew older, she'd chalked it up to depression, like anyone would. And there were foods May wouldn't eat and songs she wouldn't listen to and she always cried when she drank.

But Lou had no reason to think any of that was due to some supernatural market. No reason to even consider it.

When Lou looked at May now, she saw all the ways that she didn't know her at all. "Do you think Mom is protecting you too?"

May sighed. "Isn't she always?" She shut the laptop and stowed it away in the suitcase next to Lou's. The night was creeping on toward the witching hour, the time that May once drunkenly told her the veil between the living and the dead was the haziest, when the magic was strongest. Lou had only laughed and replaced her gin and tonic with tap water.

May ran a hand through Lou's hair, catching on the tangles. "There will be more we have to talk about," she said, her voice stalling, "but now isn't the time. Let's sleep, Louisa, and not think of the market, and not speak of it." Her eyes slipped shut. "For the next few hours, I just want to pretend."

She went off down the hall before Lou could ask what she was pretending and why. Lou swallowed her questions, choking them down. They would have to wait—what was a few hours after sixteen years of holding her questions in?

She glanced up just in time to catch the clock slipping past 3:00 a.m., and like any other night she caught it, she felt an electric shiver run down her spine.

The last time Neela had visited, Lou and Neela had "borrowed" May's car in the dead of night. It wasn't a smart decision. Neither were licensed, both were learning, and they weren't brave enough to wake Mom if there was an emergency. But after midnight, the streets of Revere were dark and nearly empty.

Lou pulled up directions on her GPS and cautiously fed them to Neela. They drove haltingly for ten minutes before they reached the beach. Lou stole into the back seat for the cooler while Neela grabbed the blanket and flashlights.

It had rained most of the day, giving way to a clear, star-filled night. The sand still held a remnant of the day's rain as Neela spread out the blanket. They shivered in their sweatshirts, laying on their backs and staring at the stars.

"I told you this would be better than a drive-in movie," Neela said. She was usually the mastermind of their plans.

Lou only laughed. Truthfully, she didn't care: that Unbelonging that pressed on her heart, the one that felt suffocating during the school year, was gone when Neela was around. When the two of them were together, Lou was back to being half of a pair instead of ripped into pieces.

"What do you think we'll be doing three years from now?" she asked in the quiet between the crashing waves.

"Like, specifically on this day?" Neela asked. She sat up to investigate the contents of the cooler and pulled out a bottle of grape soda. She always drank grape soda in America—apparently, it was really hard to find back home.

"Or generally," Lou said.

Neela opened the bottle with a *crack-hiss* and took a careful sip. She stared off into the distance, at the waves, and Lou watched her think.

Lou didn't want Neela to look over at her, to see the unthinkable longing there. Because this was the truth: when Lou thought of her future, of any time in advance, she always factored in Neela. She and her best friend would no longer be separated by an ocean or time zones or Lou's tendency toward awkwardness. They'd be in a flat in Edinburgh or traveling through South Africa or Australia or even settling at a college in California. Maybe Neela would have a partner, but it didn't really matter, because at the end of the day, when everyone else was removed, it would be her and Lou.

Lou felt dreadful anticipation growing with each crashing wave that Neela didn't answer.

"Nee?" Lou said.

"I don't know what I'll be doing," Neela said, flicking a grain of sand off her soda bottle. Her eyes looked black in the darkness. "But I know that you'll be there."

"Of course," Lou said, fighting back the surge of relief.

Her life felt like an endless path of puzzles: Why didn't she feel the same as everyone else around her? Why couldn't she just relate? But when she was with Neela, it all went away. Lou sometimes feared that she was like the much-younger sibling or cousin, the one that was impossible to shake off.

But Neela draped her arm over Lou's shoulders. "It'll be us until the end," she said, her teeth shining bright white. "Who else would keep my secrets?"

At the time, Lou had only laughed. It was her job to keep Neela's secrets.

But now, in the darkness of this Neela-less summer, Lou couldn't come to terms with this: there was one secret, one big reveal, that Neela had not told her.

CHAPTER 6

AT VARIOUS POINTS DURING LOU'S LIFE, SHE FELT QUITE LIKE SHE was coming out of a fugue state in which she'd look around, take stock of her life, and think to herself, *This is not normal. These are not things a normal family does.*

Lou and May sat in uneasy silence on the plane, waiting for it to take off. Only minutes before, Lou had spoken to her Dad on the phone. She'd left it to the last second because there would be less of a chance of him coming to get her.

He hadn't been happy. But he hadn't stopped her, either.

Now, they were past the planning and the worry. They were on their way to England whether Mom or Dad liked it or not. The only problem was Lou still had no idea what they were getting themselves into.

"Can we talk about ——"

"No," May snapped. Her eyes darted around, taking in the people around him.

They had the row to themselves, with the closest passengers being a college-aged duo wearing headphones in front of them, a family of three in the middle aisle, and a couple of businessmen behind who'd brought cocktails in a can from the terminal. No one was paying attention to them.

But May *still* wouldn't answer Lou's questions.

Too bad for her, in the body of the plane, there was nowhere to go.

"I'm not giving up," Lou said, shifting in her seat.

"Not here," May said, shooting Lou another warning glance.

But what could happen? So *what* if someone overheard them. It didn't matter. It would sound like they were talking about Dungeons & Dragons or a movie. No one actually believed in goblins.

"I'm only asking about Walmart," Lou said, raising her eyebrows. May withered slightly. But there was no way Lou was letting her out of this, and the promise of an eight-hour flight stretched in front of them. Pregnant or not, May couldn't hide in the bathroom the whole time.

"Right," May sighed, admitting defeat. "Walmart."

Lou tried to organize her thoughts as the plane raced down the runway and angled towards the sky, as Boston dropped away underneath them. She had a million questions, of course—questions that kept her up when she already had very little time to sleep, that forced her to listen to those voicemails another dozen times this morning while May was out grabbing toiletries from the pharmacy down the street.

"If you don't answer my questions, I'll have to ask Mom," Lou said finally.

May's hand tightened on the armrest between them as the plane banked. She and Mom had the same slender fingers, the same bony wrists, the same freckles up their arms.

"She's already going to kill me for bringing you," May said. "So we should probably keep questions to a minimum when we get there." May looked at her the way she used to, when Lou was a child, and May allowed her to stay up much later than her bedtime when Mom was out or when May snuck her candy she wasn't supposed to have.

"Good point. So. What's the whole point of it? And how does it work? Do you just go in? Are you invited? How do you think—why—why would . . ." The final question got caught in Lou's throat.

If Neela knew the risks, why did she go?

May snorted. "One at a time, duck. There's not a *point*. It's a market. You do get invited, and then there are . . . ways to remember how to get in and out. And ways to protect yourself."

Iron. Smudged herbs. Lines of salt and ash and pentacles. She got the feeling that when they got to York, the protections would already be familiar to her.

"Right. But if there are risks, if people don't always come back, why would you want to go in the first place?"

May rolled her eyes. "I think you're missing the point. It's not like any regular Walmart."

"Is it a super-deluxe?" Lou deadpanned.

May elbowed her.

"I just don't get it," Lou said, leaning her head against the window. They were in the clouds now, pillowy like the best cotton candy at the summer fair. "You knew it was dangerous, right? That's the whole point. So why did you go? Why would Neela?"

May was quiet for a moment, long enough that Lou worried this Q&A was over. But then, May said, "If you're so certain it's all bad, why are you flying toward it?"

Lou looked over at her. "If there's something I can do to help Neela, I'd do it in a heartbeat. And you can't pretend you don't want to be there to help Mom."

"Touché." May sighed, sitting back in her chair. She looked tired. She'd been on the phone with work all morning, trying to explain why she suddenly needed to leave for an indeterminate amount of time. Lou didn't hear the details, but when May came out of her room, her eyes were puffy and dry. Lou wasn't sure if May had a job to come back to, or if Mom did, for that matter. For both of them to up and quit their lives to go racing to the city they abandoned, without the guarantee of their jobs to come back to, even with the money Grandpa Jack left behind. . . . It wasn't a small matter.

Mom and May were sacrificing a lot for this, for whatever they would face in York.

"It's like a haunted house," May said finally. "Or, more accurately, like . . . bungee jumping or skydiving or driving in Formula 1. There's risk, yes. But you don't think the bad things will happen to you. You didn't get on this plane expecting to crash, did you? That's why people go to the market. Because they expect to leave."

Lou glanced outside again, suddenly aware of just how high they were, how far from the safety of her little room they'd already gone.

"Do you think Neela expected to leave?" Lou asked. Her voice cracked, betraying her. She clenched her hands into fists in her lap.

"Of course she did," May said, laying a hand over her arm. She closed her eyes, something clearing on her face. "My motives didn't matter when I went there," May said. "There are rules, and I broke them. But the rules don't matter in the market. They're rules set by tricksters. The gob—The *employees* don't care, duck. Not about you, not about me, and not about Neela."

Lou swallowed down the lump in her throat. "Walmart sounds like shit."

"It is," May said. She bit her lip, phasing into silence as the flight attendant went by and offered them both drinks: water for May, ginger ale for Lou.

"I need you to understand something, Lou, and this is the last I'll speak on it tonight," May said, eyes darting to the people sitting around them. The other passengers were shifting, getting ready for dinner.

"But what about—"

May shook her head. "You'll learn them soon enough. But you won't remember what you should and shouldn't do if I tell you everything. You're not afraid enough to believe me yet."

Lou didn't have anything to say to that. After all, May wasn't wrong.

"Once we're off the train in York," May said, tracing the armrest between them, "once we're within the city walls, we're in this. There is no going back. No running away."

A chill ran down Lou's spine. Last night, all she'd wanted was to run in, to get to the bottom of this, to know everything. But now that they were en route, now that Lou could study the shadows on May's face when she spoke of the market, Lou didn't know what she wanted.

Neela, safe. That was it. Neela safe and Mom not mad.

If she could get Neela back, then she'd take any risk to do it.

CHAPTER 7

May

Eighteen Years Earlier

BY THE TIME THEY GOT TO THE WITCHERY, THE FRONT ROOM was already ripe with the sickly smell of decay. It didn't matter how cold it was, how many fans they rigged using the electricity from the building above. The smell wound out from the back room and clung.

Marcus was at the broad butcher's table, washing blood off his hands in a basin. He glanced up at them, his nose wrinkling as he took in May's shorts. "You shouldn't be wearing those," he said, drying his hands on a tea towel. He hadn't done a good job with the blood removal, and dark smears now stained the cheerful towel, printed with sausage dogs wearing bow ties.

"And why not?" May asked, hands on her hips. She fought with Marcus because they had nothing better to do. Marcus, May, and Laura were the only children of the coven's witches— at least, the only children left in York, besides Neela, who didn't count. Of course they pulled at one another.

"Because it's bloody back there," he said. He pulled off his blood-stained shirt revealing smooth, dark skin and muscle. May pretended to ignore Laura's little squeak as he tossed his shirt into the burn bin, just as she'd ignored Marcus leaving their flat early one morning last week.

Before May could poke at either of them, Mum and Joss came bustling out of the back room. They both wore cloth masks, probably coated with a thin layer of peppermint oil to keep the smell at bay. Mum carried an armful of bloody cloths. Joss carried a vat of some sort of ointment or liquid or brew that smelled almost worse than the decomposition.

"Marcus, can you go up and call the coroner?" Joss asked. "We've gotten all we can from her."

He nodded, pulling on a new shirt, sparing a glance at Laura. It didn't matter. Laura followed him out anyway, mumbling about forgetting to take her apron off. May tried not to notice it too much. The three of them were apprentices of the coven they were meant to inherit and spent more time together than apart. It was no surprise Laura and Marcus would be drawn together, and May didn't let it bother her.

"How bad is it?" May asked, throwing herself down on the sofa as the two washed up. A spring dug into her back and the sofa was probably older than God, but it was better than sitting on the floor. At least here she could bury her nose in the arm and smell the musty scent of dust and old fabric rather than rotting flesh.

"Bad," Mum said, taking off her mask and tossing it in the burn bin. She removed the heavy smock she wore for autopsies and hung it on a hook near a water tank. Joss would take both of their smocks home to wash the blood-soaked clothing in a basin dedicated for such things in her backyard.

"I suspect it will be a rough year," Joss said. She took out her tobacco pouch and started rolling a cigarette. "I'm out of filters."

May tossed her a pack. Joss caught them easily and rolled two, handing one to Mum. "Can you hold it down for a few minutes?" Mum asked May, glancing toward the door. She always needed a moment to collect herself after an autopsy.

"Sure," she said.

May waited until Mum and Joss were outside and the door was firmly shut before she jumped up. She dug Mum's mask out of the burn bin and put it on. The smell would only get worse from here.

She crept down the hall. She was probably alone in the Witchery, but she never knew for sure. Angelique, the third and final witch in the coven, could be in one of the back rooms, or someone could be visiting from London or Edinburgh or Brighton—though other witches tended to avoid York at this time of year. The market made every witch tense. Even the Thaumaturge, the strongest of all of them.

May didn't blame them. If she didn't have to inherit this coven and its responsibilities, she would consider leaving town and its market too.

The body was in the last room at the end of the hall. They usually were either in this room or the one across, depending on how many there were on any given day. The smell intensified when May opened the door. She was grateful for the peppermint within her mask, even if it made her eyes water.

The body laid on a stone slab in the middle of the room. Of course, "body" was an exaggeration—the rumors had gotten it right.

Well, almost.

The girl had been reduced to a torso, with the flesh cut down the middle and organs removed. But what the rumors failed to mention was the sapling growing from the dead woman's chest or the sludgy detritus gathered in her abdominal cavity. Roots wound in her veins and jutted out in odd places, poking through her skin to wrap around her collarbones, sticking out in the torn places where her limbs once were, snaking through the middle of a tattoo on her right ribcage.

May sighed.

This was the reality of the market. This was what could happen to her if she gave in to the goblin gold burning a hole in her pocket. This was the threat, the promise, the reality.

Something clattered in the main room. May looked up just in time to catch Marcus opening the door. He let it shut behind him, knowing Laura wouldn't follow.

Laura was the strongest of the three of them, May suspected. The most fearless. But perhaps that had something to do with the fact she never looked at the bodies.

Marcus lifted the bucket of warm water and rested it on the edge of the table. "I'm here to clean her up," he said, even though May hadn't asked.

She only nodded and leaned against the rough-hewn stone wall. It was always cold in the Witchery, and today was no exception. She wished she'd stopped home to put on a jacket or jeans. She wished Marcus wasn't right about the shorts being a bad idea.

"Did Angelique stay home?" Usually, all three of them, Mum, Joss, and Angelique, were here when a body was found. May didn't think Marcus was experienced enough yet to take Angelique's place, but perhaps she was wrong.

"Christina's sitter canceled," Marcus said, unpacking his tools and laying them out. Scissors, a needle and thread, clippers.

"Angelique went to watch Neela."

Well, it was better than bringing baby Neela here, where the scent of decay hung heavy in the air. Though she was born into this legacy of blood and magic, she was still too young to inherit it. "What did they find?" May asked.

Marcus shrugged. He dipped the cloth in the water and washed the pallid skin with long, certain strokes. Once, years ago, when Marcus first started coming home from uni over the summers to help with cleanup, he'd told May he did it out of respect. The victims of the market kept York safe. If they violated the terms of the agreement, if enough of them were slain to keep the goblins sated, the witches had nothing much to worry about. It was the least he could do to make their bodies clean of magic for burial.

"The usual," he said. "Poison in the blood. Runes on the back. Your mum is working on an antidote for anything new they found."

May crossed her arms over her chest. She watched as Marcus took the set of clippers and cut the sapling from the body. He reached in and carefully untangled the roots from her ribcage. May wished she felt something, nausea or fear or anger, but she felt calm as ever.

She helped Marcus hold the skin together as he stitched the halves back together. It wasn't a perfect v-cut, like a hospital would make, but ragged and dirty. Absently, May wondered if the girl was still alive when the cut was made.

"Was there a signature?" she asked.

Marcus sighed, gathering up all the bloody tools and towels. He shucked his gloves into the basket with them. "My mother thinks it's Iark, the Market Prince," he said. "That's who came down to Petergate on the solstice."

May nodded. Every year, the Market Prince and his circle met with the coven at midnight on the solstice to ensure both sides were keeping to the Doctrine. "Do you agree with that?"

Marcus frowned. This year, for the first time, he went with Mum and Joss and Angelique to meet with the goblins. Next year, Laura would go, and May the year after.

After all, who knew what the goblins would do with their blood there, all singing to them.

"I didn't like the look of Iark's new second," he said. "She looks . . . mean."

May looked at the body again, appearing far more human now that the sapling was removed, now that the roots had been cut out, now that it was clean and sewn back together. "They all look mean," she said.

She didn't mean it. She didn't believe it. But if May kept saying she feared the goblins, if she kept reinforcing that they were the enemy, perhaps nobody would look too closely if May herself ventured down towards the Shambles one night after dark.

She didn't want to feel the pull of the market. None of them did.

May left the Witchery as the sun sank lower and lower and dyed the sky red. She slipped into the twilight, into the hour that was not good for maidens, as the stars blinked and cluttered the night sky.

She'd stayed to help with another injured girl, this one brought in alive, who sobbed as May and Marcus peeled away the metal that had been burned onto her skin. Between tears, the girl told them that she'd been punished for touching one of the goblins with a bit of iron.

Now, she walked through the streets alone. She didn't take the fast way home. There was something delicious about walking through the city at night with her hood drawn to shadow her face. Something freeing about edging around the entrances to the market.

It hadn't called to her when she was a child. She was too young then, useless to them. The market didn't go after children—goblins didn't bother with changelings.

But in her thirteenth summer, just as Laura warned her, the goblins appeared under her window one night. *Come buy, come buy!* they called, grinning up toward her. May had felt her heart thudding, her palms growing slick with sweat as she gazed out at the street below.

And the worst part? She'd *wanted* to go.

It was their magic, Mum explained to her at the table over tea, just as most mothers explained puberty to their daughters. Their magic called to May just as her magic appealed to them.

It didn't matter that May couldn't use her own magic. When she was little, they'd warded her, just as they'd warded Laura and Marcus. It made them safer here if they couldn't access their power until they were adults. Until then, she had all the side effects of being magical without the benefits of having magic.

So perhaps there was some sort of stubbornness in doing this, May conceded, creeping down the street toward the Shambles. Here, the buildings became uneven, leaning in over the streets, leering down at her.

She wasn't looking for the girl. But she wasn't *not* looking for the girl.

May paused under the overhang of one of the windows and lit a cigarette. There was a pub across the street, full to bursting. She scanned the people drinking pints outside, mostly tourists stopping for a drink. None of them looked afraid. After all, there was safety in numbers.

She glanced down the street. The danger wasn't always evident here, on the street, even in the misty twilight. Though there were entrances throughout the old part of the city, none of the market itself was aboveground. No; the streets only acted as a hunting ground.

It was only when she was alone like this that she let herself think of the coven and the weight of her blood. It was worst during the market months when May felt agonizingly trapped.

It was no secret what May's future would be. And Laura's, and Marcus's for that matter. They'd be able to go away for university, to get an education, but they'd have to return afterwards to take over the coven. That was the price of magic: loyalty.

Marcus and Laura didn't seem to fear the constraints of their bloodline the same way did May did. When she thought of this, endless markets for the rest of her life, she always felt restless. But it wasn't like she could tell Marcus and Laura that. Marcus, who was nearly finished with university, was prepared to take his place. And Laura couldn't wait to be a full witch of the coven. It was there on her face every time she helped Mum or Joss or Angelique, every time she set foot in the Witchery.

May didn't know why she felt the way she did. She only knew that she shouldn't.

She was so lost in her thoughts, it took May an embarrassingly long time to realize someone was staring at her.

The boy was leaning against the wall in the mouth of an alley. His gaze was too intense, dark enough that May felt goose bumps prickling up on her arms. He started to move as soon as their eyes locked.

"Hey," the boy called after her, his voice husky. He caught her arm, his skin cold against hers. May glanced over at the pub crowd, but none of them had noticed her.

May turned around and caught her breath. This close, the boy smelled like lemon verbena and woodsmoke. He did not smell like rot, but perhaps that was another glamour.

She shifted. Maybe he wasn't a goblin. It was possible she was wrong—the glamours were harder to strip away when her brain was clouded like this, when she forgot to wear any iron or line her pockets with oats or holly berries.

"Would you like to see something impossible?"

May leveled a gaze at him. Definitely a goblin. His eyes were wickedly black, his face narrow with fine features. "No."

The boy laughed. "Perhaps to find your own destiny, then?"

They said, in the market, you became who you really were. All pretenses slipped away. There was joy and pleasure like never before. Those who returned came back with glazed eyes, wanting to go back above all. Even if they were hurt. Even if they were half dead.

Whatever was in the market, it was apparently worth the risk.

May wanted to know who she was, under this false pretense of magic that she didn't feel ready or worthy to inherit, away from the expectations she could never meet.

"I know what my destiny is." She sighed. It didn't matter what was in the market, or what this boy or the goblin girl from before promised her. The market was death and aching and wonders beyond what she could imagine. And none of it was meant for her, no matter how much she longed for it.

Sometimes, she had moments of clarity like this, when she knew the market was a bad idea.

She gave the boy her half-smoked cigarette. He looked at it with clear distaste. "There are many finer drugs on offer than this, where I can take you," he said.

"Not interested," May said. She ignored the buzzing of her skin, the call of the market. How she *wanted* to go, especially when the invitation was right there.

She didn't trust herself to stay any longer. May nodded to him, walking backwards in the direction of home. "Good luck," she said. "I'll see you around."

"Magic beyond your wildest dreams!" the goblin called. "Unbelievable fruits! Unforgettable wines! Come buy, May Wickett!"

She blew him a kiss. It was easier to act tough when there was space between them. "Maybe next year!" she called before she turned the corner, her breath coming in one huff, adrenaline rushing through her veins.

May didn't know how much longer she could stay away from the market. And if the girl came back, even with the risks, she didn't think she'd say no again. If she couldn't leave this city behind, perhaps the best choice—the only choice—would be to embrace it.

CHAPTER 8

Lou could barely keep her eyes open as they shuffled through Border Control and then Customs, using her dark red passport for the very first time. She rested against May's shoulder as the Piccadilly line wound under the city toward the train station. She tried to look outside, but the sun had not yet risen over London before the Tube descended below the surface, so all she saw was her own shadowed face reflected back. Instead, she traced the shape of the flowers on May's tattoo over and over again, trying to keep herself awake.

May woke her again as they neared their stop, though Lou didn't even remember falling asleep. She scrambled with the luggage and followed May through the maze of tunnels and stairs and escalators, the subterranean world that existed to link the lines.

She didn't know what to expect as the pair ascended the escalator. She registered the scent of damp, of rain on city streets mingling with exhaust and cigarette smoke; of wet newspaper and the metallic Tube air. It wasn't cold when they emerged, but it was certainly colder than it had been in Boston.

"Stay with me," May urged, shooting a distrustful look at a passing group of men in suits, talking rapidly in smooth accents.

They were caught in a swell of commuter traffic as May whisked Lou into King's Cross and stationed her in front of the departure boards.

"You keep an eye on this, aye?" she said, pointing upwards. "9:57 towards Edinburgh. That's us."

Lou nodded, her words caught in her throat. May's accent was thicker here, or maybe her aunt wasn't masking it anymore. She bustled off towards the ticket kiosks, leaving Lou alone with the luggage.

Lou had seen King's Cross before in movies and shows, read about it in books, but she hadn't expected it like this. Alive and busy, not fully inside but not outside either, gray, foggy, brick and metal, abuzz with commuters. Everyone was moving, had somewhere to be, knew where they were going while Lou just stood in the middle of it. Even the people waiting near her were restless, talking on phones and shifting back and forth and walking closer to the departure boards and back again.

The board over her head changed, shifted farther to the left. They didn't have a platform yet, but Lou's blood thrummed close against her skin. It was like her adrenaline was waking up, shaking off the haze of the flight. They'd had a lull and now it was time to go, time to be there, time to help.

"For you," May said, holding out a cup. She held another in her hands.

Lou took a sip. Hot tea, a splash of milk, two sugars. The way they both drank it.

"How long is the ride?" she asked.

"Two-ish hours," May said. She took a sip of her tea and frowned. "I miss caffeine."

"It misses you too, surely," Lou said.

They stood and waited in the group of people staring up at the boards as King's Cross bustled around them. Lou felt a part of something, maybe, or like she could pretend to be a part of something. Not for the first time she thought of herself as a living vessel, of something with roots. In Boston, she felt the traceries of them, winding across the Atlantic into the damp soil of England. Now, again, she closed her eyes and reached with something inside of her. Did she feel at home? Did she understand the loss of that missing piece of her?

Maybe you don't belong anywhere, the roots whispered back. *Maybe you're cursed to wander.*

She thought back to that night on the beach with Neela. If Neela was gone, if Neela was taken, then who was Lou meant to be? Where was her pair? Whose secrets was she meant to keep?

But there was the alternative line of questioning: If Neela kept all of Lou's secrets but had hidden this from Lou, this massive part of her life . . . then what else had she hidden?

Something awful twisted in her stomach. She didn't want the same things other people did; she didn't feel the claws of desire in her throat. But she did want the clarity of someone she belonged to. She *needed* Neela.

"We've got a platform," May said, breaking Lou out of her thoughts. They grabbed their suitcases and Lou followed May through the gates and onto the train.

"Okay, love," May said, settling into the window seat and leaning her head against the glass. "I'm tired, baby's tired, and I don't think we'll have much sleep once we get there. You have to stay awake because if we both sleep, we'll end up in Edinburgh."

"But May—" Lou started. This was her final chance to ask questions, her final chance to prepare before they arrived to her mother's disappointment.

May shook her head. "Two hours, Louisa," she said wearily. "For two hours I don't want to speak of the market. After that, when we're there, we will speak of nothing else."

There was that foreign May, that haunted May. A lump rose in Lou's throat. If the market had changed May, what would it do to Neela?

"Okay," Lou agreed. "Two hours. I'll wake you up when we get there."

May looked at her for a moment longer, then sighed. She pulled something out of her bag. It was a notebook, yellowed, a little wrinkled like it had been caught in the rain.

"This will help," she said mildly.

Lou clasped the journal in her hands. Now that she had something concrete in her possession, she was afraid to open it.

May was already breathing deeply as the train pulled away from King's Cross, as the city flashed by Lou's window, as the buildings faded to countryside and Lou thought of the market and nothing at all.

It was nearly an hour before Lou opened the notebook, only to realize that it wasn't a notebook at all. It was a guidebook.

THE PETERGATE DOCTRINE

A name was signed below in shaky, childish cursive. *May Wickett.*

Lou glanced up at her aunt. May had cared about this book enough to drag it across the ocean when she moved to Boston, then keep track of it through her adult life and their multiple moves. She cared enough to bring it now.

But what was it?

The first section of it folded out to a map. Lou recognized it as the part of the city that was located within the walls. She traced her finger over the perimeter of it. There was York Minster and the surrounding yard, there was the Shambles, there was Aldwark, where she addressed the letters to Neela.

The map was dotted with icons: stars and crosses and pentacles, and one dark X over the Shambles. May had highlighted certain places in different colors: yellow over part of the Minster Yard and the section of Aldwark where Nana Tee and Neela lived, green around Church Street and Colliergate. She'd circled King Square so heavily that the pencil had nearly broken through the page.

But it was just a map. There was nothing there that Lou hadn't seen before in the hundreds of maps of York she'd looked at over the years.

She flipped to the next page. There were only three lines of text here, bold and in all caps, with May's handwriting scribbled around the edges.

1. THE MARKET SHALL ARRIVE THE EVE OF THE SOLSTICE AND ENDURE UNTIL THE TOLL OF MIDNIGHT ON LAMMAS.

2. IN ACCORDANCE WITH THE DOCTRINE, HUMAN ENTRANTS HAVE THREE NIGHTS OF SAFETY WITHIN THE WALLS OF THE MARKET. WITCHES AND CANDIDATES ARE, AS ALWAYS, FORBIDDEN FROM THE MARKET AS GOBLINS ARE FORBIDDEN FROM THE WITCHERY.

3. MORTAL VISITORS SHALL NOT HARM GOBLINS WITHIN THE
   MARKET. GOBLINS SHALL NOT HARM MORTALS OUTSIDE THE
   WALLS OF THE MARKET.

Lou shuddered. There wasn't much room for negotiation, was there?

In the margins, May had written odd notes like, *The blood calls strongest on the 13th and scarborough fair for in/out.* Which made even less sense than the rules themselves.

Lou flipped to the next page. It was an area for stamps. The top read **COMBAT INSTRUCTION**. There were ten tiny, stamped images there, all with the initials *J.M.* in blue ink.

The next few pages were filled with lyrics, cryptic words underlined in a nonsensical fashion, and the names of random assortments of herbs with gibberish.

Finally, finally, she came to something that made sense. On the eleventh page, the header was **NOTES**. May's scrawl followed, filling the rest of the little book.

July 2

Mum says I shouldn't use this as a journal, but I lost the other two and I'm not allowed to lose this so I think I should. It's got worse this year. L said it would when I'm 13. But that's not fair because I want to do fun things and now I can't.

Marcus kicked me in the head at practice earlier. I think I'm going to bruise. It's not fair because he's taller than me and can kick higher. But Joss won't let me just fight L. She says we can practice at home and I have to fight with people bigger than me because if I can't beat them then how can I beat a goblin? I don't think a goblin is coming for me and if one did I wouldn't go.

Pizza for dinner tonight!!!!!!!!!! Raj is supposed to come from Durham but I dunno if Mum will let him. He doesn't usually visit during the market because she is too busy with stuff. I like it when he comes because he brings nice presents.

July 8

Bad day. Didn't sleep much. Maybe L is right. I wish they would just stop. Raj didn't come. Mum said he had too much work to do for the end of term. But L said she heard them fighting on the phone, and Mum told him not to come. She thinks Mum thinks he'll get eaten.

Mum left really early in the evening and hasn't come home. L thinks someone died. I think she's just trying to be scary because the goblins know I'm old enough to be eaten now.

Lou shut the book. There were more entries, plenty more, but her stomach was twisting in knots and she couldn't read anymore.

May was just thirteen when she'd written these, yet it was no big deal for her for people to be taken, to be killed, to be eaten—unless that was an exaggeration, which was totally possible. But it was too much to be fabricated, too legitimate for her to throw together in the matter of hours since they'd made the plans to come.

Thirteen-year-old May believed in goblins. And judging by the entries, Mom and Nana Tee did too. Nana Tee believed enough to tell Raj—who Lou figured was probably the same Raj as Neela's father—not to come visit.

Lou studied May's face as she slept. She had a scar on her chin—was that from the market? Another scar over her ribs, one she covered self-consciously when they were at the beach, but didn't bother hiding when they were home. More on her arms, one on her collarbone, one on her thighs.

Mom had scars too. Just as many as May, if not more.

How had Lou never questioned them? Why had Lou never really worried why they left England in such a rush, why they never went back? Why they guarded themselves so carefully with iron and salt, held themselves so tight?

Perhaps, Lou thought darkly, it was because they had taught her not to question these things. It was easier to let her grow up in total ignorance.

The train slowed, and a cheerful voice announced, "We are now approaching York." Lou glanced outside, catching a glimpse of the city spreading out ahead, low buildings and old stone.

Resolutely, she buried the notebook in her backpack. She had to keep hold of it. If Mom and May refused to answer her, the notebook was her best chance to get to the bottom of things.

She nudged May with her foot. She jumped, eyes flying wide, hands gripping the edge of her seat. Her face darkened as she took in the buildings outside, as if she'd forgotten where they were and had woken up into a nightmare.

"We're here," Lou said.

May closed her eyes. "I know."

Lou watched the emotions flicker across May's face. She didn't understand them, nor could she identify what they meant.

"May," Lou said. "We don't . . ." She wasn't sure how to finish the sentence. *We don't have to go?* But that wasn't right. Of course they had to go—or, more to the point, there was no more going.

They were already here.

But there was nothing else to say. May only reached forward and grabbed Lou's hand, squeezing it quickly, as the rain slipped across the windows of the train.

Mom had done all of this, hidden everything, to protect Lou. At least, that was what she said. But studying May's face, Lou was reminded all over again that it wasn't just about her or Neela. Something had happened to May here in this city, something that had broken her. She squeezed May's hand even tighter, wishing she could somehow drive the darkness away.

CHAPTER 9

NONE OF THE MAPS LOU PORED OVER PREPARED HER FOR THE reality of the city. She was caught in the clamor of it, the smell of pies and coffee in the station and the bustling people, the scent of wet rain and the chill outside. May hustled her along, walking streets she hadn't seen in nearly twenty years as if she'd done this route every day since. The weather couldn't decide what it wanted to do, sunny but dotted with odd gray clouds and spitting rain all the same, and Lou was grateful for the raincoat May had made her pull out of her suitcase in the station.

Lou tried to watch the gray stone and listen to the people they passed, but May was going so fast it took most of Lou's focus not to get hit by a car. They passed under a section of city wall and Lou realized breathlessly that this was the old part, the part where all other Wicketts had come from, the bit she'd dreamt of for years. She paused only a moment to run her fingers along the rough-hewn stone of the wall. Who knew how old this section was? Lou had read that the oldest city walls were built by the Romans, in 71 AD or sometime near there, with many of the still-standing portions dating back to medieval times.

How would it feel to grow up here, in a city colored by history? Lou looked for May, to ask her, but her aunt was already far ahead and nearly lost in the crowd. With a sigh, Lou hurried to catch up.

May didn't speak to her until after they'd crossed the River Ouse, and then it was only to snap, "Stick close to me, there are tourists about," before she went back to her breakneck pace.

May's whole demeanor had changed since the pair passed through the city walls, Lou realized. She'd been fine when they got off the train: not smiling, not really, but she hadn't been this tense or keyed up. She'd seemed . . . okay.

Just then the Minster came into view and thoughts of anything else fled from Lou's brain.

The cathedral stood tall and proud, breaking through the clutter of the old city, alone in an open square. Lou's breath caught as she took it in, the light stone darkened and shadowed with carvings and the falling rain. She wanted to nestle into its crevices, to look out through the stained glass windows as the world passed by.

She'd seen pictures of the cathedral in all kinds of weather and from all angles, but she was not prepared for just how *small* it made her feel.

How small, and how familiar. How known.

For just a moment, she felt something within her shifting, stretching. Waking up. Some spark of electricity, quite like the jolt she'd had the night before as the clock slipped into the witching hour.

"May," Lou started, wanting to know if her aunt felt it too. If she experienced the same sense of homecoming.

But when May turned, her face was caught in an unfamiliar anguish. It took Lou a moment to recognize it: not sadness, like the other day, nor anxiety. The look on May's face was grief, the same as she wore at Grandpa Jack's funeral, the same as when she came home from work quiet and defeated and went straight to her room, when she'd lost a patient she particularly liked.

"May?"

She just shook her head. "We have to keep going. Not far now." Her voice took a sharper note when she said, again, "Stay with me."

Lou kept glancing at the Minster over her shoulder as they left it behind. Other roads snaked off to her right, rife with buildings leaning in towards the street. May seemed especially wary of this side, Lou noted. She squinted down the side streets and alleys, trying to get a glimpse of something.

No—not just something. Trying to get a glimpse of it. The market.

Fear prickled up her arms as she thought the words. The shadows seemed to darken and the buildings leaned in closer, as if by acknowledging what she was here for, she'd turned half of the city sinister.

"*Lou*," May snapped. "Let's go."

She hadn't even noticed she'd paused, caught near the mouth of an alley as she peered down it. With May's prompting, Lou picked up the pace again.

They finally came to stop at a red door painted with the number *37*. Lou looked up and down the street, surprised to realize she recognized this place. She'd seen this street in photos, and she recalled one particular picture of teenage May, slouching against this door with a cigarette glowing between her fingers.

To Lou's surprise, May pulled her key ring out of her pocket and hunted through, passing the keys to their apartment in

Boston, her car key, her work key. She selected a skeleton key and unlocked the front door.

"You still have that?" Lou asked. "It still works?"

May grimaced. "It's home, isn't it?"

Home. Would Lou still say that about their apartment after she moved out and went to college, after she had a place and life of her own? Would the space she'd occupied with May and Mom still feel like home? She thought of how suddenly their old place in Revere felt detached from her, like as soon as they packed up the furniture and mugs and wiped the scuffs out of the walls, all the memories were cut away from the body of the place. But perhaps that was yet another flaw within Lou. Perhaps not everyone felt like they'd had themselves eviscerated when they'd left their various homes behind.

But that was a question for later. She followed May up the stairs, dragging her suitcase up three steep flights of stairs.

This time, May knocked.

"No key?" Lou asked.

"I have a key," she grumbled, "but I would rather not use it this time around."

Lou didn't know if knocking was any better. After all, if Mom was mad—which she would be—she could just shut the door in their faces. And deadbolt it for good measure.

It was only when Lou heard the murmur of voices on the other side that she decided this was a terrible idea. After all of Mom's hiding, all of her partial-truths and excuses, after every protection she'd forced upon Lou, she was here now. In this city where things hunted girls like her, Lou was here, without a clue what she was doing.

She swallowed hard. She was here for Neela, not Mom. She

was here to do what had to be done, even if it was unpleasant.

The locks clattered on the other side, more than Lou expected, and the door creaked as it was pulled open. A line of salt ran along the threshold, white and new, and Mom's scuffed shoes appeared on the other side.

If Lou didn't look up at her face, she wouldn't see the disappointment.

"I'm sorry," May said, already anticipating a fight.

"Who's at the door?" Nana Tee called from somewhere deep inside the apartment. Lou held her breath at the silence. If she looked up, perhaps it would be okay. Maybe Mom would understand. Maybe she wouldn't be angry. Maybe she—

No, looking up was a bad idea. Disappointment mingled with fury on Mom's face, her nostrils flaring and jaw ticking and hands balled into fists. Lou held her breath as Mom looked between her and May, her cheeks growing ruddy with anger and the vein in her temple throbbing.

"May," Mom hissed. "I don't think there is anything *remotely* sensible about—"

"Oh!" Nana Tee exclaimed, coming around to see the three of them in a standoff. "May! Louisa! Laura, pick your jaw up and stop blocking the door, would you? They're tired and hungry, I'm sure." Her voice was chipper as always, but Lou couldn't miss the lines of exhaustion around Nana Tee's eyes. No matter how Nana Tee tried to seem casual and welcoming, the truth remained: This was not any happy reunion. This was a rescue mission.

"Mum—" Lou's mother started.

Nana Tee cut her off with a sharp look. "They're here now, Laura. Now come in, and I'll put the kettle on."

Lou felt like she'd fallen headfirst into the rabbit hole, if that rabbit hole was also a thrift store run by two bunnies on ecstasy.

When Nana Tee came to visit, she always brought a box of odds and ends for them, like herbs and weird potions and ointments that Lou avoided using in favor of Neosporin. Nana Tee's house was the same vibrant explosion of color as May's room at home, but also with the same effect as a hobbit hole: bright blankets and paint on the walls, but the earthy smell of herbs and lit candles in the windows.

The apartment was small but homey. The kitchen was just off the front door. Nana Tee and Lou sat at the kitchen table with their mugs of tea, blowing the steam and watching the street below out the window. Of course, Nana Tee knew how Lou took her tea, and somehow it tasted even better than when May made it.

Mom and May whisper-fought in the living room. Lou wondered why they didn't go into one of the bedrooms—but perhaps they were too full of old memories, both of the market and Neela. At the thought of her missing aunt, Lou felt a new lump harden in her throat.

"Have you heard any news?" Lou asked her grandmother.

Nana Tee's eyes didn't leave the window. "Nothing."

Lou followed her gaze. They faced towards a pub and a barber, and beyond that, Lou could see a section of wall.

"Where is it?" Lou asked. "The market."

Nana Tee looked at her, and all the good humor from their

arrival was gone. "Your mother wants to protect you from this," Nana said.

Lou nodded, and went to say that she understood, she wouldn't go, she just wanted to help, but Nana continued.

"This is not something you can be protected from, Louisa. It's something you must choose to avoid. You're here; you have our blood. There is no avoiding the market. There is no protecting you. The market knows you're here, just as certainly as I do. If the market chooses you, then you must not choose the market."

A chill ran down Lou's spine. This was all new to her, but it hadn't been new to Neela. Neela had probably had this speech from Nana Tee a dozen times over.

So what was Lou missing? Why had Neela known the risk and chosen to go anyway?

Mom came in, no less red than before. "Louisa," she said sternly. May hovered in the doorway behind her like a ghost.

"Yes?"

"May seems to think that you will listen to us," Mom said, vitriol creeping into her voice. "I have a lot going on right now. I don't want you to be here. If I had my way, you'd be back with your dad by midnight tomorrow."

Lou swallowed hard. She'd considered the idea that Mom would send her back, but that was a lot of money, even with the inheritance from Grandpa Jack. But she could be wrong.

"Mom, I—"

"But you're here now, aren't you," Mom said bitterly, "whether I like it or not. You're in this."

Lou didn't like the way she said that, but it was what she wanted, wasn't it? To be a part of this. To be a part of *something.*

She got up. Just at the beginning of summer, she'd surpassed her mother's height. It surprised her sometimes, when she got up and realized her mom wasn't taller or at eye level, but just slightly lower.

"You can't force me back," Lou said, watching her mother's face, "because you're here, and May's here, and Nana Tee's here, and Neela's gone. You can't force me back because I love you and I will fight you and I will not go."

Mom narrowed her eyes. Behind Lou, Nana Tee snorted. "Aye, she's you all over again," she said. In the doorway, even May was smirking.

Mom sighed, rubbing her eyes. "You're exhausting," she said, possibly to Lou, possibly to all of them. "I'll let you stay on one condition."

Lou bit her lip. "What is that?"

"You don't go in the market. You don't go near the market. You don't listen to the market. You don't ask how to get into the market. The market is absolutely off limits, even if you think you're helping. Is that understood?"

Lou watched her mother for any weakness, any break. Of course, she didn't want to go to the market. But if she had to risk that to get Neela back . . .

Well. That wasn't something she had to decide yet. If Mom was successful, then maybe it wouldn't even be an issue to worry about.

"I promise," Lou said. "I won't go into the market." She made the promise firmly, though in her heart, she knew it was probably a promise that would be broken.

CHAPTER 10

May

Eighteen Years Earlier

IN THE TWO WEEKS AFTER THE FIRST BODY WAS FOUND, FIFTEEN people had visited the market, by May's count; three had broken the rules, some part of them appearing days later in a faerie circle of flowers. There hadn't been another slip, though, so any fear from outsiders had dulled to a prickling. The twelve who had come back sat in the shadowy corners of the pub or reported to the Witchery for treatment, speaking in hushed tones of the things they saw and spoke to, of the fruits they ate, of how they escaped.

They all looked mournfully at the Shambles as night fell over the city day after day. They all wanted to go back; they all knew they couldn't.

When May was little, an old woman from the next street over used to come every week during the market to buy goblin blood from her mother. Once, May asked why she did it. What use could a normal person have for goblin blood? She drank it in her tea every morning. She'd gone to the market once, as a girl, and still felt the call begging her to come back even years later.

May thought of that sometimes as she treated people in the

Witchery night after night. Sometimes she wondered if it would be easier to succumb to the market, to disappear.

She wondered what it was like to love something so much, even though it could hurt her. Even though it *wanted* to hurt her.

And those who did not return? There were no funerals, no mourning, no stories told of them. They were gone now, lost to the market, forgotten. Any valiant rescue attempts returned empty handed. The coven passed the list of names to the police, and those cases went cold.

But it wasn't worth it to think of cold cases or goblin blood or what they could do to her. It would only lead to heartbreak.

May was still trying to convince herself not to think of goblin blood when the phone rang. She and Laura were there watching daytime TV before their respective shifts. May grabbed it—it was probably a call from someone injured, looking for Mum. After all, there was no easy way to reach the Witchery.

"Hello?"

"Coven meeting," Marcus said, breathless on the other line. He must've run to one of the cafes near the Minster to use the phone. Honestly, it would've been easier to come to the flat to get them.

May frowned. "Why?"

Laura nudged her over with her elbow and squeezed onto the chair with May so she could hear Marcus's voice. Coven meetings were rare unless there was an emergency.

"The Thaumaturge is here. She wants to see everyone." He didn't bother to explain more. The line simply went dead.

"Weird," May said. She tossed the phone onto the coffee table.

Laura was already up, pulling her shoes on. She was so dedicated to coven business. May watched her back, wishing for even just a moment she cared that much.

Marcus wasn't exaggerating when he said "everyone," May realized after they hustled back to the Witchery and darted within its stone depths. Mum, Joss, and Angelique were here, with baby Neela swaddled on Mum's lap. Joss's aunt Marjorie was also present, tucked into a corner, though she hadn't been active in the coven for at least fifteen years. Marcus, Laura, and May took the empty seats at the table.

May tried her best not to stare at the Thaumaturge. She was newish, as far as Thaumaturges went, with only five or so years in the office. And she was *young*—May had only seen the last Thaumaturge once, but she'd been wizened and stooped, with fingers that never quite pointed straight. This one was pretty, dressed smartly in a black dress and black boots. Her brown, shoulder-length hair was shiny and her skin looked healthy even in the lighting of the Witchery, which made everyone look sick.

May and Laura looked at one another. They were both thinking the same thing: she looked right posh.

Way back a couple hundred or so years ago, there was no Thaumaturge. There were only the covens, self-governed within themselves. But as the magic took longer to shift between generations and the covens grew smaller, there was need for organization. Thus, the Thaumaturge and the regions were created. It wasn't as if there were more rules, but it helped the witches to have a centralized method for the acquisition of goods and instruction and the dispersal of magic.

In other words, it made life easier. Even in York, where the witches had arguably the worst time of all.

"Thank you for coming here today," she said. Her accent was not nearly as plummy as May had expected, but she was southern all the same. "I'm sorry to call this meeting during your busiest season, but I fear it may be overdue."

If she smelled the rot emanating from the back room from the most recent body, it didn't look like it bothered her. And maybe it didn't. May didn't know what the Thaumaturge usually dealt with.

Laura shot her a look. *What's this about?* she mouthed. May shrugged. May usually dozed off whenever they were all gathered to talk about coven business

"These last few years, the market has only grown more vicious, and we want to ensure you have all the power necessary. Additionally, the time has come for one of the elders to retire." Across the room, Angelique flushed. May had expected she was on the way out, but this soon? Worry blossomed in her chest.

She glanced at Marcus. He didn't look surprised—had Angelique already told him? But he had at least a year of school left.

"As such, we've decided to fully graduate all three apprentices at the end of the week."

May's ears rang. *Graduate all three apprentices.* All three. Marcus. Laura. May.

As a full witch of the coven, she would have magic. She would have power and respect and her run of the city. No door would be closed to her. She'd get too many free pints to count during market months. She'd be able to solve most of life's minor inconveniences with the snap of her fingers.

As a witch, she'd be required to remain in North Yorkshire for most of the year, with only a few weeks of respite. She'd be paid a low salary—enough to be comfortable, but not much. She'd be expected to solve all the problems the market threw at her, and her blood would be even sweeter to the goblins. She'd probably have to go to university here. There would be no jaunts to London or Birmingham, no years abroad in France, no extended visits to Dad in the United States. There would be only this: the Witchery, the metallic scent of magic and blood and rot, the market and its horrors year after year after year.

Across from her, Laura looked positively gleeful. May worried she was going to throw up.

"But Thaumaturge—" May said, already knowing she sounded ridiculous.

"Please, call me Caroline."

"Caroline." She tried to breathe, tried to keep the panic out of her voice. "That wasn't the agreement we had. We're supposed to—I don't feel ready. Could you tell us why?"

Laura was glaring at her. *Shut up, May,* she would yell if she wasn't worried what the Thaumaturge would think of her.

To her credit, the Thaumaturge—*Caroline*—genuinely did look concerned. "I'm sorry you feel unprepared," she said. "May, is it?"

May nodded.

"The market has simply grown too violent to be handled by a coven this small," Caroline said. "We could send help from Harrogate or Leeds, but it's not consistent enough, and those are small covens as is. You three already know the operation. Angelique can phase out this year and be here to assist, but what we need is the full force of three more witches to help Joss and Christina."

"But I—"

"May." Mum's voice cut her off. She was exhausted, May knew, worn too thin by caring for Neela and keeping up with the demands of the market. She turned to face Caroline. "Thank you for coming all this way. I'm sorry if some among us seem . . . reluctant."

Caroline looked at May like she understood, like she wished she could take the weight of her inheritance away. "I know your job here is unlike anywhere else," she said, and for a moment May felt like they were in the only two in the room. "If I could take the duty away from you, I would. I wouldn't wish this job on anyone. But that's the duty of our blood. This is the sacrifice we make."

May gripped her hands together, nails cutting into her palms. She would not be weak, not now, even as her future and freedom crumbled.

May still felt the world constricting around her that night as she finished her shift. She was closing the pub by herself again. They were short-staffed, and May was happy enough to make some extra money. She didn't usually like closing shifts during the market, but what were they going to do to her? Drag her out kicking and screaming? That wasn't the goblin way.

They wanted you to choose them. They wanted you to come of your own accord, willingly.

But if she went to the market . . . would that be claiming her freedom back? Or would it be yet another foolish mistake?

She wiped down the bar aggressively, cursing the market and her mother and Laura, cursing the girl for giving her the gold and disappearing. Cursing herself for being tempted. The pub was empty. No locals wanted to be out so late on a market night, and the weather had been shite, so all the tourists ducked back to their hotels early. It didn't help that she'd had her turn at the Witchery last night and very little sleep afterwards, so she was exhausted and ready to go home.

The bell above the door rang.

"We're closed," May snarled, which wasn't quite true.

"Even for me?" a raspy, lilting voice asked. She spoke like a jazz singer.

May knocked over the bucket of cleaning solution, sending it sloshing over the bar and dripping down onto the floor.

The goblin girl stood alone in the middle of the pub. It was like the world bent around her, everything going concave to frame her in May's vision.

Today, she wore a black slip dress over tights and boots, possibly the same tights and boots, possibly stolen from a human she'd killed and eaten.

May shivered.

"Let me help," the girl said. She grabbed a towel from the other end of the bar and soaked up some of the cleaner. May watched, dumbstruck.

"I can get it," she said—too late, because the girl had already cleaned up most of the mess.

"What's your name?" the goblin girl asked, peering at May through her lashes.

May sucked in a breath. It was a useless question. The other children in York knew not to tell a goblin their name because they'd know what to call you, how to lure you, how to trap you. But of course it was useless. She was a witch's daughter. The goblins already knew her name, just as well as the boys who called her May Leg-Before-Wicket in the schoolyard did.

Besides, it didn't matter if the girl knew her name. May was already lured, already caught, already trapped.

"May," she whispered, barely audible. But it didn't matter. The goblin girl heard and smiled with her wicked teeth.

She knew. She knew that May knew and that May had told her anyway.

"A breath of spring on summer's wings," the girl said in a sing-song voice.

"Shoulda, woulda, coulda," May said before she could stop herself.

The girl's smile faltered. "Pardon?"

May shrugged, feeling small and embarrassed. It was a joke she and Laura shared, not one she was overly comfortable telling a goblin.

What are you doing? something screamed in her. Talking to this girl, telling her anything, was like holding her hand over a candle flame and waiting to be burned.

"May. Like, I may do something, I may not."

To her surprise, the goblin girl laughed. Maybe it was only for her benefit.

"You choose your own destiny, May," the girl said, and May tried very hard not to think of the way her name sounded in her mouth.

"And you?" May said. She felt less awkward when her hands were doing something, so she took the wet towel back from the girl and wrung it out in the sink, then continued wiping the bar.

"And me?"

"A name. You have one, I presume?"

May didn't need to look to know the girl was smiling; she heard it in her voice. "Eitra," she said.

"Eitra," May repeated. She didn't know many goblin names, not outside Iark, the Market Prince, or the names sobbed in the Witchery as victims recounted their tales of woe in the market. "Eitra" was unfamiliar.

"Does it mean anything?" she asked.

Eitra shrugged. "It may."

May rolled her eyes. "Why are you here, then? Want a drink?"

Eitra's eyes traced along the cask ales and bitters. "Possibly, but only if you're drinking with me."

"I can't," May said with a laugh. She glanced at the clock. "We really are closed now. I need to lock up."

Eitra rested her elbows on the bar, leaning closer. She smelled of crushed roses and steel. "I know a place," she said.

A place. May gritted her teeth. It was nearly the same invitation the goblin had given her weeks before, the night of the first body. So why was it so much more tempting now? This was what she'd been waiting for, what she'd scorned, what she'd wanted, what she'd feared. "In this world or the other?"

Eitra's smile sharpened. May wasn't sure if the lead in the pit of her stomach was fear or desire.

"You haven't thrown my coin away," Eitra said.

She hadn't. It was foolish, May knew; those with goblin gold were much more likely to be targeted. But May was already a likely target. Her blood called to the goblins, just as the market called to her, as her feet led her down the side streets to the crowded Shambles if she didn't stop herself.

"The market won't go on forever, May Wickett," Eitra said. It was a reminder that the goblin knew exactly who she was. That she should've run in the first place.

"There's still enough time for trouble," May said, putting

away the rest of the glasses. She tried to sound casual and only sounded weak.

"And plenty of time for delight," Eitra countered. She reached across the bar, laying a hand on May's arm. Her nails were painted night-black, sharpened to points.

Perhaps they weren't nails at all. Perhaps they were claws.

But then, of all things, May thought of Laura. How disappointed she'd be if May went, how much worse it would be if she didn't return. Going to market would be like turning her back on the whole coven.

Eitra must've seen some change in May's face because her own smile softened. "Just one night," she said. "Just one dance, just one drink."

One dance would lead to another and one drink would lead to a third and one night could lead to imprisonment or death.

If she trusted a goblin, she was even more senseless than Laura thought.

But this was the final chance. Once the Thaumaturge upgraded them all to candidates in the depths of the Witchery, once her fate was truly sealed, she would not be able to enter the market. Even as a witchling, there was a risk greater than that of a human. Once she became a candidate, or worse, a full witch, she'd be killed upon entry.

There were no more choices, no more chances. The market had chosen her. For the first and last time, May could choose the market.

"Before I come with you," May said, stalling, "answer me this. Have you killed one of us before?"

Eitra's smile faltered. "Sparingly," she said cautiously, "and for the glory of another. Not for myself."

If that was supposed to put May at ease, it didn't work. But at least Eitra did not deny her nature.

May squared her shoulders. "I will come with you tonight, and tonight only. We shall dance, but I will not eat or drink anything you give me. At the end of the night I will give you your coin back and I will return home and you will not seek me again. Do I have your word?"

Eitra raised an eyebrow. "Do I have your word you won't love me, then?"

Eitra was mocking her, but it made May flush red all the same. "Just answer me."

The goblin held her gaze, her eyes the bright and inhuman green of a lime peel. "As much as I can give you my word, you have it."

May sighed. It would have to be enough. "And you mustn't hurt me," she added weakly, an afterthought.

Eitra's smile turned wickedly sharp at that, sharp enough that May could imagine how her teeth would feel piercing her skin. "Only if you swear not to hurt me, witchling."

May nodded, accepting her fate and her choice and the foolishness of it all. She was due for a bollocking for this in the morning, if Laura or Mum found out. "Alright then. Let's go."

CHAPTER 11

LOU HAD MEANT TO PUSH HARDER AFTER LUNCH, TO ASK THE questions she needed answers to, but jet lag got the best of her. She lurched awake in Neela's bedroom without much memory of how she got there. She tried to catch her breath as her eyes adjusted to the room, feeling like she'd been jarred out of a nightmare. But no matter how much she tried, she couldn't recall what it was about.

Around her, the apartment was silent. She strained to hear a cough, a lurch, anything, but it was like the night had a muffled, tense quality. Even the street outside was quiet.

Lou slipped out of bed. She didn't need to turn on any of the lamps, not when the night was still dimly lit outside. The room smelled like Neela: spicy jasmine perfume and lavender fabric softener. It was like a knife to Lou's heart.

Her phone was basically useless, and she couldn't stomach listening to the voicemails again. Not here, in the place where Neela had disappeared.

The room looked like Neela had intended to return soon. A book sat open and turned over on the desk, dirty clothes were scattered on the floor at the foot of the bed, a half-eaten Dairy Milk bar rested on top of her jewelry box. Lou ran her fingers over vibrant, beaded saris and bodycon dresses and floral skirts in the open closet. Neela's beaten-up baggage was nestled in the back, still bearing tags from her last Boston to Heathrow trip.

She couldn't explain it, but it was like the house itself knew Neela was gone. As if when Neela crept out the door toward the market, the house had let out a breath and fallen in on itself. If Lou moved too many things, changed too much from how Neela had left it, the entire building might crumble under her feet.

Lou wasn't sure if anything ever would stop the aching within her.

She sat down on the floor, unable to bear the flagrant show of everything Neela. When Grandpa Jack died, Lou thought she'd understood grief. She'd felt that awful gnawing in her chest, the emptiness, the dread of waking up every day with someone just *gone*. But this was Neela, who wasn't supposed to ever leave her.

The rules in the guidebook May had given her said Neela had three nights of safety in the market. Lou wasn't sure when she'd first gone—she couldn't know, not really—but already she'd been missing for four days. If she had been safe in the market once, she wasn't anymore.

The problem was, it didn't make any sense to Lou. If she believed May's guidebook, if she believed in *goblins*, then the market was a regular occurrence. It came every year. Surely Neela knew about it, even if she'd never told Lou.

So why, then, had she gone? Why had May? What was it about the goblins that tempted them? Because Lou was here in this old city during the market, and she sure as hell wanted nothing to do with it. It was oddly infuriating. How difficult would it be to just *stay out*?

How difficult would it have been for Neela not to leave her?

She wanted to turn the room over, to destroy everything. There had to be some sort of clue, some answer, some detail Lou had overlooked. Neela was not foolish or impulsive. She didn't have a death wish. She wouldn't have just *gone*.

Somewhere in the apartment, a door creaked open. Lou froze, listening. There were distinct footsteps, probably barefoot, muffled as they tracked across the apartment.

Lou crawled over to the door on her hands and knees. She opened the door carefully, carefully, just a crack.

A dark figure crept through the living room. Her mother, Lou realized, as she crossed in front of a pane of moonlight. Her mother, with her hair bound up in a bun, dressed in black jeans and a black tank top with a beaten leather jacket slung over one arm. She bent over to rustle through a trunk against one of the walls. A pendant hung around her neck, and Lou realized there was a bundle of herbs tied to it.

She wanted to ask what she was doing or if she could help. But before she could move, Mom pulled something out of the trunk, then held it up in the light, revealing a sheathed knife. She slipped it out just enough so she could test the sharpness on a bit of cord.

Lou watched as Mom strapped the knife to her belt and proceeded to repeat the process with three more knives, hiding them up various sleeves and in her boot. With a prickling sense of dread, she realized that Mom wasn't just going to investigate what had happened—she was *hunting*.

This was what it meant to save Neela.

The moonlight made the scars on Mom's arms and back look silvery and ethereal. When she was a kid, Mom told her the scars were caused by May crashing into her, knocking them both through a window. Now, she wondered if the reality was much, much worse.

Mom double-checked the knives and patted her hair, making sure it was secure. When she was gardening in the summer, when the heat made those little hairs curl and pull away from whatever binding she had it in, Mom always cursed. She'd look at Lou with her clear blue eyes, nose wrinkled, squinting. *Pain in the arse, it is,* she'd say, wrestling with yet another headband or bun clip.

Lou wanted to run out and tell her to stop. To beg her to stay, like she didn't have the chance to with Neela.

But she only watched as Mom gripped the herb pendant in her hand, took a long breath, and murmured something Lou couldn't hear. Mom turned to look at Lou's door and Lou jumped back, hoping she hadn't been seen.

The floorboards in the apartment creaked, then the front door. When Lou went back to peek, her mother was gone. She raced to the window to see which way she'd gone, but she'd vanished without a trace. Just like Neela.

Hopefully, unlike Neela, Mom would come back.

Lou turned away, back to her scattered luggage and the room that was too much of Neela. She debated trying to go back to sleep or reading more of May's guidebook. But the decision was made for her in the form of three quick raps on the door.

"What?" Lou said.

The door opened to reveal May, dressed in jeans and a sweat-shirt. She had her shoes on. "Change in plans. We think it's best if you know what you're getting yourself into," she said. Her eyes were guarded, not quite meeting Lou's.

Lou raised her eyebrow. "Did you wait until Mom left?"

"Of course," May said. "She's got enough on her mind as it is.

Now, get clothes you don't mind ruining and put your shoes on. We have to get through the streets quickly."

Lou dragged a pair of leggings and an old T-shirt from her luggage. Truthfully, she wasn't sure what exactly she'd packed. She'd just thrown stuff in there.

It was odd, to be conspiring with May like this. She was beloved, but Lou had always seen May's allegiances lying with Mom over her. They were codependent, after all. It wasn't like May to go behind Mom's back, especially when it concerned Lou.

But it was nice to be treated like this. Like part of the big, overall picture. And it was nice to look at May and understand, to feel that glint of belonging.

"Where are we going?" she asked as she tugged the shirt over her head.

"It'll save everyone time if you stop asking inane questions," May said. She tossed Lou a thin metal chain—iron, she realized as she caught it. "Now, let's move. If Laura forgot something, I don't want her catching us on the way out."

CHAPTER 12

"I HOPE YOU SLEPT ALREADY," MAY SAID AS THEY CARVED THEIR way down Ogleforth. At the end, she turned onto a narrow street. The Minster loomed over them, imposing in the darkness.

"Do you expect to be up the rest of the night?" Lou asked, scampering to keep up with her.

"Of course. We have work to do."

May was walking too fast for any more questions. She didn't seem distressed—at least, no more distressed than she was in any other part of York.

Lou chewed on the inside of her cheek. If only Neela had told her. If only she'd shared something—*anything*—to prepare Lou for this.

Not for the first time, Lou felt a swell of anger, fierce and hollow. It was not strong enough to overpower the grief though, or the overwhelming feeling that Neela might not come back.

May slipped past a gate in the shadow of the Minster. Lou looked up at it doubtfully. Awe-inspiring as it was, she didn't want to go in at night. Not when Mom and May kept telling her to be aware, to be afraid.

"Are we going inside?" Lou asked, eying the soaring spires of the Minster.

"No. We're going to the Old Palace," May said. She glanced at her watch, then around them. Checking if the coast was clear. She led the way across a bit of landscaped grass to the building in the back corner of the Minster lot, where a stone path next to the building met a fence.

"What is this?"

May stopped, her eyes tracing over Lou. It was like she was sizing her up. Lou watched her aunt's face carefully, searching for something within it.

When Lou was little, she used to study herself in the mirror, searching for traces of Mom or May in her reflection. "Who are you?" she'd ask, pressing a palm flat against the glass until it was warm, almost like there was someone else pressing back.

Who are you? she wanted to yell at Mom, and May, at Neela, at everyone who'd hidden their entire lives from her. It was like she was seeing them all for the first time, working out the machinations in their little games.

"I'm already in this," Lou said wearily. She looked up, hunting for stars. There were only silvery, dark clouds, outlined by the moon. "I know . . . I know you two didn't want me growing up to inherit whatever shit you lived with. But it's too late for that. I'm here."

I'm here, and Neela isn't.

"That you are," May said.

To Lou's surprise, May dropped to her knees and dug her fingers under the edge of the building. A four-stone section popped up with a scraping noise, lifting on a hinge.

"You go first," May said, turning on her phone flashlight and shining it down. "Be careful on the stairs, duck."

Lou kept a hand on the rough wall as she made her way

105

down. May's flashlight only shone dimly, but the path ahead was lit with heavy sconces laden with burning candles. The floor was made of the same stone as the pathway above.

"What is this place?" Lou asked. Her voice was too loud, and she cringed a little at how it echoed. But presumably, May hadn't delivered her to the mouth of the market.

May's face was illuminated in the candlelight, flickers and shadows changing the topography of it as she frowned down the hallway. At the end, a great wooden door stood ajar. She looked like a ghoul herself down here.

"We call it the Witchery," May said. "I don't know if it's ever been called anything else."

The wheels were turning in Lou's brain as pieces slipped into place. The herbs, the iron, the weird words in the book. She couldn't quite make the pieces fit, couldn't quite make the final leap to what this all was about.

Or maybe she could. Maybe she just didn't want to.

Behind the door at the end of the hall lay the secrets Lou had been searching for her entire life. Her feet carried her closer and closer as her heart pounded against her chest, as her mouth grew dry, as she squeezed her eyes shut and wished against everything else that Neela was here.

May pushed the door open. It creaked the whole way.

The room beyond was almost medieval: sconces and candelabras provided the only light. The walls and floor were smooth stone, the ceiling carved in low arches. Lou wondered if it mirrored the arches in the Minster, the Gothic architecture that marked the city. A massive wooden table stood on one side of the room, mostly covered in herbs and jars. The wall to the left had a hewn wood counter and a big, old-looking stove. On the other side of the room, a ratty couch stood alone beside floor-to-ceiling shelves, crammed with labeled jars and books. Ahead, a long hallway lined with doors stretched into the gloom.

A tall Black woman stood in front of the stove. She wore a long skirt and a fraying, multi-colored sweater. She glanced up, making a small, strangled noise as she registered the two of them.

"May," she said, dropping her wooden spoon. It clattered on the ground, splattering dark gray liquid across the floor.

"I told you they were coming," Nana Tee said, appearing from a back room. She wore some kind of smock over her clothes, speckled with something that looked black in the low lighting.

"I didn't think she'd ever come back," the other woman said, half to herself. She recovered the spoon from the floor and tossed it into a basin.

"Of course I came back," May said. The words hung awkwardly in the air. "Ten years was a long time, but it passed."

This caught in Lou's brain. May had been gone from here for much longer than ten years. "You're being rude," Nana Tee said. She went to the shelf and pulled down an armful of jars. "Louisa, this is Joss. Joss, Lou." She nodded between the two of them with her chin. "And if the jig is up, I need help moving a patient. May, you shouldn't strain yourself."

"She isn't ready to—" May said.

Nana Tee stopped, halfway down the hall. "Did you bring her to spectate? To shock her? Or did you bring her to help?"

Lou looked between the two of them. She felt that odd sense of being very much in over her head.

May rolled her eyes. "Give me two minutes." To Joss, somewhat pleadingly, she said, "Is there tea?"

Joss nodded toward a kettle. "Darjeeling."

But Lou was over the diversions, the "we'll tell you laters" and the "after teas." She was done with *all* of it.

"No. Tell me what the *fuck* is going on." The anger was welling, mixing with the grief, an awful tangling in Lou's chest spilling out.

Neela wasn't supposed to lie to her.

Neela wasn't supposed to keep secrets.

It was Mom and May, May and Mom, the pair of them who kept their secrets in and held Lou out. Neela wasn't supposed to lie about things like this, or hide whatever this place was, but clearly she had. Neela was all over this place, from her knotted scarf on one of the hooks in the wall to her purse left on the couch, like she was coming back for it at any moment. It didn't matter how much Lou felt she did or didn't belong now. The truth of it was they had her whole life to fill her in on whatever this was, and they hadn't. And neither had Neela, or Nana Tee, or Grandpa Jack, if he knew anything.

It was embarrassing, to be so close to the middle of something that everyone knew but her. She felt small and untrustworthy, caught in the fringes.

"Your mother should've told you," May said. "I always knew she should've told you." She looked at Joss as if seeking help, but the other woman only shrugged.

"Laura had seventeen years to tell her," Joss said.

May leaned against the big table. "Three hundred years ago, the witches of York struck up a deal with the goblins who terrorized their city every year. They limited the time the goblins could come and set safety measures in place for the occupants of the city. But there was a price: the descendants of the witches, those with their blood, would be more enticing to the goblins and their market than any others. Their blood would be sweeter, fortified with magic. Their bones would be stronger for weapons or spells. And they would be more vulnerable to the goblins, more willing to follow them when called."

Lou swallowed hard. Just like that, the final piece was slipping into place. "And those witches…"

"Yep," May said, popping the "p."

"So Nana Tee is a witch."

"Yep."

"And—and you're a witch," Lou said. She felt nauseous.

"No. Not really. Magic is a fickle bitch like that."

Joss turned on May, her hands on her hips. "You're not being fair. You hid this all from her and now you won't even give her a straight answer?"

Lou didn't know Joss, but she was liking her more by the second. She made a mental note to find a way to get her alone later, to see what other information she could glean.

"Magic is not a 'fickle bitch,'" Joss said, turning to Lou. "We do have control of it. Sometimes, some of us make bad decisions and lose the ability to access our magic." She paused to smack May in the shoulder with a clean spoon. "Magic is very clear, actually."

May only shrugged. If what Joss said rankled her, it didn't show. "Okay. Laura and I broke rules. So we lost our right to the coven, to magic, and to this city."

"They were banished," Joss said flatly. "For ten years."

"Why didn't you tell me before?" Lou asked, mostly to May, but also to all the others who'd kept this from her. She did the math. Ten years from May and Mom leaving York was the year she turned nine, so they were still free to come back for almost half of her life. But they hadn't, and never said a word why.

May shrugged. "Our bloodline never mattered in Boston. It's not like the witch hunt is still on."

"I'm talking about it *all*, May," Lou said, fighting back the fierce sense of betrayal. "The market. The witch thing, yes. But why did you never say that you were taken, or why didn't Neela talk to me about it?"

May and Joss exchanged a look. Lou was so *tired* of the looks, the shrugs, the sighs. The time for secrets was up.

"Your mother wanted to protect you," May said finally, resting a hand on her stomach, on the baby. "That's all she ever wanted, Lou. To keep you safe from all of this."

"May—" Joss started, hinting at something Lou couldn't quite understand.

May's hands clenched on the counter. "And who says I *wanted* to come back? What if I didn't? What if I couldn't bear it?" She said the words like they were supposed to be fierce and angry, but really, they sounded empty.

Lou clenched her jaw. She wanted to go back to the apartment, to have time to think by herself. She wanted to burn something just to see the fire catch.

Before she could say anything, Nana Tee shouted from down the hall, "It's been longer than two minutes!"

Nana Tee's head was poking out from one of the rooms. She gestured for Lou to join her.

It was brighter in here, with both candles and battery-powered lamps. Bright enough to illuminate the horror on the table in the middle of the room.

Lou froze, shocked, in the doorway. She was certain the boy on the table was dead until he turned his head and groaned, the sound low and tortured. Nana Tee stood at his feet with a pair of tweezers and a pitcher, painstakingly pulling thorns from his legs. But it wasn't like the thorns had embedded themselves within his skin. No, they looked as if they'd grown out of him. Thousands of them in varying sizes, all over his body.

"What *happened* to him?"

Nana Tee didn't even glance up. "Drank the wrong thing, presumably." She was focused, steady, as she pulled the thorns out one by one. "His friends left him outside my door a few hours ago."

"Is that . . . common?"

Nana Tee glanced up. She had the same blue eyes as Mom and May. The trio were more like clones than mother and daughters. Lou wondered if Neela felt the same differences between her and Nana Tee that Lou did with her mother. Like they could be strangers, and no one would know the difference.

"This is what I do, Lou. Ten months of the year, I'm that old woman who has herbal remedies, who might cure a stomachache or soothe aching joints." Another thorn *plinked* into the pitcher. "And then two months of the year, I'm responsible for every goblin-induced injury the city faces."

The boy moaned again, low and awful.

Lou stared at the boy, only a bit older than her, if even. If she'd grown up here, she might have known him. Hell, Neela might know him.

This was not about Lou or Neela. This was not about witches or goblins or the secrets that had been kept from her, the wrongs Lou felt deserved retribution. Right now, this boy was suffering. It didn't matter if Lou believed in magic or packs with goblins or evil markets. She believed this boy was hurting, had come to harm in some preventable way, and they were here to fix it.

If she stripped the market down to those parts, to that negotiation, of course it was real. Of course all of this was true, and she was one tiny piece of it now, whether she liked it or not.

The fighting could come later. For now, there was work to do.

"What do you need me to do?"

Nana Tee gestured to the boy's shoulders. "I've gotten most of his front, but the back is bad. I need you to sit him up and hold him there while I pull the thorns out. Can you do that?"

"Of course," Lou said.

Nana Tee tossed her a smock like the one she was wearing. Lou grabbed a set of gloves from the box on the side table. She gripped the boy's arms, spotted and speckled with drops of blood, and heaved him up. He shouted as she did it, his agonized voice ripping through the night, and Lou gritted her teeth. She pulled him close, his head lolling onto her shoulder. He was heavy and warm, too warm. She felt his labored breathing against her neck.

"That's it," Nana Tee said, her voice soothing. She leaned over and resumed picking out thorns.

Lou lost track of time as she held the boy close against her. Eventually she began humming, the same songs Mom used to hum to Lou when she was very little. The boy sagged more and more against her, falling asleep as the thorns continued to *plink* into the pitcher.

"This is what they were trying to protect you from," Nana Tee said finally, grabbing a cloth and wiping the sweat from her forehead. She looked like a saint with the light behind her illuminating her gray hairs like a halo.

"Thorns?"

"No," Nana Tee said. She hunkered back down, shifting

the boy so she could access his lower back. "This is the price of magic, Louisa. There are worse things out there in the world, things too terrible to imagine, and you have to be the one to stand up against them."

Lou chewed on her lip. Was that a fair price? She couldn't be sure. She hadn't seen the effect of Nana Tee's magic, nor any of the benefits. She'd only seen the horror, the anguish, the cost.

But if she had magic, if she was someone with power, she knew what she'd do with it. Lou would march into the market and find Neela herself. And when they were out, when they would safe, Lou would burn it all down.

CHAPTER 13

TOO TIRED TO DRAG HERSELF INTO NEELA'S ROOM, LOU FELL asleep on the couch when they got back from the Witchery. She dreamt of thorns and smoke, the taste of blood in her mouth.

Lou jerked awake to the sound of glass shattering. Mom swore, muttering something under her breath about the Holy Trinity.

The couch sagged underneath her as she sat up. She felt bone-tired, achy, like she'd been hit by a truck. Jet lag, she figured, but she hadn't expected it to be this bad. When Neela talked about it, it sounded like something she could just get over by taking a nap rather than a multiday adjustment.

"What are you doing?" she asked, too sleepy and peering at her mom over the back of the couch.

Mom jumped, her eyes finding Lou. She must not have realized she was there.

"I dropped a glass," Mom said, gesturing to the shards littering the floor. "Don't come in here if you're not wearing shoes."

Lou nodded. She tucked her knees to her chest as Mom went under the sink and pulled out a small broom and dustpan. She watched, trying to take the time to clear her thoughts.

They hadn't been alone since Lou's arrival in York, since before Neela went missing. Now, Lou didn't know how to align the stories she'd heard of her with the woman who raised her.

Her mom was supposed to inherit magic Lou didn't understand and had hidden her entire life from Lou. But she was the same woman who'd bathed Lou when she was little, and bandaged her scraped knees, and still got her fancy hot chocolate when she'd had a bad day at school no matter how little money they had for extras.

Lou couldn't make the pieces fit together: the ruthless girl covered in scars, the one who'd saved May and now was going back for Neela, and the mother who raised her, unknowable and distant. But maybe for Mom, distance was love. Maybe, above all else, it was protection.

But the time for protection was over.

Mom finished cleaning and poured the glass into the trash, the pieces sounding like heavy rain as they tumbled to the bottom.

"Why didn't you ever tell me?" Lou asked. Because this was the biggest question, the one she could face the answer to when she could not face the others.

Mom sighed. She set the kettle to boil and opened the fridge. Shuffling, fussing, the same defense mechanism Lou used when she didn't want to answer something. If she put it off long enough, perhaps the asker would forget.

"I'm not mad," Lou said—a half-truth, if anything. It was an odd role reversal, this: asking her mother questions, declaring in advance that she wouldn't be angry at the outcome, watching her shuffle around and evade.

"I was protecting you," Mom said finally, which was the most generic answer she could've given.

It wasn't good enough.

Lou shrugged. "It feels a lot like alienation to me," she said. She looked around this place, her mother's childhood home, and felt the ache of missing Neela. Neela would've known what to say, how to attack, when all Lou felt was a growing sadness. "I could've—If the market is only here in summer, like May told me, we could've come in fall or winter or spring. I could've seen the place where you grew up, where Nana lives. I could've understood all of this before it was a life-or-death situation."

Mom's face dropped ever so slightly. "Lou, it wasn't about you. I didn't tell you about the market because we didn't have to, and because it would've made you fear something that wasn't relevant." She closed her eyes and exhaled, pushing her hair back from her face. The kettle behind her came to a boil and settled.

"Then why?" Lou asked. Her voice cracked.

Once, when Lou was nine, she woke up in the heat of August to find Neela missing from bed. They stayed together when she visited, back when they had the cramped apartment in Revere that was always too hot or too cold and smelled faintly of mothballs. Neela was not in bed, and there were murmured voices in the kitchen. Lou had crept to the door, her Niagara Falls T-shirt sweaty and clinging to her back. She'd pressed her ear to it and heard Neela giggling with May and Mom, talking about one of Nana Tee's neighbors. Now Lou couldn't remember the details of the conversation, but she remembered the stirring in the pit of her stomach, the realization that the three of them were sisters, united, sharing a mom and a hometown that Lou didn't have and never would, and something about it was sick and heavy. She'd crawled into bed, not wanting to hear more, and pretended to be asleep until Neela's knobby knees knocked into her back.

"Did you not think I could handle it?" Lou asked, feeling the anger in her bubbling like the water in the kettle. "Was this another one of those things that I, because I'd been brought up with Dad's money and Grandpa to love me, just wouldn't understand? Because I wasn't like you? Because I was soft or something?"

"That's not fair, Louisa," Mom said. "I *wanted* you to have a better childhood than I did."

Lou threw a hand out, gesturing at anything, this apartment or this city or this problem. "How is this better? I don't know anything, Mom! I barely even know you!"

Mom sucked in a breath. She turned away, using the excuse of grabbing a chipped mug and pulling it down, fixing her tea. Despite her fury, Lou wondered when Mom had last eaten. If it was any other day, she'd prod her to eat now just to get something down, but she wasn't feeling charitable at the moment.

"Who says I'm only protecting you?" Mom's eyes darted to the closed door to where May slept and back to Lou. Her voice was softer now. "This city, these things, these places, they all hold terrible memories for May. She's my sister, Lou, and I love her almost as much as I love you. If I could take away her pain, make it easier, I would do it. I would do anything for her."

"And you were banished for . . . doing what? What happened to May that was that bad?"

Mom gestured for Lou to sit at the table with her. Lou sighed, wanting to push back, but she sat down anyway. Mom fixed a second cup of tea and set it in front of Lou before she joined her.

"We went into the market when we were explicitly not allowed to. Not like us telling you not to go there; you could still theoretically pass through without issue." She made a face at

Lou, leaving the rest of the sentence unspoken: *but you'd better not do that, or else.* "But May and I . . . we couldn't go, at the risk of death, and to make things worse, they killed someone she cared about. It was traumatizing, and of course they threw us out."

Lou nodded, swallowing down the bitterness, recognizing the surrender in her mother. This was what she wanted, what she'd needed the whole time: for Mom to tell her the truth.

"Honestly, Lou, I hated it at first—resented May, even—but when you were born, I was so happy we weren't here. Sure, the circumstances weren't excellent, but we were out of this town. I never had to sing "Scarborough Fair" or "Oh, Dear" ever again. I never needed to stuff my pockets with rosemary and thyme in the dead of summer just in case I was tricked, taken, led astray."

Lou nodded. "But after you . . . after the banishment ended, why did you never come back? That doesn't explain why we were never here any other time of year."

Mom shook her head, taking a sip of her tea. "May wouldn't come back. Too much happened to her here. And I wouldn't leave her alone to come. I didn't know what me going would do to her. If she'd panic."

"Then why did she come back so easily this time?" Lou asked.

Mom sighed, sitting back in her chair. "Because," she said carefully, "she knows what will happen to Neela if I can't get her. If I fail."

Lou swallowed hard. It wasn't something she even wanted to consider. "Do you think you're going to fail?"

Mom sat in silence for a moment, turning that over. On the TV, someone laughed raucously. "I can't," she said. "I won't let the market have her, no matter what I have to do."

Lou considered this. What could be so bad about the market?

May had survived, and yet . . .

"I need to get ready for tonight," Mom said. She got up and came around to kiss Lou's forehead, her hand resting an extra second on her shoulder. "You have to be careful, Lou. There are things out there that are bigger than you."

She disappeared into her bedroom, leaving Lou alone at the table. Her mind was tripping over ideas and details, caught endlessly in a loop of "Scarborough Fair."

There was a chasm between Mom and Lou, growing even wider now that Lou knew the truth. It didn't matter that Mom hadn't meant to hurt Lou, that she'd only meant to protect her. Because by keeping this information from Lou, she'd only put her in more danger.

The market had killed someone May loved, and many others throughout the years, if the coven was to be believed. If Mom could not save Neela, they would kill her too. And despite the stirring betrayal, the truth of all Neela knew and did not share, Lou could not let the market hurt her.

If Mom failed, it was up to Lou.

CHAPTER 14

LOU SPENT MOST OF THE NEXT DAY AT THE WITCHERY, HELPING Nana Tee with another patient. This one couldn't stop vomiting sickly green sap that smelled like a mix of molasses and red wine. She brewed a potion with Joss, listening carefully to the instructions, and helped Nana Tee force the mixture down the girl's throat.

She struggled to get accustomed to the place, the stone walls and dim lighting, the lack of electricity and plumbing. When they needed the bathroom, there was a hidden stair in the back room that went to a weird staff bathroom in the Old Palace and Lou was hesitant to use it. More than once, Nana Tee sent her up with buckets to refill the basin of water. It was hard, sweaty work, but Lou was grateful for the distraction, and for the answers she managed to get from her grandmother.

They talked around the problems, but Lou managed to get jewels of information, filing each away to examine that night when she was alone. The goblins had hurt May, that much was clear. But May had chosen to go into the market all those years ago. Lou could not figure out what led her in.

That evening, she was determined to get sleep. Mom would go out whether Lou liked it or not. If she was needed to help at the Witchery, May would wake her.

She settled into Neela's bed, wrapped in sheets that smelled like her, as if Lou could roll over and grasp Neela's hand like she would when Neela came to visit. But the other side of the bed was empty and cold.

It was no wonder that, with Neela's sheets around her and that aching grief in her chest, Lou thought she was dreaming when she first heard Neela's voice.

Lou.

She rolled over, trying to follow the path of the dream, trying to follow Neela wherever the voice was leading her.

Lou.

But she wasn't asleep, was she? No. She was here, in Neela's room in York. She was awake. Lou opened her eyes, taking in the dark shapes in the room, the window propped open to let in air.

"Louisa," the voice said again. Lou's heart stuttered, then flew into overdrive, pounding in her chest. Neela. She was out there, calling from the street.

Lou launched out of bed, tripping over the tangle of bedsheets that caught her feet. She half walked, half crawled to the window and dragged herself up.

But the street was empty.

"Neela!" she shouted into the night. She threw the window open farther, leaning out, craning her head. She'd *heard* Neela. Neela was here, Neela was back, Neela needed her help.

Lou threw on shoes and darted down the stairs, not caring about the door shutting behind her, not caring about locking herself out. Neela had called to her, and Lou was going.

She sprinted out onto the street, the cold air raising goose bumps on her bare arms. Lou looked both ways, searching for any inexplicable shadow, any out-of-place lumps on the road or sidewalk.

"Lou, help me!"

Lou whirled on her heel. Neela's voice came from one of the other streets. Lou raced after it, adrenaline pumping. She didn't care that she was freezing, that she was out in the night in only a tank top and shorts. She only cared that Neela was here, Neela was calling her, Neela *needed* her.

"I'm coming!" Lou shouted. In one of the houses, a dog barked. A light flicked on in a window down the street.

She darted around the corner. There was nothing on this street either. The night was velvet and undisturbed, as if no one had shouted at all.

Lou hesitated, catching her breath. She walked ahead, examining every building she passed. It was mostly shops on this street, coffee places and restaurants closed up for the night, the windows looking into shadowed darkness.

"Neela?" Lou called, quieter this time. She didn't need anyone in the apartments coming out to investigate. There was no answer, no disturbance on the street. She could only just hear something a few streets over, carried by the wind, but it was more like party noises than someone calling for help.

She should've woken May or called Nana Tee to come investigate with her. Lou gazed down the street miserably. She couldn't believe that she'd imagined the calling, but there was no evidence to say she *hadn't* imagined it, either.

"You said you'd help me." The voice was too close, thick and sobby. It sounded as if it was coming from ahead, where the street opened up into a square. Lou jogged there, searching the shadows.

She paused in the mouth of the square. Down one of the other streets, she saw a group of people talking and smoking. But they weren't close enough, and none of them were Neela.

She clenched her hands into fists. If she could just solve this, if she could just find Neela, it would all be over.

"Lou?"

She whirled around. There, in the middle of the street she'd just come down, in the darkest of the shadows, was a silhouetted figure. Lou could barely breathe.

Neela.

Her feet were moving before she registered running and then she was crashing into her, nearly knocking both of them onto the street, Lou's arms locking around Neela's body as if she'd never let go. Neela smelled of sweat and blood and something else, something burnt. Her dark hair was a tangled mess, and her brown skin was crusted with blood and marked with lacerations.

"I'm sorry," Lou said, unable to stop the rush of tears, the battle of agony and relief. Neela held her back, not as tightly as Lou would've liked, but she was warm and solid and she was her. "I'm sorry I didn't come. I'm sorry I didn't help sooner. I—"

"Are you coming to Scarborough Fair?" Neela whisper-sung in Lou's ear, the sound haunted and thin.

"Neela?" Lou pulled back, just enough to see the features of her aunt's face. It was Neela, her dark eyes and full lips and high cheekbones, but it also . . . wasn't.

Lou felt a dark thread of fear wrap around her.

Neela ran a hand down Lou's cheek, her nails growing sharper by the second, lengthening into claws. *"And then she shall be a true love of mine. "*

Lou tried to pull away, to pull back, but the goblin held her fast as their face morphed. Lou watched in horror as Neela's bones shattered and reformed into something unfamiliar. A scream caught in her throat.

Who would save her? Who would come?

The goblin caught her arm, claws digging in. They brought their lips close to Lou's ear, close enough that their hot, wet breath stirred her hair. "We know all about you, Louisa Wickett. We know your mother and your mother's mother, and her mother's mother too." Lou smelled something rotten and meaty on her breath. She recoiled, but she could not get free. "I know what your aunt's blood tastes like running over my tongue. Sweet," they crooned, "like the finest of honeys."

She was going to throw up. If she didn't break away now, she was going to vomit all over this goblin and the street and it didn't matter, she didn't matter, because if they killed Neela, she would, she would, she would—

Get out.

"Louisa!"

The shout tore through the night, distracting the goblin. Lou wrenched her arm back, formed a fist like Dad taught her, and punched the goblin as hard as she could. The goblin staggered back, crying out in pain and surprise.

Mom stood at the end of the street, tall and strong, curly hair spilling out of her bun. Lou ran towards her. Behind her, the goblin shouted, "I have what you seek, Louisa Wickett!"

The goblin had Neela, or knew where she was—but Lou couldn't even focus on that, because wasn't trickery all goblins were good for? Mom was here. Mom had found her. She was safe.

Except, as she raced toward her mother, she took in the paleness of her face, the hand she pressed to her ribs, soaked with something dark. Lou slowed as she neared her, taking in the abrasions on her skin, the tears in her clothes, the tracks of blood under her nose.

"Lou," Mom said. She reached out to grab her and fell to her knees on the cobblestones.

CHAPTER 15
May

Eighteen Years Earlier

WHEN MUM TALKED TO LAURA AND MAY ABOUT THE MARKET, she always framed it as a choice. It was a *decision* to go, just as it was a decision to avoid it. But now, following Eitra, May felt it wasn't so much a decision as an inevitability. Had she chosen to have this dormant magic in her blood? No, she had not, just as little as she'd chosen the electric spark that flared within her as she followed Eitra closer and closer to the center of town, to the market. They stopped at home first so May could change. Eitra waited around the corner as May dashed up, silently praying that Angelique had taken the baby to her place and that Laura was out, unable to ask questions.

She got only half of her wish. Angelique was there, in the living room, rocking Neela as she slept. Angelique scowled at her and the creaking door. "Proceed with caution."

May nodded, tiptoeing across the flat.

No one else was here, and Angelique was not going to ask her questions. May took the opportunity to sneak into Laura's closet and thumb through the options there. She settled on her own black jeans and Laura's baggy black sweater, riddled with cigarette burns and holes that May thought looked cool and edgy. She didn't look as great as Eitra in her slip dress, but Eitra didn't appear to feel the damp chill in the same way that May did.

And, though she was making a ridiculous decision, she was still her mother's daughter, so she layered on silver necklaces and hid an iron one among them. She took a slim knife, barely bigger than a letter opener, from Mum's dresser and tucked the sheath into a band Mum had sewn into their bra bands to keep iron close by during market months. It wouldn't kill a goblin, but it was good enough to deter any who got too close.

And because she was a fool, she took the herbs that would get her safe entry in and out of the market, two sachets, and tucked them into her pockets.

"Are you going out?" Angelique asked in a whisper as May crept out of her room, boots in hand so she didn't make too much noise.

May nodded. "Drinks with a friend," she said. It wasn't a lie, not really.

"Be safe," Angelique said.

There wasn't a good response to that. May clambered down the stairs and back out to where she'd left Eitra. She stopped short, breath catching. Eitra leaned against the damp stone wall, collarbone limned in the light of a nearby lamp. She had her eyes closed, face turned up into the drizzle. Rain clung to her eyelashes like dew caught in a spiderweb.

She looked like a carved stone statue of a debauched goddess. Otherworldly. Impossible.

Deadly.

May shuddered. She had the sudden feeling that Eitra knew just how closely May was watching her. She looked away, at anything else, as Eitra's eyes flickered open.

"Ready for that drink?" May asked, desperate to get away from here.

Eitra nodded. "Stay with me, okay?"

The temptation of following, of refusing to run, sent a jarring thrill through May. With Eitra by her side, May saw York with a vicious new edge. The spires of the Minster looked darker against the sky. The ancient city walls constricted, threatening to fall in on York and the market and all of its horrors.

Other people must've had a predatorial instinct that May didn't, because Eitra got more than her fair share of curious and fearful looks as they passed through the streets. Or perhaps it was because she wasn't wearing a coat in the cold and rain.

May looked closer at others on the street, seeking goblins. She tried to look out of the corner of her eye, to find a flash of green skin glamoured into a human shade, or sharp teeth. The buildings of the Shambles leaned in, leering.

You shouldn't be doing this, the rain whispered on the pavement.

What do you have to lose? the cobblestones retorted.

Eitra pulled her into an alleyway, one of the entrances into the regular weekday market. Here, May smelled rot, possibly blood. She watched Eitra creep along the wall, trailing her fingers over the stones. Eitra pressed one of the stones and the glamour on the wall dissolved, revealing a squat, wooden doorway.

May bit her lip. This was it. She dipped her fingers into her pocket, touching the top of the sachet of parsley and sage. She reached for the door.

"Wait," Eitra said. She retrieved a lipstick tucked into her boots and painted her lips a dark, bloody red.

Before May could think, Eitra grabbed her by the shoulders.

She kissed May's cheek at the apex of her cheekbone. Goose bumps broke out along May's arms and she instinctively clutched Eitra's waist, feeling the texture of goblin skin and thorns through the thin silk of her dress.

"What was that for?" May asked breathlessly as Eitra stepped back, but made no move to take her hands away.

"Marking you as mine," Eitra said.

May was, quite possibly, about to die.

"Now, come on," Eitra said. She grabbed May's hands, claws digging into May's palm, and dragged her into the market.

The first thing May noticed was the smell.

It was cloying, sweet and saccharine mingled with rot, like apples candied in blood.

Inside the market, Eitra shuddered, shedding her glamours.

Her skin took on a bumpy green cast and her veins turned black under her skin. Thorns arose on her collarbone, her shoulders, along her spine. Her black-painted nails grew even longer, curving dangerously against May's skin.

As they descended the stone steps, the damp was a visceral thing, chilling May to the bone. It was like the city in November, when the winds through the streets truly began to bite.

Noises filtered up towards them: laughter and gruff voices, a stirring of unfamiliar music. May did not let go of Eitra's hand, no matter how much the claws dug into her palm.

They stopped on the first landing, even though the staircase spiraled down, down, down. May realized that there was a whole subterranean level here, the same size as the market at street level. Pillars dotted the cavernous room, and it was crammed with stalls and goblins and, May realized, the occasional person.

May froze a few steps from the landing, trying to take it all in from above. Eitra noticed this and stopped, turning to watch her. She wasn't sure what she'd expected. Fruit, yes, of course, like the legends foretold. And of course, the bodies and parts of bodies because, even though she was here, May knew what the goblins were like. But she was expecting more of a bloodbath instead of rows of stalls, sectioned off like the market in the city above. There was the collection of jewelry, then fabric, then food—which did include human flesh, May noted.

Goblins whisked through the aisles and swarmed in and out of the stairwells. Humans roamed freely, without goblin accompaniment like May had—but of course they did. They were not the predators here. The goblins outnumbered them immensely. Even unaccompanied, they wouldn't get up to much damage; there were just too many goblins haunting the passageways.

"May," Eitra said, gripping her hand. "Are you afraid?"

May glanced back to the bad section of the market, the section where they sold human flesh. She swallowed hard.

Eitra's kiss still burned on her cheekbone. She was safe, as long as she was with her.

That's foolish, a voice within her whispered, and she begrudgingly agreed. There was no such thing as safety here, especially not with a goblin.

But she was here now, and it was only the first day. She was safe. She had to be safe.

Eitra glanced back as if she could read May's mind. "Let's keep moving, hmm?" she said.

May wasn't sure how to interpret it, but they were already drawing eyes. Perhaps Eitra was being honest about wanting to keep May safe, for today, at least. The first day. Probably the only day.

"I have something to show you," Eitra said. May allowed her to drag her through the stalls, grateful when they avoided the one filled with human parts. Past that, she realized where they were going: towards goblin fruit.

May had heard about the fruit her whole life. Mum even needed some of it for her spells, collecting it either as payment for ailments or when she traded with one or two goblins—traded, but not trusted.

But goblin fruit was not for eating.

May weaved between the stalls, breath caught in her throat. Eitra watched her carefully as she took in the perfect quinces and star fruit, the plump pomegranates in shades of red, white, and black.

"Go on," Eitra said, pulling her hand from May's to grab a juicy plum from one of the vendors. Eitra punctured the skin with one claw, revealing the pale yellow flesh beneath. Sickeningly, the color reminded May of the jars of human fat a few stalls over.

"I'm okay," May said, courage faltering.

Eitra smiled and May wondered if she knew she'd say no. Maybe this was a litmus test, meant to see how much she'd ensnared May, to see just how many rules she was willing to break.

"This is fun and all," May said slowly. "But where's the real party?" She knew she had to tread carefully. She was uncertain if she was wrong in trusting Eitra, uncertain if she'd put herself in the worst position possible because she'd been distracted by her own bi panic.

For all she knew, Eitra might've singled her out because she would be the easiest prey to lure in, to keep there, to devour. May gave in too easily. She was a witchling, seeking to be led astray. She was too easily enchanted by things she was meant to fear.

"Ah," Eitra said. She turned on her heel and led the way back down the aisle of fruits. May's saliva was thick in her mouth, a hunger response triggered by the goblin fruit.

But if she ate goblin fruit, who knew what would happen? She could lose time or forget herself. She could black out and wake up four days from now, still lost in the market. They could gnaw at her body, and she'd not even notice until she came into herself, down a limb and trapped in their realm.

"Come on," Eitra lured. "I know a place."

Back to the staircase they went, and down and down and down. There were too many landings to make sense, probably using some form of magic to even exist. May peered down them as they passed, observing winding stony corridors and moth-eaten parlors filled with goblins and humans together, laughing and bleeding.

They descended into a veil of smoke, blurring out their surroundings. May saw stone walls, the same as the ones that made up most of the buildings at street level, and felt the chill that emanated from them.

She breathed in the scent of the rolling mist, tasting grit and something sweet and terrible, like chloroform.

"Eitra," May said, hesitating on the steps. "Will it be safe for me here?"

She didn't know why she asked or if she'd believe Eitra's answer.

It was better, then, that Eitra didn't give her one.

"Come on," she said, after a beat of silence. May knew she'd made a mistake. She wasn't sure if it was a life-threatening one or merely one that she'd regret tomorrow, that she'd never tell Laura or Mum about because it was so ridiculous and embarrassing.

But even with the sachet of rosemary and thyme in her other pocket, she didn't know if she could get out on her own. As they'd walked down the stairs, taking corridors and winding underground, the stairs behind them had shifted and moved, forming a labyrinth that May had no idea how to navigate. She peered behind her at the stone, just barely lit by flickering sconces. Already, the hallway she knew they took down had been replaced by stairs topped with a wood-paneled landing she didn't recognize.

The room was hazy with sweet-smelling smoke and full of people in finer and finer dress as she followed Eitra deeper. She saw a goblin girl with over-long limbs and spindly fingers, dressed in a gossamer gown of butterfly wings, chewing on a human finger like a sausage. May shudder, reaching out and grabbing Eitra's hand once more.

There was a table in the center of the room, laden with more goblin fruit and carafes of multicolored liquid. May watched as Eitra stabbed a bright blue berry with one claw and ate it, then poured herself a glass of ink-black liquid. When she drank it, it left charcoal lines between her pointed teeth.

"Where are we?" May asked.

Eitra glanced around, possibly surveying the goblins that danced around them. "Somewhere in the middle. Not too far down."

May nodded. Angelique had taught them the general shape of the market. It was like the Strid, a river in Yorkshire, feared for its vicious currents. The Strid looked like a stream, but it was really a river turned on its side, rushing in depths under the surface. The market took up the space below the center of town, but it went deep into the earth many floors down, like the Strid. A market turned on its side.

And according to those who went in, it only got worse as you went deeper. Bottlenecked, impossible to escape.

She glanced around again, trying to find another human, or anything that looked remotely safe. She saw a boy near the wall, so bone thin it looked like his cheekbones would cut through his skin. His eyes were dark brown, all pupil. Though she'd never seen something like it, May suspected he was drunk on goblin fruit, and this was confirmed when she saw a goblin woman come close and dangle grapes in his mouth. Delicately, the boy bit one, eyes closing in bliss.

May didn't recognize him. Perhaps he was from out of town.

"What is this?" a voice said from behind May. Eitra's face shifted, the green color lightening and her lips thinning into a line. "Have you brought us a toy, Eitra?"

May turned to the goblin who'd spoken. She froze—it was the boy from the Shambles, the one with the ink-dark eyes, the one who smelled like lemon verbena and woodsmoke. Here, without glamour to make him human, his skin was darker green than Eitra's and his eyes were even shinier, the iris melding into the pupil. On his shoulders he wore a cape of spiderwebs clotted with blood. His chest was bare, streaked with red from the clots.

"Back off," Eitra said, her tone taking a raspy quality. May wasn't sure if it was hot or terrifying. "Finders keepers."

The phrase had never sounded more menacing.

"I'm not anyone's anything," May said, searching for some well of courage. "I'm here of my own accord."

"Of course," the boy said, sidling nearer. "And are you enjoying the market, on your own accord?"

May clenched her jaw. She got the feeling that Eitra didn't like that this boy was talking to them. But what did that matter?

For all May knew, Eitra was just trying to earn her trust so she could eat her later.

"Would you like to dance?" Eitra asked, surprising May.

"I—"

"Dance, girl," the boy said, tipping his goblet back. "Dance, and drink, and once you have a spin with my friend, you will allow a moment of dancing with me."

"We'll see," May said.

She cursed herself as Eitra led her away, to an open space in the midst of the swirling dancers. May followed Eitra's lead, setting one hand on her shoulder and clasping her other.

She shouldn't have allowed herself to become so easily cowed, so easily frightened. She was in the market, for God's sake. She needed more steel in her veins if this was supposed to be an enjoyable experience. Or, at least, a survivable one.

"You look distressed, human," Eitra said, smirking. She started moving, and May let her lead. She seemed to be calmer away from the goblin boy.

"I'm fine," May said, but it was yet another reminder that she could not let her guard down. "Who was that?"

Eitra sighed, nearly missing a step. "He's called Iark."

May paled. She knew who Iark was. He wasn't just any goblin. He was the Market Prince, the goblin who'd fought for the title not only this year, but the three years before.

She was very relieved, then, that she hadn't followed Iark into the market weeks ago. Entering on the arm of the Market Prince? Surely, that was deadly.

"You should stay away from him," Eitra said, a note of despair in her voice.

Was that jealousy she detected? "Do you not like him?" May

asked. Her attention was briefly torn away by another human, dancing a jig out of time with the music. His head snapped to look at her, and she realized that one eye had been cut out. Black blood dripped down his cheek and over his smiling lips, catching in his mouth. His tongue flicked out, tasting the blood.

May shuddered. With any luck, that boy would be in the Witchery come morning, sobbing about his injuries. With less luck, his left hand or spine or some other part would be found in a ring of white flowers in Kings Square by the week's end.

May wondered, all over again, what she was doing here.

"We're actually very close," Eitra said, grimacing. They spun again and May could see Iark through the crowd, talking with a goblin girl dressed in a gown of oiled feathers.

"And yet, you don't think I should go near him."

She didn't know why she was asking Eitra this. Goblins couldn't be trusted—they would do whatever was necessary for their delicacies, for human flesh and blood and marrow. Perhaps she was being trapped by both of them.

"You'd be safer if you didn't," Eitra said.

May let that sit.

She focused on dancing with Eitra, on the bright vicious green of her eyes against the mist, the feeling of her thorns on May's palm, the heat of her hand. May felt a tingle down her spine, not a chill of fear, but one of desire.

May swallowed hard.

She'd never told Laura or her friends or anyone else about the things she'd wanted, the things she'd done. How she was just as likely to draw a girl into the back alley outside a club, knotting her hands in her hair, lips sucking and biting and tasting, tongue flicking out and hands gripping.

May felt that pull now, with Eitra, the want to have her alone, to destroy her and be destroyed in turn, to fall into her and be sucked under like she'd slipped jumping the Strid.

But the dance ended, as all dances did. Eitra sighed, stepped away, broke the connection, and May gasped as she swirled back into herself.

"You should dance with him," Eitra said, resigned, as if she saw the look on May's face and misunderstood who it was for. "One dance, and then remember your safety."

"Do I have to?"

Eitra stepped away. Iark was already there, watching them over Eitra's shoulder, as if she'd summoned them. He smiled at May.

"I'll keep asking if you don't," Iark said, a smile on his lips but a threat in his voice. He was already moving, stepping around Eitra, gripping May's hands and pulling her in until May's feet caught up.

May turned to say something to Eitra, but she was already gone. So much for her promise to keep May safe.

This close to him, she could smell the blood. If she moved her hand up, put it in the same place where she'd rested on Eitra's body, she'd be covering one of the clots with her palm.

"So you're the goblin prince," May said, deciding it was best to just come out with it. And if she kept him talking, kept talking *to* him, perhaps she'd cover her own fear.

"I am," he said magnanimously, one eyebrow arching. Close up, there was something handsome about him, if you didn't see him straight on. You couldn't think of goblin beauty in the same way as human beauty. It was all odd, all destructive, all rot and horror and gaudy terror. But she understood it a bit more now.

Perhaps it was because she felt the bite of Eitra's thorns on her skin, and she'd liked it.

"Do you fear me?" Iark asked, his voice lilting. He wanted her to say yes.

May only shrugged. She knew what he was, as the market prince. It was a won position, like the alpha of a wolf pack. He'd killed the previous market prince for it, and he'd remain the prince until someone killed him. Bloodshed all the way down as the power changed hands, as the chaos intensified. She wanted to go back to Eitra, who had not killed to become who she was. She didn't like Iark's hands on her.

But that felt like cowardice. She would not shudder, she would not crack, she would not break. She wanted to see the market, and this was the market in its truest form.

"Where do you go, when you're not here?" May decided a change in subject was her best bet for safety. She knew the answer to this in a clinical way. Of course they'd studied goblin history and shared what they knew of their activities, but Mum and Joss had only focused on teaching them about the market.

He shrugged as best as he could midstep. "North and south and east and west, wherever the weather blows us." He took a hand away and ran a sharp claw along May's cheekbone. "But I find that northern girls, market girls, their blood tastes the sweetest."

Another thing best to ignore. "And is this the only true market, or are there others?"

Iark laughed. He seemed delighted by her evasion. "There's no market so true as here, as York. There used to be others, but . . ." He looked off into space, remembering something that had probably happened long before May was even born.

"They're not around anymore."

The song came to an end, and Iark stepped away, just as Eitra had. "Thank you for this dance," he said. "I hope to see you here again."

May swallowed hard. "Doubtful."

He smiled wickedly. "I could send my finest singers to your window tomorrow, if that would make the decision easier."

May shuddered, thinking how terribly that would go over with Mum and Laura. "I'll decide on my own, thank you."

Iark laughed. "As you wish. All the same . . ." He took her hand and kissed the back of it, his lips dry and warm. This surprised May. She wasn't sure why, but she'd expected some sort of slime.

"May," Eitra called. She was standing just a little bit away, hands crossed over her stomach. "There's more to see."

Iark smiled, leading May back to Eitra as if she was the lady of the ball. Now that she had some of her focus back, she noticed others watching them, goblins and humans alike. She didn't like it.

"My second will take good care of you, I guarantee," Iark promised, giving her hand back to Eitra.

My second.

May felt ice settling in her veins. What had Marcus said? *I don't like the looks of Iark's new second.*

"Thank you for the dance," she said hurriedly, going back to Eitra's side. She grabbed her hand and dragged her back towards the stairs.

Eitra was Iark's second. Assistant to the most volatile, the most ruthless. May wanted to cry. How could she have put herself in her hands?

Maybe because Marcus was wrong. Eitra didn't look mean at all. She looked . . . tempting.

"What's wrong?" Eitra asked. "Wouldn't you like more amusement here?"

May shook her head. "Take me somewhere else. Somewhere less crowded."

Eitra didn't ask. She only nodded, taking them back up the stairs and through a labyrinth of corridors. They did not return to the market proper, but instead, into a snaking section of stone alleys and great columned rooms. All were empty. May wondered at this.

They walked silently through a hall, Eitra kicking the rubble that cluttered the ground. Some of it seemed to be from the market above, baubles and bird beaks and feathers, and some of it seemed to be human bones.

"Where are we?" she asked.

Eitra shrugged. "The Inbetween. It's a quiet place for thinking or feasting." The corner of her mouth tilted up. "Or seduction."

May shivered. "Is that why you've brought me here?" she asked as they left one of the great rooms behind and entered a tight corridor. "For seduction?"

Eitra tilted her head, looking at May through a slant. "That depends," she said. "Would you like to be seduced?"

Don't be this way, a voice within her whispered. It was ridiculous to want this, to want a goblin, to want something she knew only existed to hurt her.

But she wanted all the same.

It was why she didn't stop Eitra as the goblin girl guided her so her back was against the wall, why she didn't run as one hand went to her waist and the other to her hair. It was why she didn't wait for Eitra but instead dug her own nails into Eitra's scalp and pulled her close, pulled her lips down.

For just a moment, she could pretend that her own nails were claws, that the lingering taste of blood came from her own mouth. That she was strong and unbreakable and invincible, not weak and fragile and human.

She didn't know if she wanted Eitra or if she wanted to become her.

So she settled for kissing her, for entangling with her, for gasping and clawing and biting and tasting.

She settled for this, and found it to be enough.

May didn't know how long they were in the corridor, undisturbed. Eitra was right. This was a quiet place, a place for secrets. Finally, they broke apart, both flushed and breathing hard, and May stuttered, "I-I think I should go."

Eitra nodded, looking dizzy and confused. "You should," she agreed.

They didn't speak as they wound back up through the market and to the street, where the cold air kissed May's overheated cheeks. She kept a tight grip on Eitra's hand even as she shuddered back into her glamour, taking back the appearance of a human girl.

"Shall I walk you home?" Eitra asked.

May bit her lip. It was too late, too risky. "No," she said. "I don't want them to see you."

Eitra nodded. They stood alone in the middle of a street, long after the pubs closed, long after the last travelers had gone home for fear of being caught and ensnared in the market.

May didn't know what she feared anymore. Herself, probably, more than anything else.

"Tomorrow," Eitra said, breaking the silence. She closed her eyes as she spoke, as if it cost her something to say the words.

"You can come back tomorrow. To the market. You'll be safe, and I can . . . I can watch over you. Protect you."

May looked past her, at the mouth of the alley that would take her to the market. Would it be so bad to go again? She had two more days of safety.

"I don't know," she answered honestly. "I'll try."

Eitra nodded. She didn't offer May a kiss goodbye or ask for more promises. She merely stepped back, sighed, and turned back to the market.

May walked home, half-stumbling. Back in the cold of the street, she couldn't believe what she'd done—or that she'd liked it.

What was she thinking? She couldn't go tomorrow. She couldn't put her family through that if she didn't come back.

But Eitra . . .

No. Eitra was a goblin. And not just any goblin. She was Iark's second, nearly the most dangerous, nearly the most ruthless. It didn't matter if she'd been sweet to May, if she'd kissed her and whispered nice words in her ear. Eitra didn't care about her or want her. Eitra merely wanted her to trust her so May was an easier victim, and if she believed anything other than that, she was a fool.

May wound through the streets, taking the long way home, cursing every shadow that scared her.

She was a fool, she was a fool, she was a fool. And when Eitra came calling for her again, she'd make the same mistakes all over again, gladly, no matter how much it hurt, like the blood staining her hands from Eitra's thorns.

CHAPTER 16

L OU DID NOT KNOW HOW MUCH BLOOD WAS A LOT OF BLOOD OR a little blood or too much blood. All she knew was the amount of blood that seeped terribly from her mother's ribs and soaked the bandages May wrapped around her was enough blood to make her feel like she, too, was dying.

She sat by her mother's side in the Witchery, where they'd taken her to one of the back rooms. Lou barely remembered dragging Mom back to the apartment, screaming and pounding on the door until May came down, or the walk as she and May carried Mom the short distance here. She only remembered the warm flood of blood against her skin as she'd tried to apply pressure, to staunch the bleeding.

The area over Mom's left rib was a horror of teeth marks and mottled flesh and something green and seeping. It didn't look any worse than the thorns in the boy a few days before—in fact, it looked much, much better—but the sight of it had made Nana Tee and Joss exchange a look that Lou didn't like at all.

Joss prodded the area around the wound, hissing as she pulled ripped bits of fabric away to reveal the veins on Mom's stomach turning black. Lou swallowed hard.

May came over and wrapped an arm around Lou as if she'd

only just remembered that she might need to be comforted. "It's going to be okay," she said, but she didn't sound like she believed it.

"I know," Lou said. She didn't believe it, either.

"It does look bad," Joss said, more to Nana Tee than to May or Lou.

"It looks bad, but it isn't?" Lou asked hopefully.

Joss sighed, turning her attention to Mom's other wounds. "No. It looks bad, and it's probably worse," she admitted.

May's hand tightened on Lou's shoulder.

"It's a nasty bit of work," Joss said, more to herself than them. "Christina, who's the Prince this year?"

"Hilgar. But a poison like this is worse than anything we saw from them last year. Could be someone else's work."

Joss frowned at the wound. "Or maybe Hilgar grew into the title."

"I have the salve," Nana Tee said, crossing from the stove with her pot and a trivet. She rested the pot on a low table. "I don't think we have time for it to fully cool."

Joss nodded. "I'll prepare the gauze."

Nana Tee handed her the roll and a pair of scissors. She set to work removing Mom's shirt and jeans. It was odd, uncomfortable, watching this. Lou wished she could turn away, but she knew she could not. If this was bad, if this was the last she saw of her mother living—no. She could not think like that.

She was just beginning to understand the truth of her family, of her mother. She could not lose her now.

"I called down to London," Nana Tee said, hushed. "But you know the Thaumaturge passed last summer. There hasn't been a replacement yet."

"I know," Joss said. "There may not be for years."

None of it made sense to Lou, none of it mattered, because Mom could be dying—and Lou was helpless. She could only stand and watch as they applied the salve to her wounds, as they wrapped her in gauze, as Nana Tee went back to the kitchen and prepared a broth while Joss rubbed Mom's muscles with oils.

A sob choked her before she knew what was happening. Next to her, May drew in a breath. She pulled her in, pulled Lou's head into her chest, stroked her hair. Lou let herself be comforted, if even just a moment.

"It's okay," May said. Her voice cracked. Lou knew it wasn't, but she also knew what May meant. It *had* to be okay.

They were all mirrors, the four of them: Neela reflecting Lou back on herself, her worst parts and her best. Mom and May were the same way, two sides of the same coin. For the last week, Lou had felt like she'd been cleft in half, like without Neela, nothing could be worse.

But now, even with their differences and the secrets and the wounds thickly scarred, how could she go on without her mother? How could May? It was impossible to consider. It was wrong, in the same way the thorns growing from the boy's body had been wrong.

So she stayed as Joss and Nana Tee treated Mom, as time passed without marking in the Witchery. There was no way to tell what time of day it was. Dawn must've come above them by the time Joss finished her ministrations and covered Mom with a blanket. Joss's knees popped when she stood up. Lou knew vaguely that she hadn't slept the whole night, but it didn't matter. When Joss ushered her out of the glorified operating room, back to the big room and onto one of the chairs around the table, Lou let her.

May came over and pressed a hot mug of tea on her. "You should drink something," she said. Lou thought about it, but her stomach curled.

"Is there milk?" Lou asked.

"There's not even a fridge." Nana Tee sighed.

She and Joss went back to their conversation about herbs or suppliers or someone named Annika, unless Annika was an herb company. Lou couldn't quite get her head around it without caffeine.

She couldn't take it anymore. She couldn't sit here, waiting for Neela to just die or for Mom to grow worse. She couldn't go on knowing nothing about what happened.

"What do we do now?"

Joss and Nana Tee exchanged a glance. May slumped down in the chair next to Lou, resting her head on her arm. There was an abandoned plate of pastries in the middle of the table, one of the women halfheartedly trying to take care of everyone else.

"I don't know," Nana Tee admitted, wiping her hands on a towel and leaning against the counter. She looked haggard, awful.

"You don't know what to do or you don't know if she'll be okay?"

"I don't know either."

Lou took a bite of one of the croissants. Her mouth was too dry and it tasted like sawdust. She set it back down.

"We think it's poison," Joss said finally. "The tinted veins are in line with that. Laura—your mom—doesn't look good. I don't even know how she got home like this. And nothing we have is working, no charms or poultices. We might need an antidote from within the market. And with goblin poison . . . it can wreak havoc, but not for very long. Most only work until the end of the market."

"And after the end?" Lou asked.

Joss and Nana Tee exchanged a look. Lou knew what that meant: if they didn't have the antidote by the time the market left for the year, her mother would die.

Lou swallowed this down, yet another impossible truth. But she should've known. Of course it would come to this. Of course everything, everything, led back to the market.

"And we still don't have Neela back," she said miserably.

Nana Tee coughed, but it sounded like a sob. Lou couldn't look at her. If Nana Tee was breaking, if this was too much for her to take, Lou didn't know how she could go on.

Except.

"So to save Mom," Lou said slowly, thinking of the boy's voice the night before. "To save Mom, and to find Neela, someone has to go back into the market."

Nana Tee looked at her sharply. "Louisa, that's not a good train of thought."

"But you're right," Joss said quickly. She seemed like someone who liked facts and the truth. "To get the antidote, someone needs to go into the market. I don't know the likelihood of finding Neela, not after so much time in the market, but you wouldn't be able to locate her out here."

Lou put her head in her hands. Was she really considering this?

"May," she said quietly. She looked up to find her aunt watching her, exhaustion and reluctant agreement battling on her face. She had to know, to know the truth and the reality and the myths and the legends. Even though she'd already made up her mind on what she was going to do, Lou had to know more. "What's the market really like?"

May closed her eyes. Bad enough that she'd been traumatized, Lou knew; bad enough she'd left the country entirely with Mom in tow. But Lou needed her to go back there, go back in her mind to the market, and tell her everything she could.

"It's . . . bloody," May said finally, opening her eyes. Her fingers flinched, like she wanted to reach out and grab something. "Bloody and terrible. They'll cover it all for you, the first day, to lure you in. You'll only see what you can bear. Bodies, yes, but nothing horrifying. They'll lure you in with fruit and gems and liquor and dancing, merriment to remember for the rest of your life. But that's an illusion, Lou. The market is death itself."

Lou shook her head. She couldn't care about that; she didn't have the time. "That's not what I mean," she said. The decision was made. She didn't want to know how bad it would look. "I don't want to know what it looks like or what it smells like. I want to know what the goblins are like. I want to know how they'll try to trick me, to hurt me, to use me. I want to know, before it's too late, how the goblins will try to kill me."

"Louisa," Nana Tee said sharply. Lou looked at her, waiting for what would come next. But her grandmother just pressed her lips together, as if trying to hold back whatever words threatened to break forth. Finally, she said, "It's not . . . It's too much of a risk."

Fury rolled through Lou. "It's too much? For what? For me to go?" She got up, pacing the room. "Why wasn't it too much for Mom to go in for Neela? For May, even? Why does Mom have to save everyone else, but no one is willing to save Mom?"

"Lou—" Nana Tee started as Joss said, "It's not that simple."

But Lou wasn't having it. "No," she said, unable to hold back the venom. "No one else gets to decide this one. Mom has been nothing but self-sacrificing throughout this entire thing, running in to save everyone. And now, someone has to save her."

"She's right," May said woodenly. She rubbed her eyes. "She's absolutely right. Someone needs to go into the market for Laura's sake."

"And you think it should be you," Nana Tee said to Lou. "You think you can get through the market and out again."

"I'm not saying it'll be easy," Lou said. "But I'm not afraid."

"That's because you don't know what to be afraid of," Nana Tee said.

Lou shrugged. This whole debate didn't matter; it was just something she had to get through. She'd get on the other side with or without Nana Tee's blessing and tonight she'd go to that alleyway, that place, and she'd hunt down the antidote herself.

"Then tell me," she said. "Neela's already been gone too long. We have to hurry. You can tell me all those things I need to remember, the things that I never learned. Teach me the basics. The songs, the words, the spells, all of it. And tomorrow, after nightfall, I'll go into the market and do my best."

Nana Tee rubbed her eyes. She looked so, so exhausted.

"If we take a day and a half to prepare, that leaves me three full nights for the market. But first things first. I need sleep. Then, when I wake up, I need to know everything you know about the market." She held Nana Tee's eye, the only one she really had to convince. May knew she was going, knew she was just as stubborn as Mom, knew she'd leave no matter how much they tried to hold her back.

"I won't get ahead of myself," she said. "I won't let my guard down. And when I come back, I hope it'll be with both Neela and the antidote. But no matter what," she promised, "I will come back."

She got up before anyone could protest. May sighed, but she led her back down the gloomy hallway, into one of the rooms. It was small and simple: a bed, a basin of water, a candle on a nightstand.

"I'll wake you in four hours," May said.

Lou nodded. May retreated back to the big room, back to the others.

There, alone, she crawled into the bed. There were murmured voices from the other room, but Lou didn't care. She expected to take a while falling asleep, but as soon as she closed her eyes, she was falling, swirling through visions and fears of the market.

And all the ways it threatened to kill her.

CHAPTER 17

A DAY AND A HALF WOULDN'T COME CLOSE TO THE FULL SIXTEEN years of training May and Mom had. It took Lou less than an hour to realize this as she and Joss went over basic knife fighting techniques in the shadow of the Minster, battling with wooden props and fake laughing to deter any tourists who looked too closely.

Afterwards, they sat with old notebooks full of songs and riddles, repeating them over and over until the words ran together.

"The songs," Joss said, flipping the pages, pointing to annotations on the pages, "they all have secrets within them. Something that will help you or guide you along."

Lou fell back against the green grass. "How am I supposed to remember all of this?"

"Well, you won't make it out if you don't," Joss said. Her tone was light but the message was all too clear.

Lou flipped to the first of the songs. "'Scarborough Fair'," she said. Of course it was "Scarborough Fair." If she had to hear that song again when this was over, she was going to fight someone.

"That's the guide to get in," Joss said. She scooted closer. She smelled of crushed herbs and woodsmoke from the healing solutions she'd brewed early that morning while Lou slept.

"See this? Parsley, sage, rosemary, thyme."

"All nice on chicken," Lou observed.

Joss went on as if she hadn't spoken. "That's the trick in and out of the market. Parsley and sage to get safe passage in, to enter peacefully. And rosemary and thyme to leave without trouble."

Lou squinched her nose up. "How much protection can herbs offer?"

"There's a treaty, Louisa. Rules. Our magic is rooted in the safety of nature, of the natural world. Of our world."

"So herbs are supposed to protect me from goblin tricks?"

"No. Knives are."

Lou pulled out a handful of grass, letting it rain down all over her. The problem was, she wasn't good at knives. How could she be after only an afternoon of practice? And she wasn't good at the songs either. Mom and May had always hummed them to her, growing up. They hadn't taken the time to teach her the lyrics or what they meant.

In their minds, they hadn't needed to.

But now, Mom's and Neela's lives relied on Lou knowing these things. It was ironic in a terrible way.

Joss softened like she could read Lou's mind. "Parsley and sage in, rosemary and thyme out. That's the most important thing to remember. Bite down on the rosemary and thyme, and you'll find yourself safely out."

There was a lump in Lou's throat that she couldn't dislodge. "But how am I supposed to fight my way out if there's trouble?"

Joss shook her head. "They fight, sure, but goblins are prone to trickery above all else. You're a smart girl. All of this . . ." She waved towards the practice weapons, the stack of books, the basket of herbs. "All of this matters, yes, but only if you know how to use it. The best way for you might just be the unconventional way."

Lou swallowed hard. How could she know what the unconventional way was when she didn't know anything at all? "So what do I do?"

"You're safe for three days unless you actually kill one of them. Take your time. Don't drink anything; don't eat anything they offer you. That's the easiest way to lose track of time. But if you get in, find Neela, and get back out, you will be absolutely fine. Do you understand?"

Lou pressed her hands to her eyes. "But Mom wasn't in there for three nights, and they hurt her."

Joss snorted. "Yes, well, your mother and May killed a goblin."

That was a surprise. Lou levered herself up onto one elbow so she could see Joss better. "Like, before? Is that why they left?"

Perhaps Joss was the best person to probe for information. After all, she was the only one in this city who hadn't lied to Lou. If for no other reason, Lou felt inclined to trust her.

"It wasn't exactly safe for either of them here after what they did," Joss said. She chewed on her lip. "May broke a rule and was held captive. Laura went in after her. She killed the Market Prince to get them both out. They faced punishment for their actions, but they survived, and that wasn't appreciated by the market."

Lou filed that information away for later. Perhaps that was why the goblins had gone after Neela: not just for her blood, but for retribution.

Unfortunately, it seemed that the goblins already knew who Lou was. So if she was really going into the market, she'd have to follow the rules to the letter.

She looked over at Joss, feeling that rush again. Here, for the first time, was someone totally open to sharing knowledge. Lou craved answers like the earth craved water after a drought. But it wasn't Joss she wanted them from.

May was alone in the apartment when Lou went back. She sat in the chair by the window, knees tucked up under her. The TV was on but she was clearly not watching it. Instead, she gazed out at the street below, watching people walk toward the Minster.

They hadn't really left this little square of the city, Lou realized. Besides the Witchery and the apartment, they didn't go anywhere else. Surely May had people here she still cared about, old friends to visit, but it didn't seem to matter.

Lou settled onto the couch and watched her watch outside. May had heard her come in, Lou was certain, but she didn't move to speak to her. "Are you okay?" Lou asked.

May sniffled a bit. Only then did Lou realize she was crying.

"It's just . . . difficult," May said. "Being back."

Lou chewed on her lip. She didn't really know what to say, what comfort to offer. "Because of what happened? When you went into the market?"

May snorted, wiping her nose on her sleeve. "I don't know, Lou. It just . . . what was Laura protecting us from? What was the point? Of course they'd come back for us. That's what the market *does.*"

Lou considered the way May spoke of it. She was right that Mom wasn't just protecting her, but May too. Because if May had to relive whatever she'd gone through before, it was going to hurt.

She wanted to get up and sit on May's lap like she used to when she was a little kid, to lean in and smell her perfume and be comforted.

"Can I ask you something?" Lou said.

"You will anyway."

Maybe she would've, but this was sensitive, improper questioning. "Mom said the market killed someone you loved. Was it . . . was it one of the other witches?"

May sighed. She pulled the iron chain necklace from under her shirt and fiddled with the links. "A girl I cared about. She tried to save me, but it wasn't enough, and Laura and I couldn't repay her."

Lou chewed on her lip. There was more here, a story, but she would not put May through the grief of telling it. She nodded. "Thank you for telling me."

"Of course."

"Will you help me practice these songs?"

The corner of May's lips turned up. "Your mom was always far better at them. But yeah, sure. Come here and sit with me."

That night, as Lou laid in Neela's bed and tried to sleep, the goblins came calling.

The first time they shouted her name in Neela's voice, she nearly bolted out of bed as she had the night before. She bit down on her fist, trying to keep the tears at bay, but when they called her name again, there was no stopping them carving hot tracks down her cheeks.

"Help me, Lou!"

Slowly, carefully, she got up. Lou didn't really know what she was doing as she pulled sweatpants over her shorts and grabbed one of Neela's hoodies from the back of her door. She stopped at the trunk in the living room for a knife and snagged a pair of keys from the hook by the front door. Mom and May had a hook in the same place in their house, Lou realized, so even a world apart, it felt like muscle memory.

Fury bubbled in her throat, dislodging the grief, as Lou launched herself down the stairs. This time, the goblin wasn't full of tricks. They stood across the road, cast in shadows.

Lou clenched her fists at her sides. She shouldn't punch the goblin again, not if she wasn't looking for trouble. Not the night before she was meant to enter the market. She stopped a healthy distance away and examined the goblin.

"Why are you here?"

The goblin spoke in a high, lilting voice. "Your blood smells so sweet," she crooned. "And is it wrong of me to want a matched pair?"

A matched pair. The goblin meant her and Neela.

"What have you done to her?" Lou hissed through gritted teeth. *Do not fight the goblin*, she forced herself to think over and over again. *Do not fight her. You will not win.*

"Come visit us," the goblin said, flashing her a smile. She tossed something toward Lou, gold and spinning. Lou caught it in one hand. A gold coin. "You won't regret it."

Survey says that's a lie, Lou thought.

"Do you know who you are, Louisa Wickett?"

She wondered what would happen if she drew the knife and lunged, if she stopped tolerating the goblin girl's questions. "It's Wickett-Stevens."

The goblin stepped out of the shadow, into the light. Her hair was dark, nearly the same shade as Neela's even without the glamour, and she wore a shimmery green vest, like leaves covered in dew, open over her chest. Around her throat was a string of molars. She walked forward, one eyebrow raised, until she was standing directly in front of Lou.

"And yes," Lou snapped. "Of course I know who I am."

The goblin girl reached out quickly, gripping Lou's chin like Mom used to when she had a smear of ketchup on her cheek. The goblin's claw dug into Lou's lower lip. Lou felt tense, heavy, uncomfortable with the goblin so close.

"You're just a little moon, aren't you?" The goblin squeezed, her claws digging in deeper. If Lou pulled away, she had no doubt the goblin would slash her. "You don't have a self. You just orbit everyone around you."

Lou swallowed hard. *I don't know who I am without Neela.* The thought crept in before she could stop it. *I am no one without Neela.* Her breath was coming too fast, erratic.

What if there was another reason to go to the market, one that had nothing to do with Neela? What if the secret to that amorphous Unbelonging, the way to make it go away, was hidden within its depths?

The goblin girl released her hold, stepping back into the shadows. "Come buy, little moon," she said, her eyes lingering on Lou as she started down the street. "There are stories yet to be told."

Lou stood shivering in the middle of the street as the goblin retreated, sauntering back toward the center of town where the Shambles faded into the market. She tried to convince herself the goblin was lying—of course she was lying—but even as she turned back to the house, let herself in, and started up the stairs, she knew the truth.

The goblin was right. There was no Lou without Neela. She was happy to orbit, to take instruction, to follow along. She was nobody, nothing. And until now, she hadn't thought that was a bad thing.

CHAPTER 18

May

Eighteen Years Earlier

THE WITCHERY ALWAYS LOOKED STEREOTYPICALLY RITUALISTIC, but never so much as this. May tried not to think about the incessant slog of time as she stood in the middle of the room, dressed in a heavy black robe that smelled of moth balls. May, Marcus, and Laura were in a line in the place the couch usually occupied. Mum and Joss had pushed it to the side earlier that afternoon before covering every flat surface with big, waxy candles. May glanced at the table. They'd be picking dried wax off it for weeks.

It was her first real ritual—well, technically there was one when she was just a baby, used to make her magic dormant—but she wasn't pleased by any of it. Tonight was symbolic of the end of choice, the last night of freedom.

Magic restrained the way theirs was would not just come rushing back when they became witches. Tonight, the Thaumaturge had called them together to do the first ceremony. It would loosen the binding on their magic, allowing it to return in dribs and drabs so they'd actually be useful after the ceremony next week that made them into full witches. After tonight, the three of them would no longer be witchlings, but instead, they would become candidates.

May dreaded it.

Her palms were sweaty and her mouth was dry and Marcus kept clearing his throat and Laura couldn't keep still, which annoyed her, for some reason.

When she closed her eyes, she could still feel the press of Eitra's thorns on her skin. She tried to hide all signs of her distraction from Laura as they prepared for the ceremony, but more often than not, May found herself staring into space and craving. Wanting the fruit, goblin wine, Eitra.

She understood now, she thought. The call that made them all go back. If she wasn't careful, she'd find herself chained in the bottom of the market on day 4, eyes plucked out, fed her own blood for sustenance.

Fingertips touched her own, breaking her out of her thoughts. May glanced down. It was Laura's hand there, trembling. She glanced over at her sister. Her face was pinched, brow furrowed. She was chewing on the inside of her right cheek, which she always did when she was nervous.

May tried to stifle the bitterness inside her. Why would Laura be nervous or sad about this? She'd always wanted to be a full member of the coven. She'd been waiting for this day with bated breath for as long as they'd known it was coming.

To his credit, Marcus just looked stoic and impassive.

They all straightened when the far door opened. The Thaumaturge came in dressed in blood-red robes, like their black ones and the coven's white. She had her hood drawn down, her face shadowed, so May couldn't see her features. It could be anyone under that robe.

The coven whispered behind them as Caroline went through the final preparations: pouring fresh Strid water into a bowl, pressing it to their lips with the pad of her thumb, turning away and slicing her own skin with a small knife to draw blood.

May was too warm in here. She wished, just once, someone had asked her what *she* wanted.

She felt herself sliding slowly towards panic as the ritual continued, as the Thaumaturge broke the bindings of their magic with blood. Something released within her, like a joint popping, and she felt a brief flare of warmth, which only increased the panic.

It hurt to look at Laura, who regarded the Thaumaturge with an almost holy reverence. It was awful and unfair that they could have such corrupted memories of this night; Laura would always look back on this as the best thing, the thing she'd always wanted, and May would always reflect on this day with regret.

She did not feel magical. She only felt more alone.

When it was done, when the chanting ended and the candles went out and were replaced by the usual lanterns, she caught Laura's beaming smile. Laura had a hand pressed to the middle of her chest. Her cheeks were flushed with mirth or the heat of the room, and her eyes sparkled with happiness.

"Do you feel it?" she asked. "I didn't expect it to be so . . . nice."

Across the room, May registered the Thaumaturge watching them. She tried to smile back convincingly at Laura. "Yeah. I wonder what the real thing will be like."

The magic released could be contained. She didn't have to become a full witch under the light of the moon with Laura and Marcus. But no one had asked if she wanted this, or if she wanted to run. She didn't have a choice. It was a foregone conclusion, like anything else.

There was one more ceremony to get through in a few days' time, one final test, and she would be fettered to her fate.

May made an excuse to leave, citing the heat. She stripped out of her robe and tossed it on the couch and didn't run until she was away from the echoing hall of the Witchery.

Before her brain could catch up, she was running through the museum park, near the ruins. She curled up at the base of a tree and put her head between her knees, trying to catch her breath. Only then, alone, did May begin to cry.

"Has anyone ever told you that your hair is beautiful in the rain?"

May started. She'd noticed the drizzle when it started nearly thirty minutes before, but she hadn't been moved to go inside. She looked up to find Eitra standing over her in her glamoured human form.

Immediately, May felt sick. It was a rule, wasn't it? Once she was a candidate, she was forbidden from the market. Forbidden from Eitra. May wondered if Eitra could smell the magic on her, like petrichor after rain.

"Shouldn't you be partying?" May asked. It wasn't quite the term she was looking for, but Eitra belonged in the depths of the market, with the blood and bones and violence, even if she looked lovely and sweet up here.

Eitra shrugged. "I came to find you." She held out a hand and helped May up. "I suppose you're not interested in a jaunt tonight."

May shook her head. Eitra wasn't treating her any differently than she had before. Was it possible she didn't know about the transformation May had undergone? "I'd rather not tonight, thank you."

Eitra wouldn't have invited her if she knew May was a candidate and forbidden. Goblins relied on trickery, but that was in violation of the Doctrine and any agreement they had. Eitra didn't know—which meant, if she wanted, May could still go into the market. Probably.

"Are you going to leave me, then?" May asked. Eitra had started walking and May followed, going back to the path. Her head hurt from crying. She just wanted to curl up somewhere and feel bad for herself.

Eitra shrugged. "I'm not needed at the market, if you would like company." She flexed her hands, her long, dark fingernails glinting in the streetlight. "Iark can manage on his own for an evening."

May nodded. She didn't like this reminder of what Eitra was and who she served. "Does he usually make you do things for him?" She shoved her hands in her pockets so she couldn't fidget. Her clothes were damp and it was all terrible, but at least she was with Eitra.

"When he has bidding, I see it done," she said with a tone hinting at finality. May didn't question it further.

She looked at Eitra, her hair braided in a halo around her head, but frizzing in the light rain. It made that electric thrill of the magic escaping its binding within her feel liquid hot in her chest.

"Do you want to get coffee?" May asked.

Eitra raised an eyebrow. "It's the middle of the night. Doesn't coffee make you . . . go faster?"

May shrugged. It didn't matter what time it was or if they even ordered coffee. She wanted to sit across from Eitra in a dingy, badly lit booth, sleepy and unwilling to leave, like she would with any other girl she was interested in. She wanted to feel normal with her. Human.

May reached out and gripped Eitra's hand, lacing their fingers together. She wondered if Eitra could feel the thorn scratches scabbed over on her palms. "I know a place."

Ten minutes later, they were settled in a back corner at the only café open this late. May tried to keep her head down. Her mum was a frequent visitor here on the market nights, when day blended into night and back again with no regard for normal business hours. It would not be good to be caught here, but there was a good danger to it.

Eitra had a cup of black coffee in front of her. Every so often, she leaned forward and sniffed at it, cringing a little bit. May tried not to smile. She sipped at her latte in silence.

"It won't hurt you, you know," she said after Eitra's fourth sniff.

Eitra scrunched her face at May. "It smells poisonous."

"Ironic, coming from you."

They both smiled at that, but it hinted at the awkwardness between them. What were they, if not predator and prey? Outside the structures of the market, the vicious edge of want softened. May wanted Eitra to see her as something real. She reached over and traced one of Eitra's rings on her hand, flat on the table. She wore them on nearly every finger, silver and black, some plain, some carved, one or two with dark stones.

"I like these," May said, which felt ridiculous. She'd probably paid for them in blood.

Eitra shifted. "Thank you," she said. Her eyes traced over May in a way that felt not quite decent for this café. "You're still wearing iron."

May touched the chain around her throat. In truth, she wore it nearly every day, market season or not. It was habit now. "I'm sorry. Is it hurting you? I can take it off?" She reached back for the clasp, but Eitra grabbed her hand.

"No, it's probably better if you don't." The corner of her mouth tipped up in a smile. "Safer that way."

May snorted. She took a sip of her coffee. She was tired, really—she'd spent most of last night up worrying about the ceremony and how it would make her feel. It was no surprise she felt terrible now.

"What's it like, when you're not in the market? The other parts of the year?"

Eitra shrugged. She looked over May's shoulder, out at the street. "It's not comfortable, as you can imagine. We're not . . . wanted many places. There are covens keeping us out, keeping us dispersed. So we break into pairs and trios and loners, and we return to whatever hidey holes we occupy the rest of the year." Eitra looked down, her long lashes shadowing her cheeks. "I go with Iark. Do what he needs. He has a burrow in the Highlands. Sometimes, others come to visit, but never too many at a time. There are rules, you know, about how we can interact in non-market times. It's…" She paused, like she was going to say it was nice or tolerable, but she shook her head. "It is what it is. He goes into towns to wreak havoc, and I make his poisons and sharpen his knives."

"That sounds . . ." May, too, trailed off. She wasn't going to say it was nice or tolerable either. "Why do you go with Iark? How did you become his second?"

Eitra chewed on her lip. May wondered if she was actually going to answer. "We don't have families in the way that you do," she said slowly. "Mostly. My mother was a great warrior and a friend of Iark's father, and when she died, he hoped I'd be just as ruthless as her. In a way, I suppose I was always expected to end up like this."

May wanted to ask what *this* was, but she didn't know how. All she knew was Eitra didn't look confident or frightening or menacing. She looked like a scared teenager.

"Do you have to do the market every year?" May asked. "Do you have to stay with the goblins, do what they want, travel with them? Surely—"

Eitra shook her head. "It's not like that." She finally took a tentative sip of coffee and wrinkled her nose. "This is awful."

May picked up the sugar and milk from the end of the table and poured a good, long dose of both in. She stirred, conscious of the way Eitra watched her hands. "Try it now."

This time, Eitra seemed more convinced. It warmed something within May. She should not be here, in the human world, with a goblin. Every traitorous heartbeat was a betrayal of the coven.

But she wasn't going to stop.

"When I was little, during the market," Eitra said, "when they sent me out in the streets to play like a child, to lure unsuspecting victims into the market's depths . . . I used to run for the walls." She glanced out the windows. They could see one of the gates from here. May wondered if Eitra wanted to run to it now.

"I used to look over the city," she continued, "and think that I could run away anywhere. I could just leave, and forget the blood—I've never been fond of the blood, not in the way Iark is—and I could pretend to be human. Hide all of it."

"Why didn't you?" May asked.

Eitra tipped back the coffee, draining it to the dregs. May felt a weird burst of pride that she'd made it palatable to Eitra, perhaps even enjoyable. "Masochism, maybe? We all have our roles, our duties. We know what's expected of us. Some of us break that without guilt. And some of us cannot leave our shackles." She smiled, but it didn't reach her eyes. "You might have some idea what I'm talking about, witchling."

Witchling. The nickname braced against her. She was no longer a witchling, but what Eitra didn't know wouldn't hurt her. After all, after tonight, May would probably never see her again. They had this moment in time to pretend that they could choose, or be normal, or not be under the control of systems set in place hundreds of years before their births.

"And that's the only reason you stay?" May asked. "Duty?"

Eitra looked away, out the window. A couple across the street laughed loudly. May glanced over despite herself, oddly jealous of their entwined hands and easy smiles.

"I stay because I should, and because I must. Maybe I like the chaos and the blood." Eitra glanced at May through her eyelashes, like she was trying to be aloof, but the effect didn't quite work. She looked too sad.

"There's chaos out here, if you'd look for it."

Eitra chewed on her lip. "Perhaps it's not a choice, May Wickett. Perhaps not all of us can go where we please. My mother made a promise to Iark's father before she died. And he practically raised me. Now he's gone, and I can't leave Iark. He'd know if I tried." She smiled, but it didn't look truthful.

"That sounds . . . bad."

"There are promises I cannot break here."

May didn't want to press, but she had to. "And you'd stay

miserable then? Rather than trying to go?"

Eitra shrugged. "It's not all misery and despair and bloodshed. The man who sells the fruit knows my favorite. He always knows when it's too much, and he surprises me with the most beautiful raspberries. And there is honey for my bread, and fine clothing, and a roof over my head. My whole life, I've wanted for nothing. I love the twists of the market, really, and how I can find my way around even when Iark can't. I love that we rarely get ill, and that I have no worry for time. Not in the market, where I could live forever if I chose to, aging on and on but evading death. And I love the stories that are told around the fires about every corner of the world, even though I cannot go myself. I collect them. Run them over and over in my head when I'm trying to sleep."

"Will you tell me one?"

Eitra cocked her head. Her eyes were far away. May didn't know if she'd said the right thing, if there was even a right thing to say. "There's this one story my mother told me when I was younger. It's about a goblin fruit—brillberries, to be exact. The story goes that there was a goblin and a mortal girl who fell in love, but they couldn't speak of it. They arranged to run away together, for the goblin boy to leave behind his duties and break away from his oath to one of the market's warriors. Well, the girl was discovered in the market, overstaying and violating the rules, and her throat was slit. Her blood stained the white brillberries, but her body was devoured and no one was the wiser. When her lover came looking for her, he found no trace of her but the stained crate of berries. He smelled her blood on them and went on a rampage through the market, killing all who smelled of her and then himself, vowing to find her in another life. And brillberries remain blood red as a reminder of his promise."

May blinked slowly. "That is . . . something."

Eitra half smiled. "I didn't say it was pleasant." She swallowed hard, looking down at the mug in her hands. May wondered if it was still warm. "Our love stories rarely are."

May reached over the table and laced her hands through Eitra's. "We could run away," she said. "Go to America. Leave it all behind. No bloodberries or whatever to mark our story."

"And what would I do in America?" Eitra asked, raising an eyebrow.

May couldn't stop the smile that crept across her face. "I don't know. Make a coffee shop? A bookstore? Take up blacksmithing?" She felt Eitra's nails digging into her skin, like she didn't know how to love without also hurting. "We could be anything. Just two normal people who chose to be together."

"We could leave the market forever," Eitra said, but she didn't sound convinced. She looked up, her eyes dark as ink. "I would do it, you know. If Iark wouldn't find me and kill me, I would do it."

"Do you think he'd really kill you?" May asked, the illusion shattering around them.

Eitra smiled ruefully. "I'm no better than his possession, May. If he couldn't keep me as his second, his warrior, of course he'd kill me. I have no other use."

May wanted to tell her that it wasn't fair, that it wasn't true, but she knew there was nothing about this she could change. So she pretended. She told Eitra about how her father lived in America, and how they could hide at his flat and buy a van and drive to California. She told Eitra that they could be nomads, going from place to place, until they found the perfect little house in a field, in the middle of nowhere, surrounded by wildflowers. There they'd stay forever and ever, until the flowers grew around their bones.

Neither of them acknowledged the tears that rolled down May's cheeks or the hitch in Eitra's voice when she embellished the stories. May found a pen in her bag and Eitra drew wildflowers on her arms as she spoke until the sun peered over the edge of the city wall and found them there still, building a world that would never exist.

The market was Eitra's fate and magic was May's, and any diversion from those choices would be death to both of them. Any other reality was fragile as glass, destined to shatter.

CHAPTER 19

It was only right that, on the evening Lou was to make her descent into the market, May went alone with her to the Shambles. After all, they'd come to York together, and after this was done, they would leave together with or without Mom—though Lou didn't like to think of that.

But it was Lou and May, May and Lou, inextricably bound over seventeen years free of the market, who made their way through the cobbled streets as night fell over the city. Lou glanced at May as they passed through the gate towards town. She felt she understood her ever so slightly better, with her iron and her smudging and her songs and fears. After all, who wouldn't be superstitious after living through this? Who wouldn't take every opportunity for protection?

There were no more questions to ask, no more words to exchange. Lou wore tight black skinny jeans, boots, a black tank top, and a leather jacket she'd found in the back of one of the closets. She was probably overdoing the whole goblin-hunter vibe, but overdoing it made her feel less like she was about to die. She also had her knives, one sheathed and sewn into her bra band and another tucked into the top of her boot. Her fingers were heavy with iron rings, and around her neck, she wore a small, sharp iron spike. Her pockets were full of herbs, though they didn't make her feel any more or less protected. Theoretically, she knew they were more useful than the knives, but it was hard to feel that way.

She felt heavy, weighted down with protection and secrets, bearing the full brunt of the knowledge she herself had asked for.

"You'll go into the market floor first," May said, ducking around a group of tourists spilling out of one of the bookstores. "Then farther down the stairs, but beware, because they move. The lower you go, the worse it is, so be careful. And pay attention."

As they drew closer to the market, it called to her, just like the goblins outside her window every night. She could feel the crackle of it in her blood, the desire to move closer, closer, closer.

Lou and May followed the roads into the center of town, into the Shambles. Lou felt the clarity of it so much it was dizzying. It was like the market knew she was giving in and coming for a visit, like it had only been a matter of time before she was here.

She stopped and pressed a hand to the brick of a building, forcing herself to breathe. There was a crowd around; the city was still bustling with people. The flow of them wound around May and Lou like a river around a stone.

"Are you okay?" May asked, all tenderness.

Lou nodded. She wished, for a selfish moment, that she didn't have to do this. That everyone else could be smart enough to not be seduced by the body-eating goblins, but that wasn't fair to Neela nor May.

May hugged her tight. Lou breathed in the scent of her, the normal-May smell tainted with the herby remedies of Nana's kitchen. But she was still May, still the aunt she loved.

"You've gotta come back," May said into Lou's hair. "If not for me, then for your mom. Okay?"

Lou nodded, fighting back the lump in her throat. "I know."

She let May hug her tight one more time, thinking of Mom and how the two of them raised her, thinking of May's baby and how odd and terrible it would be for her to raise them alone. She hoped, this time, the kid would grow up knowing who their mother was.

Lou couldn't imagine how May felt, looking at her as she was about to descend into the market, knowing that May might be going back alone—if she went back at all.

"They'll find me?" Lou asked, the one part of the market she was afraid of. She could try to get in by herself, but according to May and Nana Tee, it was far less suspicious if she was invited.

May nervously ran her hands over her belly, something she'd been doing ever since she found out she was pregnant. "Yes." She looked down the lane at the buildings, face shadowed in the dying light of sunset. "I shouldn't be here when they do. Just in case."

Lou nodded. She didn't know the details, the specifics, but there was a goblin that she and Mom had killed. Or had led to the killing of. Lou was unclear on the details, barely able to get any of them before May shut down.

"So I'll be going," May said. She stepped back, examining Lou one last time. Lou wished May could stay, help her, guide her through the market.

More than anything, Lou wished she wouldn't have to go in alone.

But she just smiled. "I'll see you later," she said, aiming for flippancy and missing completely.

May turned and left, melting into the post-dinner crowd. Lou shifted back and forth. Alone, she wasn't sure what to do.

She could see the walls from here. Any other time of year, any time other than this summer of blood and goblins, she and Neela would walk the walls themselves, gossiping about random drama from Neela's school or comparing the best transatlantic desserts, Neela teasing her about the number of non-vegetable items called "salad."

What Lou wouldn't give for a summer like that, a week, an hour with Neela's arm linked through hers, her dark hair mingling with Lou's, their laughter sharp in the night.

She was so distracted in her own reverie, staring off into nothing, that she missed the boy's approach until he was leaning against the wall next to her, his arm pressing against hers.

"You're new here, witchling," he said.

Lou's skin prickled. No one *normal* would call her "witchling." She looked over at him, tried to make sure her gaze was dripping with derision. "And you are?"

He laughed, showing his pointed teeth. "You know what I am," he said. "I presume you're here for a reason."

Lou swallowed hard. She didn't like this answer. She wished she could turn around, run after May, dash all the way home. She wished she didn't feel the hitch in her heart, the curdling in her stomach, when she looked at the goblin boy peering down at her. She had seen what the market had done to the victims they treated in the Witchery and what it had done to Mom. She could only fear what the market had already done to Neela— and what pain it would inflict on her.

He held out a hand to her. "Would you like to come?"

"Come where?" she said, feigning ignorance. She needed to hear it for herself. To hear it from him, a stranger.

The boy smiled wickedly. He twisted his wrist, showing another piece of goblin gold in his palm, shining in the street-light. Imprinted in the middle was a pomegranate.

"To the market, of course," he said.

The boy's hand snaked out, viper quick, and grabbed Lou's wrist. He jerked her hand toward him. The coin dropped into her palm. It was warm from the heat of his skin.

"Come," he said. "There are delights waiting for us below."

She had no choice but to go, no choice but to tuck the coin deep into her pocket, to suck in a breath and hope that at the end of the night, she'd find herself right back out on these cobble-stones.

Louisa Wickett-Stevens turned on her heel and descended into the darkness, into the depths of the goblin market.

PART 2
A Lily in a Flood

WHAT BOLD ATTEMPT IS THIS, PRAY LET ME KNOW
FROM WHENCE YOU COME, AND WHITHER I MUST GO?
SHALL I, WHO AM A LADY, STOOP OR BOW
TO SUCH A PALE-FAC'D VISAGE, WHO ART THOU?

    DO YOU NOT KNOW ME? WELL, I'LL TELL YOU THEN,
    TIS I THAT CONQUER ALL THE SONS OF MEN,
    NO PITCH OF HONOUR FROM MY DART IS FREE,
    MY NAME IS DEATH, HAVE YOU NOT HEARD OF ME?

YES, I HAVE HEARD OF THEE TIME AFTER TIME,
BUT BEING IN THE GLORY OF MY PRIME,
I DID NOT THINK YOU WOULD HAVE CALLED SO SOON,
WHY MUST MY MORNING SUN GO DOWN AT NOON?

—"DEATH AND THE LADY," TRADITIONAL ENGLISH FOLK SONG

        LAURA TURN'D COLD AS STONE
    TO FIND HER SISTER HEARD THAT CRY ALONE,
          THAT GOBLIN CRY,
      "COME BUY OUR FRUITS, COME BUY."
MUST SHE THEN BUY NO MORE SUCH DAINTY FRUIT?
MUST SHE NO MORE SUCH SUCCOUS PASTURE FIND,
        GONE DEAF AND BLIND?

    —"GOBLIN MARKET," CHRISTINA ROSSETTI

CHAPTER 20

DOWN THE STONE STEPS THEY WENT, FARTHER AND FARTHER. IT felt quite like the Witchery, Lou thought as they descended, but where the Witchery smelled of clean herbs and firelight, the market below smelled of decay.

Lou was certain the goblin boy could hear the pounding of her heart as they descended. "What's your name, anyway?" she asked, trying to keep her voice as accusatory and vitriolic as possible. She didn't want to feel like she was giving anything up while asking something from him.

The goblin boy grinned at her over his shoulder. "Kildred," he said.

Lou nodded. "Kildred."

"Do you feel as if you've gained something, human?"

She swallowed hard. She *had* felt that way, but when he said it like that, all her good feelings dissolved. "No," she said. "I just wanted to know. If you know my name, it's only right I should know what to call you."

He shrugged. They came to a fork in the stairwell, with one side leading off into the gloom. Kildred led her to the right, farther and farther down. Lou felt the oddest urge to press her hand against the wall, to feel the cold of the stone leaching into her skin. She'd wanted to feel as if her roots wound into the soil here, far below the foundations of the Minster, below even the market, but always she felt as if she was just vaguely tied to the surface.

Lou pushed the thought away. It didn't matter so much where she belonged; it was more about who she belonged to. And she was going to do whatever it took to save the people she loved.

But if she was to survive, for as long as possible, she had to follow the rules.

Sounds grew louder and louder as they descended, a cacophony of voices and laughter and shouting and things being dropped and moved; heavy objects dragged across the floor and metal crashing together.

Lou thought she was ready as they came to the market floor, but of course she wasn't. How could she prepare for something like this?

It was a frenzy down below. Madness, personified. She realized that Kildred had shrugged off his glamours like a coat. He was now green and pebbled, his fingers too long, his hair a mass of ferns growing from his head.

Though the stairs descended farther into the dark, Kildred guided her to the left at the next landing. They came to a stop in a jagged, toothy archway. And beyond it lay the market in all of its terror.

But the market, the market—it was everything she hadn't known to fear. Goblins bustled around, and people too—it was easy to see which ones traveled with the market, belonged to them somehow, because they were emaciated and dark eyed, stumbling through the various stalls like ghosts. The other humans, bright-eyed, laughing, either paired with goblins or in small groups of their own, marveled at the wonders there.

It was grotesque and gorgeous, like the goblins themselves. At a far stall, Lou could see human hands hanging like plucked chickens, some of them dripping blood. The stall next door was ridden with tattoos cut from human flesh. There were bottled things Lou could only assume were human, thick blood and varieties of dark and light urine, and greasy, yellow fat, and something that Lou instinctively felt was spinal fluid. She swallowed hard and looked away from that section. An aisle over, she saw fabrics hanging down, all shades of silks and knits and intricate gowns.

And the fruits. Of course there was goblin fruit, aisles and aisles of it, rows of barrels and crates and stalls of every color. She directed them toward this aisle and away from the humans, toward the quinces and pomegranates and plump, juicy pears. They were all too bright and shiny, like plastic.

"What would you like to see first?" Kildred asked.

Neela. Take me to Neela.

Lou didn't smile—she couldn't, not here—but she said, "I don't know. What's the best part?"

Kildred followed her toward the fruit market, baskets and barrels of perfect apples and peaches and pears, every fruit Lou had ever seen and many she had not. Though she was not hungry, her mouth watered. She wondered if this was another enchantment, another glamour. Something in her itched, as if she'd never feel quite whole if she didn't have a piece of goblin fruit *right now.*

"There's nothing quite like it," he said, nodding his head toward a crate. He was trying to lure her, she knew, to entice. But Joss had warned her: *eat nothing.* She thought of the gold coin, the pomegranate on the face, and shuddered.

"What do you want?" Kildred asked. "Surely you've come seeking something."

Lou didn't know what to say. It wasn't like she could ask for Neela or the antidote. Instead, she tried to look bored, surveying the market. "This all looks so . . . pedestrian." She grabbed a peach and sunk her nails into the tender flesh. It was ripe, just in that moment between peak juiciness and before it teetered into too-soft, into decay.

"There are no delights here that I wouldn't find above," she said. She tossed the peach in the air, caught it, and let it roll off her fingers back into the barrel. The vendor hissed at her, but Lou kept her composure.

"Then I suppose we have to find you something more daring. Shall we?" Kildred said looping his arm through Lou's. It was too intimate, too much taken that she did not offer, but she merely clenched her jaw and went with him. She tried not to look at the fruit or the wares as they passed, because every time she did, she wanted them more.

They were halfway through the market, keeping to the fringes, when someone grabbed her leg.

She gasped, nearly tripping. A green, bloody hand wrapped around her ankle. Lou looked down to find a goblin woman, old and hunched, cloaked in heavy black fabric that covered most of her body.

"Beware," the goblin woman said from the shadows of her robe.

Lou gaped down at her. Kildred doubled back, laughing. "Ah, you've already attracted attention."

"Who are you?" Lou snarled, masking her fear with anger.

"She's nothing," Kildred answered for her, pulling Lou forward. "Disgraced."

The woman's hand fell free and she laughed, leaning forward onto her clawed hands. The hood of her cloak fell back, revealing her face—and her empty, dark eye sockets. Jewels and feathers fell from the sockets as she laughed, clattering to the ground and floating from the empty spaces like she was some awful, molting creature. It wasn't nearly the most horrible thing Lou had seen—the body stalls in the market were far worse—but there was something horribly unsettling about the sharp points of the woman's teeth, the lines of dried blood crusted between them.

"Come buy!" she cried as Lou and Kildred left her. "Come buy!"

Lou swallowed hard. She knew the market would be full of terrors, but this—this was one of their own. She turned forward, tried to put on a brave face, tried to follow Kildred, but all she could see was the image of the woman laughing at her, jewels and feathers dripping from her eye sockets like tears.

She forced herself to concentrate on her surroundings. Other humans were there, scattered around the market: just a few, three or four, by Lou's count. But two of them were unaccompanied by goblins. She was already uncomfortable spending this much time with Kildred. She couldn't trust him—she couldn't trust *any* of them. And there was no mention of needing a guide in any of the rules or stories she'd heard.

If there wasn't a rule about it, she was fairly certain she'd be safe. Other goblins might be more threatening to her if she was by herself, but if she didn't eat nor drink, if she didn't break the rules, what could they do?

Lou broke away from Kildred, putting space between them. He glanced at her, frowning. "Do you not want to come below?"

May had warned her about the depths of the market. It was

probably not a good idea to follow him into the deep. And Lou had three days of safety guaranteed by the Doctrine. As long as she didn't mess up, she was fine.

"I think I'd be better off on my own, actually," she said carefully. "But thanks for helping me in!"

Before Kildred could respond or catch her, she darted off into the crowd down another row of wares. This was the weapons section, she surmised, by the daggers and crossbows lining the stalls. The goblin woman at the stall closest to Lou leered at her.

"I'll give you a fine sword for your right hand, witchling," she cooed.

Lou grimaced. That was not even close to a fair trade. Also, she wasn't a witchling—any connection to York's magic had been severed long ago. "I'm okay, actually."

She tried to keep a low profile, but it was difficult when everyone kept turning to look at her. Lou did her best to hold her head high, to avoid eye contact at all costs. There was a dais at the far end of the market with a raised platform and a great chair carved of stone, dotted with onyx and rubies. The chair was empty, though a variety of goblins milled around it.

It was in her best interest, Lou decided, to stay as far away from that group of goblins as possible.

She was dawdling, wasting time. Lou tried to breathe through her mouth—it was easier to deal with the rot that way—as she cut across the aisles to the far wall. The room was roughly rectangular, with doorways and archways dotted on all four walls. On the way here, May had told her that the market wasn't *that* big, that most of it spiraled downward into the earth, but Lou was still staggered by the size of it. And she had to search the whole thing for Neela.

If Neela was even still here.

No, she wasn't going to think like that. She followed the wall toward the closest archways, constructing her own rules in her head as she went:

1. FOLLOW THE RULES: THREE DAYS ONLY, DON'T HURT ANYONE.
2. DON'T EAT OR DRINK ANYTHING.
3. ATTRACT AS LITTLE ATTENTION AS POSSIBLE.
4. DON'T GO TOO FAR DOWN.
5. KEEP A HAND ON THE KNIFE AT ALL TIMES.
6. DON'T TRUST ANYONE.

It was a long list, Lou mused. She looked straight ahead as she passed the aisle full of human remains. It was not worth looking over, investigating, psyching herself out.

Maybe if she just kept inventing rules, she would pass through safely. It was something she used to do when she was little. The world made more sense when she had concrete guidance: walk only in the center of the pavement and the universe would award her with a couple of dollars for an ice cream, keep her eyes closed when her head hit the pillow and the monsters wouldn't find her, trace the iron pentacle in the window three times every morning and her mother would be in a good mood.

They were all arbitrary, but to Lou, they'd made life easier. More predictable.

So if she followed the rules here, even if the rules were of her own making, she'd be fine. She'd find Neela and they'd get out and there'd be no reason for panic.

Lou ducked under the stone archway. It opened into a landing, forking off in two directions, both with stairs leading downwards.

Deep below, something grumbled like the earth itself was shifting.

Behind her, the clamor of the market heightened. She glanced over her shoulder to see the crowd on the dais had pulled someone up. Not a human, Lou realized uncomfortably. They'd pulled one of their own goblins up. Two other goblins held his arms as he squirmed and cried out, and another teased him, dragging a knife down his chest, leaving dark brown sap-like blood oozing down his chest.

Lou turned away. If that's what they did to their own, what would they do to her?

Right, she decided. She scampered down the stairs into the gloom.

Very little time had passed before Lou realized she was hopelessly lost. This was the problem of the market, she despaired. It wasn't like there was a map, and she was *certain* the dank corridors were moving around behind her, one jumbling into another as soon as she'd left.

Even worse, the only way to go was down. More than once, she turned to retrace her steps only to find the staircase she'd descended had morphed into a rough stone wall. If her only option was to keep descending, how could she be sure she wasn't going too far down into the depths of the market?

The other thing that terrified her, perhaps more than the constant descent, was the *loneliness*. She had on a watch so she knew that she was still well within her first night, but what if she hadn't? She kept going down these lonely corridors, all the same stone, all smelling of rot. She was pretty sure she'd even seen the same pile of abandoned bones at least three times.

It was just another way for the goblins to trap their victims. Confusion.

Finally, just as she was really starting to panic, she came to a split in the corridor. Ahead, more stairs downwards; to her left, a heavy door; to her right, an archway into a shadowy room.

She peered into the gloom. Gradually, she could make out the shapes of the room. A vast expanse of columns stretched out below her. Lou tried not to notice the decaying human body chained to one of the pillars about fifty feet away. Other shadowy shapes solidified. There, just ahead, was a table covered with a cloth with the dusted, rotting remains of a feast. An abandoned shoe to her left. A smashed pair of glasses, moth-eaten heaps of fabric—at least, she hoped it was fabric—and piles of bones dotted around the room.

If she strained, she could just hear the stomping of the market above her. Perhaps she hadn't gone as deep as she suspected if she could still hear the sound from the market floor—or more likely, the market itself was playing tricks on her.

If she was lost now by herself, how could she possibly expect to get out with Neela?

But as far as she could tell, Neela was not in this room. Lou was just about to leave to check the other room and keep going down when she heard a shuffle and a muffled clatter coming from somewhere in front of her.

She frowned, edging forward, prepared to take cover behind the table if someone jumped out of the shadows.

Something landed on her foot. Lou looked down. A round gem sat on the toe of her shoe.

There was no one around, no one who could've dropped it, and she didn't know how else it could've gotten there. Unless—unless the gem came from *under* the table.

She stooped down and lifted the tablecloth. There was a shape there, huddled in the middle. In the dim light, she could only make out the glow of sharp goblin teeth.

"What are you doing down there?" Lou asked. She felt quite like she was talking to a stray, possibly rabid, cat.

A green hand snaked out of the darkness and grabbed Lou's arm, pulling her hard. She ducked down to avoid knocking over the entire table, stumbling on her knees under the table. Her hand landed in a pile of feathers.

It was the goblin from upstairs, the old woman.

"You must go," she hissed. A ruby tumbled from one of her empty eyes, spilling onto the ground. Lou stared at her in growing shock and horror.

"I can't," Lou said, resolute. "Not until I find what I need."

"And what is that?"

"None of your business."

The goblin barked a laugh. "Here to rescue, here to steal. The little human thinks she can just take what she wants."

Lou's mouth tasted bitter, as if she'd drank some of the wine from the table above. She didn't like the goblin woman's assumptions and how close to the truth they were. She scooted back, but the goblin woman's hand snaked out once more and grabbed Lou's.

"The girl is in the level below us," she said. But then the goblin woman started gagging, choking. Lou watched in horror as she hacked up something large—a pomegranate, she realized, when the old woman sat back, gasping.

"Where?" Lou asked. And how did she know Lou was searching for Neela? Maybe everyone came here looking for someone.

But the goblin woman was of no more help. She was choking again, vomiting gold coins and what looked like tiny bones. Lou backed away, out into the shadowy room, and skittered back into the staircase.

Trust no one. It was one of her rules. But what did the woman have to gain by lying to her? Unless it was just another trap.

Lou was a guest here, though, and as lawful as could be. She wouldn't let herself be trapped by anyone. She gritted her teeth, looking back into the gloom. She could still hear the woman retching under the table, the things clattering to the ground.

Lou sighed, looking down the stairs. The only choice was to keep going. If she didn't check what the woman had told her and she was wrong, she'd never forgive herself.

CHAPTER 21
May

Eighteen Years Earlier

THE TREES AROUND THE PARK SHIFTED IN THE WIND. IT WAS FULL dark, cloudy, starless. May's mouth tasted of blood, copper and iron. Somewhere close, someone was shouting her name.

Eitra.

She whirled around. She was in Dean's Park, halfway between the church and the Witchery, and there were fingers on her upper arm, squeezing and dragging her toward the Witchery. Laura's silhouette wavered out of the corner of her eye as she begged for May to follow her, but May wasn't looking at her. Her eyes were glued to a figure back in the grass. A girl, writhing on the ground, surrounded by three others. It was Eitra, and she was screaming.

May pulled against Laura, trying to get close. One of the people surrounding Eitra hoisted something in the air, glittering in the darkness. May watched, her scream caught in her throat as the knife swung down in a smooth arc. Blood spurted from Eitra's throat as her scream was cut short. The goblin lifted the knife once more and went for her eyes.

May woke up gasping. She was alone in the room, moonlight shining through, illuminating the scarves she'd hung on her wall the summer before. She was covered in sweat.

She lowered her head to her arms, trying to catch her breath. She'd been warned that there were side effects associated with the unbinding of magic—dreams and visions and bad tastes in her mouth. She closed her eyes, trying to rid herself of the image of Eitra's blood spurting into the sky.

A nightmare. That was all it was. May tried to convince herself, tried to push it all out, as the goblins sang on the street below her window.

"You can't go back, you know," Laura said the next afternoon as they walked through the farmers' market in the city center. They were searching for leeks. May wasn't certain if it was for a potion or dinner.

May glanced over at Laura. "I know," she said, feigning innocence. Of course she couldn't go back to the market. She wasn't just a witchling anymore, and it would violate the Doctrine if she did.

But Eitra hadn't noticed. Which was a complication.

May had told Laura everything that morning—well, nearly everything, leaving out the kissing parts because they didn't bode well for her story. Laura caught her coming in at the break of dawn and was convinced May had spent the night in the market, violating rules, so she'd had to defend herself. But she wanted some sympathy too, and maybe to feel like Laura wasn't so thrilled that they were chained to this city for eternity. Instead, she'd gotten Laura's disappointment.

"But you're considering it," Laura said, stopping to look at the price of berries. "I know you are. You're going to go running in to snog some goblin, and they're going to kill you for being an arse."

She felt a flare of annoyance and embarrassment that Laura had seen right through her, even though she left out the kissing parts. And May knew she shouldn't return to the market. It was a horrible idea to return to the market. Horrible, and enticing, and as provocative as the goblin gold she still had in her pocket.

"I'll come home," she swore. "Only one more night. I just want to see the rest of it, to get it out of my system, and then I'll never go again. They have no idea what we did the other night, with the ritual. I'll be fine."

Laura put an apple back down in the bin. Being here made May think of the market—but *everything* made her think of the market. "I can't believe you'd do this," she said, mostly to herself. "I can't believe you'd even go in the first place."

May shrugged. What was there to say? She went. She knew it was bad, and yet she'd chosen to go anyway.

"Is this about the other day?" Laura asked.

"Hmm?"

"The Thaumaturge. The ritual. The reality of it." She didn't look at May. "I know . . . we don't always see things the same way."

May chewed the inside of her cheek. That old chestnut. "Not really," she said. "Though I'm not happy about it. What if I don't want to be a witch?"

"It's not about what you want."

That was easy for Laura to say, who'd never wanted anything else. But in the market, she didn't feel like a witchling, didn't feel like she was slowly losing every bit of herself for the sake of her legacy.

The only thing she'd chosen, really chosen, was Eitra. But if she couldn't go to the market, she'd never see her again freely. Once May was a full witch and truly banned from the market, she and Eitra would be worse than enemies. May swallowed hard. Eitra didn't know about the magic, about what May was now. She could risk it—couldn't she?

For Eitra. She'd go tonight to tell Eitra goodbye, to finish whatever it was that they'd started. And she'd be back in her bed tonight and never again return to the market.

She would not eat. She would not drink. She'd avoid Iark, who Eitra trusted but not with her. And then she'd . . .

She wanted to say she'd move on. She'd forget Eitra and the market, and then, when it came time for university, she'd leave York and goblins behind for good. But that wasn't an option anymore.

"I'll be safe," she promised Laura, because she had to promise something. "I'll finish what I must, I'll take the herbs and say all the right words. And I'll be safe."

Laura looked at her, eyes hollow. "You'd better," she said savagely. Without another word she turned and left May among the stands, as if she couldn't bear to look at her any longer.

That night, May prepared.

She'd spent the evening on Neela duty, holding her little sister to her chest as she ate buttered toast and went through the supplies in Mum's trunk. Neela was pretty happy, as far as babies went, besides the first month of her life, when she cried nonstop. Now that they were past that, she preferred cooing, eating, and playing with May and Laura's hair over screaming.

Angelique came at 9:00 p.m. to take over childcare. Though she disagreed, May understood why the Thaumaturge made the decision she had. May couldn't remember the last time Mum had slept at home. Most nights, Angelique fell asleep here on the sofa they'd dragged into Neela's room. During the day, Joss, Marcus, and Mum took turns sleeping and taking care of patients and the baby.

Tonight, May dressed in a pair of ripped overalls that were easy to move in and even easier to hide knives in. She sewed extra sachets of herbs into her shirt, a black bell-sleeved blouse she'd bought in Harrogate months before. She hid the iron dagger again and wore the right necklaces, tucked notes with the songs into her pockets in case she was enchanted to forget.

She was prepared. It was her second day of the market. She was no longer a neophyte, there for exploration and dancing. She was there to say goodbye.

When May checked her window just after 11:00 p.m., she was unsurprised to see Eitra leaning against the wall of the building across the street.

She hoped she wasn't making the wrong decision.

May snuck out of the apartment in her socks, heavy boots clutched in one hand, and shut the door as quietly as possible. She went down the stairs, put her boots on, then slipped out the door.

Eitra looked unsurprised to see her. "How are you feeling?" she asked.

It was an odd question, May thought, for a goblin.

"I'm fine," she lied. She held out her hand. Eitra took it.

She didn't have to follow Eitra into the market. She could've told her now, on the street, and left her in peace. But as soon as she saw the wicked smile on Eitra's face, the decision was made for her, risk be damned.

This time, May tried to be more vibrant, more alive, to commit every detail of Eitra and the streets and the market to her memory. She'd never felt so alive, with adrenaline pumping through her body as they wound down the vanishing stairs. They passed through the market floor, and she saw Iark leaning against the wall. She watched Eitra drink one glass of goblin wine and then another; she asked questions, but mostly she savored this.

Soon, too soon, they would truly be enemies.

She so rarely chose the dangerous thing, the wrong thing. She so rarely felt this afraid, like she was running on the blade of a knife.

"Dance with me," May said when Eitra had drunk her fill.

They swirled around the room and May avoided the eyes, the call of goblins, even Iark's voice calling her name, which Eitra must've told him. She ignored all of it, and when the dances were done and Eitra was flushed with wine, she coaxed her to take her back to the Inbetween, back to the cramped and warm hallway, and all she could focus on was Eitra.

She wanted the sharp parts, the things that hurt, that clawed, that dug in beneath her skin. She wanted the blood and the marrow because deep down, May knew she'd never feel like this again. She kissed Eitra harder because it felt like she was finding herself.

"They're going to make me a witch at the week's end," May

whispered against Eitra's skin. She didn't know what she hoped to accomplish with this admission, but the words were out of her mouth before she could stop them.

Eitra froze, stiff under May's hands. "What did you say?"

May drew back to look at her. "The coven is graduating all of us. I'll be a full witch. And then I can't come back again."

Eitra's skin had taken on a sickly cast. "But they can't just do that. Your magic is bound. It takes time for it to release, time before you're strong enough for the change . . ." She trailed off, her eyes searching May's face. "Please tell me you're not . . . that you didn't. Tell me they haven't made you a candidate."

May chewed on her lip. She crossed her arms in front of her chest, bracing for Eitra's reaction. She hadn't showered today, and traces of Eitra's drawn wildflowers still lingered on her forearms.

"You shouldn't have told me this."

May swallowed hard. "You knew there was the chance this would happen. You knew what I was. What I am."

Eitra shook her head, her hair coming loose and swishing over her shoulders. "No. It's—it's one thing to be a witchling. Another to be a *witch.*"

"Eitra, I-I'm still me. This doesn't really change anything."

"You should go," Eitra said. Her voice caught. Something streaked down her cheeks, the bright green of absinthe—tears, May realized. She put a hand on Eitra's arm. Eitra shook it off and turned away. "This isn't—I mustn't."

May felt her heart clench, a sharp pain rolling through her stomach. "No one else knows. It's fine as long as it's a secret."

"You shouldn't be here, May," Eitra said miserably. "You should go, right now."

"Eitra—no, wait, what? I chose to be here, to say goodbye."

"Then say goodbye," she snapped.

May was silent. She didn't have words, not right now when Eitra looked so agonized.

"You shouldn't have told me this," she said again. "Not when you know who I report back to."

May realized the implications of the statement as Eitra grabbed her hand and dragged her back through the depths of the Inbetween. Eitra reported to Iark as the Market Prince's second, yes, but what did that have to do with her? Iark didn't know May had violated the Doctrine, and he wouldn't, as long as Eitra kept it between them.

May pulled her hand back. She wasn't going this easily, not without a fight. "I came to say goodbye to you, Eitra. You don't need to throw me out. I'll leave on my own."

Eitra shook her head, laughing cruelly. "Do you think it's that easy?" She swallowed hard. "I forbid you." Her voice was choked with something May didn't understand. She watched, uncomprehending, as Eitra fought for words. "I banish you from this place, on the grounds of the Petergate Doctrine."

Eitra's face was awash with something like grief or anger or pain. She reached into May's pocket, clawing out the sachet of rosemary and thyme, and before May could say a word, she pushed it into May's mouth. May choked, biting down hard. The bitter taste of the herbs flooded her mouth.

Her body acted of its own accord and she lost time, as if she were drunk, as if she'd taken her first poisonous bite of goblin fruit.

May knew the songs and the stories, how to pass safely through the market and how to get out. Parsley and sage for safe passage in, for the three days she was welcome, and rosemary and thyme for a speedy exit until the three nights had passed. But she hadn't expected it to work like this.

Before she could blink, before she could stop or get her bearings, her feet had dragged her up the vanishing stairs and through the market, all the way up to the cobblestone street. May fell hard on her back as the market doorway shifted back into stone.

She stared incredulously at it for a moment. A minute ago, she'd been kissing Eitra three stories underground.

And now . . .

Laura was right. She shouldn't have gone back. But the way she and Eitra spoke last night . . . It had felt like they were beyond the rules of the market, like the laws didn't matter to them when they were together. Of course May had wanted to see her one last time, Petergate Doctrine be damned. And now, she'd ruined it anyway. She didn't want Eitra to hate her.

May got up, studiously ignoring the pubgoers spilling out of the street just past the mouth of the alley, laughing at her. She scrambled along the wall, humming "Scarborough Fair" under her breath, searching for a sign of anything that would get her back in.

But it was useless. Even with her words and songs, even with her parsley and sage, she could not get in without help. Not into this entrance, at least.

But Eitra had said there were more. Could she find them on her own, even after the market had cast her out?

Why are you even trying? a voice whispered in the back of her mind. Perhaps it was better this way, to be lost on the street, to be rejected by the very thing that wanted to kill her. Perhaps it was better that she didn't know how she'd upset Eitra or how to fix it because at the end of the day, Eitra was the predator and she was prey, ripe and willing for the taking.

She might not be done with the market, but the market was done with May.

And maybe that was for the better.

She took one long look at the stones containing Eitra, the stones keeping her out, and turned back for home.

CHAPTER 22

Down and down Lou went, feeling the chill in the air intensifying. There was one landing, but it went into a small chamber, lit by a single candle. A goblin woman, dressed in white, sat in a chair in the middle of the room. Her back was to Lou. She definitely wasn't Neela, and Lou really didn't want to know what she was waiting for, so she scampered past that room, farther down the stairs.

She passed two more empty antechambers before coming to a wooden door. The staircase kept spiraling down, down, down. Lou didn't know how far it would go or even if she was already too far down, into the dangerous parts. She stopped in front of the door and pressed her ear against it, trying to decipher if there was anyone inside, and more importantly, if they would eat her.

There was no sound from within. But perhaps Neela was in here and unconscious or sleeping. Lou eased the door open, but it creaked anyway.

She stood in the doorway for a moment, waiting for her eyes to adjust. She wished she had a candle with her. There was the option of her phone flashlight, but the idea of using it terrified her, as if the light would attract goblins to come find her. Lou shut the door in case anyone passed by. The room smelled of dust and something metallic, of meat left out too long, but there were no sounds. She was confident she was alone here.

But her eyes did not adjust. With the door shut behind her, underground as she was, there was no light to adjust *to*. Lou sighed and pulled out her phone. No one would find her. She would be fine.

She flicked on the flashlight and revealed the horror the room contained.

Lou dropped her phone, the light scattering across the room and landing flashlight-down. But she'd seen it. She'd seen *them*. Lou flattened herself against the door, her heart pounding in her chest.

Nothing moved. Of course they didn't. The people on the tables in front of her were all dead.

Slowly, slowly, she retrieved her phone. The screen was cracked but the flashlight still worked. She took a deep breath and shone it around the room, revealing more of the terribleness of it all.

It wasn't a morgue—no, it seemed to be more of a preparation room for the market above. A butcher's shop, even. One table held the body of a girl—or no, just the top half. The body ended at the pelvis, meaty hip sockets exposed, skin ragged as if someone had torn her legs straight off. Her head rested on her shoulder, blue eyes open and staring at nothing. White-blond curls, blackened in some places with dried blood, fell around her shoulders in a cloud. She wore the torn remains of a glittery dress. Blood crusted around a wound on her head, possibly the fatal blow.

But she wasn't Neela. And when Lou confirmed this and felt the rush of adrenaline, she knew she had to look at the other bodies in the room, if only to see that they weren't Neela either.

She gritted her teeth, swinging her light around. She'd known, hadn't she? That this was the horror of the market. It wasn't what they could do to her, or her family, but what they did to every human. The girl on the table, torn in half, probably thought she was smart enough to get out too. She probably had a mother at home who just wanted her back.

It didn't make her feel ill, like she expected, but instead she felt an unfamiliar numbness settle over her bones.

There were five other bodies in various stages of ruin and decay. A boy missing his hands and eyes; an older woman who was really just a head with gray, steely hair. Three more people in a row—but Lou couldn't tell who they were since all that remained were arms and feet.

She'd known, objectively, that the body parts from above had come from real people, people killed in the market. But it was one thing to know and something else entirely to see it.

The numbness she'd experienced before dissolved, giving way to a torrent of emotions. Lou wanted to take all of these parts, these things that decayed now but once were people, and bury them properly. She wanted to mourn. She wanted to throw up, to stifle the choked sobs that made their way out of her when she'd confirmed the faces weren't Neela's—but there were those arms and legs, unidentifiable. She crumbled against the wall, knowing that there was blood and fluid dried on the floor, that there were things she didn't want to touch, but she couldn't hold it together any longer.

The goblin woman had said Neela was below. How could Lou be sure that she'd meant she was alive?

She couldn't.

Not until she kept going, kept searching, picking this entire damn market apart until she found Neela or found enough to say she was dead.

Lou steadied herself. She had to be strong, to leave this place behind her, shut the door on what she'd seen and push forward. There was still the antidote to worry about. Time was running out, slipping away from her. She had to find the antidote too, and she had to get out of this room and really search for Neela. There were two days left, but the idea of entering the market again after what she'd seen today was nauseating.

She pushed away from the wall and went back to the door. She did not spare another glance at the bodies on the tables behind her. God knew she'd seen enough to remember it forever whether she wanted to or not.

Lou let the door shut behind her with a dim finality. Down she went: Neela, if she was alive, was below her. She had so little to believe in, so even though it was foolish, she needed to trust the odd goblin woman.

Even so, she knew it was a risky decision. She wasn't sure how to trust someone whose main character trait involved hiding under tables.

She passed another landing with no door, just a plain alcove, and then she came to a shadowy room stacked with unidenti-fiable boxes and objects. Here, Lou hesitated. Though the stairs wound down farther and farther, she could hear breathing from this room. Ragged and unsteady, but breathing all the same.

Perhaps it wasn't Neela. But maybe it was someone she could save, some tragedy she could fix, or someone that could point her towards Mom's antidote.

Lou crept into the darkness of the room. It smelled of dust and sweat, but not of decay—and for that, she was grateful.

There were cobwebby sconces on the wall, emitting a dim golden light. It reminded her of a movie she'd seen as a kid, of a cottage where all of the lost things went. She waded through piles of stuff, human and goblin-made. A goblet here, a pile of gold coins there, a stack of what looked like taxidermied animals.

The breathing grew louder as Lou made her way across the room. Quietly, quietly, she drew one of the blades she had hidden under her shirt. It was only a precaution, but Lou clung to what little protection she had.

As she crept closer and closer to the back wall, she saw a group of huddled shapes. People, taken from the market above, brought below to await the next horror.

People who were alive.

Lou's breath caught in her throat as she skimmed over the trio chained to the wall, coming to rest on a dark-haired girl crouched at the end. Lou scrambled to her, falling to her knees as she reached out to part the oily strands of hair, pushing them from the girl's face.

Neela.

She opened her eyes, unfocused, weary, as if she was coming awake from a very deep sleep. Lou held back her tears of relief because the fact was this: she was still in the bottom of the market and Neela was shackled to the wall with a very thick and heavy chain.

But she was not dead. *She was not dead.*

Relief and anxiety battled inside Lou as she lifted Neela's chin. "It's me," she whispered, her voice cracking. "It's me."

Neela's hand darted out, grabbed Lou's wrist. Her eyes were frantic now, darting from side to side. "You can't be here," Neela whispered. Her voice was hoarse and creaky from disuse. Lou had no idea how long her aunt had been here, in this damp, cold, dusty room full of forgotten things.

"I'm here for you," Lou said, searching her face. Neela's dark skin was splattered with blood and marred with bruises. A particularly nasty one swelled the left side of her jaw. Her pupils were two different sizes, and Lou wondered if she'd been drugged. "I'm here to bring you home."

Neela shook her head too fast, the ends of her hair whipping across Lou's cheeks. "You can't," she said. "I can't be free of this place."

"I will," Lou said raggedly, running her hands over the chains that bound Neela. She didn't have a key and had no idea how to get her free of them.

The person beside Neela stirred and moaned quietly. The person on the far end didn't move at all—Lou couldn't even be certain they were breathing.

"I'm theirs now," Neela insisted. She raised her face into the light, ever so slightly, and brought her hand up. She was too weak to raise the chain much, but she pointed at her throat. "They're changing me. Taking me as one of their own. Making me a part of the market."

Lou sucked in a breath as she examined Neela's throat. There was a ring of green pebbled skin around her neck, not quite closed, like a collar around her neck. She ran her fingers across it. The skin was cold and rough. Goblin skin.

"Once the ring closes," Neela said quietly, "I'll never leave the market again."

"I won't let that happen," Lou insisted, her voice turning ragged. She got up and searched the room for something, *anything*, that would get Neela free. "Where's the key? Who has it?"

"No one," Neela said. "I don't know."

She was utterly unhelpful, but it wasn't as if Lou could blame her. She went back to crouching in front of Neela, rubbing the dirt away from her eyes.

"Will they release you? There has to be some time when they'll free you."

"I don't know," Neela insisted.

Something creaked behind them. Neela's eyes flew wide, and Lou froze. They stared at each other as the creaking grew louder, as the door from the stairs opened, as something began to drag across the floor.

Neela nodded her head towards a pile of boxes. Lou nodded. Slowly, slowly, trying not to make a sound, she crept to the pile and crouched among them. It was shitty camouflage, nothing that would fool anyone looking, but she just had to hope whoever was in the room with them wouldn't look.

Something was coming. And Lou feared, all over again, that she wouldn't escape the market quite so easily as she had planned.

CHAPTER 28

Lou didn't know if her heart was still in her body. With the speed it was pounding, she wouldn't be surprised to find a bloody hole where it clawed itself out.

The dragging came closer. There were two of them, voices muttering too quietly for Lou to hear. Something clattered to the ground in the middle of the room, then something else.

"That's a despicable thing you do," a guttural voice said.

There was only a cackle in response, one Lou recognized. She tensed against her boxes. It was the woman. The one from the market floor, from under the table, the one who told her to come here to find Neela. Lou shrunk even farther back, hiding in the shadows of an overhanging shelf. She used the clatter of their movement through the clutter to disguise the sound of her burrowing into the mess.

A moment later, the two goblins came into view: the woman, as she'd feared, still dropping gems and feathers from her eyes. Lou didn't know if she'd ever get used to looking at her. And beside her was a boy, clad in a shirt of fall leaves and breeches black like an oil slick. He had a leather strap across his chest, and Lou spotted heavy rings of keys drooping from his hip.

Her stomach clenched. Were they going to chain her up with the others?

Neela, for her part, had slumped right back over, hair falling in a curtain to obscure her face. Only Lou could see the whiteness of her knuckles as she clenched her hands.

"What is it you wanted?" the boy asked.

"A lock of hair," the old woman said, "from a living girl."

The boy sighed. "I don't know why we tolerate you," he muttered. She couldn't tell if it was affectionate or long-suffering. He came close to Neela and Lou saw her aunt's shoulders tighten—hopefully not enough for the goblin to notice. He didn't use a knife, but instead, grabbed a small section of Neela's hair and yanked it out from the root. Lou's sharp intake of breath was overshadowed by Neela's yelp.

The goblin smirked, as if the sound of Neela's pain was pleasing to him. He held the clump of hair out to the old woman. She sniffed the air, then with a trembling hand, took the hair and tucked it into her apron.

"Was that all?" the goblin boy asked.

"Oh, all for now." She puttered around, feeling through boxes and smelling jars she withdrew from within. "I'll be alright getting up on my own."

The goblin boy shook his head, muttering something about old women and sacrifices as he retreated from the room, shutting the door behind him.

The woman kept fussing with glasses and jars, her eye-gems clattering onto the ground every few seconds and feathers fluttering around her. Lou tried to hold her breath, tried to be quiet and still and avoid notice as much as she could.

The goblin knew she was here, she was certain of it. And now, she was staying because . . . because . . .

Lou didn't know why.

"You can come out now, witchling," the goblin said in quite a different voice. She straightened, dropping the hood from her head. Her long hair was a light violet, her skin pale green and thorny. The hollows of her eyes weren't so scary when Lou looked at her straight on, even as the gems and feathers continued to fall from the sockets.

Lou didn't move. Neela was stock still too.

The goblin woman crossed her arms over her chest, looking quite like she'd be rolling her eyes if she had them. "I know you're in here. I can smell you. Now, don't tarry—there is work to be done."

Ice seized her heart. What did this goblin woman want from her? What could she possibly do to them?

Neela raised her head, her limp hair falling over her cheeks. She had tear tracks down her face from the pain of the boy yanking out her hair. "What do you want?" she asked.

The woman's face turned towards Neela. "I didn't know," she said icily. "I didn't know it was you. I wasn't close enough; I didn't sense it."

Neela stared at her, open-mouthed. Lou fought with the decision: Stay hidden or reveal herself? Find out what the goblin woman wanted, or wait and hide?

"Who are you?" Neela asked.

The goblin woman tried to say something and choked on the word. She gritted her teeth against it, a mockery of a smile. "Names are earned, not given."

Lou exchanged a look with Neela. There was no point fighting with the woman about that.

"Fine, then. What do you want from me?" Neela asked, her voice trembling. Lou searched her face, trying to assess if Neela was okay, if there was any way they could escape tonight.

"I'm here to help you," the goblin said. A ruby caught in her lower lip as she spoke, and she spat it out, nearly hitting Lou's hiding place with it. "Come out, little girl. I know you're here."

Neela's eyes scanned over the boxes to Lou. She looked terrified, emaciated, pained, chained to the wall. The other two humans were either pretending to be asleep or had actually passed out.

"Please," Neela whispered. Lou knew what that meant: Please, I can't do this by myself.

She had to come out, had to trust the goblin. She'd told her where Neela was, after all, and it seemed as if she wasn't here to hurt them, considering she hadn't given Lou over to the other goblin.

Or perhaps that was flawed. She couldn't forget what May had told her: Their favors were only trickery. Goblins only cared about themselves, their own well-being, their own games.

But what other choice did she have? Neela might give her away out of fear or trust or something else Lou didn't understand. Or the goblin woman—Jewels, as she thought of her—could wait her out, holding her there until her body gave her away or her three days were up. Lou didn't know if time passed the same for goblins as it did for humans. It was possible three days here was like three hours for Lou.

She had to come out.

Slowly, slowly, Lou crawled out from her hiding place. Her knee popped, and the goblin's head snapped towards the sound. She smiled in earnest now, one of her canines missing—or, Lou assumed it was a canine. All of her teeth were sharp, so it was hard to tell.

"What do you want from me?" Lou asked through her teeth. She kept the knife clenched in one hand. She didn't know what she was doing, but she was not above doing it. Even if "it" involved stabbing Jewels and leaving her here in an effort to get Neela out.

"I have what your mother needs," the goblin said.

Lou's blood turned to ice in her veins. Neela's head snapped to Lou. "What's happening to Laura?" she asked, voice ragged.

Lou tried to breathe, tried to speak, but all she could see was her mom unconscious in the Witchery and all she could think was *my mother is dying, my mother is dying, my mother is dying.* She gritted her teeth. "How do you know something is wrong with her?"

Jewels raised an eyebrow—a disconcerting motion when there was no eye to accompany it. "I saw what they did to her. And I know how to fix it."

Lou tried to make sense of this. How did the goblin know that the woman she saw was Lou's mother? They didn't even look alike. "I don't believe you."

Jewels smirked. She wasn't the same cackling hag from the ballroom. No, now she was colder, more calculating. It scared Lou. "You should. Who will help you if I don't, Louisa Wickett? Who will set you and Neela free?"

"It's Wickett-Stevens," she said through numb lips. Why couldn't any of these goblins remember that she had a dad, too?

She shrugged. "All the same." She eased herself down onto one of the boxes, flicking a feather off of one of the spines on her face. "Either you trust me or you don't. But you will not escape this market without help, with or without your friend." She nudged her chin towards Neela. "And adding the antidote on top of it? That's a tall order. One you won't come by easily."

Lou felt Neela's eyes on her, but she couldn't look. Perhaps this was how Neela had gotten into this: by trusting too quickly, by believing too much. "What do you want in return?"

"Isn't it enough for me to want the safety of two girls?"

Lou thought of the room above them, the room full of bodies, and the horror of the market floor. "No."

"Very well. Perhaps I want my own escape from this place. Perhaps you're my only way out."

So she'd have to free not only Neela, but this goblin? Could she even do that? And why did Jewels need her to do it? What did Lou have that the other humans imprisoned here didn't?

There was noise on the stairs, and the goblin woman tensed. "You have until midnight tomorrow to decide for yourself, Louisa Wickett. I will prepare your antidote and free your girl, but you must be ready to free me in return. Now hide, hide, before he returns."

Lou couldn't even answer. She just shuddered back into her hiding spot as the door creaked again, as her palms went slick with sweat. Neela squeezed her eyes tight.

"Are you finished here?" the goblin boy from before asked. "You've been requested. I came to speed you along."

There was the sound of jars clanking, of jewels hitting the ground. Lou pressed a hand against her heart, hoping to calm it down, praying that the boy wouldn't hear.

"I can be done. Who is requesting me?"

"The Prince," the boy said. "Come, and hurry."

More shuffling, dragging, as the goblin assumed the position of a frail woman once again. "You're a scourge upon us," he muttered, and this time, Lou thought he meant it.

The door shut behind them, leaving Neela and Lou alone. Lou didn't waste time; they weren't coming back. She crawled back to Neela, ignoring the dried blood on the floor.

"I'll come back for you," she promised, grabbing Neela's hand, holding it tight. She looked so tired, worn down, broken. Lou had never imagined seeing her like this, her dark skin ashen, her hair limp and oily. Lou pressed her lips to Neela's head. "I'll come back tomorrow. And we will get out of here. Okay?"

"Don't leave me," Neela begged. Her full lips were cracked, scabbed over with blood. A tear slipped down her cheek.

Lou squeezed her hand tighter. "I'll come back," she said again, her voice cracking. "You have to trust me. Will you do that?"

Neela stared at her, betrayed. "Don't go," she said. "Don't go, don't go, don't go."

Hesitantly, Louisa took the knife and gave it to Neela. "Take it," she said, even though it pained her. Lou still had to get out of the market, and though she had days of freedom left here, she wasn't sure how well that covered her if she was found lurking down here. "Use it if you need to, but only if you need to. I'll be back at nightfall."

She pulled away before Neela could hold her tighter, even though Neela cried for her, even though every sob was another knife to Lou's heart. She'd come back, she'd come back, she'd come back. With every heartbeat, she knew she had to return— but first she had to make it out.

In the end, the escape was easier than she anticipated. On the stoop of the stairwell, Lou reached into her pocket, drawing out the rosemary and thyme. She frowned at it momentarily. This was not going to be pleasant, chewing on herbs, not at all. But unpleasantness was better than death.

Lou placed the sprig of rosemary and thyme in her mouth and bit down hard. Her mind spun, the walls of the market swirling around her, her feet catching under her. She had the impression of moving very, very quickly. The next thing she knew, she was back on the street, back in the cold swirl of the York night, back staring at the stone alley. Dizzy, still smelling of the smoke of the market, but unquestionably free.

She closed her eyes. Sleep would have to come next, an hour or two stolen, but then she had to prepare. Lou rested her hand against the cool stone of the wall. It had to end tomorrow. She would have no more chances. She couldn't let the goblins lure her in for a third night and trick her into turning that third night into an impossible, unending fourth.

CHAPTER 24
May

Eighteen Years Earlier

TIME CREPT FORWARD, DRAWING MAY CLOSER AND CLOSER TO the loss of her freedom. She was distracted by her guilt, for upsetting Eitra and getting banished from the market.

It was so frustrating. And also, why was she okay with thinking about this? Why was May okay with being the prey? Worse still, why did she feel guilty? It was like the mouse begging for penance from the cat.

Maybe it was because she'd felt like she wasn't the prey. Maybe because, with Eitra, she'd felt dangerous herself, like she was the one covered in thorns.

Maybe, when she kissed Eitra, she felt like she was the one devouring, not the one waiting to be devoured.

But life went on and so must May. With or without the market.

As she dressed for work, one eye on the rain lashing against her window, she considered this. She'd been so eager to leave York, her mother, magic, and the market behind—so eager to see anywhere but here, to be far away, having adventures. Perhaps, she thought, the best adventure of all could be had here.

Or maybe she just felt that way because, when she closed her eyes, she felt the bite of Eitra's thorns, the sharpness of her teeth.

She *had* to stop thinking of Eitra. She had to stop wanting her.

May grabbed her apron, cigarette pouch, and wallet. She was halfway out the bedroom door when Laura rounded the top of the stairs. She froze, taking in May.

"Where are you going?"

May rolled her eyes. One mistake and suddenly Laura always thought she was running off to market.

"Work," May said, pushing past her in the hall. She wasn't unaccustomed to passive-aggressive stretches with Laura. They were sisters, after all. Best friends and eternal antagonists.

"Want me to walk with you?" Laura said, catching her arm.

May looked at her over her shoulder. "No. I'm perfectly capable of getting there myself."

Laura rolled her eyes. She had reason to worry, and both of them knew it. But May wasn't in the mood to admit to her own recklessness, especially when it had backfired so spectacularly— and not even in a fun way.

But she wouldn't let Laura make her feel even more miserable—or late for work.

May made her way to the pub. She didn't bring any sort of umbrella. She knew she was being dramatic, but there was something about letting the rain drench her that felt justifiably miserable. Charlotte was just getting there at the same time as May, and when May clocked in, Charlotte took a look at her and said, "You look like shite."

"Thanks," May said.

"Truly."

May rolled her eyes, tying her apron around her waist. "I got it the first time."

She pulled pints and measured gin and poured tonic. She made sardonic chatter with the regulars and told off some young guy for looking at her chest as she wiped down the bar. She took two smoke breaks and rolled too many cigarettes, stubbing them out on the wet side of the building, letting the rain wash down her face as the sky darkened and somewhere, the market woke up without her.

She kept watching the door, waiting for Eitra. Looking at everyone out of the corner of her eye, at a slant, waiting for some sort of unreliability that hinted at glamour, at a goblin trick.

She had the goblin gold; no one had taken it from her. Someone had to come for her. She was sure of it.

She had to make this right. This wasn't the goodbye she'd wanted nor needed. She couldn't keep going in this city with the market every year, knowing Eitra was just underground, her enemy.

But no one came.

Charlotte and May closed the pub together in silence, two or three regulars remaining to finish off pints and wish them a good night. May stretched out her tasks, taking extra time to mop the floor and run the dishwasher the last time.

Someone would come. They had to.

"Y'alright?" Charlotte asked as she came downstairs from counting the cash drawers in the office.

"I'm fine," May said, but she felt like she was crumbling.

If not even the fucking goblin market wanted her, who did?

May followed Charlotte out, severely regretting her choice to ignore the rain on her way to work. Now it was colder, the rain chilling deeper.

She rolled a cigarette and smoked it as she started home. The streets were nearly empty, with only a few stragglers from the closing pubs in the mouths of alleyways or staggering down the streets.

She wished for Eitra.

"Bloody hell, May," she cursed herself, kicking her cigarette down a drainpipe. "You kissed her twice."

She wanted to punch something.

"May!"

The voice came from behind her. It was unfamiliar. Someone from school, she thought. May turned. There was no one there.

Except—no. A shadow detached from one of the alleys. Glamoured, he looked like a boy, any boy, but May could only just see who he was underneath the disguise.

Iark. The Market Prince.

He smiled at her, here on the street, like he was any other boy. Like he was not a bloodthirsty goblin, there to suck the marrow from her bones.

"What do you want?" May asked, frozen in the middle of the street. She realized, achingly, that she did not have Eitra for protection. But Eitra *had* invoked the Doctrine on her. May's stomach ached. Could he come here, into the street, to punish her?

"You didn't speak to me last night," he said, moving closer to her. She glanced over her shoulder, back at the pub, but of course it was shut and locked for the night. She would find no refuge there.

She did not have any herbs or words or potions. She was just May Wickett in the rain, just a girl with a coin of a goblin girl, just a girl who'd been hurt and didn't know if she was entitled to the heartbreak of it.

"I was occupied," May said, trying to mirror his tone. Cloaked in mystery, a hint aloof.

Iark drew even closer as a pair of guys passed on the sidewalk behind him, laughing boisterously. She saw a group of three coming down the street. Two tourist girls and a goblin, she realized; all dressed, going to the market, the market, the market.

The fucking market.

May clenched her jaw. "What do you want?" she asked.

Iark held out a hand. He had a piece of goblin gold between his fingers. It glinted, catching the dim light again and again as he rolled it over his knuckles.

"I'm having a party," he said. "A soiree, even. And I'd like to invite you."

May's skin prickled. Going with Eitra was one thing. But the Market Prince, the goblin who'd earned his title by killing other goblins?

Idiocy. Her mother would have her head, if she even came home.

But Eitra hadn't known May was a candidate. Not until she'd told her. So Iark didn't either, unless Eitra had shared that infor-mation—but why would she betray May? She'd gotten May out safely. Surely that was enough.

"Why would I do that?" May asked.

Iark shrugged. "Because you desire a thrill?" he said, tossing the goblin gold towards her. She caught it instinctively, the metal burning in her palm. She felt an echoing burn against her thigh, where Eitra's goblin gold rested. "To play our games one last time, in safety?"

Safety. Was he really offering that?

May gulped. "I don't think any of those sound enticing."

She held her bag tighter against her torso and started walking. He couldn't force her into anything—well, that wasn't quite true, because without the herbs she wasn't protected from his enchantments, but she was wearing iron. That had to count for something.

And tomorrow night, she was due to become a witch. What if this was the last chance she had to see Eitra?

"Because you want to stir some jealousy, then," Iark called from behind her. May's heart thudded in her chest. "Reignite the flames of your heart's desire."

"I don't have a heart's desire," she lied.

But it was hopeless. Iark knew. Of course he did.

May cursed herself. She didn't want to have a heart's desire— she couldn't afford to—this was the truth. And she had no reason to be drawn to Eitra, to want her, this goblin fiend she'd only known for a few days' time.

But she couldn't deny that when her mind wandered, it went to her.

It was like Eitra was a shard of ice, driven directly into her heart. And May had no choice but to crave the pain, to want a stronger dose of agony.

She turned. Iark stood in the middle of the road. The street-light haloed the rain over his head, and she recalled Eitra on the first night she'd seen her, looking like a goddess.

The goblins weren't exactly beautiful, but they were other-worldly in a way that made May's heart hurt, that made her feel every heavy second of the future that awaited her after her days of the market had passed.

But Mum.

But Laura.

But *Eitra.*

She needed to see her one last time.

"I'm afraid," May lied. "I think I've seen enough of the market. How can you guarantee I won't be hurt by going one final time?"

Iark raised an eyebrow. "I'm in charge, aren't I? The market answers to me. If I guarantee you safety, you will be safe, May Wickett. No matter what you do or who you break."

She swallowed hard.

Not for the first time, May wondered if she'd been poisoned in some way, forced into infatuation when her every sense tried to push her the other way.

"I'll have your guarantee?" May asked, hating the words even as she spoke them.

Iark opened his arms wide, commanding. "I'm the Market Prince, May Wickett," he said. "If I declare you to be safe, safe you shall be."

He came close, too close, and lifted her chin with one claw. "What vassal would go against me?" he asked. His breath smelled of blood and honeysuckle. "My power may last a year and no more, but what sweet power it is. Who would dare disobey an order?"

May pulled away. Nobody, she hoped. "And Eitra . . ."

Iark smiled. It was the grin of someone who knew, without a doubt, they had won. "Eitra will be there, of course. What is a soiree without my favorite confidante?"

If Eitra was there, she'd probably try to talk May out of this.

But May couldn't predict what Eitra would do. After all, Eitra had sent her away.

"And what do I wear?" May asked. "To this soiree?"

Iark laughed, spinning her on the street. May nearly fell, but of course he didn't let that happen.

"I'll dress you in glamour and starlight," he proclaimed. "Come now, hurry, hurry. We don't want to miss too much." He put his arm around her shoulders, guiding her towards a candle shop she'd passed every day on her way to work. She swallowed hard as he withdrew a skeleton key and opened the door.

"Is this a market entrance?" she asked.

"One of many," Iark said happily, guiding her through the tables laden with candles, through a door past the register, past the stock. He came to a door in the floor and pulled it open, revealing a set of stairs hewn in stone.

"I'll go after you," May said uncertainly.

"As long as you don't run," Iark said.

May did think about it. But she was already here, with Iark's good favor—and if she tried to run, there was no guarantee he wouldn't drag her to the soiree as a snack rather than a guest.

As she followed him down the stairs, she felt a tingling all over her body. May watched, fascinated, as a delicately spun web of black stretched over her skin, replacing her clothes from the pub. The dress was sensually smooth, the gossamer of spiderwebs, catching the light and glimmering in shades of silver. Just like starlight, the night sky.

"I told you you'd have the appropriate livery," Iark said as his own human glamour dissolved. Tonight, he was dressed in a shirt of orchid petals, spotted with rain. Dark blood colored his lips and his eyelids were painted gold.

He was fierce and beautiful and terrifying.

"What is the festival for?" May asked, hurrying to catch up. She could just hear the sound of the market below, bellowing and laughter sounding on the stone stairs.

"Oh, there are soirees for all sorts of things," Iark said. "Today, we're dancing because I want to and because I have the power to order everyone else to."

May suddenly regretted this. She wished she'd left Iark in the street. Just now, she'd be going up the stairs to her apartment, opening the door to the smell of whatever potion Mum had brewed that day. Laura would be there, maybe with a freshly boiled kettle, and she'd pour May's tea. They'd talk about the pub, and the shop, and another market would be ending in just a few days and their lives would be right back to normal.

But instead, it was this: May sweeping down the stairs in her gossamer gown, seeing how the stalls had been painted with blood. Everything was sickly now. The goblins, gorged on human blood; the humans, drunk and dizzy with goblin fruit. She felt the prickle of danger settle against her skin.

There were more limbs, more blood. Iark looped his arm through hers. "I don't think," he said, "you've seen the true wonders of the market yet."

"Oh, I—"

"May," he said, "allow me to show you the finest parts."

And, of course, he set off towards the worst part of the market. Not the fruit, or the baubles, or the fabrics, but the parts.

May tried to keep steady as she walked with Iark, as the blood on the floor soaked through her shoes. There were too many smells, all of them awful, of things that were meant to remain encased in flesh. She passed specialty stalls of organs, brains and kidneys and spleens, of a shop that sold strings of vertebrae, charging extra for a full set rather than a mixed assortment. Another stall lined up pelvises next to jars of sex organs, suspended in a liquid that reminded May awfully of pickle juice.

Iark pointed to a pelvis, still bloody, with fragments of sinew clinging to the bone. "They taste better freshly cracked," he confided, "when they haven't yet been boiled clean."

May wanted to vomit.

She wanted to run, to hide, but this was the market; and not only that, this was the market that she'd chosen. She'd come here of her own accord.

For the first time, May wondered how much Iark's promise of protection meant. Market Prince or not, his promise felt far more flimsy than Eitra's mark of lipstick on her cheek.

"This is fun," May said, trying to keep her mask of composure. Maybe, if she played along, she wouldn't scream. "But this is not a party."

Iark laughed. "Perhaps not by your standard." He seemed more relaxed, as if this stroll was a test that he did not expect May to pass and was pleasantly surprised she had proven him wrong.

May wondered if that was supposed to make her feel proud. Instead, she felt ashamed and tired, exhausted to the bone of blood and magic.

She'd chosen this, she knew, and she'd have to see it through to the end.

Iark led her through the end of the stall, away from the body parts, to May's relief. They whisked down the vanishing stair, to the level where they'd danced before. May started to enter the mist, but Iark held her back. "No," he said. "My gathering is too special for here."

This made May uneasy. The danger only grew as they descended deeper into the market.

"Where are we going?" May asked, trying to sound casual.

"To my own apartments," Iark said, mirroring her tone.

Alarm bells rang in her head. "Is it much farther? Eitra said . . ."

Iark's eyes hardened. "Oh, May, I promised you my safety tonight. My own protection. Even if I take you to the bottom of the earth, do you think I would fail you?"

She swallowed hard. It was an impossible choice. She did not have rosemary and thyme; there was no guarantee she could get out on her own.

She'd followed the viper straight into its den, and now the constriction would begin.

May just wanted more sunrises, more time to make mistakes.

But she followed Iark farther down, into the cloying scent of sugared raspberries, past another floor of mist and down to a lush reception area. Here, the ground was dirt rather than stone, the walls covered in moss and lichen. She had the impression that they'd reached the bottom, that this was the end of the market. There would be no further layers.

Her mum always told her that nothing good happened past 2:00 a.m. And definitely nothing good happened after 2:00 a.m. in the depths of the market.

But they weren't alone here. Goblins, short and tall, shades of light green to dark pebbled forest to cerulean, lounged against the wall and on low stools and cushions, drinking and eating. They looked more relaxed here than in the upper levels of the market, less frenzied with blood lust. But perhaps that had more to do with the dishes on offer than the company. May spotted a full human leg on one table, gristle clinging to the exposed ball of the hip joint. Another goblin across the room ate a bowl of fingernails while his companion pulled the skin off some indeterminate body part with a fancy silver knife. He grinned at May as he slurped the strand of skin like a noodle.

Yet only a few turned to gaze at her, snidely or curiously, and she was able to hold her head high and ignore them well enough as Iark guided her farther into the cavern.

It opened into an arched ceiling, girded with boughs of pale wood. It smelled of the earth, of river water running over stones. This room was crowded with goblins, the occasional human here and there at varying levels of intoxication. May watched cautiously, trying to decide if it was worth it to ask Iark if she could intervene.

Probably not. If they were this far, they were probably brought here to die.

And then, it was like the crowds parted, like every goblin in the room knew what she'd come to see.

Eitra.

Her hair was fashioned into braids and swirls, tucked up on her head with pins shaped like tiny silver twigs and dragonflies. Her green skin was offset with oxblood lipstick, and her gown was of technicolor luminescent dragonfly wings.

It hurt May to look at her.

"Your heart is racing," Iark observed, and May hated him for knowing.

Eitra looked at her and the world fell away.

May cursed her heart, the market, and the goblin gold; she cursed whatever enchantment had been placed upon her; she cursed the beauty of Eitra's eyes and thorns and claws.

Around them, May was sure other things were happening: goblins munching on bones or spitting jewels at one another, couples swirling around on the generous dance floor, a fight in one corner between two goblin-fruit-crazed humans.

Eitra's eyes flashed with anger. May had a sudden emotion. Perhaps she'd overstepped, perhaps she'd pushed too far. Maybe coming here was a mistake for more than her own mortal safety.

But the anger was gone as soon as it had come. "Iark," Eitra said. She came close, not to May, but to the Market Prince. She kissed both of his cheeks, not leaving a lipstick mark behind. Her smile was dazzling and awful. "Have you brought us a plaything?"

"A present," Iark said, watching Eitra's face. May looked between them. It seemed as if . . . It seemed as if Iark was taunting her, somehow?

But that didn't make sense. It was May who was the fool, May who'd gone too far, May who would face the consequences.

And Eitra only smiled. "And what a fine one it is," she said coyly. "May I have her?"

Iark drew May back, nearly pushing him behind her. May grabbed a handful of his shirt just to stay upright.

"Oh, not yet," Iark said. "You had your time."

May didn't like this. Any time she was spoken of as a commodity . . .

"What about what I want?" May asked, shaking off Iark's hand.

Iark raised a narrow brow.

Eitra cleared her throat. "May . . ." she said helplessly.

May wondered if Iark could see the panic in Eitra's face as clearly as she could see it. She realized, all at once, how grave this mistake truly was.

"Go," Eitra said, her face slipping into a pallid mask. "I'll find you later."

May nodded. What else was there to say?

Iark led her away. He didn't say anything, but drew her into a dance. They circled the room again and again, and May felt a rising surge of panic. She tried to pull away, but it was no use—Iark just kept dancing.

When she least expected it, Iark leaned close, his lips brushing against hers. May was so surprised she didn't even recoil. She tasted something sweet on his tongue, sweet and hot like gold.

May pulled away. There was something wet in her mouth, dribbling over her lips like blood. She wiped her mouth with one arm. Iark only smiled at her, his teeth stained with red. Had he *bitten* her?

No, May realized as she examined the juice that stained her arm, the juice he'd forced into her mouth. It was dark, dark purple, cherry or pomegranate.

The juice of goblin fruit. And it was too late. She'd already swallowed it.

Even as she stared at him, betrayed, her mind started to turn hazy.

"What is this?" she cried out. "You promised—"

Iark only shrugged, his smile growing. "As far as I heard, the Petergate Doctrine was invoked. You have no protection here."

"But I'm not—"

"But you are." He swirled her around and around, her head growing more jumbled with each turn. "It declares who is forbidden from here. Both witches, and their candidates. Of which you are one, are you not? At least, that is what my dear second has informed me."

Eitra had told him. Betrayed her.

But she should've known—hadn't Eitra told her, warned her? She was Iark's possession, just as May was now. Perhaps it hadn't been a choice to tell in the first place. So it was May, all May, who had ruined herself, who had come seeking danger and found death instead.

May tried to say something in protest, but her tongue was too heavy in her mouth, her lips unable to move. She could only breathe in and out as he smiled terribly and whisked her back into the dance.

She was dizzy. So, so, dizzy.

Either in reality or in May's hazy, untrustworthy perception, the others in the room cleared from the center, leaving them space. They whooped and cheered as Iark whirled May around the room. Her stomach lurched, but there was nothing in it.

And every few twirls, she caught sight of Eitra. She stood still, stone-faced among the revelers, as if she was watching a sick turn of fate that only she could take responsibility for.

The first time Iark slammed on her foot, breaking at least two toes, May shrieked a sob. She tried to stop, but her feet did not obey: they only kept circling, stepping and spinning, despite the pain. Her face was wet and hot, tears spilling from her eyes, her mouth caught between a sob and a gasp.

Iark laughed.

The shouts from the crowd swelled.

May *hurt*.

Something lashed out, either a goblin with a stick or metal pole, striking May in the ribs. She cried out, falling against Iark, feeling the awful brush of his shirt against her spiderweb gown. She sobbed openly as they danced. Her ribs ached, an awful pulsing in her side.

She had not been brought here in safety. She was brought here, she saw now, to die. Whether they would beat her to death or she would live until her heart gave out, it was anyone's guess.

Another smash to her toes. May was nothing but pain, nothing but the blood on her brow as a goblin tore into her hair, pulling out a chunk of her scalp with it. She felt a tongue on her forehead and recoiled, awfully realizing that Iark was licking her open wound, swallowing down her blood.

She was going to die here in the market.

Another blow, this time to her upper arm. She was no nerves, no sense, just eyes floating, faces blurring, slumped over on Iark as he continued to circle the room.

Would he still be dancing with her, she wondered, when her body finally gave out? Would he dance her rotting corpse into the ground?

"Stop!" a voice called. Familiar. Beloved.

Startled, Iark released May and she slipped down to the ground. She curled into the best ball she could, only vaguely registering that someone crouched over her, that some great argument was unfolding over her body.

She was dressed in starlight and blood; she was a girl of the surface, a girl of the market. Maybe next year, the goblins would return to find her bones.

There was a song she was supposed to remember. She hummed it, dazed, vision tinted with blood, as she stared up at the ceiling.

Are you going to Scarborough fair?

Are you?

Are you?

"May." A voice, a hand on her head. Green eyes, the green of death and poison and antifreeze. "May, you mustn't—"

Something in her mouth, juice on her lips. Sweet and bitter

and awful and perfect, one pomegranate seed from Hades's own palm, a half year of winter.

Next year, they'd find her bones.

Was this a fate worse than magic? Could magic, imprisonment in the Witchery, the constraints of her legacy, be worse than this?

"May, come on."

Will you return from Scarborough fair?

"I don't think I will," May whispered, and then the boughs and the pomegranates and the poison all faded to black.

May came to in a burst of starlight and agony. It was like surfacing from underwater, like the pain was a distant thing and then close all at once. Her feet, her ribs, her face. Her hands and ankles, where she was bound.

She thought she knew the rules. Her whole life, she thought she'd known them by heart, and yet—

But it didn't matter, not now. Because she was as good as dead.

She sat in the middle of a room in the Inbetween, tied to a column. She was alone, she realized—no Eitra, no Iark, no other goblins there to spectate her demise.

Perhaps that was a relief.

May let her head fall back against the column. It didn't matter that it hurt. Everything hurt. A headache was no better or worse.

She did not know the time or the day. She only knew the dread at the pit of her stomach, deepening as footsteps sounded on the stairs.

It was a goblin boy, bearing a tray. There was a bowl on it and a heel of bread. He set it in front of May.

She watched him evenly. "How am I supposed to eat this?" she asked. Her voice was raw and rough.

The boy shrugged. "Not *my* problem." Without another word, he left.

May stared at the tray in front of her. The smell of the soup ignited hunger in her; she'd definitely been here for hours. And with that realization, there came a worse one: she'd overstayed her time in the market.

No three-day clause could protect her. No rosemary or thyme could get her free. The only thing to save her now would be a full-fledged rescue, and with only days remaining in the market, the odds of that were nearly impossible.

No, the most likely option was that she'd be reduced to parts by nightfall, just another pair of hands hanging from the market stall.

She wondered if Iark himself would crack open her pelvis, would smash the balls of her hips and her patella, would drink the blood as it dripped fresh from her femoral artery.

Or perhaps, she thought miserably, that delicacy would fall to Eitra.

Hot tears burned her skin. She was a *fool*. No, she was worse than a fool. She was a hopeless romantic, a child who'd developed some attachment to a monster.

May regarded her soup miserably. And now, she couldn't even eat. She'd starve with food right there in front of her.

There was a greater clattering on the steps. Two shapes emerged from the floor above, both dressed in breeches and shirts.

Eitra, she realized hopelessly. Probably here to laugh at her. And Iark, she noticed, with a greater sinking feeling.

This was worse than heartbreak. This was betrayal in its root form.

"Have you come to finish me, then?" May asked. It was impossible to keep the bitter sorrow from her voice.

Iark stopped near the stairs. "Be kind to her," he purred to Eitra. "For now."

May flinched as Eitra drew near. She looked perfect and terrible as ever. May couldn't even imagine what she herself looked like: broken, bloody, destroyed.

Eitra crouched in front of her. She analyzed May, searching for something.

"I told you not to come back," Eitra said finally.

May bared her teeth, but that wasn't good enough. She spat, hard as she could. The blood-tinged saliva struck Eitra's cheek. She recoiled, wiping it off with one clawed hand, analyzing the streaks of blood.

For one awful, intractable moment, May wondered if she was going to taste it. But Eitra only wiped her hand on her trousers and went back to staring at May.

"Have you eaten?" Eitra asked.

May didn't answer. She just stared resolutely at Eitra, her tormentor, her betrayer, her undoing.

Eitra sighed. She picked up the bowl and brought it to May's lips.

May did not drink the soup.

"Don't be a child," Eitra hissed.

"You should let her starve," Iark called.

Eitra smiled at him over her shoulder, keeping the bowl steady at May's lips. "She'll taste better if she's fed," Eitra replied.

When she turned back, the smile was gone. She looked exhausted.

"Why did you tell him?" May asked miserably, using more than the usual amount of effort to string the words together. "Why did you tell Iark what I am?"

Eitra considered her, her eyes inky and unfathomable in the dark. "It wasn't a choice," she said bitterly. "I'm his second, May. There are no secrets between us. I am bound to him, by blood and the power of my name. There cannot be secrets between us. He does not allow it."

May looked away. If Eitra was unable to keep secrets from Iark, then of course she'd had to tell him what May was—and of course, he'd known just what buttons to push to get her back, just how to hurt her.

"Listen to me," Eitra whispered, quietly enough that there was no way Iark heard her, no way that her words traveled farther than May.

May narrowed her eyes.

Eitra tipped the bowl farther, spilling soup over May. She opened her mouth, half in surprise, and choked on broth. Coughing hurt her ribs even more. She bit back a sob, looking away.

She was pathetic. She hated being reduced to this in front of anyone, but especially in front of them.

"Who will come for you, little May?" Eitra crooned.

May bit back another sob. Eitra set down the bowl and her fingers traced over May's collarbone.

"Who will miss you?" she crooned again, but there was something different in her voice, something more urgent.

May looked up at her.

Her eyes were focused, intense. Not mocking.

Was it possible . . . Could Eitra actually be asking?

"Laura," May bit out, voice too raspy for true noise. She couldn't say the name again, couldn't muster another word.

Eitra's claw snagged on one of the chains around her neck. An iron ring on a chain, May realized, with a swell of hope. It wasn't enough, but maybe . . .

Eitra pulled, snapping the chain. The necklace slithered into her palm. She only winced slightly when the iron burned into her palm.

"For your sake," Eitra said, standing, "I hope that she does."

"No," May rasped as Eitra turned, as she walked out to where Iark stood. "No, wait!"

But it was no use. Neither looked back before they turned back up the stairs, leaving May alone in the darkness.

CHAPTER 25

Lou got back to the Witchery in the hazy time of morning when the only people on the streets had either been up all night or had the worst variety of morning shift. She forced herself down the stairs and through the tunnel, braced against the dead cold of underground.

It was odd being the one everyone was waiting for. Nana Tee was still there, making a new batch of ointment to smooth over Mom's skin. She smiled kindly as Lou came in, and May's face dissolved into relief. Joss wasn't there—probably she was either getting supplies or visiting someone else who'd been brutalized by the market. Lou shuddered, thinking of the room full of bodies.

May launched across the room, nearly knocking over at least two chairs on her way to tackle Lou.

"You're back," she said, knotting her fingers in Lou's hair, drawing her to her chest even though Lou was taller. "You made it back."

May's voice speaking those words were so similar to Neela's and Mom's that it made her heart ache. If she never heard their voices again, Lou didn't know what she'd do. "I am," she said.

"Of course I am."

May held her at an arm's length so she could examine Lou's face. "What did you find?"

She pulled away to sit on the arm of the couch, unlaced her boots, and tossed them away. Exhaustion pressed heavily into her bones. She wanted to drag herself back into Neela's room, to sleep, to save all of the schemes for tomorrow. But she did have to give an update.

"I found Neela," she said. "I think I can get her out."

She nearly told them about the other goblin, about the deal she had. But what had May and Nana Tee told her? Trust no one. Make no bargains. It's all trickery, in the end.

She'd made a bargain, she'd taken the risk, she'd followed the breadcrumbs all the way to the witch's house, and if she had to climb into the oven to save her mother, dammit, she was doing it.

"She has a ring of goblin skin around her throat. It's closing. I don't know what to do about it."

Nana Tee grimaced, glancing at May. "They're claiming her," she said. "Making her a part of the market, a servant. Perhaps not intending to kill her, not yet, but there's no way to know."

"Can I stop it?" Lou asked.

There was a brief silence. May cleared her throat. "Getting her out as soon as possible will hopefully do it. And we can find some solution, some remedy, when she's back with us and safe."

Nana Tee nodded, agreeing with May's assessment, and took in Lou's appearance. "Are you okay? You're not hurt?"

Lou nodded, rubbing her eyes. She couldn't remember the last time she'd felt this exhausted, but when she pressed against her eyes, all she could see was the awful butcher's tables, and even worse: she could imagine her and Neela there, dead, dismembered side by side.

"We should make a plan, then," May said, going to the table, stopping, and turning back. She was never good at stillness when she was nervous. "Figure out what to do. Together."

Something about this annoyed Lou. "I mean, it might not be easy to stick to a plan," she said. "It might be best if I figure it out on my own."

Was it so bad that she'd *liked* making her own decisions? Even if the market was awful, even if she hated what it contained and what it represented, she'd felt free while she was searching for Neela, making decisions about where to go and who to trust. She'd been in control for once in her life.

Her whole life, she'd been digging for her own roots, searching for something that made the Unbelonging go away, something that made her feel less unmoored. Less alone. Grimly, terribly, she wondered if she'd found it.

May pursed her lips, but perhaps she saw this change in Lou, this understanding. When Nana Tee protested, trying to make a plan, May shot her a look. "She's the one who has to do it," May said. Lou glanced up, seeing a strange, delicate camaraderie between them. There were no secrets, not anymore. There was only this shared burden. "Will you tell us about it?"

Lou pulled the band out of her hair and raked her fingers through her braid as she told them about all of it: meeting with Kildred in the alley, the woman under the table, the long descent. She even told them about the corpse room, skipping over details, then how she'd found Neela and taken the herbs to return to safety.

May rested a hand on Lou's cheek. It was warm, smelling

faintly of tea from the cups she was probably drinking all day. Lou leaned into it. "You should go to sleep," May said, running a thumb over Lou's cheekbone like she did when she was little and came in from the cold after a day playing in the snow. She used to take her face in her hands and call her a little snowflake.

Lou wished someone could warm her now, could take away the achy chill that settled in her bones. "I should," she said, pulling away from May. She finished her tea, left her cup on the big table, and retreated back to the room she'd slept in previously.

May had brought a bag from Lou's suitcase. She wanted nothing more than to wash her face, to shower maybe, but she hadn't solved the running water problem and she was too tired to fill the basin of water in the corner if she used it all.

Lou shucked her clothes and pulled on one of her own T-shirts and a pair of leggings. At the very least, it would be nice to be in her own clothes.

When she crawled into the cold twin bed, Lou could only just picture how it would be when she brought Neela back. This cursed trip might actually turn into a legitimate visit. Not *fun*, but at least *better*. They'd sleep like they did in Lou's room back in Revere, crammed onto the twin bed like cogs in a clock. They used to giggle and whisper long into the night, talking about Neela's boys and escapades and planning ways for Lou to escape her boring life.

But now, Lou laid here alone, subterranean yet again. She missed the cool moonlight of Neela's room, even if it did occasionally come with the cackling of goblins outside. She could hear the gentle murmur of Nana Tee and May in the main room, and eventually, the door opening as Joss came back from treating a patient. Joss passed into the room next door, singing softly as she treated Mom's wounds with more antiseptic ointment.

Lou laid there, alone, in the dark of a room that was not hers. She closed her eyes, thinking of Neela's face marred with bruises, and of corpses hands reaching, reaching, reaching, but finding no purchase.

When she woke, May was there, sitting nearby like a sentinel. It startled Lou, but only for a moment as she blinked the sleep away, squinting in the dim light provided by the candle on the far wall.

"What are you doing?" Lou asked.

May turned to look at her. She realized May had that little notebook between her hands, the one she'd given Lou on the train. She must've grabbed it and brought it back with the bag of Lou's stuff.

"Just . . ." Her voice was different, choked. May swallowed hard. "I haven't actually looked at this in years. When we were going, I just— I felt the weirdest pull. Like I needed to bring it with me. Like it belonged here."

Lou sat up. "I didn't get to finish reading it," she said, rubbing her eyes. Every part of her body ached.

May shrugged. "In hindsight, it's not the most important thing," she said. "As long as you know the rules."

Lou nodded. Silence settled between them for a moment, a little awkward. Lou wanted to thank her for standing up for her earlier, for telling Nana Tee she could figure things out on her own. But instead, she thought of that awful goblin woman and her bargain.

"Would a goblin ever want to escape the market?" Lou asked.

May looked at her sharply. "Why?"

Lou shrugged, chewing on her lip, bluffing. "It's . . . well, you've seen it. It's awful down there. There's no way all of them enjoy it. Some have to leave, right?"

May sighed. "I don't know," she said in that exasperated voice that made Lou feel like May was shutting her out all over again. But then, a breath later, "No, they don't all want to stay. But it's hard. Some are tied to the market, chained to it. By allegiance or some other curse. So some of them do make it out—there's one who lives just past the wall, actually, and Mum consults her frequently—but if they do leave, they generally don't make a show of staying around here. But even to get out is a privilege few of them can manage."

Lou nodded. The goblin woman did want to escape, for whatever reason. So if May was right, there was something keeping her in the market, something chaining her.

"And are they all . . . well, bloodthirsty?"

"Let's not go making sweeping assumptions," May said. She held something out. It was a chain with a charm on it that caught the light. Something thin and glittering. Lou couldn't remember if she'd seen it before.

"I don't know, Lou," she said finally. "They're goblins. Not mortals. Not humans. Their morals and norms and mores are all different from ours. We can't expect the same things of goblins, just as they don't expect us to go sucking marrow out of ribcages." She offered Lou a thin smile. "The witches are sometimes quick to make generalizations. But we can't believe all the horror stories, can we? Not all humans are serial killers, but some are. Goblins are like that, but in reverse. Some have no interest in bloodshed."

Lou thought of the table of dismembered bodies. She wasn't certain how much she could agree with May there, so she only shrugged.

May got up and ruffled her hair like Lou was a little girl. "Now, get yourself cleaned up," she said, already going. "You look terrible."

CHAPTER 26

By THE TIME LOU WENT BACK TO SHOWER AND RETURNED TO THE Witchery, it was nearly four in the afternoon. The place was quiet. May napped on the couch over some sort of spell book. Joss was out on an errand, and Nana Tee was in one of the rooms, slowly setting the bones of a girl whose arm had been crushed. Alone, Lou stole into the room where Mom slept.

She was so still, like a carved statue. They had positioned her on her back, hands resting on her chest, in the same position as Grandpa Jack had been in his casket, prepared for a viewing. Lou bit her lip, too afraid to touch her, to reach out and find her cold and already gone.

Her mother took a shuddery breath. The image shattered. Lou let out a breath herself. She pulled a chair over to her mother's bed. "I miss you," she said, and at first she felt silly, talking to her mother, who could not hear her and would offer no response.

But tonight she'd return to the market, both for Neela and her mother. Tonight, there were three options: she returned triumphant, she returned empty-handed, or she didn't return at all.

Lou rested her hand on Mom's arm. Her skin was feverish to the touch. She still smelled of her shampoo and the herby scent of the ointment. She examined her mother's face. She had long lashes and graying baby hairs that framed her face. Those gray hairs were new. When Lou was little, she used to stare at Mom as she was cooking or doing work at the dining room table, trying to find any trace of herself in her mother's face. It was easy with Dad, to see the sternness of their nose, their similar dark eyes.

But Mom was different. Always straight-faced, responsible, never toeing the line or getting close to it. She wanted to shake her mother, to beg her: *Tell me who you are.* Lou lived with Mom and May all her life, and yet it was as if there was never a past before her. There was the vague shape of Yorkshire and some tragedy that Lou now knew was the market, but it was impossible to imagine Mom and May here, carefree, without the press of the market or Lou. Without Neela, even—she'd only just been born when they left.

Lou wished she knew some part of Mom, some part of the woman she'd seen coming back from the market, fierce, like she'd spent her whole life fighting. She had to find the antidote simply because she had unlocked some part of her mother she'd always searched for, some part she'd thought deep down was there but never knew how to call.

Now was her chance to know her mother outside of their dreary apartment in Revere, when unpaid bills cluttered the table, or in Grandpa Jack's house, where they were tentatively comfortable.

But more than anything, Lou wanted the truth: Was there a pre-market Laura, one who laughed without care? A Laura that didn't worry?

Neela had been carefree and easy to be with. Somehow, she'd always thought May and Mom were the same way. But perhaps, after all this time guessing, she was still wrong.

Lou traced the line of her mother's jaw with her fingertip. Everything within her swelled with the need to know, to know, to *know*.

"I went to the market last night," she said, her voice feeling odd and uneven as she spoke into the room. It was as good as empty— it wasn't like Mom was listening to her. "I'm sure when you find out about it, you'll be angry. But it all made sense there, Mom.

"When I was little, I used to look at you and May and I used to think that you loved each other more than you loved me. How could you not? You and May, May and you . . . you were inextricable. How was I supposed to know who I was, if I didn't know who *you* were?

"And I thought it was normal. I thought I had to define myself in Neela, in you, in May and Dad and Gen and Peter. I didn't know it was okay to be the person I am. What's the point of being just one person when you could be half of something bigger?"

Lou wiped her nose on her sleeve. She was exhausted, not just from the market, but all of her past rushing to her at once.

"Who are you?" she asked. She brushed the hair off Mom's forehead, the heat of her fever too warm against Lou's fingertips. "Who were you back then, before you left? Before me?"

The silence rang in Lou's ears. These were all empty questions, senseless and rhetorical. Mom couldn't answer her now any more than she could get up and dance a jig. And when she was awake, Lou didn't know if she'd have the bravery to ask all over again.

She picked up Mom's hands and kissed the back, a quick brush of her lips against her skin. "I miss you," she said again, around the lump in her throat. It was not enough, but it would have to be for now.

Someone stroked Lou's hair. She jumped, an embarrassing noise escaping her throat, and whirled to find Nana Tee standing behind her.

"I'm sorry," Nana Tee said. "I didn't mean to scare you."

Lou pressed a hand to her chest, trying to calm it. "I just didn't hear you come in. It's okay."

Nana Tee nodded. She pulled over the side table and started laying out her instruments on it: a pitcher of warm water and a couple of sponges, a new jar of Joss's ointment, a knife, a towel. Lou watched as she lifted Mom's shirt to expose the gauze and undressed the wound.

"How long have you been a witch?"

"Mm." Nana Tee disposed of the used gauze in a bucket on the floor. "Since I was . . . sixteen? Seventeen?"

Lou didn't want to just sit here and watch. She got up and took the second sponge, going to Mom's other side. "So you knew about this your whole life. Did you always know you'd become . . . this? Did you want to?"

Nana Tee shrugged. "It didn't matter what I wanted," she said. They were quiet for a moment. Lou focused on cleaning the dried blood around Mom's wound. She tried not to think too much about the blackened veins that led away from it.

"I did the work because my mother did it," Nana Tee said, "and her mother before her, and a great aunt before that, as far back as anyone can tell."

Lou tossed her used sponge in the bucket and accepted some of the ointment from Nana Tee. She tried to rub it into Mom's skin in a soothing way, like Mom rubbed Vicks VapoRub into Lou's chest when she was a child. "And what will happen to the coven after you?"

Nana Tee sighed. Her eyes flicked to Lou, then away. "I don't know," she said honestly. "Responsibility like this is usually inherited, not chosen. I wouldn't have chosen it if I didn't have to," she said, winking at Lou. "It couldn't go to Laura and May, not after what happened, and Marcus—that's Joss's son—helped for a while, but his wife wanted to go back to Spain when the babies were born. Neela grew into this, but I don't know if she feels the same pull I do. I think she's going to choose to leave, to give up her magic forever instead of inheriting all this trouble. I don't know what will happen after that."

Nana Tee handed Lou a rag to wipe her hands on as she set to rebandaging the wounds.

"Does it scare you?" Lou asked.

Nana Tee tsked. "I'm afraid of what will happen to this town without protection," she said. Her weathered hands didn't shake as she taped down the gauze. "But that's the way of things, isn't it? Maybe there will come a time when we're not needed, when the market doesn't hurt so much. And maybe soon the magic will all run out. Who's to say?"

"Indeed," Lou said. What would she do, if she had the choice? Lou chewed on her bottom lip. "And do I have magic? Or can I, if I learned to use it?"

Something in Nana Tee's gaze shifted. "I don't know, Lou. Perhaps? But it would take so much training to find out, and it might be all for nothing."

Lou shrugged. It was fair enough; she didn't know what Mom and May had done, how they'd lost their magic, but it was obviously permanent and possibly took her chance away too.

But she couldn't deny the peace here in the Witchery or the steadiness she felt here within the walls. When she'd arrived, she'd lamented feeling rootless. But maybe it wasn't York that grounded her. Maybe it was this: the market and the magic, the constant push and pull of it all, and the life her mother had left behind.

It hadn't been difficult to coax May to go on a walk. It required some guilting, certainly, but nothing that wasn't true. After all, it was Lou's first transatlantic trip, her first big stay in their ancestral home, and she'd spent most of the time trying not to die. The least May could do was buy her a coffee and take her into the Minster.

It was after closing time, but May had some sort of secret way through the crypt. Now, they sat in the empty nave. Lou kept looking up at the soaring arches, the intricate carvings in the stone. She couldn't help but be in awe of it all—they didn't make them like this in Boston.

"Who's buried here?" Lou asked, scanning the great stained glass windows.

"Bishops," May said. "Archbishops."

"Hm." Lou fidgeted in her seat. She'd asked May to come with her for a specific reason, and it had nothing to do with Costa lattes or dead archbishops. "May?"

May sighed like she already knew what was coming. "Yes, Louisa?"

"Can you tell me what happened?"

"You've got to be more specific."

Lou didn't think she did. She traced the lid of her coffee cup with the tip of her finger. "Why did you give up your magic? Why did you go?"

May shrugged. She was reigned in now, not so open. But then she sighed again and said, "Can we walk and talk? I don't like the echo. It makes me feel . . ." She shuddered. "Fourteen again."

"Fair." Lou got up and followed her aunt down the aisle and across toward the south transept.

May was quiet for a minute. Lou thought about asking again, pressing, but she recognized the look on May's face. Mom made the same one when she was thinking of the right thing to say. It happened often when they were at dinner with Dad.

"Where should I start?" May asked finally.

"Why did you go into the market? Clearly, you knew that would . . . cause a problem."

May snorted. "Yeah, I know. I knew the risks. I watched Mum basically transform glamoured hedgehogs back into humans for the better part of my childhood. But . . ." May tried to smile, to laugh, but it fell flat. She looked at Lou, searching. "I don't know if I can explain it to you. There's a draw, isn't there? To the market and its magic. I knew it was the wrong thing, and I wanted it anyway."

Lou nodded.

May chewed her lip uneasily. Lou gave her time, gazing up at the stonework, the stained glass windows. She wished she could remember how old the Minster was. Here, in the middle of it, the building felt ageless.

"But I was lured too, though that may not be a fair statement." She stopped at one of the racks of candles, meant to be lit for prayers. May slipped a couple of pounds into the donation box and grabbed two of the candles. She lit them and carefully positioned them in the holders.

"By a goblin?"

May sighed. "You're going to think me a fool."

"Just tell me."

"Yes, I was lured by a goblin. And I—listen, I know how it sounds. But I came to care for her. And I accidentally violated the Petergate Doctrine—"

"Ah. The big rules."

"Yes. I violated one of the rules—don't worry, you can't make the same mistake—and I was imprisoned. So Laura came to get me, and we ended up killing a goblin, and it didn't matter because—" May's voice caught. She cleared her throat and glared off into the distance, as if that would ward off the tears. "The goblin I cared about died helping us escape. It's my fault. And there was a price on our heads, and since we'd violated the market rules, we couldn't stay here safely."

"So they shipped you off to the States," Lou said.

May shrugged. "I mean, we agreed to go. Not that we had much of a choice. But by the time that was up, you were already too curious, and Laura wasn't willing to risk coming back." May bumped Lou with her hip. "And it wasn't a big deal to take Neela for the summer, either, until she chose to be a full member of the coven or leave. So you both were safe away from the market."

"Well." Lou craned her head up, up, up, to the crisscrossed stonework of the ceiling far above. "For a time."

May draped an arm over Lou's shoulder. Lou leaned into her. She was soft, comforting, smelling of home. "We just wanted to protect you, Lou. Both of you."

"But did you ever think about what I wanted?" Lou asked.

The question hung in the air, unanswered. May's hand tightened on Lou's shoulder. "Not when it came to the market," she said finally. "And if . . . if you choose to be a part of it now, I think we'd both understand."

Something prickled under Lou's skin. She was surprised May could see to the thoughts she wasn't yet willing to admit to herself.

"I have something for you," May announced, no preamble. She withdrew her arm to dig through her small purse.

"Oh?"

She pulled a tiny tissue-paper wrapped item from the front pocket. "I was saving this as a last resort," she said. "Mostly because I don't know—" She stopped, took a deep breath, as if she was on the edge of tears. When she picked up again, she said, "I didn't know if I could part with it. It's from someone who was very dear to me. But I hope it will get you out, as a last resort."

Lou bit her lip. She'd never been good with heirlooms. She'd lost at least three things Grandpa Jack had given her from his family. "Thank you for trusting me."

May snorted. "It's a big thing, I know."

They smiled at each other, that smile of knowing, of shared memories. It helped Lou relax.

Maybe there was room for healing.

"Here," May said, opening her palm. Something glittered in her palm: a shard of glass, Lou thought. She leaned close to look. It was clear-ish, glimmering, pulsing with some odd sort of light.

"It's goblin ice," May said. She twisted her hand back and forth, letting the ice catch the light. "But don't let the name fool you. It won't melt or anything."

Lou ran her finger along the edge. It was rounded, but pointy at the tip and cold to the touch. She couldn't imagine how it could be helpful to her if she really had to fight her way out of the market. "What does it do?"

"It will freeze the heart of a goblin."

Lou regarded the ice shard skeptically. It didn't look like much. "Will that . . . kill it?"

May rolled her eyes. "Yes," she said. "If you stab a goblin with this tiny little thing, it will kill them. Get them in the thigh? Over. The arm? Over."

"Efficient," Lou observed.

"It's there as a last resort," May said. "I wouldn't recommend using it unless you need to. Though you didn't grow up here, your blood is still linked to the coven. You're one of us, whether you like it or not. You have to follow the Doctrine. You mustn't kill any of them, Lou. Not unless you have to."

Lou chewed her lip. The sun was setting outside, throwing imprints of the stained glass in dazzling shades of red and orange. Soon, it would be time to descend into the depths of the market, into the rot and the madness. "And if I have to?"

May leaned in to kiss Lou on the forehead. "Then you must run very, very fast."

CHAPTER 27

May

Eighteen Years Earlier

IN THE DARKNESS OF THE INBETWEEN, THE PLACE WHERE THE goblins deigned to imprison May, she lost all track of time. At first, she hummed to herself: *Oh, dear! What could the matter be? Johnny's so long at the fair,* but her patience grew thin as the hours dragged on.

She only had herself to blame. Not even Eitra had tried to save her—not that May could blame her. She was a goblin. Trickery was in her nature.

It was May's fault for being a fool, for letting a goblin trick her out of her own heart.

Some indeterminate time after her imprisonment, something stirred in the darkness. Something . . . flickered.

May opened her eyes, trying to see in the dark gloom. Above her, the market was in full swing; night must've fallen. But now, there were sounds nearer. Small sounds, filtering through the bones and the rubble. She squinted, trying to see through her pounding headache.

She'd lost too much blood. She had too many broken bones. Whatever was coming to kill her better do it quick.

She didn't realize she'd said that thought out loud until a soft voice replied, "I'm not coming to kill you, May."

Laura.

May strained to see her. The voice, quiet as it had been, had come from behind her. May turned her head. She could just barely make out the flickering candle, the pale skin of Laura's hands.

"Laura," she tried. No sound escaped.

"Hush, now," Laura whispered. She dropped to one knee behind May. May felt a sharp bite of metal and realized that Laura had cut her bindings. Blood came rushing back to her hands, terrible and painful. She fell forward onto her face, too numb to catch herself, and sucked in a breath as every hurting place moved.

"We have to go, May," Laura whispered.

May turned her face, one cheek pressed into the dirt. Something bit into her cheek—a bone fragment, probably—and she tasted dust on her lips. "How did you find me?"

Laura stood. She looked angry but resolved. She was dressed in all black, belt strapped with an arsenal of knives. May saw the bulge of herbs in her pockets.

They won't work on me, May thought bitterly, thinking of rosemary and thyme in her mouth. *I've overstayed my welcome here.*

"Come on," Laura said. She stooped down to get her hands under May's armpits, and it took all of May's waning strength to not cry out at her touch.

"I know," Laura said, sounding on the edge of tears herself. "I know."

May buried her head in Laura's shoulder. "I can't," she muttered.

"You *must*," Laura insisted.

Every step was agony. May didn't know where they were going or how Laura got in, and she didn't care. Laura was here, they were moving. Perhaps she was already dead, perhaps this was hell, but they were moving.

They came to the bottom of a set of stairs. They were impossibly high, May mourned. Far too high.

"We'll crawl if we have to," Laura said, like she could read May's thoughts.

"Where do they go?" May asked. If they were anything like the vanishing stair, they could deposit the pair straight into the market, and then when where they be? Both dead, eaten by goblins.

No. Laura was healthy, she was safe. It was her first day in the market.

She could make it. Without May, she could get out.

"You have to go," May mustered. "You can't—you can't get both of us out. You have to leave me."

Laura squeezed May's arm tighter. "I'm not doing that. Listen to me, May. I'm not leaving you here."

There was something savage and unfamiliar in Laura's voice. May only nodded, barely protesting as Laura pushed some herbal remedy into May's mouth and forced her to chew.

It didn't make her pain go away, but it cleared her head a little.

They took one step at a time. May crawled, Laura pushing her, stretching and reaching for the light. Every move was agony. She wanted to give up; she wanted to sleep. They would find them anyway, the goblins. There was no way out of the market.

"What's up there?" May whispered. There were so many

floors, so many rooms—if even this was a struggle, how would they get out alive?

Laura shook her head. "It goes back to the market floor," she said.

The market floor. It was so close to the surface, but crowded with goblins who wanted nothing more than to kill May.

"You go to the top," May said. "Keep watch. I won't move quickly."

Laura nodded, but she seemed unwilling to leave. Either way, she took a few more steps and hesitated just below the landing, still in the shadows.

May forced herself up—this staircase had to be bigger than the other ones, covering more ground, like a game of chutes and ladders. They bypassed other floors that May explored in the days before.

She could hear the sounds of the market more clearly now. It could've been her headache, but to her, it was like everything was louder, rising to a new frenzy. She could smell the rot from above—or maybe she only smelled her own mortality.

She finally made it to Laura, who dragged her back up to her feet. "It's clear enough," Laura muttered. "They all seem to be occupied."

May thought back to her other experiences of the market. There were humans there, walking freely, injured as badly as she was. The only time anyone had paid her particular attention was when she'd been with Iark.

Of course they would. He was the Market Prince.

Be brave, she told herself, though all she wanted to do was return to the Inbetween, to lay down and hide. *Be brave and survive.*

"Laura," May said, gripping her sister's arm, leaving a bloody handprint. She hadn't realized her head wound had opened back up again.

"Yes?" Laura asked, tearing her eyes away from the market.

"If anything happens," May said, "if they take me, you must go. You must leave me."

Laura opened her mouth to protest, but May stopped her.

"No. These were my choices, not yours. You must." She would not allow her to argue.

Laura frowned. "If it will get you moving," she said, "I'll agree to it."

"Good."

Three steps stood between them and the market, their last bit of protection.

"Are you ready?"

"Yes," May answered, because she had to be.

Arm in arm, they stepped into the flickering light of the market floor.

It was like a glamour had been removed. The fruit was sickly and rotten, smashed and imperfect. The delights she'd marveled at before were now torn and moth-eaten, and even the horrifying human limbs were worse, discolored with rot. Goblins leered over baskets and barrels of produce, their laughter as sickening to May as the fetid juices that dripped from the tables.

May's stomach turned. Even when she'd thought she'd seen the truth of the market, she'd only seen an illusion.

Yet the only thing that mattered was this: no one turned to them. The market was clotted with goblins and humans alike, enjoying the final nights. The air was thick with blood, and screams sounded just as often as laughter. And an injured girl, May realized, was no novelty in the market.

Hope swirled in her, strengthening. "I think there's an exit there," May said, nodding further down the wall, to the mouth of a dark stairway upwards.

"I think you're right," Laura agreed. She steered them in that direction.

May clung to her, putting as much of her weight as possible on Laura. She was a mess in her black gown, torn and dirty, but freedom was bright and sharp, close enough she could taste it.

As they walked, Laura pulled a hand away to take out the sachet of herbs.

"They won't work on me," May lamented.

Laura frowned. "It's worth a try."

They were so close to the door. May wanted to plead with her, keep going, we're nearly there, the herbs don't matter.

But Laura commanded, "Open your mouth."

"Laura, I told you—"

"Just do it."

May did as she was told. She opened her mouth, and Laura put the small bundle of rosemary and thyme between her back molars.

"Bite it," she said.

May did as she was told. Nothing happened. There was no draw to move, to escape, that she'd had days before.

May shook her head, spitting the bundle out on the market floor. "It doesn't work. There's no safe passage for me. Only trickery."

Laura grimaced, taking May's weight back on her shoulders. "Trickery it is, then."

A sudden, sharp pain hammered through May's head, like she'd been punched in the upper temple. She gasped, staggering against the wall.

"What is it?" Laura asked.

"Oh, my pretty," a voice said before May had the chance to answer. The pain radiated outward, striking every nerve. A goblin woman, hunched, pointed one gnarled finger at her. "You're a market girl now."

Laura straightened, wrapping one arm protectively around May. "She's fine," Laura lied. "She's only been here a night— she's only drunk."

The goblin woman cackled, throwing her head back. She drew even more attention to them. "Market girl!" She laughed, pointing and howling. "Market girl!"

There were more goblins then, coming to see the commotion.

"Go," May pleaded, and Laura made a run for the stairs, dragging May along with her. Laura passed through the arch into the stairwell with ease, but May slammed into something hard and flat and invisible—a wall, a ward, a deterrent. She clawed against it with what little strength she had, feebly scratching, but it was as solid and transparent as glass.

It was the same sort of wards the witches used to guard the Witchery from goblins, May feared. Only this time, it was there to keep her out of the mortal world forever.

"May!" Laura called. "Come on!"

May slammed herself against the wall again, feeling the impact jarring every single one of her wounds. It *hurt*.

But there was no use. She was stuck. Trapped.

She was a market girl.

Laura ran back and tried to grab May's hands, tried to pull her out through the wards. She only succeeded in further bruising May's knuckles. Behind her, May heard the laughter multiplying, growing louder as the entire market turned its attention to her.

The goblins loved a spectacle and trickery. Of course this was how Laura got through and down to the Inbetween so easily. It was a trap. Perhaps, the whole time, they were meant to die here together.

"Oh, fuck this," Laura snarled. She came back into the market, back into the horrors. Her eyes were furious, full of molten anger. She lowered May to the ground and moved to stand in front of her.

"Who must I talk to?" Laura shouted at the wall of laughing goblins. "What must I do to take her away? I will not leave her here! I will not leave her to the market!"

The laughing only grew louder.

May swallowed back her bile, her resolve deepening. There was no way out of the market. She pulled herself into a sitting position, trying to grab Laura's leg or hand as she paced in front of May. She had to go, to cut her losses, to get out of here before she was taken too.

Furious, Laura drew her blade. Her voice was steadier, low and deadly, when she spoke. The goblins hushed to hear her. "I will kill who I must," Laura promised. No, May thought, crawling forward, trying to stop her. *No, no, you mustn't.* "I will maim whoever stands in my way. But I will take my sister home."

The blade glinted dangerously in the high candlelit chandeliers of the market hall. May knew the knife; it was from the back room of the Witchery, where they hadn't been allowed to go until they were ten because it was so full of sharp, pointy objects. They'd studied fighting alongside Marcus and the children of the other covens. Every Sunday from the time May was a child until she was sixteen and too busy to care, the scraggly group gathered and practiced fighting skills. May was never very good.

But Laura was.

Now, she wielded the blade with a certainty May never had. She had always been afraid she'd cut herself or someone else on the training knives they used, but Laura never seemed to care.

But this was not practice, and Laura wasn't facing off against May or Marcus or even Sadiq, their instructor. No, it was Iark, the Market Prince, who separated from the crowd.

"Me," he declared. His grin was awful, sickening. May shivered, recalling again the pain of her broken bones.

Laura stood tall and strong. May stared up at her. Her sister was not cowed; she did not bend nor break. She did not even look afraid.

That was a mistake.

Iark circled, coming closer. "You think you could best me, human?"

Laura jutted her chin stubbornly. "I don't see why I couldn't."

He regarded her. "I will fight you, then," he said. "And I will eat your molars alongside my evening meal after I defeat you."

Laura pulled a second knife down from the sheath on her forearm, the smooth sound overloud in the new silence of the market. Both of her knives were steel, inlaid with iron in the shape of runic magic. May recognized the set. Reserved for dire consequences, they were rumored to have been charmed by the Thaumaturge of 1834.

Iark pulled his own daggers, slender, twisted things, fashioned from bone. Knowing him, it was probably human bone.

All May could do was flatten herself to the wall before Iark lurched toward Laura. May's heart flew to her throat.

Around the room they danced, just as May and Iark had at the ball on the night he took her prisoner—but this time, Laura lunged, slashing his upper bicep and leaving a sickly streak of greenish-black blood behind. Iark howled, fighting with renewed ferocity.

She could not watch. She could not look away.

Iark finally hit Laura, slashing her ribs, spilling ruby blood that stained her shirt a darker black. She hissed through her teeth, but she did not falter. Even though the goblins were now pelting both her and Iark with rotten fruit, she did not lose focus. She jumped on top of a table, scattering silver rings into the crowd.

May pressed a hand to her chest as if to calm her racing heart and felt something under her gown. She stilled. Her fingers dug out the iron chain she'd worn to the market, the same chain that Eitra had stolen from her in the Inbetween—but now, the chain did not have a ring on it. No, instead something pointy and sharp was wrapped in a leather cord and attached to the chain.

Goblin ice.

Strid water, frozen and cursed by strong magic, forever solid and cool. It was impossible to make anymore—none of the witches in the coven had enough magic left for it. May had only heard rumors of its existence. All known pieces had been pilfered by the market nearly a century before. And yet . . . here it was.

It was the only weapon guaranteed to kill a goblin. Of course there were other, less reliable, ways: decapitation and stopping the heart and whatnot, but goblin ice was simple in comparison. And Laura would tire far before Iark.

May squeezed her eyes shut. There was no reason for this bloodshed, this terror. There was her mistake. Her choice.

Using the goblin ice would be her choice too.

No one was watching her. Everyone was watching the fight.

She crawled forward, keeping to the edge of the crowd, keeping low. No one noticed her. Perhaps no one knew this was the girl they were fighting over. She was already forgotten, a relic of the market, already dead to the crowd.

May wrapped her hands around the ice shard as tight as she could hold it.

She tried to forget the pain, the agony of simply existing. She watched Laura, watched Iark, inching ever closer to the two of them as they circled, striking and missing, dancing back then striking again.

May could not hesitate. Could not let doubts stay her hand. She lunged forward and slashed, catching Iark's ankle, severing the Achilles tendon. He stumbled, fell. Blood moved sluggishly over his foot, turning copper, reacting with the ice. Only then did his veins begin to darken.

Iark looked down at her, shocked. May wondered what he saw: a victim, a demon, a terror. His veins bulged, turning black, and he fell to his knees. His knives clattered to the ground.

Laura stood tall, panting out breath, watching as Iark's veins began to burst.

May scrabbled for Laura's hands as the room erupted into chaos.

They crawled together, May coughing as goblin feet ran over her fingers. They were far from the door, too far, and a cry went up to find the assassin.

"I'm sorry," May sobbed.

"Just fucking move," Laura hissed.

She tried, she tried, but it was all too much.

"Go," May pleaded. She could not imagine moving that far, could not imagine making it to the door on her own.

"The assassin!" someone in the crowd called. "The assassins are escaping!"

But they were lost in the chaos, in the rush. Laura scrambled up to her feet, trying to pull May up, but she could not.

May had used her last store of energy. She was bleeding again, from her head and from her ribs, and bright splotches crowded her vision.

"Go," a savage voice above her said. Laura's face turned odd, trusting but not. Someone picked May up, held her to her chest, someone with thorns, who smelled of metal and cigarette smoke and blood.

Eitra.

May could barely focus as Eitra dashed after Laura. She was not held back by any invisible walls, she was not hit with goblin fruit or assailed. She ran freely, catching up to Laura easily on the stairs.

"We have to move," she urged.

"You're here," May said. She wasn't sure why this shocked her. Where else would Eitra be?

"You thought I'd leave?" Eitra asked, her voice softer than usual. "You thought I'd leave you like that?"

May didn't know what she thought. She was tired, aching, past the point of pain. She floated somewhere between sleeping and waking.

"Can you manage her?" Laura asked. May realized they'd slowed down, no longer running.

"I need a moment," Eitra said.

May opened her eyes as Eitra sagged back, releasing her, nearly dropping her. They were in a side alley somewhere near the Minster.

"We have to get her to the Witchery," Laura said, pacing back and forth. Eitra breathed heavily, trying to catch her breath from running with May.

May didn't know how much longer she could stay conscious.

"I'll try," Eitra said, but she sounded hopeless. "We have to get her off the streets."

They hoisted her between the two of them. May's head lolled on their shoulders. She saw bits: the trees outside the Minster, branches looking like fingers stretching for the sky; a pair of tourists who looked at them oddly and called after to ask if they needed help. She vaguely remembered holding her hand in front of her face and looking at the blood in the cracks of her skin and barely noticed as Eitra held up the chain with the goblin ice still attached and returned it to May's throat.

CHAPTER 28

T ONIGHT , L OU DIDN ' T BOTHER WITH THE GOBLIN GOLD OR Kildred. Nana Tee told her of an entrance to the market floor. She wasn't breaking any rules; she didn't have to be incognito. So Lou found the door nestled between an oddities shop and a bookstore and let herself in.

She took the stairs and found herself in a corner close to the dais. It was still early in the night, so the market floor wasn't nearly as packed with goblins as it had been the night before. Groups of two and three milled about down the aisles, bartering over wares. Lou noticed a trio of school-age girls giggling near the fruit vendor. She frowned, but there was nothing she could do about it. Tonight, she had other missions to accomplish.

Lou tried to look confident and at ease as she strolled down the wall, away from the dais. May had confirmed that the staircases did shift and move, so it was unlikely that Lou would be able to follow the same path to the place Neela was held. No, it would be easier if she found the goblin first, even though that made her uneasy.

She was suddenly too aware of someone walking behind her.

Lou turned. A goblin girl was there, her hair braided into two thick plaits and embellished with dragonflies. She wore a dress of unlined silver chainmail. Lou swallowed and looked back up at her face.

"Hello, little moon," the goblin said archly. "I thought I might see you here."

It was the goblin who'd pretended to be Neela, the one who'd haunted her from the street outside Nana Tee's house. The one Lou had punched.

"I don't have to talk to you," Lou said. She turned back to her mission and pressed on, but the goblin girl kept up with her.

"Are you enjoying yourself?"

Lou didn't see the point in answering her. If she kept quiet, maybe the girl would leave her alone and move on to more interesting prey.

"Have you come to find the other witchling?"

At this, Lou glared. "Why does it matter to you?"

The girl smiled, all teeth. All that metal made a distinct rustling noise as she walked. "Because she's mine," she said.

Lou shrugged. "I'm not here to break the rules." She did not let any panic slip into her voice. She did not slow her pace or quicken it; she kept everything level and even. Boring. That was the game to play.

"Oh, you're no fun," the girl laughed. Lou didn't feel like pointing out her idea of "fun" had nothing to do with dismembered bodies or rotting fruit, but it was pointless. "My friend Kildred tells me that you've caught the old woman's eye."

"What does that mean?" It was totally possible the goblin girl was just trapping her. Lou regretted speaking as soon as the words were out of her mouth—interest was the worst route.

"The old woman. Eitra."

"Mm." Lou paused at one of the stalls, this one packed with

textiles. She ignored the vendor leering at her and ran her fingers over a bit of trim. She couldn't keep going with this goblin girl following her about. She'd lead her straight to Neela, and the game would be up.

The girl poked her claw through a bright red strawberry from the stall behind her. She bit into it, the berry staining her teeth red. The fruit seller didn't seem to care that she'd stolen from him, but perhaps that was the way of goblins.

"Don't you want to hear a story, witchling?" she asked.

Lou shrugged. "Doesn't matter. You all have so many stories. You'll tell me if you want to."

The girl leaned against the fabric stall, her thigh so close to Lou's that she could feel the heat through the girl's chainmail. "There are things forbidden to goblins, you know. We have rules like you."

"Shocking," Lou said dryly. She really did like one of the silks, but it wasn't like she could actually buy it. God, she was succeeding in boring herself. It was a wonder the girl didn't just leave her alone. Lou moved down to the next stall, this one dedicated solely to buttons. She tried not to look too hard at the box dedicated to transformed human molars.

"It is said by those who know better than I that the goblin woman, Eitra, stole the Market Prince's new partner, who was property of the prince and the market."

Lou inspected one of the buttons, navy with a gold center. She did not let it show that she was interested at all. "Sucks for him. I'm sure the girl was better off free."

The goblin girl's hand snaked out and wrapped around Lou's wrist. Lou looked at her. "Who said she freed her?" She laughed, low and throaty. "No, little moon. She *ate* her."

Lou swallowed hard. Joss had told her, theoretically, that goblins ate people: cracked their bones and sucked the marrow out, melted down the fat, roasted organs and ingested flesh like bacon. But she didn't like to think of it when she was here, in the market, with the body parts—and she didn't like knowing that she'd made a bargain with a goblin who'd broken her own rules.

"And the Market Prince cursed her for it. Took out the eyes that had coveted his prize. And then, they say, she killed him, roasted his flesh on the market pyre, and ate him too. It was a whole bloody business, I've been told."

Well, shit.

"Enjoy the market," the girl said. As quickly as she'd come, she melted into the growing crowd, leaving Lou behind.

It was totally possible this was just another trick, Lou thought as she turned away. Possible that this was just a lie.

But that was the problem with goblins. She'd seen the place where they kept the butchered dead. When reality was that bad, how could she *not* believe the story she'd been told?

The bargain with Eitra guaranteed the goblin woman freedom from the market. But she'd been cursed because she'd been so terrible she'd broken rules of the market—and the rules of the market were already fairly brutal.

What if Lou released Eitra and she wreaked havoc? What if she followed them back and ate May or Nana Tee? What if this was just another goblin trick, and she didn't know how to heal Mom at all?

But May had said not all goblins were bloodthirsty. Was it possible Eitra was one who didn't want to hurt anyone, who only wanted to live peacefully out of the market? Lou thought of how the goblin boy had ripped Neela's hair out and cringed.

She'd have to figure out a solution later. Right now, she had to move. The faster she got to Neela, the faster she could get them out. And if she needed to return for the antidote, dealing with Eitra would be easier without dragging a sick Neela along with her.

It took the better part of an hour for Lou to find her way back down the shifting staircases to the room where Neela was held. She hurried across the room full of junk to the wall of prisoners. Except instead of three prisoners, now there was only Neela.

Lou knelt in front of her. "I'm back," she said, reaching to touch Neela's thigh.

She jolted awake. Lou recoiled, shocked at the change. Her lip was swollen, split in two, and there were new bruises blossoming down the side of her face. Lou sucked in a breath.

"What happened to the other two?" she asked.

Neela looked at her like she was seeing something else, something Lou would never be able to see. "They came for them."

Lou thought of the body parts in the market above, how fresh they looked. She shuddered. "We're going to get you out," she said, moving to Neela's side to examine her wrists.

Neela was quiet even as Lou probed her bloody flesh. The restraints had chafed; her wrists were a ruin of blood and blisters. Neela had probably spent most of her first day imprisoned here pulling against them, trying to get free.

"Do you remember the songs they used to sing to us?" Neela asked. Her voice was rough from blood and disuse, or perhaps, from screaming.

Lou's fingers paused. If Neela brought up "Scarborough Fair" here, in the pits of the market, Lou was going to scream. "They sang us many songs."

Raspily, quietly, Neela began to sing:

"'O what a bright, bright hill is yon,
That shines so clear to see?'
'O it is the hill of heaven,' he said,
'where you shall never be.'
'O what a black, dark hill is yon, that looks so dark to me?'"

Another voice cut in, dusky, like the smell of the scotch that Mom and May drank in the deep of winter.

"'O it is the hill of hell,' he said,
'Where you and I shall be.'"

Lou froze. She looked up to find Eitra in the middle of the room, face shadowed by her hood. She cursed her slowness, her clumsiness. After what the goblin girl had told her, she'd meant to do this *without* Eitra.

"Aye," Eitra said, answering a question neither of them had asked. "A market song, it is. From the days when the market traveled up all the way to Inverness and farther north, when we sailed to the Orkneys and back again."

Lou sat back on her knees. "Do you have the keys?" she asked. She didn't like the song they'd sung; she didn't like knowing it was a market song. She would not be stuck here on the shores of hell with Neela. She would drag them both back into the light, fighting all the way if she had to.

Eitra held up a silver key. Lou was about to ask for it when she tossed it. The key clattered to the ground in front of Lou.

"I don't know how much good it'll do," Eitra said. "Your kin smells of goblin blood already."

"My neck," Neela said, her voice hushed as if she'd already given up. "My neck has been burning all day."

Lou stopped fussing with the key to look at her neck. Sure enough, the pebbled skin around Neela's neck was nearly closed. Only a thin path of smooth brown skin bridged the gap.

"If it closes," Eitra said, "it will be a greater restraint than any binding or cuff."

Lou bit back her frustration, her anger. May had told her that if Lou got Neela back to the Witchery in time, they could find a solution. But the binds of the market were already closing around Neela's neck, and the Witchery and any antidotes were too far away. "What can I even *do*?" she asked, the words coming out in nearly a sob. She'd come so far, she'd nearly made it, only to be stopped now.

"You have to stop it or reverse it lest the market claim her. The only way to get her out after she's been claimed by the market is to kill the Market Prince."

Lou groaned and closed her eyes, leaning her forehead against Neela's shoulder. She had to think, which was nearly impossible to do with Neela's rough, panicked breathing and the gentle sounds of the jewels falling from Eitra's eyes.

"Is that ice I smell?" Eitra said, startling Lou. Lou's hands went to her pocket, where the shard dug into her thigh.

"Goblin ice?" Lou asked.

"Aye. It'll be enough. To break the market's hold, to get her free." Eitra's nostrils flared as she sniffed the air. Her face was unreadable, caught somewhere between distress and hope. "I've only seen it used once before—I had a piece, but lost it."

May had said it would be enough to freeze a goblin's heart—would it be enough to stop the progress of the skin? Lou scrambled for it, pulling it out of her pocket.

What if she caught an artery, or hit Neela's vocal cords, making her unable to speak? What if she really, really, hurt her? What if the goblin ice killed Neela?

What if she's trapped here forever?

Lou gritted her teeth together, getting a good hold on the shard. "Okay, Nee," she said, rubbing the spot of skin with her opposite thumb, making sure she knew exactly where to pierce. "This is going to hurt."

Neela eyed her. "Worse than everything else?" she asked.

It was a fair point.

Carefully but forcefully, Lou pressed the tip of the ice into the hollow of Neela's throat. Neela drew a sharp breath, pulling back, but Lou did not relent. She *could not* relent. She pushed the needle-like tip in until it was firmly lodged but probably, hopefully not hurting anything major. A perfect drop of blood slipped down Neela's throat, over her collarbone.

Lou looked in her eyes. "Can you breathe? Is it bearable?"

Neela's eyes were wide, wet with tears. "I can bear it," she said. But Lou knew it wasn't about what she could bear, it was what she had to.

Lou peered at her handiwork. The pebbled skin looked like it had blued on the edges, possibly even receded. "I think it's working," she said. She turned to Eitra before she could lose her nerve, before she could think too much about the story she'd been told.

"Do you have the antidote?" Lou asked. "To save Mom?"

Eitra nodded, either smiling or bearing her teeth; it was hard to tell the difference.

Lou took the key and unlocked Neela's restraints, trying to

be insouciant about the whole thing. "Great," she said through gritted teeth. Neela looked at her questioningly. Lou shook her head.

She didn't know what to do with Eitra. And if she wasn't careful, whatever curse had befallen Eitra could harm her and Neela too.

CHAPTER 29

HER BRAIN WENT IN CIRCLES AS THEY MADE THEIR WAY BACK TO the door. Without Eitra, she likely wouldn't be able to escape; if she brought Eitra out with them, then there would be trouble. Eitra had the antidote for Mom, so Lou couldn't leave her here in the market, no matter what she'd done; but, oh yes, *she'd eaten one of her own.*

All Lou wanted was five minutes alone with Neela, five minutes to figure out what the hell she was supposed to do. Best case scenario? They got out without Eitra but with the antidote. But how? Lou gritted her teeth. She was exhausted of games, of riddles and tricks. She just wanted to be *home.*

"We're going to look suspicious," Lou said, hesitating near the door to the room of lost things. She scanned over the three of them: Eitra in her cloak, looking more limber today than she had the day before; Neela, with her blood and dirty clothes and the ice half stuck through her neck; and Lou in her black garments with her hidden knives and probably murderous expression.

Eitra waved a hand, dismissing her worries. "I've haunted this market for longer than you've been alive," she said. "There are as many secret passages as there are traps."

Lou swallowed hard. She and Neela exchanged a glance. Lou

hadn't encountered any traps, but as much as she didn't want to trust Eitra, what she said made sense. Trickery was the nature of goblins, after all.

"If you insist," Lou said. She checked her watch. It was nearing two in the morning—she'd spent more time searching for Neela than she'd meant to. "But we have to move. Are you sure you want to lead?"

"What, because I don't have eyes?" Eitra turned back to Lou, and for a terrible second, it was almost like she was evaluating her. Like she could see after all. "I've also been blind longer than you've been alive, girl." She tapped the side of her head with one gnarled fingernail. "I've got other senses to rely on. More than you, human."

Lou didn't answer. It was better not to, so Eitra led the way out. Lou wrapped Neela's arm securely around her neck and helped her hobble up the stairs. Neela was breathing hard by the time they were even at the first step. Doubt darkened Lou's mind. Could Neela make it out on her own? Lou didn't know if she was strong enough to carry her.

They went up a flight, and then instead of straight up again, Eitra felt along the wall for a stone. Once she found it, she rapped on it three times with her elbow. A low door scraped open, half the height of the regular corridor.

They'd have to crawl.

Lou hated the idea of it, but Eitra had the antidote, and she was already hunched in the opening. The tunnel was dark and when Lou ducked down to peer inside, she couldn't see anything past the gloom.

"Are we really doing this?" Neela rasped. She looked like she was about to be sick.

Lou grimaced. "I'm not sure we have much of a choice." She glanced up the stairs, lit with torches. Far above, stone scraped against stone as something in the stairway shifted. "You go first, okay? I'll follow."

Lou helped Neela to her knees, then nearly pushed her into the tunnel. She made a low, uncomfortable moan as she crawled forward.

"Hurry, girl," Eitra snapped.

Lou frowned. She didn't like this, not one bit, but she had to trust that Eitra wanted out of the market more than she wanted to eat them.

Cursing this whole city, Lou lowered herself and crawled in after Neela. As soon as she cleared the entrance, the wall rumbled back into place, sealing them off. But Lou realized the darkness wasn't complete. Up ahead, nearly too far to see, there was a light in the distance.

The air in the tunnel was dry and awful, and in places the tunnel was so narrow that both arms and her back scraped against it. The gentle sound of jewels clattering on the ground from Eitra's eyes every few seconds accompanied Neela's pained grunts and Lou's own heavy breathing. She cut her hands on more than one of them as she crawled, sharp little gems that didn't even glimmer in the low light. She could just barely hear rumbles from the market every now and then, and her chest was tight with terror at the thought of the whole thing crumbling down on top of them.

"Eitra," Lou whisper-called, breaking the silence. "What is this?"

"Used to be a sewer," she said.

Lou gagged.

"Probably not for a while," Neela muttered. "And at least it doesn't smell like shit."

Well, she supposed that was fair. They were probably still crawling through centuries-old shit, but it was better than being flayed on the market floor.

An immeasurable amount of time later, they drew nearer to the light. It came from a staircase, Lou realized, leading up. She tried to assess how far they'd climbed. Had it been across the entire span of the market?

"And now we go up," Eitra said, crawling the first few steps until she had space to stand.

In the dim light, Neela looked even worse. Lou touched Neela's ankle as she started up the stairs. Neela looked back at her.

"Are you okay?" Lou asked. She jutted her chin upward, towards Eitra, still climbing. "Can you do this?"

Neela pursed her lips. "Do I have a choice?"

Another fair point. "Just think of the shower you'll have once we get out of here."

That garnered a small smile from her, the first Lou had seen from Neela. A surge of relief rushed through her. They could do this. They could be free, and maybe Nana Tee would know what to do about Eitra.

They followed Eitra up, up, up. Unlike the stairway Lou had taken to Neela's holding place, this one had no splits, no landings, no diversions. It spiraled upward in high, tricky steps. Neela had to take a break every few minutes to catch her breath, but slowly they made progress. If Eitra was impatient with the two of them, she didn't show it. Every time she heard their shuffling steps stop behind her, she, too, paused.

"So," Lou said. "The antidote. What is it? What happened to Mom?"

Neela had to stop again. Lou stood beside her, helping her stay upright, running one hand up and down Neela's back for comfort. Above them, Eitra waited.

"It was an old curse," Eitra said. "Meant for market traitors. It doesn't hold her captive here, but her body belongs to the market. As long as she is away from it, she will rot from the inside out."

Lou shuddered. That explained the awful blackish lines of Mom's veins and the green tint of her skin. But how far had it progressed? Could they still save her? "And what's the antidote?"

Eitra grimaced. "Goblin blood. The juice of seven goblin pomegranate seeds. And a lock of hair from the Market Prince."

Lou felt cold dread in the pit of her stomach. According to the goblin girl, Eitra had eaten a previous Market Prince. Did she do the same to this one?

"And you managed to get all of that?" Lou asked.

Eitra shrugged. "Not easily." Her lips split into an awful smile. One of the feathers floated down and got stuck on her lip. "Now come. We're nearly to the Inbetween. From there, we'll take a back stair that diverts around the market floor."

Lou couldn't imagine Neela's agony as they kept climbing up. Her breathing grew more labored, and her hand clutched at smooth stone on the wall. Lou climbed close after her, one hand out and poised to catch Neela if she fell.

They came out in that cavernous room full of columns, the one with the table where Eitra had hidden the night before.

"It's easier from here," Eitra said, already starting across the expanse. Lou glanced over at Neela. She was sickly and pale, gaunt from her days in the market. Lou wasn't sure how much farther she could make it.

"Oh! Isn't this fun!"

The voice came from the shadow of one of the pillars. Lou could only just make out a glint of silver before the goblin girl stepped into the light.

It was the girl from above, the one in the chainmail dress. Lou felt sick. She was so foolish—of course the girl knew what she was here for. Wasn't that how she'd tried to lure Lou here in the first place? And she'd only made it worse by talking to her about Eitra.

Eitra moved faster than Lou thought she could, putting herself in front of the girls. It was oddly protective—oddly in conflict with what Lou knew of goblins.

"Good eve, Hilgar," she said, her voice detached.

Hilgar. The name was familiar. Lou wracked her brain trying to remember. Beside her, Neela drew a sharp breath. She reached down and squeezed Lou's hand.

Why would she have heard a goblin's name? Unless . . .

Well, shit. Apparently "Market Prince" was a gender-neutral title.

"Are you that eager for another sentence?" Hilgar said, drawing closer. She spoke only to Eitra, her eyes glittering in the low light. "Do you want to see what new punishment I can find for you? Is a full year of solitude, of starvation not enough?"

To her credit, Eitra didn't cower under Hilgar's gaze. Lou probably would, in her position.

"We have to go," Neela whispered to her, so quietly it was almost as if Lou had thought the words herself.

"Eitra has the antidote," Lou muttered back, despairing. She took stock of the doorways around them. There was no way to tell if any of them led out or if all went to the market floor.

There was the sound of metal on metal—Hilgar had drawn a sword. "It's pathetic, how much you want to be a witchling," she said, easing closer to the three of them. "They don't want you. They never wanted you. Why do you think they left you here to rot?"

Eitra doubled over, hacking something up. Before she could stop herself, Lou lurched forward to help her. It was instinctual.

There was blood coming from Eitra's mouth. Blood and coins and bones and pomegranate seeds. She grabbed Lou's hand when she was close, forcing something into it. A vial of some sort, splattered with the sappy blood from Eitra's mouth.

The antidote.

Only a few feet away now, Hilgar laughed as blood trickled from Eitra's empty eye sockets. Eitra tripped forward, catching herself on Lou's shoulder. Lou tried not to gag as sticky blood soaked her shirt.

"The staircase with the skull over it," Eitra muttered, the words garbled around whatever she was choking on now. A coin slipped down the back of Lou's shirt, slick with blood. "Run. Straight up. Don't stop."

She pushed Lou away, back toward Neela, and coughed hard. Lou staggered back, grabbing Neela's hand, as Eitra coughed and coughed and coughed.

Hilgar pointed a taloned finger at Lou and Neela. "I'm not done with you yet, witchlings," she said. "Tonight we shall feast on——"

Her voice broke off into a scream as Eitra launched forward, biting hard into the Market Prince's neck.

"Come on!" Lou grabbed Neela's hand and raced away, scanning the staircases. There—the one with the skull above wasn't far. She glanced back to see Eitra still latched onto Hilgar, her claws digging into the girl's face and arm. But Hilgar wasn't going down easily. She'd drawn a knife and was bringing it down, down, down—

Lou turned away, clenching the antidote in her fist. She hauled Neela up the stairs, struggling to bear the majority of Neela's weight. Lou was running on her last reserves of adrenaline. They passed a landing to the market floor, but Lou didn't even look. She just raced up, up, up, ignoring the ache of her muscles. Her ears rang—or maybe she could still hear Hilgar or Eitra screaming below.

At the top of the stairs, there was a heavy wooden door. They pushed through it and found themselves in a storeroom. Lou could make out the shape of wooden rocking horses in one corner and boxes of dolls in another. They were in the back room of a toy shop.

"Fuck," Neela hissed, letting the door shut behind her and falling against it. *"Fuck."*

"We've got to keep moving," Lou insisted, grabbing her hand and pulling her forward. She didn't care what alarms she tripped, what CCTV videos she showed up on. She scrabbled at the door, managed to open it, and pulled Neela out onto the street.

The rain was a drizzle, clinging to their clothes. Neela was breathing hard, possibly on the verge of a panic attack. Lou dropped her head back and gazed at the stars.

CHAPTER 30
May

Eighteen Years Earlier

SHE CAME BACK INTO CONSCIOUSNESS THINKING OF SACRIFICE and sisterhood, and maybe a little of Eitra too. There was cold, damp grass under her cheek. May wasn't certain where she was, but at least it wasn't the market. She felt the press of her scratchy T-shirt and jeans—the clothes Iark had glamoured into a ballgown returned to their natural state after their escape and now clung to her skin, torn and stiff with blood.

Eitra and Laura hovered over her, in and out of focus. She realized that Eitra was chewing something, every now and then pulling thick, green saliva out of her mouth and applying it to May's forehead.

Hazily, she remembered she'd *been* here before. She'd seen this, in a dream or a nightmare, soaked with blood.

May made a noise of disgust.

"It's my turn to spit on you," Eitra said tenderly, applying more plant saliva.

But it did feel better, May realized, as if the weird spit-plant-situation was leeching the pain from May's body. She felt the same cooling effect on her feet, now bare, and her side, where her shirt had been pulled up to show her broken ribs.

"What are you doing?" May slurred. Her tongue felt too big in her mouth.

"Magic, innit," Laura said. She sat on her butt, knees tented in front of her body. She looked exhausted.

"Are you a witch now, then?" May asked.

Laura didn't meet her eye. "No." She didn't elaborate.

May sat up, allowing Eitra to help her. "Thank you," she said to her, but she wasn't sure what exactly she was thanking her for. Blinking away the last of the confusion, May was able to decipher that they were Dean's Park, near the hulking shadow of the Minster, in the bit near the Old Palace. She understood why there were here. On the other side of the Old Palace was the four-square of false stone path that lifted, revealing the tunnels that led to the tunnels to the Witchery. Perhaps Laura had brought them here with the intent to seek the Witchery, then aborted the mission when she remembered Eitra wouldn't make it past the wards.

Awkwardness settled over the three of them. May stared at her hands, still marred with blood. She'd done it, though she'd had so little strength. She'd killed Iark, the Market Prince; she'd forged the path to their escape.

But she wouldn't have made it out of the market if Eitra hadn't carried her. May didn't know if she was supposed to hug Eitra or accuse her, if she wanted to thank Laura or curse her for coming after her in the first place.

It was good that Laura broke the silence. "Eitra came to find me," she said haltingly, offering an answer to the questions May hadn't asked. "She told me where you were. What they did to you."

This surprised May. The last time she'd seen Eitra before the fight, she'd had been with Iark, deadly and threatening as May sat chained in the Inbetween, waiting to die.

"Why?" May asked.

Eitra shrugged, evasive. "You came back because of me. Didn't you?"

The answer was too close to home. Yes, she'd gone back for Eitra, to make her jealous or win her back, to say goodbye. She'd gone back because Eitra had sent her away so easily, had made May feel worthless when she forced her out of the market. Because she needed to prove to herself that something had existed between them.

"It doesn't matter," May said bitterly. "You're going back now and I'll never see you again." *You told Iark what I am,* she didn't say. *I love you, and you nearly killed me.*

Eitra sat back on her heels, looking like she'd had the wind knocked out of her. "I can't go back," she said.

Laura and May stared at her. "You can't?" Laura asked finally.

Eitra shook her head. She looked so lost, so forlorn. May had always thought Eitra was infallible, but clearly that wasn't true.

"I've betrayed my own kind," Eitra said. She shrugged. "The market runs on blood. Yours, mine. Human and goblin alike. If I go back, after what I've done to help you escape—"

"You barely broke the rules," Laura protested. "You didn't kill anyone."

"I helped an assassin escape," Eitra said. "You're now untouchable, out of the reach of the market. But I am not. If they find me or if I return, they will kill me."

May stared at her, something clenching and burning in her chest. She wondered if, all over again, her heart was breaking.

"What will you do, then?" May asked.

Stay.

Stay here. With me.

Eitra looked up at the great round moon, as if to ask it where she could go. "I don't know," she answered honestly. Blood still crusted over her thorns, her cheekbones. May wondered what she'd been doing before she carried her out of the market. Had she been feasting like the rest of the goblins?

Did saving May erase all the terrible things Eitra had done as Iark's second? Did she need human flesh to survive? How would she even function?

"The market is all I've ever had," Eitra said.

What could they say? That they could give her more?

There was Mum to contend with, who probably wouldn't take well to housing a goblin, and did Eitra even want to go with them?

Once, on a night that felt ages ago, May and Eitra had talked about all the ways they could escape, could leave this town and run away together. Then, it had seemed like an impossibility, but now, May could almost smell the wildflowers growing around a cottage far away.

Maybe Eitra didn't have to be a goblin here, a relic of the market. Maybe May didn't have to be a witch.

"Come with us," Laura said, so May wouldn't have to.

Eitra looked between them. "For tonight, at least," she agreed hesitantly. "To make sure you recover, May."

May nodded. It was sensible, even if it made her long to be able to ask for more than that.

Eitra gently wiped the green mixture off May's skin with a torn shirtsleeve and they prepared to walk home. May thought she caught the hint of a shadow moving under one of the trees across the park, but she couldn't be sure.

May could mostly hobble on her own now, thanks to Eitra's treatment, but she kept between Eitra and Laura as they made their way over to the path. She marveled at the night, cold and crisp, the outside world she never thought she'd see again.

They were nearing the Witchery when Eitra tensed. "Wait," she whispered.

"What is it?" May asked. Something within her was coming awake, some sense of déjà vu growing stronger. The hair prickled on the back of her neck.

But she didn't need to, really, because they all saw the same thing. Goblins, on the drive that led to College Street, toward home.

Waiting for them.

Three goblins leaned against the wall of the Minster Yard. May glanced over her shoulder. They could double back across the park, but they'd already been seen.

"The Witchery?" Laura asked, somewhat hopelessly.

May pressed her lips together. There, they'd be safe, but what about Eitra?

"Eitra." But the voice did not come from the group in front of them.

She whirled, nearly knocking May over. There, fanned along the park behind them, were three more goblins.

They'd been ambushed.

May tasted bile. They hadn't escaped, not really. How could they ever escape something that horrible? They might never put it behind them, and it was all her fault.

"Eitra," the goblins called. They were taking their time,

spreading out, sauntering closer. Eitra's hand tightened on May's.

Eitra closed her eyes tight, and May saw the shimmer of tears on her cheeks. Her thorns cast long shadows over her temples.

"What do we do?" Laura asked uncertainly. There was no way they could run. The goblins would catch them. They were faster, stronger. Hungry.

And they seemed in no hurry. The goblins closed in at a leisurely pace. Moonlight winked off one of their knives. May swallowed hard. She understood what they were conveying, what the goblins were doing.

May, Laura, Eitra—there was no way out. They were at the goblins' mercy.

"We'll make you a deal," the sharp-toothed one with the knife said. He was all edges, like Eitra when May had first seen her unglamoured. "You surrender to us, Traitor, and we'll let the humans go free."

"No," May hissed, clutching Eitra's hand. There had to be a better way out, something they could do, something that made sense. She tried to catch Laura's eye, but her sister would not look at her.

Eitra shook her head, wiping tears away. The goblins were coming closer, closer, closer. "Keep eyes on them, Laura," Eitra said. Her expression shifted into something new and awful.

"Come back to the market," another goblin crooned. He swung a mace lazily back and forth in front of him. "Tonight, we'll feast on our own."

"A choice, Eitra," Knife Goblin said. He seemed to be the leader. May could hardly breathe, panic pressed so tight against her chest. "Come with us, or we shall crack all of your bones tonight."

This was not the frantic, bloody battle they'd fought before. This was slow and slick, the goblins in their trickster mode. They were teasing, taunting, tormenting. May thought of Eitra coming to see her in the Inbetween, of her claws on May's collarbone, of the laughing tilt to her voice. She stole a glance at her. Had she been this, sometime before? Had she been in a hunting party just like this?

The idea made her sick.

But no—that was not Eitra, not the Eitra she knew. Not Eitra in control of her own choices.

"Go," Eitra said, teeth gritted, resolute. "Get out of here."

"May, the Witche—"

"*No,*" she insisted, ignoring Laura's suggestion.

"Stay then, human," Mace Goblin crooned as the circle grew ever tighter around them.

Something hit May hard in the cheek. She gasped, drawing back, but it was only a mushy, rotten peach. Goblin fruit. The goblin who'd thrown it cackled into the night.

"Don't you want to come play, human?" the tallest goblin said, breaking the circle to come within reaching distance.

"They're not yours," Eitra snarled, lunging.

The tall goblin lashed out with a serrated whip, barbs biting into Eitra's skin. She cried out.

May grabbed Eitra, pulling her back between her and Laura. She could just see Laura out of the corner of her eye, squaring off, knives drawn. May put her hands on Eitra's shoulders, disregarding the thorns to turn her toward her, forcing her to meet May's eye.

Eitra lifted her hand and cupped May's face, claws digging into her skin. Her voice was fervent. "I will find you," Eitra promised. "In this world or another, in this lifetime or the next. I will find you, May. I promise it." Her voice was thick with tears, impossible.

May shook her head, gripping harder. Eitra didn't understand. She couldn't just—she couldn't just *give up.* "You can't. We will get out." Behind her, Laura was as tense as piano wire, gearing to fight. Again.

Because of May.

It was an awful thing to know that she was at the center of this, to know she could not fight, could not escape, could not abandon. That she had to stand tall and face the worst of the consequences.

As if she could hear May's thoughts, Eitra's eyes were wet and dewy. "It's what I deserve," she said softly, so quietly May almost didn't hear, "for what I've done. I told you I couldn't break my promises."

Eitra pulled her in and kissed her, hard. Her other hand moved down, grabbing May's. Then she pulled away.

"Eitra," the goblins crooned. It was a suffocating susurrus, the voices tripping over one another, all repeating her name over and over again. It made it impossible for May to *think.*

Eitra's fingers danced across one of the chains May wore around her neck. It took May a second to realize that she was touching the goblin ice on its chain, clean of Iark's blood, cool against her chest.

May lifted her hand and gripped the ice. "Don't let them take you again," Eitra said.

She pressed it into May's hand. "Don't let them take you again," she said.

May clenched it tight in her palm, feeling it press into the abrasions from Eitra's thorns.

"May, we've gotta go," Laura hissed, grabbing May's bicep.

Eitra pressed her hand to May's cheek. "Go," she said. May stared into Eitra's awful green eyes, unglamoured, waiting for the world to end.

She'd been here before. She'd done this.

The goblins laughed; the moon watched over the shadows of the Minster. May clawed against Laura as her sister grabbed her, dragged her out of the encroaching circle of goblins and across the park, as Laura scrabbled for the stone that lifted to reveal the tunnel to the Witchery. May fought and screamed, yelled for Eitra, even as a goblin boy drew out a twisted onyx knife and took it to one of her eyes.

"No!" May shrieked.

Her arm ached as Laura pulled her down. A girl in the grass. Three goblins above her. If May watched any longer, she'd see the spurt of blood against the darkness just like she'd dreamt—just like she'd seen.

Laura slammed the door before May could see any more, slicing Eitra's scream down the middle. They were surrounded by stale, dusty air, and the half-heard scream echoed in May's ears.

May turned on her, fists pounding into Laura's chest. She shouted every curse word, every awful thing she could think of, as Laura dragged her farther down the tunnel into the cold stone confines of the Witchery.

Mum and Joss were already there, waiting, with a poultice. May crumpled to the ground. There were no windows, no ways to see what was happening. But she knew what there would be: a smear of goblin blood, black in the night, and a shred of Eitra's shirt. Not that it mattered.

She was gone. They had taken her back to the market, to her death.

There were hands on her shoulders and in her hair, but May did not see them. She did not hear the voices that murmured over her.

Eitra was dead and May was not.

Eitra was dead, and May could not move, could not breathe, could not think over the echoes of Eitra's screaming. She couldn't stop hearing it, the sound ricocheting off her brain.

Eitra was dead and it was all May's fault.

CHAPTER 31

SLOWLY AND WEARILY, THEY MADE THEIR WAY BACK TO THE Witchery. Lou was certain there'd be goblins sent after them, but either they didn't know that Neela was gone and Hilgar was harmed, or they didn't care.

Neela was quiet all the way, as if the strength had been leeched out of her. Lou didn't blame her. After all, she'd spent days chained to a wall and now she had a needle in her throat, just barely keeping her alive. Halfway back, Lou realized she was holding the bloody vial. She tucked it into her pocket, where she had less chance of dropping it.

But eventually, they made it. Lou pulled up a stone and helped Neela down the stairs, using the last store of her strength to get her down the tunnel. She barely remembered pushing open the door, May pulling them inside, Nana Tee weeping over Neela, the joyous reunion of all of them. She knew she set the green antidote bottle on the table, but she couldn't remember doing it.

She just picked her way through the main room to the back hall, brushing May off, and let herself into her mother's room. In here, it was cool and silent. Lou let herself fall to her knees at her mother's side, let herself break. She grabbed Mom's hand, burning hot.

"Lou?"

She didn't look up at May, hovering in the doorway. It didn't matter. May came to her, laid her hand on Lou's back. "What is it? What happened?"

Lou shook her head. What had happened? She saved Neela. She brought back the antidote to save Mom. So why did she feel so incredibly awful?

Eitra had saved them. Maybe that was the problem. It felt like some sort of prank, a goblin trick, and Lou couldn't wrap her head around why she'd done it.

It just didn't make sense.

And worse: Lou had just let her. She'd left Eitra behind.

There were rules to the market, rules to her life, rules for her personal brand of kindness. She hadn't broken market rules: she had not killed any goblins nor had she overstayed her welcome, and since she'd made Neela whole again with the goblin ice, she hadn't taken anything of theirs. Nana Tee and May wouldn't have sent her after Neela otherwise.

And she hadn't trusted Eitra either, following her own set of rules. But even if she hadn't fully trusted Eitra, Eitra had, for some reason, sacrificed for *her*. Eitra had told her how to save Neela, had found the antidote for Mom. All she'd wanted was her freedom.

What if Hilgar had lied to Lou? And even if she hadn't, why did it matter? Eitra had shown kindness to Lou, mercy Lou didn't deserve.

Before she knew it, she was crying, tears pouring out and burning the raw skin of her face. May crouched next to her, shushing and rocking her, but Lou just couldn't stop.

Because even though Eitra was a goblin and a traitor, Lou

had left her there to die. There was something so awful about it, of the damp of Eitra's blood on her and the terribleness of the sticky coin in her shirt and the ache of her wounds and her heart.

Eitra had helped her. Even though Lou had reasons for not helping Eitra in return, leaving her the way she did made her feel terrible.

"Hush, now, love," May said into her hair. "It's over. It's done."

Lou only cried harder, clutching May. It was over. It was over. It was over.

But it was the market, fierce and terrible and alive. It would never really be over. And if the coven dissolved after Joss and Nana Tee, if all the magic faded, it would grow and grow and consume everything in this city.

CHAPTER 32

L OU DID NOT WAKE UP ENTANGLED WITH N EELA OR TO THE NEW
dawn of a better day. She woke on the floor beside her mother's
sickbed, still gritty from the market, the door half-open. In the
other room, she could hear Joss and May, possibly arguing.

Lou sat up. Everything ached. She knew she should check on
Neela, or do anything other than stay here on the floor, but the
future tasted bitter on her tongue.

She looked at Mom. All her lacerations from the market
had scabbed over. They looked to be in the process of healing.
Everything, it seemed, was healing, except for the wound that
mattered. The wound that poisoned her.

Lou dragged herself out to the main room. The antidote
sat on the middle of the table, surrounded by gauze pads and
syringes. May and Joss sat, eating and drinking tea and reading
the paper, as Nana Tee brewed something in a great pot. Neela
was probably still asleep.

Lou slid into a chair. She felt nearly as bad as she had last
night, but May didn't question her on it. Joss only offered her a
kind smile and pushed a fresh box of croissants over to her.

"You did well, love," Nana Tee said, coming over to kiss Lou
on the forehead.

Lou shrugged. She couldn't fight the feeling that she'd somehow failed. Maybe this was just the dread of the market. It was possible the feeling would never really leave her.

"Why haven't you given the antidote to Mom yet?" she asked around a mouthful of croissant.

"We did. Just a tiny test dose, to make sure it worked," Joss said. "It did. There was a small improvement in the wound, and we're about to administer the second dose now."

Lou nodded, relieved. So it had worked after all.

"We'd best do it now," Nana Tee said, banging her spoon on the pot. "I have to go back to the Gulliver boy in a few hours. He ate an entire persimmon." She sighed, shaking her head. "Going to need to spend most of the night with that one."

They made their way into the sickroom like a funeral procession. Lou leaned on the sharp edge of the wardrobe and watched as Joss carefully peeled away the dressings on Mom's wound. It was sticky with blood, blacked with rot and infection except for one small spot that shone pink and new. Mom's ribcage looked necrotic, like something was eating the flesh from inside out.

Lou looked away. She couldn't bear it.

But there was a murmur as the full syringe was handed over, an intake of breath as Joss injected Mom with it.

Lou squeezed her eyes shut. *Please, please, please . . .*

Nana Tee sucked in a breath. "It's working."

It was like everything came out of Lou at once. She made a noise, somewhere between a whimper and a cough, and buried her face in her arms.

It was over. It was finished. She would never have to go to the market again.

Lou went back to the apartment with Neela to shower, half because she was worried about Neela passing out on the way there, and half because she was also disgusting with dust and grime.

After her shower, Lou dressed in jeans and one of Neela's T-shirts, featuring a cricketer with the phrase *I swing both ways*. It didn't actually make sense to her since she'd resisted all cricket chat whenever possible, but it was soft and comfortable and Lou loved it all the same. She made a cup of tea and settled on the couch to wait for Neela, scrolling through her phone to answer Dad's many texts and a few from Gen and scrolling through social media to see what her classmates were up to.

It was oddly surreal, this reminder that other people had normal lives like Lou did only weeks before. Lives without the market, without blood. Without the need for folk songs and herbs and salt.

Neela emerged from the bathroom in a cloud of floral-scented steam. She was sniffly and red; she'd been crying in the shower, Lou figured. Lou's eyes went to the patch of skin around Neela's throat. It was dry and scratchy, scabbed over, but the traces of goblin skin were fading and the ice was gone. May or Nana Tee had it, or maybe Joss. She scooted to one side of the couch and patted it to have Neela sit down.

"You shouldn't have come for me," Neela said, not taking her up on her invitation.

It wasn't worth responding to. Of course Lou had come for her. There was no other choice.

Neela's eyes traced across the trunk where Nana Tee kept her herbs, the hangings on the wall, a picture that Lou now realized captured the witches in Nana's coven. "I can't be inside during daylight. Not now. Will you come walking with me?"

"Of course," Lou said. "Where do you want to go?"

"Have you been to the walls yet?"

Lou shook her head. There hadn't been much time for exploring. And it was good that they'd be away from the others for a while, out where Lou could ask Neela her questions.

It took a few minutes for Neela to dress in black jeans and a white T-shirt and pull her black hair into a braid, then another few as they slowly walked to one of the staircases leading up to the walls. Lou didn't miss how Neela hesitated, how difficult it was for her to get up the stairs with her injuries even after Joss had treated the worst of them.

"We don't have to do this," Lou said.

Neela didn't bother to answer that.

They made it to the top and Lou gazed out over the city, surrounded by the wall. The height offered a great view of the Minster but also of the workings of the city. Here, Lou could see into people's back gardens and the outdoor seating areas of pubs and restaurants. Normal people milled about, conversing and laughing and drinking as if they had no idea of the devastation occurring underneath their feet. And maybe they didn't.

She read a plaque about the Romans. The words barely made sense in the jumble of her brain.

Neela seemed to benefit from the breeze that glided over the ancient stone, blowing tendrils of her still-damp hair over her head. She gripped the wall every now and then, either to help her with moving or to ground her.

"Neela?"

"Hmm?"

"Why did you go?"

It was the question that had plagued Lou. Neela had been raised here, in the shadow of the market and the watch of the coven. She'd known the rules and the risks and yet she'd gone all the same.

"One of my friends wanted to," Neela said, looking away toward the Minster. "She said I didn't have to go. But I was—" Here, Neela paused, swallowing hard. They came to a rounded expansion in the wall. Lou leaned against the old stone, gazing out, waiting.

Neela leaned her head against Lou's shoulder. "I was trained," she said, almost in a whisper. "I was sure it would be okay, that *we* would be okay, because I knew what to do. So we went and it was fun and a bit scary, and then she brought another friend and we went again, and she promised not to go the third day, but she did. So I went after her."

Lou didn't want to ask the next question, but she had to. "Did they take both of you? Or did she get out?"

"I don't know," Neela confessed.

All Lou could think of was that horrible room of bodies, the ones she could possibly identify and the ones she couldn't. "Do you have a picture?"

Neela nodded. She pulled out her phone and scrolled through her camera roll, past laughing shots with her friends in the grass of the Museum Gardens and shots of them in school uniforms with skirts hiked too high on their thighs. Lou felt a surge of jealousy, but it didn't have the same bite it used to when she thought of Neela's other life. Now she knew the truth of it, some part of it. The secrets were unveiled.

Neela brought up a picture of her friend. The girl was white, with curly white-blond hair and a dusting of freckles over her nose. Bright blue eyes. Lou had seen those same eyes, dead and staring at nothing.

It was the girl from the table, the girl from the butchery in the shiny silver dress. The one missing her bottom half.

For an awful moment, Lou thought she was going to be sick.

Neela must've caught the change in Lou's breathing, some hitch, some giveaway. She pulled her head up and looked at Lou, scanning her face. "Did you see her?" she asked, breathless.

Lou could only grimace. What was there to say? She couldn't tell Neela the details. But she had to tell her the truth. "I did," she said.

Neela's face fell, taking in Lou's drawn, sad expression. "Oh," she said. She sagged against the wall, leaning on her elbows. "Oh."

"I'm so sorry," Lou said. She wasn't sure what else there was to say. Words evaded her, but the image of the girl's body stuck in her mind.

A muscle in Neela's jaw flexed. "No," she said. "I mean, it's not okay. It's fucking awful and I don't know what I'm going to do and—" She caught herself, her nails scratching against the old stone. "We were supposed to go to uni together. In Glasgow. We were supposed to leave this all behind."

Lou nodded, uncertain what to say. This was an unreliable, awful sort of grief, unexpected and too soon.

"What was her name?" Lou asked.

"Charlotte," Neela murmured.

Lou wrapped an arm around Neela, and Neela leaned her

head back on Lou's shoulder. She didn't cry. Perhaps it was from guilt or shame or exhaustion, or perhaps Neela wasn't ready to cry until it was over and finished, until the market was gone for good.

Mom finally woke up just before the Minster bells rang for 3:00 p.m. They'd moved her back out to the couch, where she was easier to monitor. Lou and Neela sat on the ground, wrapped in blankets, watching a movie on an ancient battery-powered DVD player that May had found in one of the drawers. They had the same catatonic, exhausted mood. May was at the kitchen table, washing and sharpening the weapons Lou had taken into the market. Joss had left to report back to another coven, and Nana Tee read the paper she'd abandoned.

Mom came to in a sharp breath, eyes opening blearily. Lou was on her hands and knees, moving before anyone else could react. She crawled to the edge of the couch and grabbed Mom's hand.

Mom's breathing was unsteady as she looked around her, like she was searching for something. She looked at Lou, then May, then Neela—and then she sat up, wincing at the pain in her ribs.

"Eitra," she croaked, her voice raspy and barely there.

Lou looked behind her. May was pale, paler than she'd been even when Mom came in half dead. "What?" she said.

Mom coughed, wincing harder. "You're hurt," Lou started, laying a gentle hand on the wrappings, trying to get Mom to lay down again. But she only shook her head, running a hand through her sleep-matted hair.

"Eitra's there," she said, a little stronger. "She's alive. She's in the market."

CHAPTER 33

It only made sense, Lou thought, sipping at a too-hot cup of tea, that it would come to this. That they'd be assembled all over again, planning all over again, to go back within the market to save one of their own.

But not a witch. No, it just so happened that they were planning to go back to save a goblin.

"I'm going to be honest," Neela said. She was clean, wearing a pair of leggings and an oversized black sweatshirt, chewing on her nails from her perch on the windowsill. "This doesn't sound like a good idea. And if Lou's right, and Eitra's the same goblin who helped us, I can't guarantee she . . . well, she got into it with the Market Prince. I don't know if she's even still down there."

May made some sort of noise that Lou had never heard from her before. Mom only sighed. She was holding a cold compress to her head. Apparently, a headache was the only side effect remaining from her injuries and the magical healing.

"It's far too dangerous, and the market ends tonight," Nana Tee said. "There isn't anything else that can be done about it."

"Tell me what you saw," May said, ignoring her mother. For a second, Lou thought she was talking to her, but no, she was focused on Mom.

Mom rubbed her eyes with her other hand. "I have a very limited grasp on what happened. But I went through one of the lesser-known entrances to the market, through the cellar of The Thorne and Crown. I made it into the market without much notice, but I got stopped in the Inbetween."

The name of the room sent a chill down Lou's spine. She and Neela exchanged a glance—all Lou could think of was that skeleton, and how it could've been her mother.

"There were three of them. I tried to fight my way out, but—" Mom shrugged. "One of them bit me. The fucker. And that's when Eitra came. At first I didn't realize it was her, but she told them that I was hers, and to back off, lest she'd eat the lot of them."

Eat the lot of them. Like Hilgar said Eitra had done. All over again, Lou saw Eitra's teeth sinking into Hilgar's flesh. An odd, creeping dread started in Lou's stomach. "Is it normal for goblins to . . . cannibalize one another?"

Nana Tee shrugged. "Not unheard of, but they prefer humans."

"But you said it was Eitra," May snapped, clearly annoyed they'd gotten off topic. "Are you sure?"

"She . . . she helped me through the market," Mom said, staring off into space. "I wouldn't have made it on my own. But she promised . . ." Mom looked away, swallowing hard. "She promised to look after Neela. Until one of us could come back."

And she had. She'd waited for Lou, then helped her through the market, and Lou had just left her there.

But why had she been willing to sacrifice herself? How did the others know her? Something came into horrifying clarity in Lou's mind. "But who is Eitra?" she asked.

There was a long pause. Nana Tee cleared her throat and went back to the stove, where she was working on another day's worth of potions.

"She saved us from the market the first time," Mom said, but Lou knew her well enough to know that wasn't the whole truth.

Lou sat, rapt, as May told the story: How she met the goblin and allowed herself to be lured in, how she came to care about Eitra even though she knew she shouldn't. She told them of Mom's fight with Iark, the Market Prince, and how Eitra got them out in the end. And then, haltingly, she told them of how Eitra was cornered and captured—how they thought she died.

"But they must have cursed her," Mom said, "and gouged out her eyes."

A fight with the Market Prince, one that ended in his death, one that began with the goblin girl stealing his prize. Gouged out eyes. A punishment. There was no way the similarities were a coincidence.

Lou felt sick to her stomach.

"Why didn't she say anything to me?" Lou said, despairing. They could've saved her. They were so close to saving her—if only her own fear hadn't gotten in the way. If only she had just trusted the goblin.

"Maybe she can't," Neela said, chewing on her thumbnail.

Nana Tee was watching May. She sighed, setting the water to boil. "I know what you're going to say," she said. "Think twice before you do."

May was up on her feet, back to pacing. "If Eitra's alive, I have to go back to her."

"But the baby—" Nana Tee started.

"She's right," Mom said, clearly exasperated. "Obviously

the market has become torturous to her. We can't just leave her there." She looked at Neela, at Lou and May, then back at Nana Tee. "Without Eitra, none of us would've survived the market."

Nana Tee shook her head. "That could be true, but what are we going to do? It's the last day of the market. *You* can't go."

"I'll go," May said, resolved.

"Think of the baby," Nana Tee snapped.

It was a dreadful, horrible thing. But Lou knew—she gritted her teeth even as she thought of it, as she remembered the oppressive smell of rot—she *knew* she was the only one with a chance. "I have a day left," she said. "And it's not like they can keep me longer on the last day of the market. I'll go and get her. It's my fault we didn't save her in the first place."

It was a wrong she had to correct. She'd let her fear overrule her good sense, her desire to help. And she'd left Eitra behind.

Mom shook her head. "That's not fair," she said. "Just because they can't keep you, it doesn't mean they can't hurt you. I'll go."

"You're still healing," Lou protested. "And Neela isn't fully healed from the goblin skin. Who knows if she'll be okay going back? I'm the only one who can do it. Joss and Nana Tee are witches, so they can't go. You and Neela are healing and have already pissed them off. You have to let me go. I'll be in and out, quickly. If it's the last day of the market, surely there will be something else there to distract them."

"I don't know," Nana Tee said, uncertain.

Lou got up. They were wasting time debating it. The sky outside was already darkening and May looked like she was about to jump out of her skin. "You agree with me, don't you?" she asked.

May bit her lip. "There aren't any other choices."

"Then I'll get ready," Lou said, slipping back to don her black clothes, her knives, her iron—but this time, she did it with an odd sort of glee.

This was her duty as a Wickett, as the granddaughter of a witch. She'd been born into this, just as she'd been born to be stubborn like her mother.

Lou glanced up to see Nana Tee watching her. Though she'd worn her smock, some of the blood from a patient had seeped through, blotching her white shirt with blood. She wore it like it was a normal thing to do.

"I'll be okay," Lou promised.

"I know," Nana Tee said. The corner of her mouth tipped up into a smile. "Don't forget your rosemary and thyme, witchling."

In the end, May went with her. "To show her The Thorne and Crown," May said, avoiding eye contact, "and to wait, in case she needs help getting back. No more." But Lou noticed what May shoved in her pockets.

"Will you wait for me outside?" Lou asked as they walked down the streets. It was raining tonight, not terribly, but a persistent drizzle that clung to Lou's hair and eyelashes.

"Kind of." She opened the bag, pulling out a woolen cloak. She pushed the bag towards Lou and swept the cloak over her shoulders.

"What are you doing?"

May looked at her evenly. "Did you really think I'd let you go alone this time?"

Lou raised an eyebrow. "You shouldn't, May. There's the baby to think about. And I'll be fine—seriously, I'll run in, get her, and run out."

"I don't think it'll be that easy," May said. She steered Lou through the Shambles. Lou was so rarely on these streets, never by herself. She wondered if they were actually confusing or they just felt that way to her. York was not big. Perhaps in another time, another life, she would've learned the turns and alleys in a day. Perhaps she'd come back and learn them in earnest, without fear.

May led the way into the pub. It wasn't crowded, but it wasn't empty, either. May certainly looked out of place in her cloak, and Lou was pretty sure the bulge of one of her knives was showing. She pressed a self-conscious hand against her thigh to cover it before anyone saw.

May went right up to the bar. She leaned her arm against it, her mouth promising mischief but her eyes as dark and hard as flint. A young girl with a red ponytail came over.

"Hiya, y'alright?"

"We're here to investigate something," May said, leaning closer. The girl looked taken aback. "An infestation? In the cellar?"

Realization dawned on the girl's face as she took in the clothes they wore and the look on May's face. "Um, I'm not sure we're . . . allowing amateurs in."

May smiled, the edges wicked in a way Lou did not expect her aunt to be. Ever. But perhaps this was the May the market unlocked, the girl who snuck in, the girl who killed a prince, the girl who would sacrifice everything.

"We are not amateurs," she said. May moved her cape off the arm she had draped over the bar, revealing an iron spike strapped to her forearm.

How had Lou not *noticed* that?

Either way, the display worked. The girl nodded quickly, waving them through a section of the bar that lifted to let them pass. They followed her back through a squeaky swinging door and down a stairwell smelling of beer and cold. She punched a code into the door at the bottom and stepped aside to let them in.

They stood in a chilly stone cellar. Damp clung to the walls, and the room was dimly lit and cavernous, with low ceilings and cinder block walls. Lou could hear the hissing of CO_2 pushing beer through the lines.

"Left past the wines, and don't you take a thing. There's another set of stairs to the bottle room. Back right corner. And you can't come back this way, aye? Pub locks at eleven, and I won't let you out."

May nodded. She pulled something out of her pocket. It was a charm, Lou realized, made by her grandmother. May handed it to the bar girl. "Keep it on you on your way home, and for next year. It'll keep you safe."

The girl weighed it in her palm. Lou wondered what the charm was. Iron, probably, paired with some sort of herb for protection. "Thank you," the girl said. She started back towards the bar, but hesitated at the last moment. "Ye be safe, alright?"

"Of course," May said. The door shut, and they were alone in the cellar.

May deflated. "Watch for roaches," she muttered. Lou barely flinched. After the week she'd had, roaches were nothing.

They made their way down the stairs. Lou kept her hand on the wall, though it was damp and cold and oddly slimy. When she thought of restaurant cellars, she thought of order and clean spaces and stacked shelves and freezers, not this.

There was a cart over in the corner, and when they pushed it away, they revealed a wooden cover in the floor. Lou swallowed hard.

This was it.

"Do you think they're right below us?" she asked.

May shook her head. "I don't think so." But she slid the iron spike into her palm all the same, because after all, it was best to be prepared. She looked at Lou evenly. "Are you sure you want to do this?"

It wasn't something she *wanted* to do, but May knew that. Neither of them would be going through this if was merely a passing fancy.

May lifted the trap door and let the wood fall against the floor. Stairs awaited them in the dark mouth of the hole, with the vague promise of torchlight flickering ahead through the corridor. Next to her, May was tense as a piano wire.

"Well," she said, "I suppose we'd better get to it."

Lou nodded. She went first, slipping one of her daggers into her hand. She felt an icy prick of dread curling in her stomach. Somewhere ahead, in the rooms where Lou never wanted to be again, the market clamored: *come buy, come buy, come buy.*

CHAPTER 34

TWO CHOICES PRESENTED THEMSELVES AS THE TUNNEL ENDED and branched in opposite directions. Lou, sweat slick on her palms, was reminded of the story they'd read in English class the year before.

The lady or the tiger? she thought.

"I think we should go right," May said, turning to look back the way they came and then peering down the two pathways. "I think it will take us closer to the market."

Lou nodded. "How can we be sure Eitra will be easy to find?"

"We can't," May said. "We just have to keep going."

She was right, but she was also in an odd position. "May," Lou said, laying a hand on her shoulder. May looked back. "You've gotta go, even at the first sign of trouble. It's not about you anymore. I'll figure it out, but you have to leave. Okay?"

May bit her lip. The reality of it warred in her eyes, but finally she sighed. "You're right," she said. "Okay."

Lou dropped her hand and let it be.

They made their way down the stairs, careful of the damp, treading softly so their footsteps didn't echo. It didn't matter much. The noise of the market grew ever louder as they descended, as did the scent of rot. Lou wondered if it would be worse today, if all the glamours would be removed, cast aside. She wondered if today, the last reckless day, was really the most dangerous of them all.

There was a landing ahead, and an archway to the left, spilling light across the stones. This was the market floor, Lou was pretty sure, judging by the trampled petals and drops of blood that marred the stones, some leading farther downstairs.

"Let me," Lou said. She skirted around May, keeping to the wall, and peered into the market. It was as if all the goblins from the other levels had converged here tonight, packing the aisles between stalls. There was laughing and dancing, wares flying—and not just fruit, Lou realized, watching a silver knife pinwheel through the air and stick in the arm of a pale gray goblin man. He cried out, pulling the knife out and searching for the person who'd tossed it.

Lou peeled her eyes away. They were all here, probably close to two hundred of them, all half-drunk and chaotic and hungry for flesh as the market came to a close. She scanned over the stalls, pausing for a moment on the row that sold human parts. Not only were the hands and legs and flesh discolored with rot and stinking, but they were heavily depleted.

She swallowed hard. It would not be good to get caught, she thought, when there was a lack of flesh to be had.

"Do you see her?" May asked.

Lou jumped. She'd almost forgotten the point of the mission. "Not yet," she whispered back. She scanned the market anew, searching for any trace of Eitra. She kept her gaze low, hunting along the floors, but she saw nothing.

"I don't see her," Lou said.

May sighed. "She might be on another level."

It was possible. "Should we go down to check first?"

May nodded. "At least to the Inbetween. If they've taken her prisoner, she'd be there."

Lou turned away from the market and led the way down three flights to the vast, cavernous hall of columns and deeper down to the room of things meant to be forgotten. Lou shuddered, taking in the columns. Next to her, May reached out and squeezed her hand.

In the middle of the room, Eitra was tied to a column. They'd surrounded her with spikes radiating outward in concentric circles, secured to the floor, sticking up. Iron-tipped, Lou realized, which surprised her. She hadn't expected them to use something like that on their own kind. The setup reminded her of a documentary she'd seen about Vlad Dracul, who impaled his victims on spikes. Eitra was one bad escape attempt from being impaled.

She raised her head at the sound of their footsteps. When she opened her mouth, flower petals poured to the ground. That was new, Lou thought, observing the fluttering path of one to the damp stone floor.

"Stay at the edge," Lou said, nodding to May.

May didn't respond. Lou looked over at her. Her eyes were wet and her expression was impossible to read. Lou was not used to seeing May like this, crumbling, coming undone.

"You didn't find me," May said. "You promised you would."

Eitra's head snapped to the sound of her voice. Her lips, which Lou had never truly looked at, were beautiful and full, and now they curved into a smile. When Eitra set aside the act, when she wasn't pretending to be wrecked, Lou could imagine her . . . well, she could imagine her the way May first saw her. The way May fell in love with her.

"You were better off without me," she said. "I only would've brought you more wreckage, May Wickett."

May scoffed, pressing a hand to her mouth. But both of them were smiling in that way that May never did, that she'd never seen any of the Wickett women smile before.

Lou took a deep breath. She had to focus. She could turn sideways and move through the spikes easily enough, but if one grazed her, it would be game over and it would be even harder to get both herself and Eitra back through. She had no idea if Eitra could sense them well enough to pass safely.

She assessed the spikes. They seemed to be dug into the ground and coated with something. Maybe she could pull them up, form a narrow path between her and Eitra? Or snap them? She looked up, checking out the ceiling. There were beams, but nothing to secure a rope to—not that she had a rope to begin with.

Perhaps she'd watched too many spy movies as a kid.

Occam's razor, Lou decided. The simplest explanation was the right one—the simplest solution was the most possible. The goblins hadn't anticipated anyone would come back for Eitra, so maybe they hadn't taken as many precautions as were necessary.

Lou wrapped her hands around the base of the closest spike and pulled. She hissed as splinters found home in her palms, but with some wiggling and profanity, the spike came up from the earth. She staggered back under the sudden weight, very narrowly avoiding May.

"Great," May said flatly. "One down, thirty to go."

"Progress is progress," Lou insisted through gritted teeth, stepping forward to pull the next one.

She pushed through the pain as the wood cut into her hands. May pulled her own jacket sleeves over her hands and helped, pulling out spikes until they'd accumulated a rather untidy pile on the outer edge, like a giant's game of pick up sticks. Eitra was quiet through the endeavor, wincing every time she heard one of Lou's brief exclamations of pain.

"Is this your punishment?" Lou asked. She couldn't bear the silence. "For saving Neela and me."

Eitra snorted. "No, actually. They do this every year, on the last day of the market. Tie me up, taunt me, leave me here to rot until the next market."

Behind her, Lou heard a sharp intake of breath. She glanced back to see May's horrified face. "They *leave* you here? All year? How do you survive?"

Eitra shrugged. "It's not like I can starve, is it?" She leaned her head back against the column. "It's a fair punishment, I suppose. We killed the prince, so they mean to kill my spirit." She leaned over to retch up a nearly full orchid. Lou noticed how the petals were flecked with blood.

"Has no one," Lou huffed around another pole, briefly stopping to wipe the blood on her hands, "done this before?"

"Done what?" Eitra asked.

"Tried to set a cursed goblin free?"

Eitra bit her lip. Her brow was still furrowed, her hands crumpled limply against her chest, but now Lou wondered if that was all part of the act. Become seemingly feeble so no one could believe she could save herself. "Who would come for me?" she asked. She shrugged, barely noticing as the cuffs around her arms cut deeper. "I can't get out on my own. And who would try to save *me*?"

She let that hang in the air. Lou risked a glance at May, who'd retreated from the final circle of pikes, back to the edge.

May. May was meant to save her.

"Keep watch," Lou said to her aunt, if only to break the tense silence. She discarded the last of the spikes, her path to Eitra finally clear.

Above, something crashed onto the floor, and they all froze for the barest moment, none of them breathing, until the sounds continued. The market was a clamorous, living thing, and Lou did not want to be a part of it any longer.

Lou knelt down, avoiding the spikes still on either side of her, to examine Eitra's hands.

If she'd thought Neela's wrists were in bad shape, she was horrified by Eitra's. She was bound with rope wound through with thin iron wires. Lou hissed, examining the bloody and puss-filled burn marks that covered Eitra's skin. There was no knot that she could see: they must've been magicked closed, forming one continuous, unbroken loop.

"This is going to hurt," Lou said, drawing one of her knives.

"I expect nothing less."

She worked the knife under the ropes, trying to saw them apart.

Eitra hissed. Dark blood slipped over Lou's fingers. "You lied to me," Lou said, quietly enough so May wouldn't hear.

"My curse prevents me from speaking of what I did. What we did," she muttered back. "How was I supposed to say anything?"

Lou grimaced. "But you said you'd take care of Neela. Why? You didn't have to do anything else, and there was no guarantee of us saving you." She almost had the restraints cut; she was working on one last thread of iron. It was like sawing through the wires Grandpa Jack used to secure Christmas garland to the fireplace. Outside the circle of spikes, May paced. The last thread snapped before Eitra could answer. She sagged forward, catching herself on her hands.

"Because I knew, if either of you were hurt, it would destroy May."

Lou rose from her crouch. She considered Eitra. She knew she'd come here to save her; she knew how May felt about her, and what she'd done for them years ago. But until now, until she heard it from Eitra's lips, she wasn't sure she'd believed it.

But here was the truth: Eitra cared about May enough to save her, to risk everything, and then to do it all over again twenty years later. She'd turned her back on her kind twice, now. Thrice, if Lou counted Eitra getting Mom out of the market when she was injured.

Lou reached down and pulled Eitra to her feet. The hood fell from her head, revealing curling violet hair that tumbled free over her shoulders. It was caught through with feathers from her eyes. But she was tall and strong, nothing like the thing that had grabbed Lou's ankles under the wine table.

"Thank you," Lou said.

Eitra smiled. "We're not out yet, Louisa."

"Lou," she corrected. "Just call me Lou."

Eitra nodded, bowing her head like the name was a gift. And for goblins, for the folk like her, perhaps it was.

"We have to get through the spikes," Lou said, turning back to face the circle. May waited anxiously on the other side. "Will you be alright?"

Eitra's mouth thinned into a line. "I have to be, don't I?" She reached out and took Lou's hands. The thorns that lined her skin dug into her palm, but Lou squeezed back even tighter.

She didn't know how they made it. It was a slow process, Lou stepping forward and Eitra following her exact footsteps, each breath caught as a spike grazed Eitra's arm, relief when it didn't pierce the fabric of her cloak. But then, with one final tug, Eitra was free of the spikes, free of the restraints, free.

May laid a hand on her cheek, ignoring the thorns. Eitra smiled, and the gems and feathers and flowers spilled out with renewed gusto.

"Do you fear me?" Eitra said. "Like this?"

Lou felt she was watching something indecent. She stepped back.

"Never," May said. She rolled up onto her tiptoes, hands pressed to Eitra's shoulders, and kissed her gently.

"I thought you might come back."

Lou's heart froze over. The voice came from the stairs across the room. She looked up to see a familiar form illuminated in the light of the stairs. He stepped down into it, smiling.

Kildred.

"I knew you weren't here for me," he said, crossing the floor. "But I didn't suspect you were here for her." He smiled terribly. "I should eat the lot of you. I wouldn't even need to share."

Lou darted a glance at the stairs behind them. There were no goblins there. This was not an ambush, not yet. She didn't give a damn what the pub girl had said. "Go," she hissed to May and Eitra.

She turned to follow, to get out, but a hand caught her forearm. She looked back. Kildred moved fast, faster than she'd expected.

"Lou," May said, caught between the door and the wall.

Lou shook her head. "Go," she said. What she meant was: *Trust me.*

"You don't want them," Lou said, looking back at Kildred, following his gaze as he tracked May and Eitra across the room.

"What use are they? A cursed goblin and a useless old woman."
She was sure May was going to fight her for calling her old, but
it didn't matter. Right now, Lou just had to focus on getting *out*.
The running footsteps behind her grew fainter and fainter. With
her free hand, Lou reached for her packet of herbs, pulling them
out of her pocket. She only needed to get them into her mouth.

He grimaced. "And what are you?"

Behind her, the door slammed as Eitra and May escaped. Lou
was well and truly alone with Kildred.

She curtsied, even as her heart sunk, even as she thought of
all those bodies in the room below her feet. "I'm just a girl," Lou
said. "I'm just a girl here at Scarborough Fair." She pushed a
hand deep into her pocket, feeling the jab of rosemary against
her fingers.

Kildred lurched forward, bearing his teeth. He ripped the
herbs away from her hand with a swift motion. When he bit into
her shoulder, it *hurt*.

She gasped against the pain, fumbling to grip him, to push
him away. But it was no use. He was stronger than her, bigger
than her. He was a goblin, hungry for flesh he didn't have to
share, and she was a mere mortal.

His teeth dug in. Pain arced even higher. But she couldn't just
let him consume her—she had to do something.

Lou tried with all her might to stop focusing on the agony
and to *think*. Her hand went to the knife on her thigh and she
raised it to strike. But what if she really hurt him?

She couldn't punch back or attack him in any way, not in the
market, not on his turf. Her breath was coming too fast and her
heart was pounding and she had to think of something, anything
that didn't break the Doctrine—

"The Doctrine!" Lou shouted, her voice coming out a piercing wail. Kildred lurched back, his mouth covered in her blood. She didn't dare move her arm. Hot blood pulsed down her shoulder. The knife fell from her free hand. There was no sense using it.

"What?"

"I didn't violate any rules," she said. Her voice was too shaky, unreliable. She clapped her good hand to her shoulder to staunch the bleeding. "I didn't hurt you. I didn't trespass. You're breaking the Doctrine."

Kildred seethed, his teeth clenched. "Oh? You wish to plead your case?"

She didn't want to plead *anything*. She just wanted to go.

Kildred's eyes took on a wicked glint. "Come on," he said, grabbing Lou's arm roughly, dragging her through the Inbetween toward the steps that led to the market. She cried out as he jerked her along, as the blood slicked her fingers.

Lou didn't fight him. This was what she'd been prepared for, wasn't it? The market would not let her go so easily. "Where are we going?"

Kildred flashed a smile over his shoulder at her, full of deadly, pointed teeth lined with Lou's blood. "To the Market Prince."

CHAPTER 85

THE MARKET FLOOR WAS IN A CATASTROPHIC STATE OF DISARRAY.
Lou staggered to keep up as Kildred dragged her through
the mess. She slipped on a mash of bloody-red berries on the
floor and fell against him. Kildred only slowed to right her and
continued on his march toward the front of the stalls.

There, closest to the stalls that Lou had most tried to avoid,
she spotted their destination. At the end of the aisle between the
rows of body parts, stood the dais. This was the center of activity,
the churning mass of whooping and laughing goblins.

Kildred pulled her through the clot of goblins, who made no
move to part for her. In fact, it was as if they pressed closer, claws
scratching and voices screeching as Kildred dragged Lou to her
fate. He threw her down in front of the dais, and she didn't have
anything to catch herself on. Lou sprawled down on her hands
and knees, cutting her palm on something white and jagged. A
bone shard, Lou realized, as bile rose to her throat.

Shiny boots appeared on the ground in front of her. Lou
didn't dare look up, didn't dare face Hilgar.

"It appears you orbit everyone else, but no one is here to orbit
you, little moon."

Lou didn't answer. The first time Hilgar had told her she

relied on everyone else, she'd realized it was true. But not now. Lou felt cut free from her orbits. At first, probing the feeling, she felt like she was floating without purpose—but that wasn't true. She still had Mom and May and Neela and Nana Tee. But she didn't have to constantly redefine how much she reflected them.

"I hear you've released my prisoner. That's a pity."

"I've brought you the human, Hilgar. She's stirred up quite a lot of trouble," Kildred said, sounding odd and eager. There was a beat of silence. Lou finally glanced up. Hilgar's face was mottled with bruises, and she had a very uncomfortable-looking wound on her neck where Eitra had bit her. Lou was sure her shoulder looked nearly identical. If only goblins' first fight or flight instinct wasn't *bite*.

"Did I ask you to speak?" Hilgar said finally.

Kildred stuttered for words, but in the end, he was not the Market Prince and was not willing to level with her. He faded back with the other goblins.

Lou had to be *smart* and think of something. There was no one left to come for her. Eitra would be killed if she returned, May and Neela had already used their three days of freedom, Mom was too ill, and Nana Tee and Joss would violate the Doctrine by entering. Even if they tried to send someone else, they were out of time. She had no magic and Kildred had taken her rosemary and thyme. There were still daggers and the goblin ice, but Lou was facing a room full of goblins alone. Even if she took one or two down with her, she had no chance of escaping.

Her train of thought splintered as someone kicked her in the ribs. Lou gasped, skidding and colliding with one of the partially destructed stalls of human body parts. She choked on air, fingers clawing for purchase. Pain radiated out from her side.

Around her, the goblins only laughed. Lou looked up, but there was nothing to save her here; there were only the hands of the dead, dangling in front of her eyes, fingers reaching, as if to say *we claim you, we claim you, you will never leave the market again.*

Lou pushed back to her hands and knees. Hilgar stood watching her, head cocked, hands on her hips. She had a wry smile on her lips. "Kildred," she said, not taking her eyes off Lou. "Fetch me my sword. I want to see this one bleed."

Kildred emerged from the crowd momentarily before turning on his heel and making his way to one of the archways.

The goblins converged into a circle around Lou and Hilgar, laughing and shrieking. Lou tried to catch her breath, tried to *think,* but everything was muddied with pain.

"You shouldn't have come back," Hilgar said.

Lou didn't bother with a response.

Something hit her from behind, knocking her forward. Her face smacked against the floor at Hilgar's feet. From the juicy *splat* and sickly smell, she realized she'd been hit by a rotten melon.

Maybe it was better to stay down. Maybe that would make it all end sooner.

Lou turned her head—and nearly shrieked. There was someone *looking* at her from the shadows under the stall, someone laying on their side like Lou, someone with curly hair and—

Someone whose body ended at the neck. A clean cut had been made at the point where her neck would join her shoulders, severing it from the rest of her torso. A goblin butcher had done their job on her.

Charlotte's head, brought up from the butchery, lay on its side next to Lou.

Hysteria bubbled under her skin. She pushed up, gripping the stall to pull herself to her feet. She would not stay here and die, like Charlotte; she would not let them take her. If fighting was the only option, she would go down with blood in her mouth.

Lou whirled toward the encroaching goblins and pulled one of her daggers. Most of them were bigger than her, and older, and armed with goblin weapons. "Stay away," she seethed, turning slowly, jabbing her dagger at anyone who moved closer. "Stay away from me."

"Or what?" Hilgar laughed. "You'll scratch us? Do you mean to harm us?"

Lou was not her mother. She would not win in a fight; she would not win by cleverness. Goblins did not play by the rules. They lived to trick, to lead astray, to lower inhibitions.

There was no battle she could outwit them in, no riddles she could spin to argue her way out of this one.

But maybe she didn't need to outthink them. Maybe . . . maybe she only needed to follow the rules.

The rules.

She'd followed the rules. If she struck out now, if she harmed one of the goblins, she'd violate the doctrine. But who was to say they'd keep their end of the bargain? Hilgar was only trying to trick her, to convince her she needed to fight.

Lou was still within her three allotted days. She had not harmed a goblin within the market. And though she'd unchained Eitra, she hadn't taken her out of the market. May had. Even if she'd bent a few rules, she had not violated any laws laid out by the Doctrine herself.

Lou swallowed hard, ignoring the pain pulsing all over her body. She brought her hands down, put her knives away.

"There are laws between your folk and mine," she said. She

tried to stand tall as Hilgar came closer with her bloody, beringed hand around her sword. "I have not violated my end of the Doctrine. And yet you're threatening to kill me."

Hilgar stopped an arm's length away, one eyebrow curving into an arch. "And what of my prisoners?"

"What of them?" she asked. "Show me the written law about releasing humans from the market. There is none. And as for Eitra, another mortal left the market walls with her. I am not responsible for that." She hoped it was true enough. From what she could remember, there really was nothing in the Doctrine preventing Lou from freeing Neela. It had been about her getting Neela out before the goblins killed her, or worse. And May had crossed the boundaries of the market with Eitra, even if Lou had been the one to free her from the trap. But where was the rule about that?

If the market ran on the written rules between the goblins and the witches, they couldn't go enforcing laws that didn't exist. Lou had to believe in that.

Hilgar bared her teeth. Lou was conscious of the market growing quiet around them, of the goblins watching her. But this time, she didn't feel overwhelming dread or fear. She felt alive. This was her strength: negotiation. Figuring it out.

"You tried to defy me in my own court," Hilgar hissed.

"That's not a rule." Lou licked her lips, tasting blood. She was feeling very woozy from being knocked around and losing blood in her shoulder.

"I'll keep you here until you die, Louisa Wickett, and then I'll wear your ribcage as a crown."

Lou shrugged. It took all her effort to appear unaffected. "Unfortunately, you can't. But I'll take that threat into consideration when I speak to the coven."

"Hilgar," someone said very quietly. Lou noticed Kildred standing nearby, looking uneasy. "Unfortunately, she's right. She, erm, hasn't violated the doctrine. We can't keep her. And if we hurt her—"

"She's already half dead," Hilgar snarled.

"Yes, well. If we hurt her *more*, then *we* violate the doctrine."

Lou just focused on standing upright as the pair glared at one another. The mood in the room was changing, goblins turning away to go back to their own delights. There was no longer the bloodthirsty roar; no one threatened Lou.

"Then what was the punishment for the violation eighteen years ago, when *they* violated the doctrine and killed one of our own?" Hilgar cried out. The longer Lou looked at her, the more she appeared quite like a child throwing a tantrum.

Another goblin, an older one, cleared her throat. "The witches were dealt with in accordance with their laws. They were banished; their magic was stripped. And Eitra was dealt with here."

Hilgar's eyes bored into Lou's face, the hatred in them nearly hot enough to burn. "Are you telling me," she said, each word terrible, "that we truly cannot kill her?"

There was a silence. In that moment, Lou felt a surge of relief. She was not a fighter, she was not a witchling, not a little moon in orbit. She was a force to be reckoned with.

Lou took in the market for the last time, thinking of how May had looked at Eitra, thinking of salvation, of Neela's wrists, of the smell of death and rot.

She nodded, trying to stay steady. "Well, I wish I could say it's been a pleasure, but it hasn't. Perhaps I'll see you again next year. Kildred, I believe you have something of mine."

Hilgar and Kildred exchanged a glance. Lou's heart caught, waiting in the breathless moment before Kildred shook his head and tossed her the herbs. Ignoring the ache in her shoulder, Lou caught them.

She shoved the packet into her mouth. She bit down, hard, catching the edge of her tongue, only just catching Hilgar's eyes widening in anger as the world seemed to tip under her feet.

The market rushed by in a *whoosh* as Lou was dragged by some unseen force. She flew through the market, the crushed stalls of rotting fruit and flesh, of bone and marrow and teeth, the calls of *come buy, come buy*. She smacked her knees on the stone stairs as the force dragged her up, the force of the witches of Yorkshire, of her ancestors who would not leave her here to die even if she lacked the magic they themselves bred.

She landed flat on her back on the cold, wet walkway. The door to the market slammed shut in front of her, the wall fading back into solid stone.

Louisa Wickett-Stevens, the daughter of the witches who refused to fall, stared up at the cloudy midnight sky, seeking the stars. When she dug her fingers into the stones to push herself upright, she felt a flicker of light deep within the earth.

Below her, the market seethed and roiled. It would leave, she knew; it would abandon the bodies and the fruit and those who were cursed, leave them behind to wait and rot. It would leave and next year, it would be back again to claim new victims.

But the market, the market, the market: it would never have her again.

CHAPTER 36
May

Eighteen Years Earlier

When May slept, she dreamt of Eitra.

She was killing her, or kissing her, or maybe both. Maybe all of it at the same time, Eitra's blood running over May's hands as Eitra's fingers tangled in her hair. May wasn't sure what was real and what was not, if any of it had happened, if she'd survived at all.

She felt Eitra's fingertips, soft despite her claws. It was a fallacy of course—Eitra was not suited for tenderness. But dream-May did not care. When Eitra kissed her neck, May did not feel the bite of teeth. There was only sweetness and want, mixed with a soft sadness of realization, even in sleep, that this would never come to pass.

May opened her eyes, slipping out of the dream and sleep itself like passing through a curtain. Because no matter how much she didn't want to, on the day after the market, when the smoke had cleared and the rubble had settled, May woke up.

There was a shuffling, scuffing noise of someone tripping on stone. The heavy wooden door swung open, revealing Laura's face. She held a cup of tea and wore a mask of pity. May felt the full press of her weariness, of the knowledge there would be more days after this one, more and more and more days without Eitra, with only this ice shard and this goddamned city and its cursed market.

"May." Laura came in, quiet and cautious. May wasn't sure what her sister expected to see, but it was just her, as always, breakable and frail.

"It's cold here, at night," May said, drawing the blankets back over her shoulders.

Laura smiled. "It's half two."

May pursed her lips. She felt the press of the Witchery's magic around her, useless even as it crackled in her blood. She bit her lip and recoiled, finding the skin already broken.

"I just need to know . . ." May said, but she couldn't finish the sentence. *I need to know what happened. I need to know that you saved me. That you're here. That you're real. That this is not another goblin trick.*

Laura hesitated. She scrutinized May in the flickering candlelight. They couldn't have electricity, not without catching the notice of the people who ran the Minster. May tried to imagine what Laura was looking for. Wounds that she didn't have, that Laura wore instead of her? Marks of Eitra or the Goblin Prince? Any suggestion that May was well and truly gone to market, to market, to market?

"You okay?"

Never.

May nodded.

Someone cleared their throat in the doorway. May looked up. Marcus stood there, looking uneasily between the two of them. "They've made a decision."

May glanced at Laura, fear rising within her. A decision? Who had? Why? Were they—had she violated some rule, some law?

Would they be forced to send her to the market? If they did that, at least, she'd be reunited with Eitra's bones. The pair of them could rot into eternity together.

"Thanks," Laura said. She shot Marcus a glance that May only barely understood. Marcus disappeared back down the hallway.

"What is it?" May asked when they were alone again.

Laura looked at her unhappily. "You'll see."

Nothing about that sounded good. But she pulled the blankets tighter around her and slid out of bed. The stone floor was freezing against her bare feet. Laura walked ahead of her, head held high, out into the main room.

May didn't like the scene she walked into: the Thaumaturge was back, as were a few representatives from other covens. May hadn't studied well enough to tell where they'd come from, but she'd learned enough to know this did not bode well.

Mum, Joss, and Angelique stood against the far wall. Marcus was near the table like he was caught between the coven and Laura and May.

"Is this . . ." May looked around. Surely they weren't going through with the ceremony to make them into full witches now— May couldn't bear it. She barely felt well enough to stand.

Everything hurt.

The Thaumaturge stepped forward. Her shiny hair was pulled back, and she wore ceremonial robes. May wanted to grab Laura's hand, to ask someone what was happening, but she didn't dare speak.

"May Felicity Wickett. Laura Elizabeth Wickett."

May didn't like the way the Thaumaturge said their names, the way Mum wouldn't make eye contact with May. The night before, after treating her wounds, Mum and Joss barely spoke to her. She'd fallen into a grief-stricken sleep soon after she was healed.

She also, May noticed, had not spoken Marcus's name. This was no graduation ceremony. Now, fear did strike May. She reached forward, but Laura was already reaching back. They laced their fingers together.

Caroline looked unbearably sad as she locked eyes with May. This, she knew, was her punishment.

"You have been found guilty of breaking the Petergate Doctrine and risking the safety of your coven. This reckless behavior cannot go unpunished. As a result, both of you will face a ten-year banishment from the area within the city walls."

May felt numbness and ice in her veins, creeping along. Banishment? *Banishment?* She'd never heard such a punishment for a witch, never knew it was possible.

Where were they supposed to go? What were they supposed to *do?*

But that wasn't all. Laura sucked in a breath, looking away from May like she already knew what was coming.

The Thaumaturge cleared her throat. "Additionally, your power will be removed. Permanently. Never again will you be able to practice magic, and you will never become full members of the coven."

There was a home video of them when they were younger, shot in Joss's back garden. It was a normal autumn day. May, who couldn't have been older than three, toddled after Laura and Marcus with her arms outstretched. "I curse you!" she'd shrieked.

Laura had turned around and gathered her up into her arms. "No!" she shouted, too seriously for the game. "No cursing, May. We're *good* witches. When we grow up, we're supposed to be *good* witches."

May couldn't look at her now. She barely felt Laura's hand in hers—it was possible she'd taken it away.

They'd never be good witches.

A second dream, this one of Iark, the Market Prince.

"You thought you could escape?" Iark asked. May felt the press of his skin against hers—they were dancing, waltzing, just as they had at the fete. Her ribs were already broken, blood trickling from her scalp. She tried to pull away, but realized the flesh of her hands was molded to Iark's body. She could not break free. They were combined, one flesh and one blood.

May was at the mercy of the Prince.

She swallowed hard as they spun. A headache pulsed against her temples. She remembered how it felt, to be like this as they'd danced. To be destroyed.

Iark smiled. His teeth were lined with blood.

"Where is she?" May asked, searching the room. There could be salvation yet. If Eitra . . . if Eitra was there. She scanned over the lines of goblins, short and tall, illuminated by the candlelight, watching.

"Who?" Iark asked—no, not Iark.

May's head snapped forward. It was Eitra who danced with her now, grinning triumphantly. May pulled her close, pulled her mouth down, but all she tasted was blood and rot.

May gagged, choked on the blood. Horrified, she looked up.

Eitra's face had rotted away, leaving behind only her skull. "I did say I'd find you."

The second time May woke, she was far from the Witchery, back in their flat. In Mum's room, Neela was crying.

Someone, either Laura or Mum, had scrubbed the blood from her skin and changed her clothes. She remembered flashes of it, of the blood on the stone floor, of Laura's hands on her cheeks, wiping away tears.

There was still blood under her nails.

In the kitchen, Mum and Laura were fighting. "But we've *never* lived with Jack," Laura insisted, referring to the father they shared, the stranger who lived an ocean away.

"This isn't a discussion, Laura."

May stared at the ceiling, thinking of blood and Boston and the Witchery and the market. She was banished from this place. Already, someone had packed her bags. They stood like sentinels in the middle of the room. It was only a matter of where to go.

"You're going," Mum said, and the decision was final. "Now, go check on your sister."

Laura's stomping was louder than Neela's crying as she threw open the door. "You're awake," she said, but it was less of a statement and more of an accusation.

May looked at her head on. There'd be no Marcus in Boston, no magic, no witchery, no market, no goblins.

"Do you hate me?" May asked.

Laura blinked at her. "What?"

May hugged her knees to her chest. She felt split in half. After the trial, after the magic had been dug out of them like a tree root, she felt even emptier than before. There was no doubt

Laura felt the same way, unmoored, uncomfortable without her magic. She pressed a palm to her chest where she could feel the goblin ice hanging on the chain around her neck. She'd hoped it would ground her, but it only made everything worse.

"You gave up your magic," May said. "Because of me."

Laura stared at her for an immeasurable time. Finally, she crept past the suitcases and over the piles of clothes. She climbed onto the bed beside May. "I would give up *anything* for you, May."

May nodded. She didn't ask any more questions. She only leaned her head against Laura's shoulder as the waves of grief roared ever higher.

They were leaving this place, maybe for good. Soon, May would not wake to the goblins, to the scent of rot, to the crackle of magic. They would not stay in this city where the market haunted and lingered, where the blood stained the cobblestones for the better part of the summer if you only knew where to look.

Laura wrapped an arm around May. May wondered if she was thinking the same thing, of blood and magic and endings.

"We're going to be okay," Laura said, her fingers digging into May's skin like she had to be certain May was real and whole and next to her. "You and me. We'll always have each other. We don't need magic. We don't need anyone else."

May nodded. She didn't believe Laura, but she knew it was easier to agree. Even now, she felt the creeping fear the market had left behind in her, the unending cold. Even now, she knew the truth: no matter how far she ran, no matter who she did or didn't trust, the market would come back for her.

It always claimed what it was due.

EPILOGUE

THEY ASSEMBLED IN THE TRAIN STATION, THE WHOLE MOTLEY crew. Mom looked so much better, the color returning to her face. She hadn't said anything to Lou, but she knew Mom was happy to be going back to Boston, back to her version of freedom. May was off printing the tickets, her dark hair still wet from the shower. Eitra stood with Mom, quietly tapping her fingers on a set of luggage Nana Tee lent her. She'd disguised herself incredibly well, her skin medium brown, the thorns tucked away, and her hair the same violet, but now it looked hip and intentional rather than unnatural. She wore a pair of sunglasses and, every so often, she raised a hand to catch whatever it was coming out of her eyes. Since leaving the market, it was mostly gems and petals, getting less and less frequent. It was a part of the market curse, Eitra had told Lou the night before as Lou had helped her pack. It would wear off eventually. And until it did, they'd build up a tidy collection of jewels to sell or keep or throw into the Charles.

Lou caught Mom staring at her. "You okay?"

Mom nodded. "Are you sure you want to do this?"

Lou looked up at the high ceiling of the train station. It smelled of fog and coffee. The station wasn't bustling now, in the middle of the afternoon, but soon she had no doubt it would be.

"I'm sure," Lou said. It felt weird to have a choice, to make the decision, to speak it out loud.

When she looked back at Mom, the corners of her mouth were turned up. Mom leaned forward and kissed her on the forehead. "I'm sorry," she said, possibly for the thousandth time since Lou had returned two days before. Lou hadn't yet asked what she was sorry *for.* She wasn't sure she wanted to.

Lou laced her fingers through Mom's. Later, when she went back, there would be time—time to talk about what Mom had been through, and May too; time to stitch up all the old wounds, to probe at the scar tissue of their relationship as it strengthened.

"Are you going to be okay?" she asked Mom again.

Her nose scrunched up. "Not when I talk to Gen. She's going to have my head when she finds out you're not going to Yosemite."

Lou nudged her shoulder—not hard, as they were both still a bit too achy for that. "I'm old enough to pick where I go," she said.

"True. But you explain that to your stepmother." Mom's tone softened as she looked at Lou, as she swept the hair away from her face. "I always wondered what you'd be like if you grew up here," she said. Lou had spent so much time trying to imagine what Mom was thinking, what was possibly going on in her head, that the idea of who she might have been had they stayed in York had never occurred to her.

"Laura!"

Mom and Lou turned to find May, frazzled, standing with Nana Tee. She looked a little bit wild. "I'll see what that's about," Mom said, squeezing Lou's hand once and stepping away. "Why don't you take Eitra for some tea?"

Lou nodded. She and Eitra headed up to the Costa near

the platform. Eitra listened to the sounds of the station with an odd kind of reverence as Lou ordered, adding various milks and sugars to their drinks.

"Does it scare you?" she asked as she handed two teas to Eitra. "Going so far away?"

Eitra's lips curled into a smile. "No," she said. "It'll be an adventure. And I assume there will be food involved."

Lou snorted. It hadn't been an easy thing, she'd surmised, to get travel documents for Eitra, but there was some sort of liaison between the coven and the government and Lou didn't bother asking questions. There would be plenty of time to learn all the ins and outs, to probe how and why the coven operated.

Eitra sipped her tea, made a face, and dumped at least eight more sugar packets in. Lou did not question it.

"Do you have any advice for me?" Lou asked as they descended the stairs, back toward her unruly family.

"Hmm." Eitra coughed into her elbow, catching a fat emerald in the crook of it. She shifted the teas around in her hands and shoved the stone in her coat pocket. "Don't eat anything given to you by anyone you don't know. Listen to your grandmother. Most goblins think she's terrifying."

Lou couldn't imagine how Nana Tee could terrify anyone, but she nodded along.

"Keep a dagger in your boot and follow the rules." She smiled wryly. "But I suppose I don't have to tell you that, do I?"

She walked the path home from the train station on her own. The sun was out in earnest, for once. Lou looked at the shops and restaurants and cafes as she passed—not because she was searching for goblins or gauging safety but because she was making a mental note of places to visit, maybe with Neela or Nana Tee or Joss, or maybe by herself.

Back at the Witchery, Joss sat on the sofa, sewing a spring of rowan berries into a child's coat pocket. Neela was at the flat, recovering from her injuries. She'd promised to give Lou an introduction to British TV later that night by way of some sort of show where a bunch of people watched TV shows and commented on them. They'd eat popcorn and drink tea or possibly a few beers that Neela was legally allowed to buy here, and they would not talk of the market.

But here, in the Witchery, the work was only just beginning. Joss smiled at Lou as she shut the door behind her. "I found some books that would be helpful," she said, nodding to the towering stack on the big table. "Don't look so worried. We have time."

"Thank you," Lou said. She pulled the first of them off the stack and cradled it in her hands. The title read *Magyc and Ritual.* It was old and heavy, smelling of dust. She opened it up and flipped through the pages. There were words she didn't understand scattered throughout, much like the ones written in May's old notebook.

"Lou?"

She glanced over. Joss was watching her carefully. "You don't have to do this, you know. This isn't . . . it's not something you have to inherit."

Lou smiled. The others had been telling her that for days, ever since she asked Mom if she could stay, since she asked Nana

Tee if there was the possibility that maybe, just maybe, she might have some of the magic herself.

"I know," she said. "I want to see if it fits."

Joss nodded. "There's a note for you too." She waved her hands and muttered under her breath, and a square envelope whirled through the air toward Lou. Lou caught it neatly.

It smelled of dirt and rust, as if someone had sprayed peculiar perfume over the paper. Lou unfolded the note.

Felicitations to you, little moon, on your cleverness. I hope this is not our final meeting. Next year, it seems we both will have some changes to introduce to the Doctrine.

Until our next meeting in the moonlight, I shall think on you fondly. Perhaps there will be time to wear your ribcage yet.

—H

Lou shuddered. She didn't know what it meant to receive something from the Market Prince—but she certainly didn't enjoy it.

A door opened in the back room, and she heard quick footsteps on the stone. Nana Tee poked her head out. "I thought I heard you," she said to Lou. She was dressed in her smock and gloves, splattered with blood. She nodded to a clean set, folded, on one end of the table. "Can you help me?"

"Sure," Lou said. She grabbed the clothes, nodded to Joss, and followed Nana Tee down the hall. It was the first day of her official training, the first day she was an apprentice of the coven. Lou couldn't detect it on her own yet, wasn't fully familiar with it, but she could smell the tense static in the air.

"It's not a pleasant one," Nana Tee said apologetically. "We'll have to start with a cleaning spell, then one to get rid of necrotic flesh. And we have to find a way to get vines to stop growing from his sinuses."

Nana Tee opened the door, leading the way in. The patient laid on the table. Nana Tee had done a spell already to put him to sleep and laid out the necessary tools. She opened her case of herbs and pre-made ointments and looked up at Lou, eyes wide and expectant.

"Are you ready to begin?" Nana Tee asked.

Lou could feel the roots under her feet, the tendrils of magic reaching up, seeking her. Coming home.

"I'm ready."

ACKNOWLEDGMENTS

My editor, Lauren Knowles, has been a lifeline through the last year as I've worked on this book. Thank you for being patient even when I took way too long to complete simple tasks and worked my way through Book Two Syndrome. I would not have gotten through Book One without the support of my amazing publicist, Lauren Cepero, who dealt with my five daily emails with grace and patience. Huge thanks to Will Kiester, Tamara Grasty, Mary Beth Garhart, Meg Palmer, Lizzy Mason, and Lynne Hartzer. Sincere thanks to Julia Tyler and Peter Strain for creating the most gorgeous cover in existence.

A sincere and heartfelt thank you to my agents, Dr. Uwe Stender and Amelia Appel. I've been so lucky to have you both in my corner for the last five years, even though I panic about everything. Thank you to Brent Taylor for being a superstar and the rest of Team Triada for all the help and support.

Thank you to my parents and family, who have always supported me. So you can find your name, thanks to: Jane and Vic; Lex; Grandma Peg; Dana and Tony; Kim and Craig; Susan; Lindaly and Win, Jeanna, Justin, Win, and all family; Stacey, Doug, Jacob, and Squid; Jeff, Britt, Chris, and Taylor; and all others. To Grandma, Dada, and Papap: I so wish you were here to experience this with me.

Thank you to my dear friends: Becca, Kat, Rebekah, Erin, Lara, Mike, Kali, Katina, Joe V., Rachel, Julia, Shakira, Michael, and Kish.

Special thank you to Elizabeth K., Briston B., Leah T., and Elle T., whose notes shaped this book into something comprehensible. Thanks to Kelsey R., Alechia D., Courtney G., Allison S., Chloe G., Alex B., and Lili for being incredible friends. Without weekly discussion with Tasha, Daphne, and Kat, I would never have made it through lockdowns, let alone finished this book. Thank you to Avi and Seolin, who are the best writers I know. Thank you to all of the booksellers, bloggers, bookstagrammers, booktubers, and booktokers who supported my work along the way. Special thanks to the team at RHUL who have supported me on this path.

Love and thanks to my fiancé, Matt, who supported me, listened to me ranting, and helped me write cricket jokes. I don't know what I'd do without you. Thanks to the Moss/McKenzie/Mutchell/Bird conglomerate yet again for endless excitement and support. MAC, someday I'll write a book appropriate for you to actually read.

And thank you, reader, for picking up my book and trusting me. I hope I didn't let you down.

ABOUT THE AUTHOR

Tori Bovalino is originally from Pittsburgh, PA and now lives in the UK with her partner and their very loud cat, Sir Gordon Greenidge II. Tori loves scary stories, obscure academic book facts, and impractical oversized sweaters.